PRAISE FOR KRIST

"Impeccably researched and highly inspirational, [...] shows the complex political and human plight of those fighting for freedom in World War II Italy and how personal sacrifice and daring can have an impact on generations to come. Cambron uses her considerable talents as a writer of historical fiction to bring to life a large cast of characters scattered across the globe in several different time periods, each of the 'good guys' someone we would be honoured to call a friend. An uplifting tale that educates, energizes, and comforts the reader. I was captivated from its enigmatic, action-packed beginning to its most wonderfully satisfying end."

—Natalie Jenner, author of the international bestseller
The Jane Austen Society and *The Bloomsbury Girls*

"With rare insight and remarkable finesse, Cambron excavates the forgotten fragments of history and crafts them into a sweeping masterpiece. Encompassing decades and inspired by a true story of extraordinary audacity, *The Italian Ballerina* explores how the ripples of the past merge with the present and reminds us of the capacity of ordinary individuals to rise against darkness and leave a legacy that outlasts their generation. Intricate and transportive, soaring and deeply resonant, this is Cambron at her finest."

—Amanda Barratt, Christy Award–winning
author of *The White Rose Resists*

"Incredibly researched and emotionally evocative, Cambron—once again—takes us into the depths of war as well as to the heights of love, bravery, sacrifice, and devotion. I thoroughly enjoyed every moment within this story and must warn readers—you'll completely lose your heart to young Calla. Enjoy!"

—Katherine Reay, bestselling author of *The Printed
Letter Bookshop* and *The London House*

"Gripping and atmospheric, *The Italian Ballerina* explores the collective, intercontinental strength and struggle of those brave men and women who stood up against injustice to end the horrors of World War II. Cambron centers her story on civilians transformed to heroes—the prima ballerina turned nurse, the farmer turned medic, the small child turned pillar of strength, the soccer star turned caretaker—and readers are reminded that there are no small parts in this life. Though Cambron shines a spotlight on the vileness of hatred and war, she equally illuminates and emphasizes the way an 'ordinary' gift, if used, can be a lifeline to hope for generations. Awash with vivid characters and exceptionally well-researched, *The Italian Ballerina* is an outstanding work of historical fiction."

—Joy Callaway, international bestselling author of *The Grand Design*

"Poignant and inspirational, *The Italian Ballerina* captured my heart and wouldn't let go. Told in a non-linear style, the stories of Court and Julia in the past and Delaney in the present are woven into the life of Calla, a little Jewish girl caught in the horrors of World War II. Cambron's extensive research is evident, but it is the individual journeys of the characters that make this book special."

—Robin Lee Hatcher, Christy Award–
winning author of *I'll Be Seeing You*

"Based on true events, this exquisite tale impresses with its historical and emotional authenticity. Historical fiction fans won't want to miss this."

—*Publishers Weekly*, starred review, for *The Paris Dressmaker*

"Told with precise details of the Nazi occupation of Paris, the story moves swiftly along, alternating between Lila's story and Sandrine's. The pacing is good, the characters entirely believable, and the revelations of the French underground's workings are fascinating."

—Historical Novel Society for *The Paris Dressmaker*

"In the timeless fashion of Chanel, Ricci, and Dior, Cambron delivers another masterpiece in *The Paris Dressmaker*. Penned with unimaginable heartache, unforgettable romance, and cheering defiance against the oppression the Nazis inflicted on Paris, readers will be swept away into a story where battle-scarred good at last rings victory over evil. *Tres magnifique.*"

—J'nell Ciesielski, author of *The Socialite*

"Kristy Cambron's masterful skill at weaving historical detail into a compelling story graces every page of *The Paris Dressmaker*. A thoroughly satisfying blend of memorable characters, evocative writing, and wartime drama that seamlessly transports you to the City of Light at its most desperate hour. Well done!"

—Susan Meissner, bestselling author of *The Nature of Fragile Things*

"Rich with evocative descriptions of Paris and harrowing details of life during the German occupation, *The Paris Dressmaker* satisfies on all levels. *Tres magnifique!*"

—Sarah Sundin, bestselling and award-winning author of *Until Leaves Fall in Paris*

"Destined to delight fans of Melanie Dobson and Natasha Lester, *The Paris Dressmaker* is a well-researched and beautifully interwoven treatise on courage and conviction in the midst of oppression."

—Rachel McMillan, author of *The London Restoration* and *The Mozart Code*

"Cambron rises to a new level with this intriguing, well-written story of love and triumph."

—Rachel Hauck, *New York Times* bestselling author, for *The Paris Dressmaker*

"Stunning. With as much skill and care as the title's namesake possesses, *The Paris Dressmaker* weaves together the stories of two heroines who boldly defy the darkness that descends on the City of Light. This is Cambron at her very finest. A luminous must-read, and a timeless reminder that light conquers dark."

—Jocelyn Green, Christy Award–winning
author of *Shadows of the White City*

"Another page turner! Kristy Cambron will enthrall readers with this gripping tale."

—Kate Breslin, bestselling author of *Far Side
of the Sea*, for *The Painted Castle*

"Meticulously researched, intricately plotted, and elegantly written, Kristy Cambron weaves a haunting yet heartwarming tale that spans generations. Highly recommended!"

—Sarah E. Ladd, bestselling author of *The Letter
from Briarton Park*, for *The Painted Castle*

"Enchanting and mesmerizing! *Castle on the Rise* enters an alluring land and time with a tale to be treasured."

—Patti Callahan, *New York Times* bestselling
author of *Becoming Mrs. Lewis*

"Cambron's lithe prose pulls together past and present, and her attention to historical detail grounds the narrative to the last breathtaking moments."

—*Publishers Weekly*, starred review, for *The Illusionist's Apprentice*

"Prepare to be amazed by *The Illusionist's Apprentice*. This novel will have your pulse pounding and your mind racing to keep up with reversals, betrayals, and surprises from the first page to the last."

—Greer Macallister, bestselling author of *The
Magician's Lie* and *Girl in Disguise*

"With rich descriptions, attention to detail, mesmerizing characters, and an understated current of faith, this work evokes writers such as Kim Vogel Sawyer, Francine Rivers, and Sara Gruen."

—*Library Journal*, starred review, for *The Ringmaster's Wife*

The
ITALIAN
BALLERINA

ALSO BY KRISTY CAMBRON

STAND-ALONE NOVELS

The Paris Dressmaker

The Illusionist's Apprentice

The Ringmaster's Wife

THE LOST CASTLE NOVELS

The Lost Castle

Castle on the Rise

The Painted Castle

THE HIDDEN MASTERPIECE NOVELS

The Butterfly and the Violin

A Sparrow in Terezin

The
ITALIAN
BALLERINA

KRISTY
CAMBRON

THOMAS NELSON
Since 1798

Library of Congress Cataloging-in-Publication Data

Names: Cambron, Kristy, author.
Title: The Italian ballerina / Kristy Cambron.
Description: Nashville, Tennessee : Thomas Nelson, [2022] | Summary: "A prima
    ballerina. Two American medics. And a young Jewish girl with no name... At the
    height of the Nazi occupation of Rome, an unlikely band of heroes comes together
    to save Italian Jews in this breathtaking World War II novel based on real historical
    events"-- Provided by publisher.
Identifiers: LCCN 2021061545 (print) | LCCN 2021061546 (ebook) | ISBN 9780785232193
    (paperback) | ISBN 9780785232209 (epub) | ISBN 9780785232216
Subjects: LCSH: World War, 1939-1945--Italy--Rome--Fiction. | World War,
    1939-1945--Jews--Rescue--Italy--Rome--Fiction. | LCGFT: Historical fiction. | Novels.
Classification: LCC PS3603.A4468 I83 2022 (print) | LCC PS3603.A4468 (ebook) | DDC
    813/.6--dc23/eng/20220218
LC record available at https://lccn.loc.gov/2021061545
LC ebook record available at https://lccn.loc.gov/2021061546

Printed in the United States of America

22 23 24 25 26 LSC 5 4 3 2 1

For my mom.
And for Marilyn and Harriet—
librarians who placed the beauty of words
into grateful readers' hands,
having become lifelong friends because of it.

Many cities of men he saw and learned their minds,
many pains he suffered, heartsick on the open sea,
fighting to save his life and bring his comrades home.
—HOMER, ODYSSEY

Prologue

But go ye and learn what that meaneth, I will have mercy,
and not sacrifice: for I am not come to call the righteous, but
sinners to repentance.

Matthew 9:13 KJV

18 May 1944
Tiber Island
Rome, Italy

Never open a locked door unless you're certain death doesn't
lurk behind it.

Fine advice if you weren't being hunted down by a swarm of Nazi
soldiers. And if Private Courtney Coleman wanted them to survive
longer than the next five minutes, there was only one chance to break
through locked steel and roll the dice on what they'd find.

"Come on!" He rammed his shoulder against the steel door at
the end of the hospital ward, then brushed blond hair back from his
eyes so he could see to wedge the chisel into the rusted knuckle of
the upper hinge.

Calla stood at his side. Watching. Hushed. And proving far braver than a five-year-old kid should be as chaos erupted in Fatebenefratelli Hospital's halls. But the dread that flashed in her violet eyes told another story.

She'd been through the same trauma before. Had swallowed the same gut-wrenching fear as the uniforms hunted her.

And anger pumped through Court's veins to see the child's ivory suitcase with the splash of cherries on its sides clutched in front of her like a shield. She hugged it as if she'd protect it with her last breath—open door or not.

Another metal hospital bed was flipped on its side behind them. The patients weren't as quiet now, as men crashed bed frames to the tile floor to arrange as barriers between the front of the quarantine ward and the locked door at the end.

"Don't worry, kid." Court glanced over his shoulder in the direction of the activity. "They're just making a big mess is all. It'll be over soon."

Yeah . . . I know. Not much in the way of reassurance.

Calla understood Italian. He couldn't speak but a few words of it. And it didn't help that their hospital ward was now in upheaval. Men organized against the impending threat with barked orders and turned IV towers and bedpans into makeshift weapons. Match that with the untamed popping of gunfire as partisans battled their Nazi overlords in the streets, and it seemed the powder keg of Rome was poised to explode.

"We . . ." *Pound.* "Promised . . ." *Pound, pound.* "To keep you safe," Court said, all calm-like, hoping she'd at least draw comfort from his tone. He turned to look back in those wide eyes. "And we will protect you. Trust me. *Sì?*"

She nodded. "*Sì.*"

Good thing the door, sealed a hundred years or more, didn't

prove shut up forever. The bolt let go with a final frustrated *pop* and fell to the tile at their shoes. Calla reached down to her scuffed Mary Janes, picked it up, and presented the rusty trinket in her palm.

"Would you look at that?" Court flashed a spontaneous smile and rushed to kneel at the next hinge. "This might actually work." He began *pound, pound, shove-pounding* again, forcing the chisel into its rusted knuckle. With more zeal now because they knew it was possible.

The lower hinge followed suit and went easier. Dislodged steel coughed out age-old dust, and Court threw his arm out in a protective arc to back the kid up as the door jerked catty-corner in its frame. He muscled the portal open and poked his head inside. A set of wooden stairs teeming with cobwebs and musty air led downward, with morning sun piercing a single barred window set high against the roof rafters.

No escape there—too small, even for Calla.

Court peered into the stairwell's abyss.

The mystery of where the dark staircase led wasn't ideal. At least it was down. And anything was better than Gestapo flooding into a ward packed with Jews. If Providence smiled, then the escape route would work. And the quarantine ward on the opposite side would have been opened too. At that very moment Julia could be freeing the Jewish women and children to escape down to the ground floor, while AJ and the medical staff distracted the Gestapo until everyone was out.

"*Scappa!*" He ordered Calla to run all the while hoping he'd remembered the right Italian word. When she didn't move, he pointed to the darkness. "You heard me. Scappa—go!"

Her answer was to reach down, pick up the second bolt, and drop it in the front pocket of her sailor dress. Gripping the suitcase, she shook her head with soft brown waves defying him as they danced against the firm set of her chin.

"Fine, kid. You win. We go together." No time to argue about it. Court eased her against the stucco wall just inside the door. Palms out, he commanded, "Just stay, okay? Out of sight. I'll come back for you."

Calla slunk back into the shadows, and Court signaled the rest of the ward, alerting the men: *"È aperto!"*—the door was open. And an order of *"Corri!"* for them to run fast.

One after another, he waved them through. Men trekked down the stairs with their medical-supply weapons. Others fled empty-handed, not flinching between the barricades and any freedom they could grasp. The last to go was Aleksander, the young anti-Fascist leader who pulled his worn leather messenger bag over his shoulder but paused to look Court in the eye.

"The Ponte Cestio," he said in his thick Polish accent. "Get out, and get to the bridge. We'll give you cover as you cross."

Nodding, Court vowed, "Right. We'll meet you there."

He patted Court's shoulder before he darted off behind the rest.

A check of the front row of overturned beds signaled all were out. They were minutes away from freedom—seconds maybe—when the sharp sound of jackboots clipping tile echoed against the high ceiling at the front of the ward.

Court dropped to the floor.

Hard.

He pressed his back into the striped mattress of the nearest bed barricade and shot a glance to the stairwell door. Calla's doe-eyed glare met him across the twenty-foot span, questioning what had happened to make him fall.

"Shh . . ." Court pointed behind him, then pressed a finger to

his lips, entreating silence. When she nodded, he took the compact mirror from his pocket and angled it around the edge of the metal bed frame.

A lone figure stood in the doorway.

Judging by the silhouette of the officer's hat and uniform, it must be Patz—the SS captain with the soulless eyes and Reich-poisoned heart. The Nazi leader would have known by now that male patients had escaped through the open door and he, locked behind the cage wall of metal grating fixed at the front of the ward, could do not a thing about it.

The figure stepped forward. Slowly, moving through light that pierced the edges of the drawn shades. Sunlight flashed against the officer's litzen collar and glinted upon metal as he stepped through the stream, showing a Walther P38 raised in his hand. And now Court could see better that the figure had met with some kind of blow to the face, with a bruise and cut that trickled blood in a crescent under his right eye. The officer tapped the barrel against a tine of the metal grating and peered into the ward.

Court pulled the mirror back.

Before he could pocket it, the figure gave a furious rattle of the cage. The jolt sent the compact from Court's palm to skitter against the floor tile. He palmed it and looked up as Calla buried an inaudible sob with her chin turned down to her suitcase.

For a battle-worn soldier who'd never been a praying man, Court found the surprise of words waiting inside. Prayers—not for himself, but for her. They broke free from some unknown place and spilled out . . .

Please, God—tell the kid not to be brave.

Not this time.

You're the only One who can save her . . .

When Calla finally looked up, Court pointed over his shoulder and mouthed the code words, *cattivo soldato*—it was, in fact, the bad soldier she'd feared. Waving her on, pleading with each try, Court ordered her to leave him behind.

Scappa! he mouthed again.

She shook her head in furious defiance, inching forward in the glow of morning light now streaming into the stairwell, enough that Court could see tears tracking down those little olive cheeks.

Per favore . . . Court mouthed the silent plea again, emotion tripping him as he begged with the thinnest whisper, "Calla. Please go! Scappa—to the garden. Find Julia."

Court stopped short then, hair standing on end, his words cut off by an eerie fall of silence.

The figure had stopped. No more cage rattling. No more pacing. It didn't even sound like gunfire echoed in the streets at the same decibel as before. All Court could hear was the drumbeat of his own heart and the dull echo of the Gestapo's activity in the halls. He stared back at Calla, both of them listening. Waiting. And he holding his breath as her panicked glance darted from the man she trusted to the uniform she most feared.

"*Eine Jüdin! Sie ist da!*" the figure called to the Nazi police teeming the halls. "*Sie ist da!*"

They'd found their prey.

A girl.

A Jew.

Without thinking, Court jumped up.

He ran headlong into the space between the barricade and Calla's little form hovering in the doorway. A bullet couldn't find her if he used every inch of his body to block it first. He'd pulled her back from the fray once before.

If he could just get to her again . . .

The ward split then with deafening sounds Court would never forget: a child's scream, a single gunshot to pierce the air, and the telltale *thump* to the tile as a body fell.

One

As the first streaks of morning light stretched across the horizon, Luftwaffe bombers stormed the skies over the beachhead at Salerno, painting the sand crimson.

Private Courtney Coleman coughed against grit that smashed into his teeth seconds after a bomb blast left him face-planted in the surf. With ears ringing and senses jarred, he stared out at the cadence of waves churned up by Allied destroyers offshore.

The ratcheting sound of machine guns played their horror-filled melody across the beach as 88mm shells whistled down from behemoth cliffs and exploded upon the dunes from the steep banks of the Sele River to the sea. A haunting voice still looped over a loudspeaker, the same mocking as when bow ramps had lowered near the shore and infantry regiments had deployed before dawn. Bullets pinged the waves around him as a thick German accent invited them in English to "come in" and "give up" for attempting to gain the upper hand with what should have been a surprise attack on Italy's mainland.

Waves of milky fog swept over them, the usual camouflage of hexachloroethane—HCE the boys called it—fanning out to obscure a water landing. And the sea air was overtaken by the woodsy scent of camphor and burnt cordite as German artillery swept the beachhead, pitting the soldiers with fire from above.

And their medic teams were called in to mop up hell's hallways in the center of it all.

Rolling onto his shoulder, Court reached out for the wounded soldier they'd tried to carry out from Blue Beach. Wire mesh laid out for the makeshift road lay twisted at Court's side and cut into the canvas of his uniform jacket, leaving his left arm limp and useless. But still, he couldn't feel an onslaught of pain and knew by now he should have. Court fisted another cough in the sand just to be sure he wasn't imagining things.

Liquid rolled off his chin, puddling in his good palm in a pool of crimson.

This is real.

This is happening . . .

I'm hit.

White-hot pain chose that instant to sear through Court's defenses. An armband stamped with a red cross appeared through the chaos—someone shoved the mangled mess of a canvas-and-aluminum litter out of the way to check on the still soldier next to him.

"He's dead."

The figure passed the body, then rushed to Court. Easing him onto his back in the sand, the medic pushed Court's combat helmet aside and ripped his shoulder seam as pain strafed him.

"Ah, no . . . *Court!*"

To everyone, he was Private Coleman. Or a nameless Allied medic. But under the shadow of a red cross–bearing combat helmet, it could only be their medic team leader—a friend, Sergeant AJ Nelson—who'd never called him by name.

Wet sand caked the side of AJ's face and fell from the damp black of his hairline. With Neptune grass wedged in his helmet strap and a cut trickling blood above his eye, he'd been caught up in it too. Seemed in one piece though, thank God. He brushed his own blood away from his eye and went to work ripping off his uniform belt to bind Court's arm.

The lure to drift off grew stronger. Court's eyelids fluttered, closing against the merging chorus of pain, machine-gun fire, and the rhythmic crash of waves . . .

"No, no, no!"

A smack to the face and Court opened his eyes again.

AJ spread two fingers in the shape of a *V* and pointed at his own steel grays under the brim of his combat helmet. "Right here, Soldier! Look at me." AJ turned, gestured out with a prompting wave of his crimson palm, then brought his focus back. "Remember that dish you got at home? The, uh . . . pinup in that photo you carry?"

"She's . . . *not* . . . a pinup."

"'Course not." So like their peacemaking leader to agree, if only to make a soldier's last moments happy. AJ clamped down on Court's shoulder with a terrifying mound of white gauze that grew blood red against the fringes of his peripheral vision.

"Tell me her name again?"

Court welcomed the memory of the peach grove . . . a dusty orchard lane . . . a soft gauze dress . . . and autumn sunset playing with the fire in Penelope's hair. She walked in front of him—barefoot, smiling, reaching back—fingertips drifting a dance along the uneven tops of orchard grass.

"Penn."

"Right. Penelope. That farm girl." AJ looked to someone off to the side, then added, "*No*—if it was the carotid he'd have bled out by now. We used the last tourniquet, so I've got my belt above the brachial. Keep pressure at the neck. Here. And watch it—he may have damage to the spine."

A pair of hands clamped down with choking pressure on Court's collarbone, causing him to roil and cough. And spit more blood.

"Court—your legs. Can you move 'em for me?" AJ watched, seconds only, as Court tried to get his wits about him enough to make his limbs respond. Their leader shook his head. "No? Right."

Court's lower half was shifted to the side of the bombed-out road as the tires of a DUKW chewed over wire mesh at eye level. AJ thundered out a stretcher order, then an explosion lifted a geyser of water and sand some twenty yards out. The medics flattened over Court for a breath's respite, then rose and went back to work, AJ digging in his medic pouch as bullets whistled by their heads.

"You know the drill, Soldier. Keep talking. Tell me about that girl."

Court lay still, unwilling. No one else's business but his.

"You think this is a joke? That's an order. Talk." AJ gave a three-count and the team transferred Court to the litter. Turning to another litter bearer, AJ ripped into a packet with his teeth. "Yep. Morphine. Just one syrette. Along with plasma and this—he's going to need both."

God, no—that's sulfa powder . . .

This is bad.

AJ sprinkled antiseptic powder over Court's collar and arm, then wiped blood on his thigh before he pulled an EMT book and pencil from his medic pack.

Shaking had set in with searing pain, making Court's thoughts too muddled to nail down which medic casualty form AJ was filling out. "What are . . . you . . . writing?"

AJ ignored him. Kept jotting notes as Tenor applied bandages and Dean got the plasma infusion started in his other arm.

"Tell me, Romeo. You goin' to marry her?"

"No."

"Why not?" AJ shook his head. "Bravest man in Clark's 5th Corps can storm a beach mined by the Boches but goes yellow when it comes to a dish? How does that work?"

Court smiled in spite of himself. "Didn't . . . ask." Court drank in a ragged breath through pain, and the remembrance that Penn would always be far too good for the likes of him. "She'd have said . . . no."

"You mean those movie star looks the ladies are always swooning over couldn't charm at least one female on this planet? Thought we might as well have Gary Cooper in the unit. But you'll have to pay off the rest of us drips to keep this headline quiet." AJ finished writing on the tag and twisted the wire onto the button on Court's front patch pocket. "On three, boys."

The ground left Court then.

Or he left the ground.

For the first time he saw his litter bearers on three sides: AJ in a haven over Court's head and shoulders. Dean's tall Iowa-farm-boy build as he carried out front. Their young Bronx crooner, Tenor, marching alongside the IV tower fixed to the litter, with a soldier's body draped in a fireman's carry over his shoulders. Their team of noncombatants were caked in sand and blood and smears of ash as they carried casualties out from the front lines.

Only this time, they carried *him*.

The crew took off up the ridge—the main service road that cut north to the field hospital. Court could feel the telltale suction of boots sinking in and being freed from sand as they trekked over the uneven terrain, the men marching in their trained off-step cadence to minimize jostling. And then there were the courses of pain in Court's body. The shaking. The smoky burn in his nostrils plaguing his lungs' battle for each breath.

The sky shifted from Salerno blue to matte fatigue metal—an ambulance.

Court had seen enough of the nightmare to know he'd been loaded and where it was headed. They'd been piling up Salerno's dead at Red Beach since the first ramps dropped at half past three this morning. Rumor had it doctors there had lost most of their supplies in the predawn landings and had to perform surgeries draped under blankets for cover. Seemed true with makeshift graves lined with helmets ripped wide by shell fragments and rows of combat boots stilled in seagrass. Hours later, they could do little more than patch men back together with spit and Beemans before the worst of the wounded met transport out.

Red Beach would be worse to Court than dying right there in the surf.

"No jeep?" AJ shouted over the rhythm of battle in the background.

A soldier answered, "None available, sir."

"These tires will have trouble slogging through the mud. But if it's the best we've got . . ." AJ climbed up in the truck and squeezed in beside Court. He rapped his palm on the inside of the metal wall. "Let's go—this one can't wait!"

"Don't take me there."

AJ ignored Court's pitiful command. Even refused to meet his eyes. Instead, their sergeant focused on the IV as the engine chugged forward and the beaches of Salerno wept smoke from a thousand fires behind.

Desperate, Court reached out, found AJ's uniform shirt, and fisted it in a vise until the leader was finally forced to look him square in the eyes.

"I said . . . don't take me . . . there."

"So you *can* move your limbs. That's good news." AJ smiled. No doubt in an attempt to hide concern veiled behind his usual dose of brevity. "Very good in fact."

Court muscled AJ down until they were nose to nose, gritting out his words through clenched teeth. "I won't . . . go. Let me die . . . here. D'ya hear me?"

AJ eased Court's fist free and edged back, ignoring his attempt to sound brash.

"I hear you, Soldier. But you aren't dying today. Not on my watch. Just lie back."

Court fell back, body spent. How could he say that? Men died in war every day. In every mission. And on the beaches? Seemed two bought it every second. Yet they somehow managed to weather the near-impossible standard given a medic to judge mortality at a glance. They'd pass over one soldier. Move to the next with the higher survival rate. It was a cruel calculation of fate. And in the hours waiting out the next battle in a foxhole or sleeping in a ditch, each soldier's mind would be plagued with the faces of the nameless dead in a bitter replay reel. Those moments Court kept buried within himself, pushing them back until the next time they donned combat helmets and charged into the fray.

It was to that flicker of humanity he appealed now.

Even if Court survived the field hospital, he could be evaced to a carrier sitting off the coast. And from there, home. Or if fate smiled and he was cleared for service again, it would almost certainly mean reassignment to a new unit. Either scenario he couldn't abide. It was stay with their team or ship back in a pine box. That's what they'd agreed to. Surely Sarge could understand that.

One way or another, Court was in it until the bloody end—the war's . . . or his.

Morphine began to dull the edges of pain, forcing Court to battle against drifting off. He blinked at the ambulance ceiling to stay afloat.

"Promise. Me," he whispered.

AJ tipped his medic helmet back off his brow and flashed a stern glower. "Afraid I can't do that, Private. You'll go where the big brass tell us to take you and that's flat."

Court reached up to his chest pocket and felt around. Nothing— save for the cushion of bandages and the flutter of the medical tag AJ had affixed to him.

His one lifeline was gone.

"Where is it?"

AJ shook his head, then patted his own chest pocket. "Looking for that silver pocket watch of yours? You told me to take it if you ever went down. Remember? If you want it back now, you'll have to earn it." He stared down at Court, still tough as nails.

But as AJ turned to scan the bomb-blasted landscape out of the back of the truck, something flashed in his profile. A darkness that took AJ's steely eyes a fraction deeper into the abyss of war as the maze of makeshift roads snaked them through Salerno's hairpin twists and turns.

"Just stay alive, Court." He squeezed Court's good shoulder without looking down. "Let the morphine do its job. We'll do the rest."

In the blur of artillery fire and the welcome abeyance that finally convinced Court to fall away, AJ's voice faded and was replaced by the memory of haunting words Penn had said the day he'd walked out her door:

"You can't keep living for yourself, Court. Once you figure out what that means, you'll finally find home . . ."

Two

A ballerina ought to have mastered the art of patience.

In Julia Bradbury's profession it was a longtime companion, if not an acceptable overlord. But to find the lack of it within herself now was maddening—especially if she must endure Winston Peterbrooke's grumbling when she did appear, dripping rain-soaked puddles on his talent agency doorstep.

Rather than go straight on to morning rehearsals, Julia made a snap decision to push her way off the packed train and exit at the High Street station. The march to west London offered little reassurance, greeting her with an unseasonably chilly rain and insufferable gusts of wind that twisted her umbrella inside out. And there she was after, tracking rain in the lift and tapping a gloved index finger against her chin as she watched the lights ping with the rise to the third floor.

Oh dear . . . Whatever will Winston say?

As one of the shrewdest talent agents in the London entertainment world, Winston Peterbrooke was renowned for undercutting the competition to shave off a percentage here, another hundred pounds there. But to the ones who really knew him, he was tireless in his efforts to angle for his clients. But those clients might not know the true manner of the man underneath the rumpled suit and outwardly boorish manner, unless of course they had been a client as long as Julia had.

Or a friend.

Winston was the only person left in her life she could fully trust with a terribly important matter such as this. And whether it was proper to arrive unannounced, if he did indeed have news . . . it could change everything.

Julia bustled through the frosted-glass door into the office, shaking the last spray of raindrops from her rubbish umbrella onto the art deco tile. Unbelting her trench gave a good excuse to hang back and glance around the reception room. Empty chairs stood like a row of overworked soldiers, their worn wood and garish primrose brocade faded under years of use. Two high-arched Georgian windows permitted the tiniest glow of light from the streetlamps below. And the longtime secretary sat alone at her post behind the desk.

What a relief. No inquisitive clients to root out a burgeoning story about London's ballet circuit.

Julia exhaled. Short. Shaky. Yet hopeful.

"Why, Miss Bradbury." Mrs. Entwhistle's eyes brightened when Julia stepped up. "Lovely to see you, dear. As usual."

"And you, Mrs. Entwhistle. Good morning."

The old secretary never missed a trick—and certainly not with that hovering, half glimmer of a smile. Something had obviously stirred, and it wasn't tipple in Winston's morning Darjeeling.

"I awoke to a message in my box?"

"Yes. I telephoned your Mrs. Bloom's boardinghouse with it

yesterday eve. But we advised Mr. Peterbrooke wished you to stop in this afternoon."

"Right. This afternoon." Julia looked down at her disheveled state. "So . . . naturally I arrived on the first train, through our fair city's most hospitable nature, I might add."

"Of course you did." Mrs. Entwhistle tossed a sidelong glance at the frosted glass that read *AGENT* in thick, Roman block letters, then didn't even try not to beam back. "Well, you'll be no worse for wear. Not with this news."

Julia anchored a gloved palm at the belted waist of her suit, gripping the peplum like a peacock-blue lifeline.

"A message. From whom?"

The secretary lowered her voice to a whisper, mouthing the words *"Vic-Wells."*

Julia's heart soared, and she instinctively held her breath.

"I normally haven't time to make sense of the lot that passes from my desk to Mr. Peterbrooke's, as you know how busy we are. But I did look over this one. And saw the name Margot Fonteyn alongside Robert—"

"Helpmann." Julia's stomach flip-flopped at the mention of such top-tier names in their performance world. "Oh my word."

"You see? It was only a matter of time for the right eyes to take notice of your talent. And now you shall dance under the stage lights at Covent Garden."

Mrs. Entwhistle reached for Julia's hand and gave a right proper squeeze. Winston's door opened then, the old hinges screeching like an angry owl. He appeared in the doorway in a starched white shirt, navy polka-dot bow tie, and the usual bedraggled tweed waistcoat over wool trousers—not unlike a wise old sage who appeared at precisely the right time.

"Mrs. E—where on earth have you hidden the steno pads?" He held a sheet of paper in one hand and a pair of gold wire-rimmed spectacles teetering in the other, reading whatever had caught his attention.

"Where I always do, sir. Your desk. Left side. Bottom drawer." She winked at Julia. "And your nine o'clock has arrived."

"I haven't a nine o'clock." He checked his wristwatch.

"You do now, sir."

"Winston. Good day." Julia stepped forward, smiling sweetly and without guile, for the man with the rumpled suit, graying temples, and dwindling roster of reputable clients was still the oldest of old benefactors in her life.

"Ah . . . Julia. Why am I not surprised?" He sighed, exaggerated though it was, and then remarked, "And must you always look like that?"

She patted the coil of chestnut hair pinned in a pert bun under her rain-speckled tam, as if checking to see whether the rain had done irreparable damage.

"Look like what exactly?"

"Like I'm Father Christmas and you've just won the sweepstakes all wrapped up in one. Well, you're here now. So I suppose you must come in."

Julia trailed him into the office. The aged swivel chair creaked when he settled his weight on it, and he gestured for her to close the door. After clicking it closed, she slipped into one of the chairs opposite the desk. She waited as he took two aspirin from a jar in the drawer of the old walnut desk and downed them with the last swill of liquid from a teacup.

Done and dusted, Winston cleared his throat and turned to inspect the haphazard pile of papers upon the desk.

"So. We received correspondence from Ninette de Valois."

"I see. And?" Posture pin straight even as her insides melted, Julia removed her dove-gray gloves. Slowly—forcing herself to go one finger at a time as she waited for him to continue.

"Yes. Markova has gone on to Ballet Russe de Monte Carlo and is quite happy to tour as their star. As such, Vic-Wells is looking to add new names to the roster alongside Margot Fonteyn and Robert Helpmann. And it seems they are interested in exploring what we may have to offer."

He looked down to a card-stock missive in his hand, giving it a skim. "De Valois says: 'Miss Bradbury has shown herself quite clever and technically proficient. She possesses a genuine level of artistry well beyond her years.'"

"Really? She said all of that?"

"Mm-hmm." He dropped the card on the desktop and laced his fingers over the pile. "Audition must have gone alright then."

"It did."

A thousand tiny longings had shot through Julia's heart after her tryout at the famed Vic-Wells Ballet a fortnight ago. And just two days prior she'd been called back for a second tryout, but this time with the enigmatic company head Ninette de Valois herself. And now as Julia sat in Winston's office, the news she'd been aching to hear forever was poised to fall from his lips . . . a placement with one of the top companies in London. In the world, for that matter.

The years of study. Of sacrifice. Of dreaming . . . all hinged on this moment.

"I wish you'd spit it out, dear girl. I haven't got all day."

She leaned forward in her chair, nearly sinking off the edge of the leather cushion as she braced a palm on the front of the desk, fingernails digging into the wood.

"Oh, alright. You want me to beg, and I will! Whatever did they say?"

Winston's face warmed with what looked akin to pride, and he slid the card across the desktop in front of her. "Congratulations."

Julia swept it up and shot to her feet, pressing the card stock to her heart.

"You darling, darling man! I'm not even cross with you for putting me through the paces. I'm so happy, my heart could burst!"

"Yes, yes. Sit down." He waved her off, the mock peevishness taking over again as she bit her bottom lip and sat back again like a good girl. "Down to brass tacks. It's a *pas de deux*. They wish to engage you for the 1940 season, and we shall see how it goes for a new contract after that."

"A *pas de deux*?" Julia shook her head. "I don't understand. I auditioned for a *pas seul*—the variation for the Bluebird. I prefer solo pieces."

"I am aware of that. So you must unlearn and then learn again. Quickly in fact. It seems they have selected you for Aurora."

"The lead. In *The Sleeping Beauty*. At Covent Garden. You cannot be serious," Julia breathed out as tears wet her eyes, and she seriously considered pecking a kiss to that shining bald head of his.

"Then I shall tell your company you will not be renewing your contract with them. And you'll begin with Vic-Wells first of the year. Though they'll have you in for rehearsals in a thrice, no doubt. So be ready to get straight to work."

"Vic-Wells . . . ," Julia whispered.

The air seemed to shift as she said the words aloud, as if the stacks of old books and ledgers suddenly had a shimmer of magic about them, and the dim light from the desk lamps seemed romantic instead of working overtime to compete with the sullen skies outside. Rain if it must; nothing could dampen her spirits this day. And hopefully, not if the year brought . . . who knew what, given the rumors splashed upon the front page of the *Daily Herald* each day.

"But what if . . . Is war really coming? Won't that change things?"

He stared back, in a far-stretching gaze that suggested he hadn't shed the ghosts of the first war.

"I shouldn't fret about it now. If there is a war, we shall take it on the chin and chuck everything we've got at the enemy, as we did the first time. And press on."

"Yes. I suppose we must." The wall clock chimed nine, cutting the moment with its cry. Julia rose. "Oh dear. I'm late."

"Your company will understand."

"I daresay they will." She hurried to the door but turned, beaming back at the figure of the man who in so many ways had been the captain steering the ship of Julia's and her parents' dreams. "Winston. You know I've waited so long for . . ." She sighed, her eyes daring to mist again. "Thank you ever so much."

"Do not thank me, my girl. Just get on and blow out the lights on that stage, hmm? Make your dear father and mother proud. They would be, you know, if they were here."

"I should hope they would."

She slipped her gloves on as quickly as she could, not thinking of the years her parents had dreamed their daughter would make it to this day, only to be two years shy in seeing it for themselves. Julia belted her trench and hooked her satchel in her elbow, preparing to make a run through the deluge outside.

"Then endeavor to give London a show not soon forgotten. And do not be intimidated by Anton. No matter what the company heads say, yours is the star that is rising. And you will surpass him one day.

He's a proficient talent but hasn't near as much grace and not half the grit. That, at least, I do remember about the chap."

Julia froze, her fingertips drifting off the edge of the brass doorknob. He couldn't possibly have just spoken that name—not in tandem with the news she'd waited to hear all her life.

She turned back.

"Anton . . . Vasile?"

"Well, not Anton Dolin. Vasile is the one still trying to make his mark. Surely you remember him. You've danced in the same circles for enough time now. Didn't your paths cross a few years back, in New York perhaps?"

"Yes. In New York."

The ghostly memory of a dashing young *ballerino* flitted through her mind—the blond crown, molten-chocolate eyes, and lean build. The effortless, elegant perfection to every move. The way his hands found their target of her fingertips or her waist, always with pinpoint precision and ease. And then there was the arrogance. The entitlement. And the liberties—a remembrance that was fast making Julia recoil as if the doorknob had seared her hand.

Yes, he had talent. But something said his aspirations didn't stop with a starring role in New York or London. He wanted more. And he'd do anything to get it.

"If I'm Aurora, then Anton is . . . ?"

"Prince Désiré." Winston swiped his glasses down the bridge of his nose, with a glimmer of actual annoyance on this go. He peered over their top rim. "Is there a problem?"

"No." Julia painted a smile to her lips. "None at all."

"Grand. Then I shall telephone de Valois and tell her she has her stars. And in the meantime, I suggest you find your scruples and give them a good talking to. A prima ballerina must be confident.

And you *are*. Let's see you summon that air going out of here that you had dancing in."

Winston didn't look up after that.

The pile of papers on his desk lured him back, and the teapot on his desk invited him for a second cup. What choice had Julia but to nod, smile, and obey? And summon a façade of confidence as she stepped out in a driving rain with her grand news—even if, deep down, she was left broken by it at the very same time.

Three

PRESENT DAY
ST. JOHN ROAD
STARLIGHT, INDIANA

Delaney Coleman eased the turquoise '46 Ford truck to a stop on the gravel drive, then cut the engine. A breeze swept in when she opened the door, rustling her shoulder-length blonde waves and stirring leaves to swirl in front of the windshield like falling snow. She paused in the cab and watched them fly, her fingertips frozen to the keys still in the ignition.

It hadn't hit until that moment—this would be their first harvest without Grandpa. The first holiday season without Dr. Coleman to flip the switch on the Christmas lights illuminating the town square. And the first time he wasn't standing on the porch in one of his old flannel shirts, waving to greet her when she came home for a visit.

It would be the first of many firsts that now stretched before them.

A drive down the long lane on their property had shown that the orchard had fared well, thanks to Dad and the loyal employees who'd kept the business going since Grandpa's heart trouble had started up in the spring. And they'd taken it over completely after the shock of a funeral so soon after. But now that Delaney's short visit had stretched into weeks of doing normal things to help aging parents—like heading to town for coffee and cleaning supplies or worrying about the piles of leaves that had gathered around the porch steps—the thought of going back home to Seattle felt further away. And wrong somehow. Like a rust-patched truck without an owner and a tired old farmhouse that couldn't go on as it once had.

Delaney sighed, pocketed the keys as she hopped out of the cab, and headed up the covered porch steps. She'd expected to paint on a brave smile to face her parents, not to be hit with the scents of bacon, brown sugar, and vinegar the instant she stepped up to the screen door. She peered over the crate in her arms to the disaster area that seemed as if a mad scientist had invaded the farmhouse kitchen and set up an experiment on every available space. And on counters that had been neat as a pin when she'd left.

Oh no. Momma's canning again . . .

This was never good.

"Shoo, Sherlock!" Delaney eased their eager tabby aside with a nudge of her work boot and tugged the screen door open. He slipped in past her as she looked around, and her heart sank.

When Grandma Penn had passed from cancer so many years before, Edie Coleman had stayed busy. Taking care of everyone. Making arrangements. And she'd holed up in the kitchen and canned half the county and probably a third of their peach harvest in a single funeral weekend. Now after having lost Grandpa too—but so suddenly—it looked as though she'd reverted to "busy" again, with a forty-quart stockpot simmering away on the stove and rainbow-hued bowls of late-season peaches, beans, and a basket of apples—only half peeled—left abandoned on the counter.

Delaney wedged the crate into a space on the butcher's block island, nudging back a white porcelain colander of beans that still needed to be snapped. It tipped before she could catch it, sending Sherlock to skitter down the hall and a mass of green shoots to fan out across the floor.

"Great. Way to go, Del." Kneeling down, Delaney scooped up the mess as she called out, "Momma? You awake?"

"I'm back here!" Her mom's voice carried from the valet pantry's open door.

Delaney carried the colander to the sink and switched off the burner to the boiling stockpot on her way back. She found her momma sitting cross-legged on the hardwood, clad in mechanic coveralls and worn Stuart plaid, a pencil stuck through the sugar-blonde twist knotted with a rubber band at her nape. She pecked something on the laptop keyboard splayed on her lap, then swiped the pencil and went about ticking an invisible line against a row of peach preserves.

"What are you doing?"

"I got to canning and realized we don't have enough labels. I thought I'd go ahead and order them."

"Labels?" Delaney crouched down and glanced over her shoulder to the kitchen. While a stockpot had been boiling away and half the orchard was strewn about the counter space, it was labels that needed her undivided attention?

"Does Dad know you're doing this?"

"Oh, he went out to the orchard hours ago. And why not do it now? Good a time as any. How else will we get these jars ready to sell? Christmas-basket packing will be here before we know it, and we'll need labels to do it."

"Yes, but we have a team for that. Workers in the orchard and a canning facility at the farmers' market. They've been planning for the harvest and holiday seasons all year. And they know what they're doing. So you really don't have to do this right now."

"Please, Del. Don't start." Edie waved her off with a flick of the wrist and tracked back over the rows of jars, starting her pencil eraser down the next line. "If I'm not allowed to put my oar in with you, we're not putting one in the water on the other side of the boat."

"I'll pretend that's not a remark about me being thirty, newly single, very likely unemployed, and sleeping in my old bed again."

Even though Delaney might as well call a spade what it was. She didn't know which break was easier: To attend a funeral by herself meant she learned just how much her boyfriend wasn't in it for the long haul. Or to be on thin ice from prolonged bereavement leave from her dead-end junior editor position for a small magazine . . . She didn't have the foggiest idea what to do with her life now. In the end Delaney had never expected a clean slate to come like it had. And she certainly never expected so many things to be upended at once.

Living out of her old bedroom again was the least of her worries.

"I'm sorry. I didn't—" Her mother stopped short, creased her brow, and slapped a palm to her leg. Seemed grief was an unpredictable trip wire for all three of them these days. "I didn't mean that, Del. You know how glad we are that you're home."

"I know."

"And it's not the labels I'm concerned about."

"Don't you think I know that too?"

Momma sighed through the obvious—that someone or something else was at the forefront of her mind—but pulled a folded piece of paper from her front coverall pocket and handed it over.

"What's this?" Delaney unfolded the paper and scanned the missive printed on official company letterhead.

"We received a letter forwarded from the town museum to the Jenkins' Orchard company address. It seems the sender didn't put it together that the Jenkins name had turned to Coleman a generation back, and they tried to track down your grandfather at his medical office instead. They didn't know he'd passed and that his will left the clinic building to the museum."

"This is signed by a Frederick Wilson, attorney-at-law, on behalf of his client in . . . Rome, Italy? And it's dated over a month ago! Momma—why didn't you or Daddy tell me?"

"Your father thought it would blow over."

Delaney nodded and offered a faint smile. Just a little show of support. What good did it do to pass blame? "And let me guess—it didn't?"

Momma avoided her stare. And it shattered Delaney to watch her mother's chin quiver a little before she continued. "No. It seems this attorney is attempting to make contact for this client of his—a family who claims your grandfather had property that belongs to them. As your grandfather's will stipulated his medical office building be donated to the museum on behalf of the town, everything inside went with it. When the museum staff searched the attic, they found some things. And now that lawyers are involved, they've handed the items over to us to manage."

"What items? What is it this client wants?"

"There's a box in the mudroom, so that must be it." Momma pointed to a box tucked back by the kitchen door, teeming with books and worn wares and what looked like a stack of old editions of *The Saturday Evening Post* peeking out from the top. "The museum dropped it off last week. We called your aunts Mary and Agnes to see what they might know about it, but they didn't have a clue either since they'd married and lived away all these years. So that stuff's just been gathering dust in the clinic attic—mainly books and magazines, some old papers and photos . . . We didn't look through it in detail because your father just found it too difficult right now. But there was something special in the box: your great-grandfather's pocket watch. Your father always wondered what had become of it. Now we know. And it's the only thing of value there, but this attorney says his client has the right to choose what he wants. They claim to have letters from your grandfather saying so."

"Have you seen their letters?"

"No. And we're not certain we want to, not if they expect your father will let his family heirlooms go just like that. At least not to a stranger." She openly brushed away a tear now, giving a soft shake of her head. "It'd be like losing your grandfather all over again. And I don't think he could take that."

"Well, nothing leaves this house unless we say so."

"We may not have a choice, Del. They're moving forward and they say they'll do it in court if they have to," her mom tossed out, walking out of the pantry with the laptop still open. "The orchard business account received an email with a video call invitation to hash it out, but your father's been putting off sending a reply. You know his pride—he was afraid he wouldn't be able to hold his tongue, and I can't say I blame him for it."

"A video call?" Delaney trailed her into the kitchen. "When?"

"Ten o'clock I believe."

"You mean today?" Delaney glanced up at the kitchen clock on the wall. "Momma—that was five minutes ago!"

"We'll just send an email back that says we won't be bullied. And if this client—a Mr. Santini—wants his attorney to try again, then we'll lawyer up too."

"I won't be bullied either. But you'd better believe I want to talk to this guy face-to-face. This is no time to be terrorizing a grieving family for the last memories of Grandpa. If you don't want to make the call, then please let me. It's better to see where they stand, even if we are late."

"You never were one to back down from a fight."

"That's right." Delaney shot her a smile as she stooped under the table to plug the laptop power cord into the wall outlet. "And I'm not about to start now."

Delaney retrieved the box and set it on the counter behind the kitchen table. She angled the laptop camera so it would have a perfect view behind her—a little enticement for whoever this creep was. If he wanted any of her grandfather's things, he'd have to go through her to get them.

When her mother squeezed onto the stool beside her, Del whispered away from the camera, "You don't have to do this. I can handle it if you want."

"Maybe I'd like to look this gentleman in the eye. You know, guilt-trip him for picking on a grieving family for their patriarch's good name? And if that doesn't work, at least he'll see we Colemans stick together in a fight. He doesn't know how lucky he is it's not your father sitting here." Her mother adjusted the rolls on her shirtsleeves and calmed wisps of hair around her face before squaring her shoulders to the camera.

Delaney connected the call, and a picture flipped to a calendar-worthy Italian scene staring back. The camera's view was set in the midst of a magical courtyard at a rustic wood table, backdropped by vineyard hills and villa walls bathed in golden sunshine. Italian string lights interlaced the branches of a knobby old tree, their bulbs dancing with a gentle sway in the breeze. Lemon trees yawned over the borders of a high stone wall, and parasol pines created shadows over a weathered iron gate—left ajar—flanked by bronze lanterns on each side.

It was breathtaking . . .

It was Rome . . .

And it was *perfect*.

"Hello?" Delaney waited until a pair of jeans and a washed-out blue tee crossed in front of the camera, blocking the blast of sun.

"*Buongiorno*. One moment, per favore."

Thank goodness. The guy spoke some English, even if he did own a slightly incredible—and somewhat distracting—Italian accent.

A digital camera came into view as it was set on the rugged wood tabletop. He followed that with a toss of a military-style jacket over the arm of a metal chair and set a glass of golden wine on the opposite side. Sun-kissed arms and a rough unshaven face came into view as he muscled a canvas messenger bag to hook on the back of his chair, then dropped down in the seat. The man's attention was still focused on setting his space as he looked away and ran his hand through unruly, deep-chocolate curls that hung over his brow.

Momma flicked Delaney's kneecap under the table.

She gave her mother an exaggerated eye roll that said, *"Yeah. I get it. A bit of a looker. So what?"* And she prayed that would be the end of it. The last thing Delaney needed was to come out of a failed relationship and a potential cross-country move to enter right into some scheme at video matchmaking. If she had her way, this was a temporary headache to battle through—nothing more.

"Well, I've seen quite enough," Momma whispered on a silent clap of her hands. She rose and started to leave. "I'll just—"

"Where are you going?" Delaney whispered.

"I have calls to return."

Calls? Really? Delaney mouthed, stopping short from shouting,

"What happened to the Colemans stick together in a fight?" as her mother waved her off, chuckling as she disappeared down the hall.

Delaney cleared her throat. "Mr. Santini?"

"Sì. I am here. You were late, so—"

"I know. And I'm sorry for that. I just found out about the call this morning and had to rush to make it."

"It's alright." He was still searching through his bag, digging until he found a pen. "And it's the old joke, but Mr. Santini is my father. So Matteo will be fine."

He pulled out a legal pad with paper worn and curled at the bottom, then rolled a page over the top and held it ready. Odd, but he still didn't seem to want to look into the camera. In fact, he seemed to want to look anyplace but at her, and kept his eyes drawn down.

"Okay. I'm Delaney, but everyone calls me Del."

"Fine. Del it is. You ready?"

"Yes. I'm sure you're busy, so I'll make this brief. I'd like to talk about your letters first."

Matteo finally sat straight and looked square at the camera, giving her a true shot from ice-blue eyes. "I'm sorry, who are you again?"

"Delaney Coleman." When the name didn't break any ice through his blank stare, she tried again. "Dr. Courtney Coleman's granddaughter?"

"You're not from the museum?"

"No. We were forwarded a letter from your attorney, indicating you believe our family heirlooms belong to you. And that you have letters from my grandfather stating so. I'd like to see proof of that claim." Delaney swept unruly waves behind her ear, blinked back calmly, and raised her chin a little for good measure.

He sat through a few seconds of the uncomfortable silence that followed, then darted his gaze off camera. After a few short whispers and a curt nod, he came back. "And should I have invited our attorney to join this call?" Matteo tapped the pen on his tablet and half smiled. "I thought this was just to catalog items the museum found."

"You mean property the museum gave back to its rightful owners? I don't think we need lawyers to do that. Do you?"

"No. I suppose we can hold off for now. But to answer your question, yes. Nona wrote letters in her day. It was kind of her thing." Matteo shrugged. Lazed back in the chair a little. "And we have quite a few to her from your grandfather. So yes, we can back up every claim."

"I'd like to see the letters."

"Of course. I can email copies. But you'll need a little luck to get through them. We just found them in Nona's things ourselves and some are many decades old, so in poor condition. Oh—and . . . they're in Italian."

Italian? That seemed a little far-fetched. The grandfather Delaney had known all her life didn't speak any other languages, except for reading the occasional Latin in his old medical journals.

Delaney crossed her arms over her chest. "That's not possible. My grandfather wasn't fluent in Italian. We'd have known if he was."

"Well, he must have learned. Because we have letters from a Dr. Courtney Coleman of Starlight, Indiana, stating that my grandmother—Mrs. Calla Santini—can have her property back at any time. And she's asking for it now."

"Really. Why now after all this time?"

Maybe you just found out what something in that box is worth.

"That's immaterial. The point is, she's asking for it. And before I make an effort to recover *our* property, she wants to see what you have."

She wants to see . . .

Delaney edged forward in her chair, instinct ready to carry her straight through the camera. Someone was obviously with him.

"Wait—is your grandmother there right now? Can I speak with her?"

"No."

"No, she's not there? Or no, I can't talk to her?"

He clicked his pen. "Just a run-through of the items will be fine. And I'm recording this, unless you have any objections."

"No objections. So we'll just start with the items on top then." Delaney turned, leaning back to the box and thumbing through what was there. "There are some old magazines . . . a cigar box that looks like it is filled with old family photographs . . . a few books that seem old enough to go back to wartime. My grandfather was a World War Two vet. And quite the reader, so it fits. And my great-grandfather's pocket watch should be in here too. I just haven't found it yet."

It didn't take long to unearth a crimson ribbon–bound stack of papers—indeed, letters—buried under the mound of magazines, and her heart started to flutter enough to cut off her voice.

"Um . . . just a moment." Carefully, Delaney pulled one from the stack, its yellowed envelope marked with Grandpa's telltale hand-writing on the outside. She opened it. Hands shaking. Forgetting for a moment that she was still on camera. Then she sank back on an exhale. "I can't believe it. There are letters here too. You were right. They're in Italian. At least that's what it looks like, because I can't—"

"Wait—what is that?"

Drawn back by his missed opportunity to gloat, Delaney looked up again. "The letters? There's a stack of them here."

"No—*that*." Matteo pointed with his pen, as if he could push her out of the way and reach straight through to what interested him on the kitchen wall behind. Delaney walked fingers over items until she came to a cracked leather suitcase handle, and he shouted, "Whoa! Right there."

Delaney lifted it out—cute little thing. Even if it was yellowed with age and had faded red-leather piping along the seams, the cherry bundles on the outside reminded her of a case that might have once held a Shirley Temple doll in the 1930s or '40s.

"You mean this old thing? I don't know. Looks like a child's suitcase maybe."

Matteo darted his hand so fast it knocked the glass to one side, spilling wine across the tabletop. He jumped up, grabbed his camera to save it first, and then rescued the legal pad, fanning paper as liquid dripped off the table's edge.

"You alright there?"

"Yeah. Sì—fine." Matteo looped the camera strap over his neck so he could mop and move items.

Matteo Santini might have said he was fine, but he clearly wasn't. It was the hardest thing not to laugh at the man. He'd gone from Mr. Cool and Casual to looking like someone had just set off fireworks under his chair. He moved to one side and sat again, angling the laptop away from the spill. And leaned into the camera with a much more attentive air. "Is there, uh . . . anything inside it?"

"I don't think so." Delaney shook it, then tried the latch. "It doesn't feel like it, but it's locked. And I don't see a key in the box."

"*Grazie.* Just a moment, per favore."

Looking off camera again, he half covered his chin with curled fingers to shield his lips, then came back. He leaned forward, folding fingers on the dry corner of the tabletop.

"So we're prepared to pay for shipping and offer a generous finder's fee for your trouble. But that package needs to be insured and tracked when you send it. Maybe have the museum ship it to make sure it's not damaged coming over."

"I'm sorry—a finder's fee for what?"

"The suitcase. It's ours. And we want it back."

Del set the suitcase aside, extra careful this time as she positioned it just at the edge of his camera's view. "No."

"No what?"

"No, we're not ready to part with this. It was my grandfather's after all."

"That's not possible," Matteo cut in, proving he was not very schooled in keeping his irritation at bay. "Not when it's *my* nona's."

"Mr. Santini." When the business side of her reverted to using his surname, his face seemed to ice over even more. "I've just learned of the existence of these things today, so I'm willing to consider that we may not have all the information there is about them. But to be honest, we're going through a difficult time right now and I need absolute proof that anything here belongs to your nona before we'll even consider parting with a family heirloom. And if this suitcase is caught in the cross fire, I'm sorry."

He tipped his brow a fraction higher, either at the challenge, her using the endearment belonging to *his* Italian gran, or both.

"And who said we're willing to agree to anything when we have proof that we own it? Our lawyer is ready to go to court if need be."

Before he could bully his way into ownership of the suitcase, a loud bark of a woman's voice cut the speaker with *"Silenzio!"*

Matteo cleared his throat over the rebuke and said, *"Mi scusi."*

Delaney heard his name and then the lyrical notes of what sounded to be an Italian female talking a mite too fast to be commenting on the weather. Though Delaney could make out a stitch of it, it did sound like someone was giving him the business.

Oh, to see who it was and shake her hand.

"*Va bene*, Del." Matteo came back and flexed his jaw like the next bit pained him considerably. "We'll agree to whatever conditions you want."

"That's good to hear. But I've already said I'm not ready to send this over."

"I know that. So we'll pay your way to bring the suitcase here to us."

Delaney blinked back, staring into that gorgeous Italian landscape. She must have dreamed he'd just said that. "You mean to Rome?"

He nodded. "Sì."

"You're saying you'd actually pay for us to bring this suitcase to you?"

"Tivoli to be exact. And no matter the cost."

Right. And that turn of events was even more unexpected than a tug-of-war for a worn-out old suitcase.

"Well, I'd have to think about it."

"Of course." Matteo looked off camera, then smiled to someone. And nodded slightly, as if resigned. "Talk about it with your spouse or, uh, your family. We'll pay for someone to travel with you if necessary."

It was then that Momma's shadow emerged and she poked her head in from the hall, nodding like her chin had been mechanized. She mouthed a furious repeat of, *Go! You go!*

"No spouse. So if I did come . . ." Too much to explain. And if her momma's jumping jacks in the hall said anything about it, she'd more than given her blessing for Delaney to make the quick trip and smooth out things for them on her own. "It would probably just be me. As I've said, our family has a lot to deal with at home right now. How soon?"

"I hate to put pressure on you because I don't know how you're fixed, but the sooner the better for us. We need this resolved as quickly as possible."

"We do too. At least that we can agree on."

"*Bravo.* The museum will have our address here in Tivoli. And our references, so either they or you can see that all checks out. Shouldn't take more than a few days. It's really just for you to give us your travel dates, and we'll send you the ticket." Matteo paused in the back-and-forth, and something in the way his gaze stayed on her whispered there was more to the story than an old suitcase could reveal at first glance.

"And you don't want anything else in this box?"

"You can bring it if you'd like, but no. All we want is the suitcase."

"And you'll help me translate the letters when I arrive?"

"I will." He nodded. Just once. As if that was a bargain struck. "If it's what you want."

The sun burned bright behind his shoulders, casting the glow of gold upon the trees and villa walls. Delaney ran a fingertip over the suitcase handle. How could the innocent little thing be lost for more than half a century and only after her grandfather was gone decide it was time to go home? If that's what Rome really was.

It might have been locked, but the suitcase opened up a host of questions to which she was now curious to find answers.

"Okay, Mr. Santini." Delaney nodded. *Deep breath.* "I accept. I'll meet you in Rome."

Four

R egret was a killer—especially the morning after.

Court sat in the passenger seat of his father's Ford Deluxe, debating which was the more sobering cure for a hangover: another bout with a busted-up kisser or rattling around in the old tin can with Dr. Henry Coleman after he had to bail his son out of the county lockup.

Again.

The coupe rumbled over bumpy wagon roads, shooting pain through Court's side with every jounce of the tires. He eased his hand up under his armpit but kept his shoulder pinned against the door. Best to hide the evidence of a support palm to bruised ribs if he wanted to save any face at all.

"Hurts, don't it?"

Great. He noticed.

Court kept quiet.

"Do you have sharp pain on a deep breath?"

"No."

"Cough up any blood in the night?"

"No. Look, I'm fine. Nothing's busted up inside. It was just somebody's fool attempt to feed a bruised ego. Nothing I can't handle." Court grimaced again—the inopportune timing of the road sent the jalopy over a divot that seemed bent on punishing him for his third brawling arrest in the last year. Probably a record for their little town, if not a routine for Court, since the night before had been his first back in town after a few months' absence.

"I shake my head at what you can actually handle in this life. And to think you once wanted to go to medical school—to help people." He stared out the windshield, as if unable to see anything but his son's string of failures laid out before them.

"Things change."

"You can say that again. So how did it start this time?"

Besides Guthrie Jenkins walking into the bar and ripping me from my stool without warning?

Court shrugged. "Try asking the guy who actually started it."

"Do not get clever with me, my boy. You know it matters a great deal in this community. I want an answer."

They'd done this song and dance before. Many times. And badly at that. His father would never believe the truth from Court's lips. Not now. Not ever. So Court opted for the predictable avenues of avoidance and sarcasm to do the rescuing for him.

"I don't know. I'd knocked back a few. He had too. And we settled a disagreement like two men in a bar."

"Two men in a bar, hmm? Not men. Boys."

Court sighed. Rolled his eyes, but only to the cornfields out the window. "Look. I didn't come back to fight—not with you or anybody else. Guthrie Jenkins just found me first is all."

"We thought you were gone for good this time. So why'd you come back?"

That was miles past the line Court was prepared to admit to.

He knew the truth of Dr. Henry Coleman's infirmity, even if the rest of their small farm community didn't. Court had lived with the man. He'd read enough medical journals to know the extent to which his eyesight was failing. That, taken with a request from Court's mother to look after the adoptive father who would need help after she was gone, added up to one thing: before long, he'd probably lose his sight altogether. But how did you look after a stubborn man who didn't want help—especially not from the adopted son who'd disappointed him at every turn?

Court shrugged. "Business."

"And what business would that be when we haven't seen hide nor hair of you since the funeral?"

"Doesn't matter now."

"I'd say it does when I had to make a house call to Patrick Jenkins's place middle of the night to set his son's broken nose. Then to find out you were back in town and responsible for it. That warrants more than excuses in my book—not to mention an assault charge and jail time in the eyes of the local sheriff."

"I don't recall the sheriff was there to see who threw the first punch."

"And with your track record, who do you suppose that was?"

"If it makes you feel better, Guthrie landed a few on me too. In the end he oughta be thanking me. That nose of his never was straight. And I aim to keep doling out corrective fists until it is."

Dr. Coleman slammed his foot on the brake so fast, Court about flew into the chronometer embedded in the dash. He braced a hand to the timepiece to keep from slamming clean into it.

"Hey—watch it!" Court clamped his eyes shut, pain searing through his side as the car idled in the middle of the dirt road.

"It stops here, Courtney."

"What does? Please say the cockeyed driving."

Knowing the man's secret, Court immediately regretted the slip. He sighed and stared out as a tractor gnawed over the fields at the top of a long drive. A dust cloud formed, wafting over hills of orchard rows—peach and apple trees lining the backdrop of the *Jenkins's Orchard* sign nearby.

"Look. I'm not asking for anything except an aspirin and a few winks in my own bed. Shouldn't be too hard to offer your only son. And if you still want me to be on my way after that, then fine. I'll go."

"Not this time, Courtney." Dr. Coleman turned to stare straight ahead, index finger tapping out the engine's melody against the steering wheel. "Get out."

Okay . . . no bluff.

He's serious. Or thinks he is. And that's the last thing I need right now.

"And I'm supposed to . . . what? Walk home?"

"Try pretending you're walking away from your responsibilities again. Should be easy. You've done it enough times before." Dr. Coleman pointed to the sign over the top of the steering wheel. "And this is the last time, even if Patrick Jenkins did speak up on your behalf."

Court sighed again, annoyed that do-gooder Jenkins had managed to strike again. "And why would he do that?"

"You got me. I told him not to. Told him you'd never change. Not after you walked out on them and left the orchard the first time. And not even after my Maddie asked you to stay."

The mention of his late mother's name sent a twinge to Court's chest.

My Maddie . . .

The name that was so sweet once was now used to inject a rebuke. That was how he'd said it—like Court had no claim to the ever-present ache in his own chest since her years-long battle with diabetes had finally taken its toll. Even with the wider use of the drug insulin, her poor body could no longer withstand the fight. And as she weakened and wasted away, their adopted son had now become but a bitter pill to be endured without her.

And maybe it was true.

The tractor continued to kick up dust in the field, its cloud fading in the wind that swept the long lane that split the orchard rows.

"Jenkins says he won't press charges as long as you agree to work off your debts at the orchard. There's payment for Guthrie's medical bill." He clicked his tongue in obvious disapproval. "And the bail."

"He paid it." Court slammed his fist against the door. If his father had paid again, Court could have just owed him. But if Jenkins had decided to pony up, there was no easy way out of that obligation. "Fine. How long is this servitude supposed to take?"

"That's up to Patrick. Because if it were me, I'd have had the judge throw the book at you so fast, you'd be the one waking up with more than just a headache. Regardless, this ride is the last handout you'll get. From me, anyways."

One thing they had in common—neither was willing to give an inch. Maybe he was refusing a handout, but Court was just as sure he'd never again ask for one.

"And if I don't go back?"

"No one says you have to. Whether you walk down that road to the orchard or end up one of a hundred other places, that's up to you. But you're getting out of this car. Now."

What else was there to do? Court lifted the handle and slid out, then slammed the door behind him without looking up. The engine idled, and he shifted three-quarters to the left, staring out at the long road of dirt beneath his shoes. "She was my Maddie, too, you know."

The car pulled off and Court was left standing there, deciding whether he should walk the long road alone. In the end there was nothing else to do.

His ribs throbbed with each step. That familiar road meant nothing except he'd truly be free at the end of it. Court had tried to make it there once. It didn't work. Never would—not when he and his father were fire and ice trying to exist in the same town. At least this way he could work off the debts, leave, and never again feel like he had reason to look back. Maybe Court could hitch a ride across the river to Louisville. Catch a bus south. Shake off the dust of rural Indiana roads and just go live his life . . . whatever he might make of it.

The tractor called louder around the bend, and Court turned to find it chugging to a stop by the ditch and a row of mailboxes bolted to a rusted milk can.

"You looking for work there, cowboy?" a worker called out from the tractor seat.

Court clamped his eyes shut for a second as the voice registered. "Uh . . . yeah," he shouted back.

The worker cut the engine and jumped to the ground, petite work boots and denim coveralls landing in the field grass. Her ginger braid flopped over the shoulder of her blue gingham shirt. She swept it back before squinting sharp green eyes into the bleeding rays of morning sun.

"Well, you'll have to go on up to the house—just keep on that road there. Though I don't think we're taking any on just now. You should've come by over the summer. That's when we really needed the help."

Court stared back, the familiar sensation uncanny for how it could twist his gut in knots just to see her again.

She pulled off her work gloves and walked closer. "You from around here?"

When he didn't answer, she eased up.

It was then she seemed to notice the bloodstained shirt collar. And that he carried no belongings save for a dusty suit jacket hooked over one shoulder. Her palm fixed on her brow to block the sun enough to give her the first true look at his face. And she stopped.

Cold.

The easy smile faded. Her feet froze in the orchard grass. And her fingers tightened in a death lock around her worn leather work gloves.

"Why, if it isn't Court Coleman." She crossed her arms over the front of her coveralls. No mixed messages about what emotions his presence conjured. "What on God's green earth do you think you're doing back here?"

The world flooded back then—the sharp sting of memories . . . the sweet familiarity of her voice . . . the years of ancient history and the chasm between them still as wide as the Grand Canyon. Court recognized the fiery glint in her eyes that said if he didn't answer in a satisfactory manner—and quick—she might drive the tractor clean over him.

He'd deserve it too.

If regret was a killer the morning after, Court was sure he didn't want to entertain it months down the road. He shifted his stance, turning his chin so his busted face pointed to the fields instead of to the woman he'd walked out on.

But he wasn't hiding anything. Not from her. And they both knew it.

"Hello, Penn. I'm back."

10 September 1943
Paestum Beachhead
Salerno, Italy

"You heard what I said. He's here. Saw with my own two eyes."

Court drifted out of the heavy fog of morphine. Mortar blasts echoed in the distance as a pair of scatty soldiers talked loud enough to wake the dead nearby.

A second voice chided the first. "I could believe a lot of things about this war . . . but not that. And not at this shoddy field hospital."

A fire welled up within Court.

I'm at Red Beach . . .

They left me behind.

"True as I'm standing here. John Steinbeck is working as a war correspondent for the *New York Herald Tribune*. Washington may have tried to chain him to a desk, but he lobbied to be sent to the front lines. Stormed the beaches at Sicily and now he's here with us in Salerno. Rode off in a jeep toward the fight stirring up over at the tobacco factory. He needed a shave well enough, but I saw. It was him."

The second soldier whistled low. "Persano's gonna be tough to bust the line off the beaches. Hundreds of litters coming here by the hour, and word is those Brits still can't keep control enough to even use Montecorvino Airfield. You think FDR knows his prized writer's headed into a storm like that?"

"I'd bet my ma's house he don't. But listen to this—one of the docs here says he played in an after-hours poker game with officers bragging about Steinbeck. The doc laid down a royal flush right there on the hood of the jeep. Bet was, the junior officer who lost had to prove it and give up the name of the leader Steinbeck's been working under."

"Which was . . . don't tell me. Clark Gable?"

"A film star it is, but this one's Douglas Fairbanks Jr. Seems he's leading some swashbuckling unit offshore."

"You lie!" he hooted. "This ain't Hollywood. And it sure ain't no movie set."

"That's closer than you'd think with all these celebrities in uniform," the storyteller said, though he'd dropped his voice this time. "Steinbeck's headed to Rome with some commando unit. Got his own private medics tagging along just in case he takes a bullet in the wrong place. Ordered by Lieutenant Commander Warren himself. All hush-hush. The Germans bombed out so many bridges in their retreat, we need recon so our engineers can de-mine the roads and do a quick rebuild. And that sergeant you crossed a while back—named Nelson?"

"The one tough as nails with the ego to match?"

"Yep. Rumor is his unit's heading out with 'em."

The mention of AJ was enough to break through and stir Court's senses, causing his eyelids to flutter. He blinked, finally awake.

Overhead stretched a fatigue sky—a field-hospital tent fluttering under gusting wind along the beachhead. He could have cursed AJ for dropping him in the nightmare at Red Beach, leaving him behind while they trekked off to Rome without him. And that wasn't going to happen. Fighting alongside the boys in his unit for years and watching soldiers die in their hands—it was enough to motivate Court to do anything to get back to the front lines.

To help. To fight to the death.

To do what they'd all come to do and not back down—no matter what.

Court gritted his teeth. Using his good arm to reach across his body, he fumbled his fingertips over his left side, tracing the bandages down. Shoulder . . . to elbow . . . to wrist. Though there were stabs of pain, his fingertips moved on command. He could feel his legs. Could wiggle his toes. And God help him—the pain in his neck was welcome because it meant everything he owned on his body at birth was still accounted for now.

Thank the Almighty.

"Steinbeck's going behind the German line? Why? To write the Jerries' letters back home?" The second soldier snorted out a laugh again, then cut it short. "Oh—hey. Looks like that soldier over there is waking up. They told us to flag down one of the skirts if he did."

Someone whistled with the shrill cry of pinkie fingers stuck in teeth. Court looked over in the direction of the skirl.

One soldier stood at the opening of the tent—bandaged up, white rows of gauze covering half his head and over an eye, but under a combat helmet—smoking a cigarette in the open air. The other was a sad lot too. He leaned on a crutch, missing a limb under the knee on one leg and bandaged up pretty good on the other.

"You awake there, Soldier?" The legless soldier took a drag off a cigarette hanging from his bottom lip and blew smoke out the tent flap. "Nurse is on her way. Hold on. They'll be shipping us out on the boat tonight, so it's almost over."

Recall flooded. From the blast that took Court down on Blue Beach. The pain . . . The wash of fear . . . Even what it felt like to get close enough to spit death square in the eye. And then the greater fear of living but being shipped Stateside, only half the man he was when he'd shipped out. Court wasn't out of the woods yet—not unless he could walk out of that tent on his own terms.

He had to get moving.

Rubbing a palm over his face, he told himself, *Wake up . . . Wake up!*

"Nurse—that soldier over there. He's awake."

"What are you two doing here? You know this entry has to stay clear."

A nurse blasted the soldiers with hellfire for clogging her area, even if it looked like the whole beach had tried crowding into this one tent. Court fixed his gaze on the casualties. Everywhere. On cots. Sitting on the ground. Some standing room, if they could still stand.

"Where are we supposed to go?" the crutch-bearing soldier shot back. "The Donut Dollie trucks aren't here yet. And good thing those Red Cross volunteers haven't rolled out on the beaches because planes keep strafing the supply pallets. We step outta here and we're all sitting ducks."

"And we're sitting ducks in here if those cigs catch something flammable! You know smoking isn't allowed. So please. Out! Take it someplace else."

The nurse huffed and moved over to Court's cot, then eased him back down with a firm hand to his good shoulder when he tried to rise. "Just lie back for me now."

"I'm alright," Court said as firmly as he could over the gravel in his throat.

"Let me be the judge of that. You're not long out of surgery. I just want to see how you're doing." She leaned over to check his bandages. Hourglass figure. Dark brown hair—pinned back in a style too old for her face. Looked like she might own a sweet smile, too, but in that tent probably found few opportunities to show it off.

She put the stethoscope earpieces in and pressed the drum over his heart. Court stopped resisting and allowed his head to fall back on the pillow.

"Lieutenant Commander Warren."

"What was that?" She pulled the stethoscope tips from her ears.

"I said Lieutenant Commander Warren. I need to speak with him."

"Well, you don't hear that pickup line every day." She laughed and grabbed Court's wrist, staring at her wristwatch to keep time on his pulse. "If you do manage to get an audience with the commander, kindly tell him supplies are in a dead slog between the boats and this tent. And what does come through is so riddled with bullets we can't use much. It'd be killer-diller if we actually had what we need to do our jobs."

"I'm assigned to a medic unit under him, so I'll be sure that gets back."

"Are you now?" She straightened. Walked to the metal cart wheeled between his cot and the next one over. She pulled out a clipboard and flipped through the mess of papers, then took a pencil from behind her ear and scribbled something down.

"Well, Private Coleman. All it says here is that I have orders to prep you for evac. And you'll have a full post-op eval on the boat."

"No, ma'am. I'm assigned to a unit under Sergeant Nelson in the 36th. By order of Lieutenant Commander Warren. That's why I need to speak with him. I have to be ready to head out to Rome tomorrow."

"You say you're going to Rome . . . tomorrow?" She lowered the chart, doubt tracking over her face.

Seemed he'd hit on a trip wire of some kind. She stared back for a breath, deciding. If he knew that much, then he'd have to have received official orders. Right? Court only hoped she believed a shred of it so he could get out of that bed and back to the line. "Yes."

"And why is that exactly?"

Court shook his head. "That's confidential, ma'am."

"Well, sounds like quite the tall tale seeing as you just woke up.

I'd say you're talking clean out of that head of yours, even if it is one of the most handsome mugs we've seen in here. The good news is, those boys in your unit got you here in time to save your life. So you and that smile of yours got nothing else to worry about."

Great. Another thing I'll owe AJ for.

"Pass me. I'm fine, see?" Court pushed himself to a sitting position. No grimace. And no submitting to pain. He aimed to show he could handle it. "Seems like you could use the extra bed anyway."

"Oh no you don't." She eased him down again. "Look—I can't promise anything. I'll talk to the doctor, but nobody's getting passed out of this tent unless he says so. Period."

"Donna! We need you!"

The pretty smile whipped her head around at someone's call as another soldier was carried in, lifeless on a litter. Court scanned the faces of the litter bearers. He didn't recognize them; no one from his unit.

"I have to go." She dropped his chart back on the cart. "You just hang tight, Soldier. We'll get you on your way when they say you're ready and not before."

"Wait—Donna? Is that your name?"

She eased up. "It's Nurse Henson."

"Sorry. Nurse Henson. On the cart there might be a jacket. Could you hand it to me?"

Court's plea struck a chord because she sighed and then stooped, pulling out a jumble of fatigue, a red cross armband hanging just out of the chest pocket. She winked when she handed it over and swept off again.

Trying not to think too much about the torn sleeve and dried blood spatters on the side, Court felt around the jacket, running his palm over pockets, searching for weight. Until . . .

There you are.

He pulled out the pocket watch, gripping the lifeline tight in his palm.

AJ must have been by. Must have left it, knowing when Court woke it'd be the first thing he'd look for. And the one thing he needed.

Court held on to it for a long minute, then clicked the knob so the cover popped open. Though his vision was still a little fuzzy, he saw Penn's photo on the inside. Staring back. Giving him strength. He pressed a thumb to her smile—like he always did, for years now since he'd left for war—and would have closed it again if a heady beach wind hadn't torn through the side of the tent.

Papers flew from the carts. Gauze rolls bounced on the ground like popcorn in a kettle drum, causing chaos with the nurses beyond the bed row. The gust had aired out the tent and ruffled his hair, at the very least making Court glad he was alive and able to see his girl. But when he did look back, her smile was gone—blown free from the cover.

Court searched his blankets, heart beating wildly until he found the little photo had flipped out and landed in a woolen fold. He swiped it up. He'd need to find some gum before he had to head out again. If Court could muster the strength to pass a physical exam and get reassigned on the trek all the way to Rome, he'd need Penn to go with him.

To tuck the photo back for safekeeping, Court flipped the watch and looked inside the cover again. Only this time, a hidden-something he'd never seen before lay taped under the lip where the photo had protected it: a tiny lock of russet curls.

Every thought stalled as he ran fingertips over the soft lock. Court knew what it was. Penn was asking him—telling him maybe, from far across an ocean—that if he wanted the job of husband and father, the lock of the baby's hair meant he could have it. That is, if he was man enough to ask her, to step up and stay for good this time, and be a father to another man's child.

Well, Soldier . . .

What are you gonna do?

Court could turn the tides in another boy's life in a way he'd never had. And the rush of fear that accompanied the realization made everything he was fighting for feel like home was not just across an ocean. Now, it was more like a million miles away.

Five

*I*n *this grave hour, perhaps the most fateful in our history, I send to every household of my people, both at home and overseas, this message . . ."*

Julia paused in the back hall of Sadler's Wells Theatre, listening as the measured words of His Majesty King George VI lifted over the scratchy frequency of the backstage wireless, the sound of a high-pitched schoolgirl giggle rising with it. It confirmed where the missing pair had fled to, and Julia was quite sure it wasn't to take in the state address from their sovereign in a private backstage audience.

"Lillie?"

The young chorine in the blush leotard jumped out of her stupor as Julia turned the corner into the backstage dressing area. Anton, however, stood still as the king continued his address, with one arm snaked around the small of the girl's back and the other palm anchored to the brick wall above her head.

He whispered something with lips grazing her temple.

"Did you not hear the address, Lillie?" Julia paused long enough to glance to the wireless posted against the wall as His Majesty continued. *"For the second time in the lives of most of us we are at war . . ."*

"Yes, of course. We're listening." Lillie beamed up at the ballerino. "And it's marvelous, isn't it?"

Yes, of course. Isn't war marvelous?

Their stares confirmed they thought Julia cold, prudish, and quite meddlesome. But she couldn't care. Not when doe-eyed Lillie hadn't a clue what she was doing. Nor when she'd be the one to wake up one day and thank her lucky stars someone walked around the corner at that very moment—that someone being a ballerina who had the unfortunate knowledge of exactly how Anton Vasile operated.

"Lillie? Madame has paused rehearsal. Given the seriousness of the king's address, she thought the cast ought to listen together. I've been sent to fetch you." Julia fixed her glare on the swagger in Anton's smirking profile. *"Immediately."*

Without looking up he said, "Thank you, Julia. You may scurry off now with your message that Miss Hall is rehearsing her steps with Prince Désiré. And she will rejoin the cast after her tutelage is complete—not before."

Just like him to slither in the dark backstage, wooing his next conquest with dust and canvas backdrops, a smattering of old costumes piled around like some haberdashery's stockroom instead of the honeymoon suite he'd no doubt promised the girl.

Enough.

Julia walked to the wireless, the king's ominous declaration of *"there may be dark days ahead"* cut off when she flipped the knob. She waited, icing her stance with arms folded over the ivory satin and Chantilly-lace bodice of her rehearsal costume.

"Must I remind you, Anton? This is the ladies' dressing area. No men allowed. Madame will have your hide if she catches you behind the curtain."

"Come now, Julia." The velvet in his voice made her skin crawl. Even more so as he fingered a stray lock of Lillie's chocolate hair back from her forehead with a very determined pinkie. "Can you not see Miss Hall and I are engaged in private matters that should be quite outside anyone's notice?"

"Not whilst the rest of the cast is waiting. Including Madame, who signs Lillie's pay voucher. And yours. It would be in everyone's best interest if she were to rejoin us. Her absence will be more than noted."

Anton released his hold and bade the girl to go with a flit of his chin, but not before his hand caught the chiffon hem of Lillie's skirt and pulled in a playful tug as she swept by.

"Later. Hmm?"

Once Lillie was gone, Anton's mood shifted. He set about a rough tightening of his necktie and turned his back on Julia as he pulled suspenders back up over his shoulders.

This she knew well enough as Anton's punishment for an ill-timed interruption. The whiplashing of his manner would befit a petulant child because his plans—whatever they could be in a handful of stolen moments backstage—had been delayed. By impending war. By the gall of their sovereign to have chosen his timing such for a speech. Or by Julia thwarting his intentions.

Anton kicked a wooden crate that dared to exist in his way. It shook, teetering as it considered falling to one side. He turned then, stilling the crate to sit down. He unrolled his shirtsleeves and gave a harsh fasten to the buttons at his cuffs, still too irritated to look her in the eye.

"Tell me, Julia. Will there ever be a day in which you relinquish your self-appointed post as my jailer? Or my priest?"

"Your actions could have you dismissed. No fraternization amongst the cast. You know this."

"And what of it? The girl is of age. So am I. If we wish to see each other, that's our affair."

"I'd wager it's more Lillie's affair than yours. But not under the rule of Madame's law. She won't have her employees make her a fool. Not even one of her stars."

"Julia, stop this." And he did look at her then, his head snapping up with a pinched glare meant to accuse her. "We must find a way to work together. With civility."

"You dare speak to me of civility?"

"Yes. And the class our position demands. After all, this is what you said you wanted in New York. Remember, those years ago? To be prima ballerina. To honor your parents' dreams. And now you have it. Do you intend to throw all that away by stirring up trouble because of some churlish, lovesick pining from our youthful days?"

Don't you dare mention New York. You do not get to attach yourself to my dream.

Or define my past.

"Lovesick pining? How different our remembrances are."

"That's what this is, isn't it? Hmm? Jealousy? I've moved on. You ought to grow up and do the same."

It shamed Julia that she knew him so completely.

As was his usual manner of projecting the picture-perfect image—just as in in his studio headshots that the ballet company flouted—Anton appeared polished on the outside in his impeccably tailored suit. Almost civil once he'd decided it would benefit him more to soothe the rough edges of his temper rather than engage in a full-on tantrum. But underneath? He was always set on his own aims. This she knew firsthand.

Anton sighed and reached for the suit jacket he'd draped over a nearby makeup chair. "I have no wish to fight with you. In fact, I've come bearing news. Lillie just happened to find me first." He retrieved a piece of folded paper from his jacket's inside pocket. "Here. Read it."

"What is it?"

When Julia made no move toward him, he smirked and dropped his hand to his side. "A telegram with an official invitation to join a traveling troupe."

"No thank you. I'm contracted here."

"Not for long. With war, the ballet will shut down. Mark my words. Everything will. But if we're clever and remain forward-thinking, this post will cement us on the stage. That's what you want, isn't it—to dance?"

"You know it is all I want."

"And this ticket will take you from London to the provinces to start. And then if we play our cards right, Milan. Even Rome. And eventually Germany if all goes tick-tock—there's rumor of a ballet envoy of international stars who will travel with the eyes of the world watching. Like at the Berlin Olympics, it would be a goodwill tour with dancers from all nations, coming together to show that this kerfuffle with Hitler will be over soon."

"What makes you think I'd go?"

He ignored the question, flipping the conversation back to his whims. "It's rumored that even Margot Fonteyn is considering signing on. I thought perhaps that might sweeten the deal enough for you to accept."

Julia wasn't fooled. No matter how pristine the exterior, she knew the man behind the mask, and she knew exactly what he was about. War was inevitable now, and he was about any manipulation that would keep him as far from the front lines as possible.

"You mean this is your chance to remain free from conscription, which you cannot do as only half of a famous pairing?"

"Ah, Julia." He laughed this time and tossed the telegram on the makeup table. "So practical. And blunt. It's what I've always admired in you, your great predictability."

"You forget. *I know you.* And now that our nation is at war, you mean to profit for your own gain. But you cannot control all the world, even should you wish it."

"No. But I control my world. And regardless of the fear the king attempts to stoke over that wireless, I submit this offer as evidence that any conflict might be resolved in a civilized manner if both parties are in agreement. Don't you see? We are bonded, you and I. Your fate is tied with mine and mine with your own. Regardless of what the future brings for this country—or the world—our star is rising. But it only rises together."

He stood and slipped arms in sleeves to fill out his jacket. Then tucked his collar and ran a palm down canary silk, smoothing his tie as he stared back at her in the reflection. "I've not come to fight with you, Julia."

Always with the professional veneer—so that in the event anyone were to walk in there would be nothing untoward for them to claim—Anton turned and closed the space between them.

Julia inched back in response, until she bumped a barrel. It teetered against her backside, locking her in place.

When he'd hemmed her in, he reached up to run a finger around one of the wisps of chestnut that had escaped her bun to curl at her nape. "But if you think for one moment that the name Bradbury is responsible for a tenth of the ticket sales I've brought to this company," he said, leaning in until his breath warmed the delicate skin of her ear, "I invite you to speak your piece with Madame. But know that I will no longer protect you from the hellfire that should come upon you after. And the childhood dream your dearly departed parents had for you . . . Well. Do you really want to risk public ruin for a little indiscretion from your past? I wonder what the performance world would say should that pop up in the newspaper headlines."

Julia chanced it, looking up. Staring back into those dark and deceptive eyes with a glare she hoped could chisel stone. "Is that a threat?"

"Not at all. Merely an elegant observation as we're facing the very inelegant prospect of war. Don't turn this into a faff. Just think about it, yes? I'm confident that in time, you'll change your mind and accept this generous offer."

Anton stepped back then, straightening his cuffs with silky movements. And with a palm smoothing a wave of combed hair back to ensure its perfect part, he strolled to the door. "I have no wish to go to war with you, Julia. But I will if I must."

She kept her eyes fixed on the telegram that lay butterflied on the makeup table as he left, the sound of his whistling carrying down the hall. She stepped over to the wireless when he'd gone, hand shaking as she turned the knob back to the On position.

The king continued, admonishing his subjects with a slow and steady call to action: *"If one and all be resolutely faithful today, ready for whatever service or sacrifice it may demand, with God's help . . . we shall prevail . . ."*

With God's help.

Julia flicked the knob, again cutting the sovereign's voice dead.

For the resolutely faithful, the king's words might have proven a great comfort. But what of the already broken? What of the ones who hadn't any hope left before the battle had even begun? Everything had changed after New York. And Julia didn't know which road was worse to travel—the road to a war the whole world might see or the road through the harrowing reality of the private war only she knew of.

Six

*I*n *Italy, every sunset belongs to the one who stops to enjoy it.*"
        That's what Grandpa had once told Delaney. It just never made sense until that moment. Set against the backdrop of a sweeping cerulean sky, the setting sun painted a sheen of gold over Roman ruins and centuries-old olive groves, like it was completely normal to have ancient treasures mixed into a rural landscape.

Delaney tapped her fingertips to the top of the duffel bag holding the old suitcase as the chartered vehicle left Rome's main city center and took her deeper into the heart of rural Lazio. The driver pointed out the estate grounds of the Villa d'Este—the grand villa and lavish hillside gardens she recognized from a map in the guidebook she'd picked up at an airport shop. They passed through storied streets of the old city, and roads became hairpin turns along the River Aniene that snaked around Tivoli. And though she would have liked nothing more than to see a trip to Italy as an adventure, the reality of home nagged at her heart, and her reasons to be there at all took precedence over any enchantments on the side of the road.

"*Ci siamo, signorina.*" The driver pointed out a hefty iron gate on their right as they drove through. "We are here, miss."

"Grazie."

The driver slowed to a stop at the end of the winding drive and stepped out to help with her suitcase in the trunk.

This must be it—Villa Adriano. The name engraved on a bronze plaque affixed to the wall behind weathered stone stairs looked like a famous one in the guidebook. But this was definitely not the Roman ruins of Villa Adriana. It was a provincial villa with high-arched windows that stretched along the ground floor, blooms in flower boxes under the panes of open leaded-glass windows, and curtains that danced in a gentle breeze. A wooden pergola braided over by vines through trellis panels gave shelter to twin potted lemon trees framing a round-top front door.

The door seemed to swing open on cue, and *he* stepped out.

Welcoming a complete stranger to his family's Italian country home appeared business as usual for Matteo, as he wore the same uniform of a casual canvas jacket, worn-in tee, and jeans from their video call, except he also had a black ball cap with a frayed bill pulled down low over his brow. He trotted down the stone steps and gave a half wave in greeting to Delaney as she gathered her things in the back seat. He addressed the driver, laughing about something-she-didn't-know-what in Italian, signed something for the man—maybe a tip?—and handed it back with a "Grazie."

Duffel in hand, purse hooked over her shoulder, and with a deep breath, Delaney stepped out of the car. She turned back to take her suitcase from the driver but found that Matteo had already retrieved it as he walked around the auto's side.

"Buongiorno. Del Coleman?" The way her name rolled off his tongue revealed only a hint of the Italian accent. But still, it sounded kind of nice. "Glad you finally made it."

"Buongiorno, Matteo," she said, trying out her own Italian. "Nice to meet you. And I'm glad I made it too."

He towered over her and at the same time seemed to be making an admirable effort not to fix his gaze on the duffel bag. He did have a genuine smile, though, that said he might have been more relieved to see her and the suitcase than he dared let on.

"We thought for a minute you might've changed your mind."

"*You* thought," a petite woman called from the porch, with a thick Italian accent but graciously in English. "I knew she would arrive safe and sound. And here she is. Buongiorno, dear."

Delaney held her breath.

Is this Calla Santini?

The age was almost there—gray hair pinned at her nape and creases at the outer corners of her amber eyes made Delaney believe she'd probably enjoyed many a good smile in her time. Drying her hands on a tea towel that she flipped over the shoulder of her violet oxford, the woman, too, came down the stairs.

An almost poodle-type roan with warm-chocolate markings sailed down the steps after her until it reached Matteo's side. He gave the dog a good pat and it sniffed at Delaney, with cautious bobs of its head, then backed off and danced around the fringes of anyone's reach with its tail in a soft wag.

"They say every Italian home has a dog. The brown Lagotto over there is called Ghost—she'll make sure you find out why in your own time. And walking this way is Sabine, my nona's assistant. You'll get used to both of their noses pushing into anything they please," he whispered, then called back, "Fine. *I thought* she wasn't coming. But can you blame me?"

"*Zitto, giovanotto.*" Sabine sounded like she chided Matteo, even if it was done with a smile. She offered her hand to Delaney and she accepted, finding the woman's grip matched the warmth on her face. "Miss Delaney. Matteo here tells us you go by Del. Sì?"

"Yes. I mean, sì. I'm sorry about coming in late. We had bad weather for the connecting flight from Paris. It put everything behind." She turned to Matteo. "Thank you for the car, by the way. Do I owe you money for the tip?"

"A tip?"

"Yes—is that what you signed for the driver?"

"Do not concern yourself about that, my dear," the woman cut in. "I am Sabine, Mrs. Santini's personal assistant. And we received your text messages about why you would be late. This young man is just on the impatient side. When there is something he truly wants, he cannot wait for it. Not even for a day." Sabine reached up with a patronizing pat to his cheek. "Matteo will carry your luggage. You know which room for her. Grazie," she said, without waiting for an answer.

He pulled his cell phone out of his back pocket, checking its face. "And then I have to be off. I'll lose the light."

"Sì. Sì." She waved him off with a soft flutter of her fingertips. "This I know. *Non preoccuparti*—don't worry. We'll get her settled without your help."

Matteo obeyed, trotting up the stone stairs with the suitcase, and whistled out loud as he headed through the door. Ghost thundered up the steps behind him, then disappeared into the villa's shadows on his ankles.

"Come on then." Sabine offered Delaney an arm up the stairs to the door. "I will show you to your room."

She nodded and stepped in behind Sabine. It was fine to think of settling in, but Delaney was more eager, if anything, to simply drop the bags in her room and find the nearest desk to set up her laptop. She'd already photographed the letters found in the box from the museum and emailed those to Matteo. And translating the connection between their two families in those letters meant she was increasingly impatient to see what that was in real life.

"Will he be back soon, you think?"

"Matteo? He'll find his way down the back stairs and then return in time. He always does."

The Santinis had made certain Delaney and the suitcase had a comfortable trip in business class, at what must have been an exorbitant cost. And anyone could guess a hilltop hideaway in Tivoli proper wouldn't come cheap. All considered, that suggested they were well off. But the villa contradicted that notion, more a humble home than the lavish country manor she'd expected.

Terra-cotta tile stretched through the front entry to a sun-warmed sitting room with white stucco walls, a high beamed ceiling, and a stone fireplace to one side. Ocher wingbacks flanked the hearth stones, and rows of books were wedged into the built-ins under the windows. A breakfast table took up the back of the room, with olive-wood chairs tucked in tight and a bowl of Italian lemons in its center. But it was the open patio to a cobblestone courtyard that drew her attention, and Delaney watched as men set up chairs at a long farmhouse table outside.

"I'm sorry—you have guests. Is this a bad time?"

"Certainly not. It is the perfect time. And we always have guests."

Sabine gripped the curved iron stair rail as she led Delaney to the upper floors. "When we are preparing for *la cena*."

"La cena? What's that?"

Sabine didn't hear Delaney's question, as she was already trekking down the hall like a sergeant running drills. But the view upstairs was even more exquisite than the welcome had been because of a stunning mosaic of framed photos that adorned the length of the stucco wall.

The images stopped Delaney in her tracks as she sought to capture each one. She lingered over golden sunsets. Vibrant-hued gardens. Iconic shots of sunlight bleeding through Roman ruins. And intermingled with the landscapes were black-and-white snapshots of guests of all ages and walks of life—always seated at a long courtyard table, with wineglasses raised and string lights in the background. Each was more intriguing than the one before it, covering decades of sunsets and smiles.

She paused at the last photo, drawn in as it hung over a table with a lamp glowing against the fall of twilight out the window.

The snapshot had a grainier quality, and a couple in '60s dress suggested this photo was older. A tall, lean gentleman with peppered hair, a vintage suit, and thick, horn-rimmed glasses stood arm in arm with a beaming woman in a rose-gold gown—shimmering, mod in style, and quite stunning to look at.

Delaney squinted, trying to read the sign affixed to a stone building behind the pair.

Accademia di Balletto . . .

Ballet?

The woman was petite. More than graceful enough. And entirely charming as she leaned into a generous hug at the gentleman's side. Delaney could believe she'd been a ballerina, perhaps for the elegant presence she had. It shone out even through an old photograph.

"Miss Coleman?"

"Yes?" Delaney jumped at the sound of Sabine's voice. She turned to find the woman waiting in the doorway to a cheery yellow room, with a stack of towels in her arms.

"Ah. You have found yourself taken in by the photos, hmm?"

"How could I not? They're beautiful. Who took them?"

"Some Matteo. Some others. But enough of that for now. This is *La Gialla*—your room. And the washroom is just through there, with extra towels in the bureau. You will let me know if you have need of anything? I am needed in the kitchen, and I suspect they'll send out a search party if I don't appear soon."

"Yes. Of course." Delaney took the stack of towels. "Thank you." And then because of the "When in Rome" saying that floated in her mind—and she actually was in Rome—Delaney added, "I mean, grazie."

"*Va bene.* Why don't you freshen up? And come down when you are ready." Sabine winked as a swell of laughter floated up from the ground floor, through the open terrace door in her room. "And then we'll show you what la cena is all about."

Seven

Three things Court remembered about walking into the Jenkinses' farm kitchen: You put in a hard day's work even before breakfast. Eat up because you're gonna work hard after. And wipe your feet, or Sunday school teacher June Jenkins would have your hide for tracking up her clean hardwoods.

Looked like nothing had changed.

Penn marched up the porch steps and sailed through the door, leaving Court standing on the other side of the screen. Invisible hat in his hands, Court waited on the mat. How long would he have to eat crow on the porch before someone acknowledged his presence?

From his seat at the end of the oval breakfast table, Patrick Jenkins, with sun-weathered skin, plaid shirt rolled at the wrists, and a full head of coarse gray hair, kept his bifocals focused on his newspaper. And kept on stirring the cream in his coffee without looking up.

Penn turned her back on the door and moved over to the sink

to pump water over a colander of apples. Guthrie yanked a chair out and plunked down at the table. It shouldn't have made Court feel better to see the purple tint of racoon eyes shadowed next to Guthrie's nose as he loaded his plate with bacon and cornbread.

Shouldn't have made him feel better.

But it still did.

A few long seconds later, Patrick sighed. Folded his newspaper. And, probably figuring no one else would do it, walked over to the door. He stopped and looked back at Court, equal height putting them eye to eye through the screen. "Morning."

"Sir."

Patrick clicked his tongue as he surveyed Court's busted face, which was justified. Court held his chin up. Stood still. Blinked back. Didn't hide anything from the man. After all, he'd put up the bail money, so the man had earned a once-over to see what he'd paid for.

"Come on in. Breakfast's on the table." Patrick pushed the screen wide and held it open. He pointed to the seagrass mat beneath Court's shoes. "Wipe your feet."

Maddie Coleman didn't raise Court to disrespect a man like Patrick Jenkins, no matter their history. So he gave his dusty shoes a good swipe on the mat, then stepped in. The same Philco radio he'd remembered from before hummed in the corner of the adjoining sitting room. It played some kind of Glenn Miller Orchestra tune, floating a happy melody. He saw the same evergreen sofa and tufted side chair sporting a lace doily on the back. Shelves of Patrick's Farmers' Almanacs and old books still lined the far wall, and high windows had the curtains pulled back so morning sun streamed in.

June stood at the stove in her usual navy polka-dot farm dress, the family trademark ginger hair tied back in a tight bun so she could give attention to something sizzling in a cast iron skillet. She turned, offering the welcoming smile she always had, even when broken-down sinners had the gall to step back into her kitchen.

Wiping her hands on a linen towel, she came to meet him. "Court. Good morning."

"Morning, ma'am."

Court thought he caught Penn's shoulders stiffen at the sound of his name, even as she lifted the apples from sink to counter to start peeling the skin clean off a Red Delicious with military precision.

"We've got a place for you at the table if you're hungry. But first . . ." June took a porcelain bowl from the countertop and handed it over. "Here."

Court hung his jacket in the crook of his arm and, even though it took effort, made no grimace at the pain that shot through his ribs when he accepted it. He balanced the basin in his arms, trying not to show surprise to find it held a roll of bandages, glass bottle of peroxide, shaving kit, comb, toothbrush, and short stack of clean towels. They were crisp white—the kind you left hanging in the guest room. Not given to the likes of him.

No doubt the Jenkins family didn't have all those supplies lying around the medicine cabinet. But how they'd managed a trip to town between the late-night arrest and sunrise that morning caused pangs of remorse to fire through his gut.

When the gift was firm in hand, he looked up. "Thank you."

"Guthrie set up a cot in the tack room in the barn. You've got the pump out back for washing up. Breakfast is at seven sharp. Every day. You're not here, you don't eat. You missed going to town yesterday, so let us know if you need Patrick to pick up anything this week. And we leave for services at nine o'clock."

Great. A hangover in the church pew. Exactly the place Court didn't want to start out his stint as the new field hand.

"You got a clean shirt?"

Court looked down. Bloodstained with an impressive rip where Guthrie had fisted his collar to yank him off the barstool. It was the best—and only—shirt he owned.

"No, ma'am. Just the one."

"You best give it up then so I can get it mended and out on the line for next week. We'll find you one of Guthrie's in the meantime. Patrick will loan you a tie. And Guthrie will show you to where you'll be staying."

Before Guthrie could protest what must have been a blast of steam rising from his insides, Penn cut in. "No. I'll show him."

It wasn't like Penn to contradict any word of her parents. But what did seem off was the odd silence in the room that followed. Penn set the apple and peeling knife down, then turned around slowly to face him with . . .

Was that fear in her eyes?

Penn was pretty—that he knew. Everybody knew. And a darn sight prettier than Court had remembered from the image tucked away in the back of his mind. With those intoxicating eyes and that disarming smile. When they'd gone out to the picture show once, she'd said the dash of freckles over her nose made her look common compared to the likes of on-screen sirens Hedy Lamarr and Veronica Lake. Imagine that. *Common.* The complete vision standing before him.

Why Court remembered that little detail now, he didn't know. But those pretty eyes staring at June with a mix of dread and anger weren't Penn's usual response, no matter how humble the breed of her confidence was.

"Alright then. Penn will take you out. And then you've got enough time to eat before we leave."

Penn nodded. Even adjusted her jaw a little. Something was ticking through that mind of hers. She passed by him now, cold shoulder to the door, and Court moved to follow at a safe distance.

"Courtney?" Patrick looked up from his newspaper this time, glaring over the top frame of his glasses as he said Court's full name, and with as much stone-cold emphasis as he'd deemed necessary.

"Yes, sir?"

"No drinking. No brawling. And short of a tornado blowing that barn down outside, I don't want to see you with an excuse to set foot in this house. Not unless it's for a meal here with us. Do you understand me, son?"

Court stole a glance to Penn and then looked away just as fast. A little voice inside said this was no warning to ignore—not if Court liked having breath in his body. And even with the bruised ribs, he did.

Liked it just fine.

"Yes, sir. I understand."

"Alright then." Back to his newspaper. "Go on and get cleaned up."

Penn led him outside and grabbed a bucket hanging off the end of the fence on the way to the barn, then scattered feed to the chickens in the yard without a word.

Court followed her through the wide-open barn doors as she led him toward the back, passing Duke munching oats in his stall. The horse seemed to remember him, offering a soft snort over the rail. Court balanced the bowl in his elbow, enough to give a quick rub to the white patch on his old friend's ebony nose as they swept by.

"Here it is." Penn pointed to a room that opened up beyond the doorway, its entry tucked under stairs. She braced her arms over her waist—maybe showing off a little of that characteristic moxie as she waited for him to walk through. That, at least, was familiar.

Court stepped through to a tack room with a high ceiling, odds and ends of bridles and saddles organized on one wall, a window cutout on the other, and a cot with a pillow and quilt spread over the top in a smooth flying geese pattern. It was simple. Clean. No fuss. And too good for a man like him. He was about to make a crack like that when he spotted the bedside table and what lay atop it, just like it was waiting for him.

Any ease he might have had melted away.

The book.

The old copy of Homer's *Odyssey* with the worn oxblood cover. The tome that had once been his prized possession. Court's only possession really, besides the old photo he kept tucked in its binding.

Was it still there? Court set the bowl down, and the edge of the porcelain knocked the book off onto the hardwood floor. He knelt by the side of the bed, picked it up. Remembered what that worn binding had felt like in his hands the hundreds of times he'd turned to those pages over the years. And felt the edge of the photo peeking out from the front cover.

Court tucked it back in and turned to face her. "You kept it?"

She shrugged. "Thought if we ever did see you again, the right thing to do would be to return it. No matter how things ended between us."

Penn stared up at him from the shadow of the stairs. It took seconds only for the past to come flooding back.

How could a mere couple of months away seem like an eternity without looking in those eyes? All of a sudden Court couldn't remember why it had seemed like such a good idea to go from his mother's funeral straight to the bus station to hop on a Greyhound with a one-way ticket out of town. And without saying goodbye.

Everything in those eyes now trying to hold back tears said he'd hurt her more than he could have realized.

"So that's it," she said, turning to walk out. "And the water pump's out back."

"Penn, wait." He stepped forward, reaching out with his fingertips to brush her elbow from behind . . . and grazed her side without meaning to.

She froze.

Court blasted back. One step. Then two, and braced a palm to the doorframe like an anchor, because without it a puff of wind could've knocked him clean over.

"There's nothing to talk about," Penn whispered, her back still to him, arms hugging her waist like a wall.

"What . . . What's going on here?"

Heaven help him when she turned and stared up at him, and he saw those green eyes had somehow gone a shade darker. And were more distant than the look he hadn't seen since they were kids. Maybe this was what scared looked like.

Call Court scared too.

Call him a scoundrel. A rake. Or a troubled drifter with one shirt and an old book to his name—that and a stubborn constitution that said he was never gonna change. Not in this lifetime or the next.

In that instant of Penn's slow unfolding of her arms to her sides, Court begged God to call him a thousand things. Whatever He wanted, just not the one thing Court knew he could never be.

A father.

"Penn?" Court whispered as he chanced a look to the rise at her middle, pleading with her to tell him he was flat wrong. That he hadn't messed up again—this time with something that would do more than just ruin him. It'd ruin her too. "You're expecting?"

77

14 SEPTEMBER 1943
ALTAVILLA SILENTINA
CAMPANIA, ITALY

Court marched into the roadside camp to find Allied jeeps lined up like a circus caravan along the side of the road. He pocketed his map. Didn't need it trekking across a field anyway.

The boys he'd joined up with had moved inland from the beachhead, along the Alburni Mountains that spanned the backdrop with their jagged rise. They'd avoided roads watched by the crow's nest of Germans entrenched in the mountainsides and, for the last couple miles, had gone cross-country instead. Now he marched through Italy's golden fields to follow the veil of smoke that drifted up from the heart of the valley.

Service trucks stalled in rain-tracked mud. Soldiers dug out tires with picks and shovels. Some with their bare hands. Other uniforms walked back and forth over the road with metal detectors, the machines hungry to root out buried mines. And Allied patrols stood guard over the caravan, weaving paths across the rise, their hawk eyes searching for movement along the outskirts of the nearby village of Cerrelli.

Court searched the faces of the soldiers camped out along the stone façade of a country chapel, looking for medic crosses.

Soldiers were still on the alert, with combat helmets on and packs at the ready. But they'd managed to dig into the hillside, hunched over K rations and card games like the advance had been held up for some time now. And no wonder. The deep crevice of a rocky streambed came into view. Soldiers were hard at work rebuilding the bridge the Germans had bombed after they'd retreated across it.

That rebuild could take ten hours or more.

Court looked in the direction of uniforms crowding the front of the line of vehicles. A radio operator stood by the hood of a jeep, hand-cranking the dynamo on an EE-8 field phone for an officer to use the hand unit. Other combat helmets were bent over a rolled-out map, organizing the activity with the paper held against the wind by rocks pinned at the corners.

Engineers.

That meant Steinbeck had to be close by . . . and his medic team too.

"Hey." Court got the attention of one of the nearby helmets, a soldier tinkering under a raised Jeep hood.

"Yeah?"

"The medics from the 36th under Sergeant Nelson. They here?"

"That'd be above my pay grade," he said, a cig drifting dangerously close to falling off his bottom lip. He pointed his wrench to the back of the line. "But follow the smoke and you should find the wounded before you get to it."

Court took a step in that direction but stopped. "What's the smoke? Village bombed out?"

"Nah. Funeral pyres." The mechanic took a deep drag and blew smoke in a cloud. "Not much we can do for dead civilians. But medics should be back there treating the boys who landed on the wrong side of an ambush outside Altavilla. Word is couple units got busted up pretty good. They're patching 'em up before we send 'em back to the beach. Then we move out."

The setting sun blasted Court in the eyes as he thanked the soldier and moved on, worsening an already piercing headache. He cupped a fist to his mouth over the stench of smoke and burning flesh that carried on the wind and looked out over a field for the wounded.

Sarge came into view first. Couldn't mistake AJ's black hair, wide shoulders, and familiar tall frame—even as he'd taken a knee by a litter to wrap gauze around the arm of one of the wounded. So Court marched up. Saluted. And waited.

When AJ made no move to acknowledge him, Court flitted his glance over the uniforms until he spotted Tenor and Dean. They were working on a soldier, too, but not focused enough to miss the fact that Court had appeared again, seemingly out of thin air.

"What are you doing here, Private?" AJ finally tossed over his shoulder, like he had eyes in the back of his head to see who'd come trekking over the ridge. Knowing him, he did. "Thought you were supposed to be on a boat by now."

"No, sir." Court unbuttoned his chest pocket, pulled out his orders, and waited, holding out the creased paper. "Passed back to active duty. Lieutenant Commander Warren signed off himself."

"You don't say?"

AJ squeezed the soldier on the non-wounded shoulder—the tiny tick of reassurance Court had received once—then stood tall. He dusted his palms on his uniform pants and reached for the orders, reading over them with a characteristic scrutinizing eye. "Says here you're reassigned to me. And the engineer unit pushing northeast."

"Yes, sir."

"We're headed to Naples. And even though the Germans are digging into the north and pulled Mussolini out of prison in a one-two punch, the Allies still plan to push on to Rome. No matter how long it takes."

Court drew in a sharp breath. "Yes, sir. I know."

AJ handed the orders back, through with the confirmation of the big brass's passed inspection. Looked like he wanted to conduct an inspection of his own. "Just how'd you manage to find us out here when you're supposed to be in surgery at Red Beach?"

"That's done. I'm a fast healer. And they needed the bed."

AJ crossed his arms over his chest and flitted his glance to the bandages peeking out from Court's shirt collar. "Most boys sent back out are reassigned to a new unit. What makes you special to get orders tracking down your old one?"

"Warren agreed."

"After you suggested it?"

"I wouldn't say that. He merely saw reason. It's easier to go from a field hospital cot back to a foxhole if it's with a unit you've worked with for the last two years. They knew you'd gone as far as Persano, but the radio said the line got stalled when you had to patch a span."

"And that meant you could catch up."

"Yes, sir. I tagged along with a team going in. We were told to follow the smoke once we were in range. We're in range and here you are. That's it." Court looked over the field of wounded and a tent shielding the worst of the fire's activity far off. "Heard a unit was shredded at Altavilla. Is that this?"

"Yeah." AJ tipped the combat helmet back off his forehead and pointed up the ridge. "That action's only about a mile from here. Straight up. And the Germans left a little present of a razed village and a bombed-out bridge down here. We got held up with repairs and agreed to take these boys in. Get 'em ready to go back before the engineers move on."

Curious, Court glanced around. "And the journalist? He here too?"

"The, uh, Typewriter, you mean? That's what we call him," Tenor cut in, smiling wide. So like him to find a joke in anything, even while Court's place hung in the balance. "He's here. Is that why you're back?"

Court shrugged. "Maybe I want an autograph."

Seemed AJ had had just about enough of his cheek. He tilted his head for Court to follow him to the tree line. Once out of earshot from the others, their leader stared back, not a flinch from a hard jaw as seconds ticked by between them. "Your injuries should have qualified you for a ticket Stateside. And I'm convinced you're the last person on this planet who'd be starstruck by anybody—unless your girl came walking down that road over there. So what's the real story?"

"Anybody can recover."

"Yeah. But not that fast. You should have died, Court. You know it and I know it. I took your watch, remember?"

Court pushed that memory back as quick as he could. Last thing he wanted to be reminded of was how close he came to meeting his Maker on Blue Beach. "I remember, sir."

"And I'd bet my life you'd have needed more advanced surgery than you could get with a quick patch job at a field hospital. Yet here you are. So why don't you tell me another one?"

"Sir, every man in this unit agreed we'd stick together. That's what we said at the start of this thing. We're not going home with half the job left out on the field. All I'm asking is to keep doing that job. To see it through, no matter what. I want to fight, as much as any noncombatant is allowed. And I only want to do it under your command, sir."

"Why?"

"I have my reasons for staying. Same as you. All I know is I can't go home. Not yet."

AJ sighed. "Maybe some junior officer fresh out of medical school cleared you. But it's not the same thing as working for me. I don't have time to play nursemaid out here—not to you or anybody. Not when boys are dying before our eyes."

"And I'm not asking you to. This is where I can do the most good, and do it with men I trust."

"If I let you back in, it's still my rule out here. That means if you have any symptoms—dizziness, loss of balance, pain. I don't care if you sneeze the wrong way—you tell me and I'm pulling you out. Do you understand me, Private?"

The pocket watch suddenly made the front pocket of Court's uniform shirt feel like it was lead lined, and his head pounded in time with the sound of bridge-building hammers in the background. But in war a soldier did what he had to do to survive. Whatever it took to fight. Court would, too, especially now that he knew how much he had to fight for.

"Yes, sir."

"Right. Then is there anything you want to tell me?" AJ's steel eyes met Court's in a vise hold. "Anything I should know before we put you back to work?"

For the first time since they'd headed into the battle's fray more than two years before, Court looked his superior officer straight in the eyes . . . and lied.

"No, sir. Let's go to Rome."

Eight

L ondon held its breath.

All of England did, truth be told. The disillusioned flocked to the cathedrals for Sunday services, to mourn and to pray, even as bomb damage was being assessed and fires still raged in parts of the city.

Julia, too, might have gone to light a candle for those caught in the first wave of Hitler's blitzkrieg bombings the day before. But that had changed with an urgent summons slipped under her boarding-house door with instructions to appear—in full ATS uniform—at the Whitehall War Office at nine o'clock sharp the following morning.

The trek from Marylebone had taken dreadfully long, as petrol was already in low supply and repeated air-raid sirens and craters marking thoroughfares ensured transit schedules became useless. Piccadilly's usual bustle was to be expected, as were the horn honks and coughing motor engines that contributed to the music of their fair city. But all was cast in a shade of somber as pedestrians stepped around fresh rubble piles littering the sidewalks. And with high-explosive bombs that had rained down, the Luftwaffe's planes shattered all hope for a continuance of what the newspapers had dubbed the last many months as England's "Phoney War."

Julia caught her breath at the intersection, adjusting the strap on her obligatory gas mask satchel as she waited, watching as the Ministry of Information's "Keep Calm and Carry On" slogan swept by on the side of a double-decker trolleybus.

War was not just rumor now but reality.

As if any soul needed the reminder. A regimen of nighttime blackouts had already seen reams of black and navy fabric become a sought-after scarcity in millinery shops. Curbstones and traffic light bollards painted in bold black-and-white stripes now checkered the city, their patchwork quilt designs aiding motorists who had to turn headlamps down to a nearly invisible point. And the heady wartime headlines splashed across the likes of *The Daily Herald* and *The London Times* now decried Hitler's brazen Luftwaffe attacks from every newsstand corner.

Entertainment, too, had acquiesced to war's pressure.

Theater and ballet companies had dispersed months prior, including Vic-Wells, with contracts expunged as ballerinos shipped off to war and ballerinas were left to seek another berth. Like Lillie, who at no surprise had broken with Anton and, instead of continuing with her dancing aspirations, had signed with the Auxiliary Territorial Service—the women's branch of the British Army. She'd already sent Julia a letter from France, being part of one of the first waves of wireless operators posted there before the events of Dunkirk. And if Hitler's new bombing tactic was any indication of what was yet to come, it was likely Julia would find herself expedited to her own post as well.

The traffic light flipped and Julia hopped off the patchwork curb, followed the flow of foot traffic as she crossed the intersection, and hurried up the sidewalk. A department store not far off looked to have taken a direct hit. Julia joined the rest, trying not to gape as they angled around debris—gloves and handbags, broken glass and singed paper, and the eerie sight of mannequin legs strewn about the sidewalk as if the bombs had unearthed Dr. Frankenstein's secret laboratory belowground.

Posters came into view behind the fractured glass at Frank's Hairdressing Saloons and papered the ground outside what had once been a cozy corner bookshop. The advertisements boasted bright young things with ebony hair rolls, smiling cherry-red lips, and smart military uniforms to usher recruits past Leicester Square to the official Whitehall War Office complex up ahead.

Julia followed them too.

She took a deep breath and paused outside the building's massive rounded turret corner to straighten her smart military jacket and skirt and smooth hair pinned in a chignon under her uniform hat. A stop at the security desk for a check of her credentials and the issuance of a temporary pass card meant it was a quarter after the hour before Julia was soldiered through the necessary security checks back to the office of recruitment processing her assignment.

The charge looked up when Julia was brought back.

Mrs. Flynn was the no-nonsense, middle-aged officer Julia had worked with at the recruiting office the first time, and the person she was told to seek out at the post for this urgent summons. The woman fixed her eyes over the top of her bifocals, inspecting her wristwatch to find, no doubt, that it had indeed ticked well past the top of the hour.

"Miss Bradbury."

"Yes, I'm terribly sorry I'm late. But the trolleybus schedule was off and I had to—"

"Don't trouble yourself. On a morning like this, we're all sideways." She set a determined pace beyond the reception desk and down the hall. "This way."

Even for a Sunday morning, war refused to sleep; typewriter keys echoed in the halls, telephones rang somewhere from a switchboard closet, and conversation hummed with the voices of those now fully inducted into the frenzied war effort.

"Do sit, Miss Bradbury." Mrs. Flynn didn't look up as she took her seat behind the desk. After opening a folder, she took out a document and slid it across the desk. "We asked you to return so soon, even given the events of yesterday, because there has been an error. We shall need to right your paperwork immediately and issue a new identification card."

"Oh. I see . . . That part wasn't in the message left to me. Just that I was to arrive here this morning."

"We cannot leave official military orders in a public boardinghouse, can we? While this reassignment is a mere formality, we'll need your signature in order to move forth. Then we shall take your photo and you'll be off, aptly in His Majesty's service."

Julia scanned the missive, finding words like *envoy* and *peacekeeping* standing out among the paragraphs of type, and nothing that looked close to the description of training for a wireless operator—which had been the post assigned at her recruitment appointment.

"I don't understand. It appears as though this is a reassignment for domestic service . . . in the provinces?"

"Yes." Mrs. Flynn pulled a second sheet from the file. "Here is your travel itinerary and performance schedule for the next year. Though if these horrid bombings are repeated, I daresay we should all remain fluid with our expectations in the future. Schedules are likely to change. And if new orders are issued, you'll receive them straightaway."

"I don't understand. I thought I was to train as a telephonist?"

"Your tutelage in languages—particularly Italian and French—is a background that would indeed serve as a valuable resource for communications in the women's branch of the British Army. But it has come to our attention that your skills are more valuable to the ATS if used in another capacity."

"And what might that be?"

"Miss Bradbury, if I may be frank." Mrs. Flynn stared at Julia, her face carved from stone. "A prima ballerina has no place at the front. Even in a noncombatant role."

"I see."

"We assume this was modesty on your part not to have relayed your rather illustrious career achievements before now. But when we were alerted of the error, it took only a telephone call to your listed next of kin—a gentleman by the name of Winston Peterbrooke—to get it sorted."

Julia's lips parted, but she could find no words in reply.

The turn of events had all the hallmarks of intercession by a gentleman who knew how to game the system and then play his own odds. And his name certainly wasn't Winston Peterbrooke. As London was bombed, more men would surely be called into uniform. The strategy to use the advantage of dance—or to use *her*—in order to avoid conscription . . . it left all the breadcrumbs of an Anton Vasile trail.

"And who alerted you to this error?"

"I shouldn't know, just that Mr. Peterbrooke confirmed it for us."

Julia swallowed hard. "Could you look again, please? You're quite certain it was not a gentleman by the name of Anton Vasile?"

Mrs. Flynn scanned the paperwork, with its typed forms, a handwritten notation tacked to the front page, and the snapshot photo of Julia that had been paper-clipped to the folder's inside cover.

"No. Not a mention of any gentleman. Just that the error was brought to our attention in time, or you'd have shipped off tomorrow for basic at Guildford and we may never have been the wiser about the mistake." She looked up, her brow furrowing sharply, seemingly after having taken in the hot-cold reaction that passed over Julia's face. "Are you quite alright, miss?"

"Yes, of course. Do go on."

In truth, Julia shifted in her chair, the information niggling. A last-minute change of assignment—to one with a quite mystifying likeness to what Anton had once proposed—didn't sit well at all.

"Given this information, Miss Bradbury, the British Army cannot rightfully position you where you might meet with harm. As I've said, an assignment anywhere near the front, even in a support role, cannot guarantee your safety."

"Whilst London can no longer assure it either."

"That may very well be, but this office agrees that a reassignment is necessary. At this juncture the ATS is employing only cooks, waitresses, shopkeepers, and the occasional telephonist, but only if her skills warrant the assignment. I'm afraid we haven't a full training regimen developed for them yet, let alone for as unorthodox a placement as a classically trained ballet dancer. I am merely following orders by passing this information on to you and obtaining your signature for it."

Julia straightened her back. "And if I should wish to render an appeal? To whom would we send that?"

Mrs. Flynn picked up the pen from the desk and unscrewed the cap. She held it out and offered a gentle nudge. "I am confident you will not. Not when you've already signed on to do your duty for king and country. And to receive your post with the ATS—whatever that post may be. It appears fate has seen fit to send you back to the stage, Miss Bradbury, so your gifts might serve as a harbinger of peace in these troubled times. You ought to find great value in that."

With naught else to do, Julia nodded, accepted the pen, and inked her name. The rest was a daze as she stood for the obligatory photograph for her identification card, then accepted a train ticket and summons to appear on the platform at nine o'clock sharp the following morning.

Julia stepped from the building out to the patchwork curb, the wail of sirens echoing in the background. Passersby hurried along Whitehall, brushing her shoulders as she stood on the sidewalk and crumpled the orders in her fist.

It wasn't the dancing—Julia would have welcomed a summons with nearly any opportunity that would keep her aptly employed on a stage. But this envoy was to ship out with Vic-Wells's former stars, with the illustrious names of Vasile and Bradbury confirmed to go with it. And if Anton was indeed involved, it meant Julia was nothing more than a puppet on a string. She knew where that road led. To Milan. Perhaps even Rome, just as he'd once said before war had begun. And a commission that had about as much to do with Mrs. Flynn's definition of fate as the sun rising and setting each day. Though the woman had been correct on one point—ballet was a gift. It had once saved Julia, and, it appeared, it must do so again.

Fate indeed.

No one knew where fate chose to play its little games—not even in war. In the matter of a day, Julia had gone from free to caged. And in another twenty-four hours she'd step onto a train in uniform, with a man whose whims kept a tight hold on her tomorrows.

All Julia could see now was how fate tried—and failed—to claim a starring role in her life.

Nine

Delaney slipped on the only packable dress she'd brought to Rome—a long wrap design in black pindot she'd tossed in her suitcase just in case. It seemed a last-minute save over jeans and flats now that she'd followed the sound of laughter down the villa stairs. Instead of a quiet dinner she found a gathering the size of a small wedding reception stirring in the courtyard.

Glass lanterns flickered candlelight along the cobblestone path, lighting the steps of guests who carried serving bowls out from the kitchen. Sabine was there with a French-blue dress and her welcoming smile, lighting candles in glass hurricanes running the length of a rustic wood table. Guests claimed seats one after another and wasted no time filling appetizer plates from overflowing antipasto chargers.

Behind them stretched the backdrop of stone walls and the same scrolled gate Delaney recognized from the video call with Matteo. It seemed unbelievable now, to be standing in the exact same spot that had first taken her breath away. And though Delaney had hoped there might be time to review the letters before dinner, there was no chance of that now by the look of things—even if she had made an error and brought her laptop along. She paused in the doorway, tucking the laptop against her side, unsure of whether to walk in or hang back and wait for an invitation.

Matteo was easy to spot from behind, having taken a seat across from a man about the same thirtysomething age as he, with a beard and dark hair knotted on his crown. Noticing Delaney hovering on the fringes of the action, he whispered something to Matteo and tipped his chin in her direction. Matteo turned. And it calmed her a little that he didn't hesitate to hop up and walk her way with a welcoming smile.

"*Buona sera*, Del," he said, and then spotted the laptop. And tried to hide his amusement, as if he was absolutely questioning the decision to bring such a thing to dinner but thought it best to keep the opinions of a stranger to himself.

"Buona sera." Knowing she was caught, Delaney smiled too. "So . . . obviously I'm the girl who brought a laptop to her first dinner in Rome. Is that a fatal mistake?"

He held his hands out, arrested. "I didn't say a thing."

"And that was kind. Because I'm pretty sure you could have." Delaney surveyed the scene of flickering candlelight, wine bottles meeting glass rims, and seats filling up along the length of the table. "I'd hoped maybe we'd have time to look at our letters. But now I think I've severely underestimated the definition of an authentic Italian dinner. Have I interrupted a private party?"

"May I?" he asked first, holding his hand out.

"Of course." She handed the laptop over. Matteo set it on the sideboard just inside the door, then extended a hand toward the courtyard for her to step out with him.

"You didn't interrupt a thing. The villa's set up as a guesthouse, so we have people in for dinner on a regular basis, especially this time of year when the weather cooperates. But I will say that's the first time I've ever heard this villa described as anything close to private."

"So this is what Sabine meant by la cena?"

"It's what we would call *gioie della tavola*—'the joys of the table.' Nona's famous for her dinners in Tivoli. She may be slowing down a bit, but she still insists on doing the cooking—authentic fare like we've offered at this table for the last sixty years. And as long as Calla Santini is here, Villa Adriano will always operate with the heart to welcome every guest. Especially the first-time ones."

Matteo walked her toward the gathering, though his gaze drifted more than once to the open gate and the direction of where the path curved and disappeared.

"Will Mrs. Santini join us then? I so want to meet her."

"Sì. We sometimes get started without her." He looked down at the path for a breath, as if something weighted had captured him. Then, without missing a beat, he replaced whatever it was with another easy smile for the party before them. "But she'll be along soon."

Looking to the only empty seats left at the far end of the table— and the one next to his—Delaney chanced asking, "Is that her chair on the end then?"

"No. It's yours. Being guest of honor and all." Matteo ticked his head to the side, squinting just enough to show a little mocking in his profile. "Or I could just be trying to get in your good graces so you'll give us the suitcase right out of the gate."

"Oh. You didn't mention it when I arrived, so I thought maybe you were trying to play hardball. You know, lull me into a false sense of security so I'd hand it over, only to go home and see it sell for a million dollars at Sotheby's a month later."

"Not likely. We'd never sell. And I'd bet you've done your homework by now and know that other than obvious sentimental value, the suitcase isn't worth very much. But enough business talk—you must be starving. Come on. I'll show you around."

There were names and faces to greet: a pair of honeymooners from Massachusetts. A jolly gentleman Brit who was a repeat guest on frequent business trips to Rome. And neighbors with children and grandchildren running about the courtyard, chasing a bashful Ghost who weaved about behind the seated guests. Matteo introduced a woman with a pink paisley scarf over a gray bob and a deep crimson smile as Mirena—a cousin his nona had grown up with and apparently whose name seemed the perfect match to the depth of wisdom in her eyes. And reaching the end, Matteo pointed out topknot guy.

"This is a friend from the days back at uni." Matteo gave a light tap to the open chair on the end and pulled it out for her. "Finn Hunt, this is Delaney Coleman."

"Right. The mysterious stranger in the doorway. Nice to meet ya." Finn revealed a deep Irish accent and a wide grin. "An' you're here with our Matt then?"

"Del's just stopped in for a few days, on family business." Matteo cut off Finn's insinuation at the knees. He gave her a little side-eye as he sat though, and Delaney read it as she might need to be on her toes with this one.

"Business, eh? Sounds like that's code for she's single and can scoot closer to me. An' as for going back to our university days, we'll wait for those stories 'til I'm a couple glasses in. The tales are a little more interestin' if I remember to make myself the hero."

Matteo tossed a mock frown in Finn's direction. "Just so you know, you and your stories are on their best behavior where this guest is concerned."

"Yeah? And why is that now?"

"Orders from Sabine. We don't want to scare this one off."

"Fine by me, boss. Less talkin' means more eatin'." Finn winked at Delaney as the first of family-sized bowls was passed down their way. "And I never heard of an Irishman who couldn't enjoy a bit of *craic* if the company is as lovely as this."

Delaney smiled when Matteo tossed her a look that said, *"See?"* and she hid a laugh as she laid a napkin in her lap.

Okay . . . noted. Quite the flirt.

Finn chatted on, which Matteo didn't really seem to mind despite the lighthearted warning, and took the liberty of spooning heaping portions on his plate while pressing Delaney with endless questions and recommending the dishes she shouldn't dare pass up. The advice proved helpful in the end, as she'd never have made it through bowls of *carciofi alla Romana*—Italian-style artichokes—alongside sautéed eggplant, pesto pasta, mussels with olive oil, and the mountains of antipasto and savories on her own.

Time swept away. Candles burned low. And plates were passed until waistlines were forgotten. The conversation softened to a hum and the party began its slow ease into a break for the night, with bottles that offered the last of the sweet Sangiovese and guests who savored a lemon-infused *pastiera napoletana* for the final complement to a perfect meal.

"So you mentioned you have a journalism background, Del. What is it you write?" Finn seemed content to keep talking, even after the table guests had thinned and the candles had nearly served out their purpose.

"I've been an editor at a small lifestyle magazine in Seattle for the last few years." She gave a polite smile of course, pausing as she tiptoed around what was too much to unearth in small talk with strangers. Though the surroundings had pricked her thoughts a little. Between their family's loss and the potential do-over of returning home, Delaney wished she knew what her new chapters might entail. Even if predicting was proving harder to do. "And I am a writer, but one who's probably in between pens, let's say. Right now I'm helping to manage the family business back home while I figure a few things out."

"Sounds like that's code for she doesn't want to wade in any deeper, Finn. Maybe give her a pass, seeing as she is a guest?"

Luckily she was saved by Matteo's defense and didn't have to answer.

"That's alright. We've heard a bit about this lovely lady here. And some of my life in Ireland and yours in New York—these days, that is. But you haven't said . . ." Finn paused, swirling wine in a circle at the bottom of his glass before looking up. "Does our guest here know about Brazil?"

"No."

"What's this about Brazil?" Delaney asked innocently between bites of dessert, her interest piqued as she glanced back and forth between them. Matteo didn't look away, however. Instead of the light and easy conversation they'd enjoyed over dinner, he now bristled at his friend. Across the table he sent Finn a glare that said his loose tongue might have crossed some sort of invisible line—a forbidden one if looks could be judged at all.

"Why don't you tell her? She's obviously interested."

"I think that's enough ancient history for now." Matteo took a last sip of his water and stood. "Excuse me, Del. It's usual to snap a photo before we break for the night."

"Sure." She watched as Matteo moved off down the table.

He cleared a few plates, whispering something as he handed them off to Sabine in exchange for his camera. He directed the table for a few photos and then thanked the guests before they set off, offering another one of those smiles that seemed genuine but still layered behind reserve. Finally he gave Ghost a whistle, the roan following as he trailed off and disappeared through the iron gate.

"What was all that about?"

"Don't mind him." Finn sighed. Hard. And tossed his napkin on the tabletop in defeat. "That was directed at me. Matt gets it in his head that nobody wants to hear about old times, just because he doesn't want to relive 'em. And he won't be pushed into anything, even if a well-meaning friend tries to look out for his best interests where living an actual life is concerned."

"And what does that mean?"

"It means, Miss Coleman, if Mrs. Santini hasn't joined us by now, he gets a little testy. And I'd say he's gone off to the garden to look for her."

"So that's it . . . behind the wall? It's a garden?" Delaney stared through the shadows beyond the pines, along the path Matteo had just taken. "Can we go inside?"

"Like Brazil, I think it'd be Matt's place to be decidin' on that."

"Oh. Of course." Delaney tried not to make it evident that her eyes were glued to the garden path as she toyed her fork in the last bites of dessert on her plate. "Matteo said he lives in New York but he's here in Rome right now for some photography work. Is that what you do too?"

"What I do? Right." Finn's face brightened in the flicker of candlelight, morphing into a wide-eyed grin. And when she didn't respond, the laughter in his smile faded just as fast.

"Wait—you're serious?" Finn set down his glass, by this time drained of wine, and leaned forward on a hushed tone. "You mean that wasn't some polite act that the women always do when they're sittin' next to Matt? You really don't know who he is? Or . . . her?"

"What should I know?" Thank heaven Delaney stopped short of blurting out, "I couldn't find anything on them when I checked online." It had seemed off at the time, that a man with a common name could have an invisible internet footprint. Neither he nor Mrs. Santini seemed to own even a dormant social media account, at least not one that her journalism background could dig up. And at least for Matteo, that was about as close to a unicorn as she could imagine in their modern world.

"Sweetheart, that woman is ballet royalty around these parts, even if they do like to keep it quiet. And even if Matt's learned every bit of how to do that from his gran." Finn chuckled and leaned back in his chair. "I'd say most everyone at this table knows his story, but they're just respectful enough to pretend they don't. Guests here just enjoy each other's company and leave him alone otherwise. That's the only way he'd agree to make an appearance at things like this."

Now that Finn mentioned it, there did seem to be some whispers when Matteo's back was turned. Delaney hadn't thought much about it, other than he wasn't very hard on the eyes, and if she'd been at dinner with her girlfriends, they might have whispered too. But now . . . something definitely didn't add up.

"Why would he have to agree to dinner at his own home?"

"Well, that'd be another thing you'll have to ask Matt. We've been friends a long time, so at least that I do know about him. If there's talkin' to be done, he'll want to be doin' it himself." Finn tipped his chin to the garden path. "Here they come."

With slow, careful steps over cobblestones and circled by Ghost trotting around, Matteo emerged from the garden shadows with a petite woman on his arm, the top of her head just grazing his shoulder.

Snow-white hair was rolled in an elegant French twist. Pearls shimmered in a single strand around her neck, and her pale-rust dress danced waves around her calves with each step. And gran and grandson seemed at peace with their world, as he cradled her elbow and led her back through the gate. He whispered something down in her ear when they reached the stone walls and she nodded, then opened glass doors on the hanging lanterns and blew out the flames flickering in each.

With the lanterns cold, Matteo closed the gate with the aching cry of rusty hinges. Delaney rose and set her napkin on the table as she stepped toward them, drawn their way until the three met under the canopy of string lights laced in the trees.

"Delaney Coleman . . . this is Mrs. Calla Santini. Nona." Matteo extended a protective hand behind the woman's shoulders. "She's been waiting for you."

"It's so nice to meet—" Delaney stopped and looked to Matteo. "Will you tell her, please, that it's nice to meet her? And you said she's been waiting for me. Is that right? And not the suitcase?"

"No. She hasn't asked for the suitcase." He paused. "She asked for you instead."

If Delaney were a betting person, she'd have staked all on the fact that Matteo was opting to choose his words very carefully. He slipped his hands in his jeans pockets as Calla stepped forward on her own and smiled when she said something to Matteo in soft, lyrical Italian.

Delaney caught only one word: *Coleman*.

She looked from grandson to Nona and back. "What did she say?"

"She asks if it's true, you're Dr. Coleman's granddaughter, come all this way from the United States to see her."

"Yes. I mean . . . Sì. I am. I did."

Matteo remained silent this time, as Calla read Delaney's return smile with a nod. Beautiful and slow. And her face warmed with soft, almost violet eyes that looked so youthful in their depths. Not even the years that had smoothed lines over her face could rob the innocence in them as tears began a silent build.

"*Salvatore* Coleman," she whispered, and reached up to pat Delaney's cheek.

A wave of vanilla and sable perfumed the air from her wrist, as she nodded and studied Delaney. Calla's chin quivered as she took in the contours of her face. And nodded. As if memorizing. Or somehow . . . remembering? Even though that wasn't at all possible when they'd never met before.

"*Amica mia*. Grazie," Calla whispered, her voice catching on emotion. "Grazie."

Delaney stood frozen as Calla cupped her cheeks between her hands. *Grazie* was easy to decipher. But for the other word, Delaney looked up to Matteo again, who'd eased a step back and was watching in what seemed an almost stunned silence.

"Salvatore?" Delaney shook her head, overcome. "I don't understand. What does that mean? What does she want?"

"She doesn't want anything, Del. She's, uh . . . thanking you. And she's thanking him."

"Who? Not my grandfather."

Matteo swallowed hard and nodded. Just once. And paused until at last it seemed he found his voice. "*Salvatore*—it means 'savior.' And *amica mia* is . . . 'friend.'"

Ten

21 SEPTEMBER 1941
ST. JOHN ROAD
STARLIGHT, INDIANA

Where've you been all day?"

By the time Court found Penn, she was sitting in the bed of her daddy's old Ford truck, legs curled under her as she leaned into the weathered wood slats. It was where she always was at sunset, watching fire paint across the sky. "I've been around."

"Around, huh?" Court set a folded quilt on the tailgate. When she opened her mouth to object, he added, "And before you say no, this wasn't my doing. June thought you might be cold. Sent me to see to it."

Penn accepted the quilt on a technicality, Court knew. Fine by him. As long as she took it in the end. The temperature had a habit of falling fast once the sun went to bed over those hills, and he couldn't stand the thought of her catching a chill.

"Well, you'd think Momma could try to be a little less transparent." She draped the patchwork over her shoulders.

"Don't you think she's right? That we should talk?"

Court would have rather faced another fist in a bar than have to buckle under the pressure of her silence, which was ten times worse. He slid his hands in his pants pockets. Then realized it would look weak when he was trying to show her he could be as bullheaded as she. And took them out again.

"You didn't go to services this morning."

"I thought something was different about you." Penn side-eyed the new shirt as he eased up to sit beside her, silently adjusting for the pain in his ribs. "Is that Guthrie's Sunday best you're wearing?"

"It is. Even though it likely killed him to give the enemy the shirt off his back."

"That, too, was Momma's doing, no doubt."

"Yeah. Seems I needed something proper to wear for listening to Father Daniels talk his way through fire and brimstone. All while staring down at me because your daddy saw fit to post us in the first row. I thought Hades would open up beneath me and take out the whole pew. Sure would've given this town something new to talk about other than how the sinner came home."

"If you put it like that, I'm sorry I missed it."

"Why did you?"

"Oh, they don't need my situation on display." She shrugged, as if rolling more off her back than she was willing to say. But he could guess. "Besides, I can do my praying right here. I like the view better anyway. Upturned noses at the ladies' league haven't got a thing on the sunsets at Jenkins' Orchard. Just look at that."

Waiting on the emergence of a starry sky was the last thing he cared about at the moment; the splashes of color against a growing wave of night triggered a memory or two.

"I always liked it out here when I was a kid. The sky opens up over this land like nowhere else in the world. I used to pretend if

God were real and was involved in any of our lives, He'd have made the stars in the night sky just for us. Maybe He was peering down. Watching. And waiting to see who'd stop and look over a sunset to notice His handiwork."

"Hmm." Penn sighed. "Maybe."

"You don't think so?"

"The handiwork, yes. But I *know* God is real. And I think He's far more interested in seeing us enjoy something He's created than ever getting credit for it. I never heard of a Creator who did it for the bragging rights. Only One who did it for the love."

Love.

Court thought he knew something about that. Maybe when he looked at her. But certainly not from any Creator who'd never paid him notice before. Seemed a higher power had seen fit to let him be. And that had always been just fine by Court. Kind of an understanding they had not to get in each other's way.

Penn leaned into the side of the truck, still staring up as if lost in the moment. And Court took the chance to look down. She probably didn't realize it, but her hand rested on her midsection, cradling the rise under denim coveralls, her thumb brushing over her belly in an absentminded caress. There was an unexpected sweetness to it—an innocence Court doubted she even knew was there.

And something he certainly wasn't ready to feel, causing his insides to lock up in response.

"Why didn't you tell me, Penn?"

She caught him staring and pulled the quilt tighter around her front, hiding her body under the patchwork cape.

"Don't you dare go getting any notions this is your responsibility."

"Isn't it? If I'd known, I wouldn't have left. I'd have—"

"—done the right thing. I know." Penn finished his sentence with a rough shake of the head. "And let me trap you? No, sir. Even if this baby was yours, I won't be the girl who tied Courtney Coleman to a rail. I'd rather be notorious for anything in this town than that. And I don't plan on wearing a scarlet letter all my life either. It's done. And I'm going to own up to it. I believe grace can cover all things—even this."

The wind could've been knocked clean out of him.

To take a few shots in a bar and wake up the next day on the wrong side of the law was one thing. But to be slapped with her circumstances, then spend all day making peace with trying to do right by her, only to find out it wasn't his duty to bear after all? Penn must have thought a man could absorb a heck of a lot more than those shifting sands beneath his boots.

"What do you mean, 'even if this baby was yours'?"

She stared at the horizon like the answer could be found drifting out there somewhere. Then looked up, sad eyes looking back at him through the waning twilight. "What? Didn't you think after you left that anyone else could love me?"

"This is love?" Court's fists balled at his sides, the cold metal of the truck bed all of a sudden feeling like it was asking for a stiff right hook. "No. It's not. I'll kill him. Where is he? *Who* is he?"

"You won't do a thing, Court."

"You expect me to just let this go?"

"Yes. I do."

"Why?"

She sighed. "Because I'm asking you to. It's why I offered to show you out to the barn instead of Guthrie. I'd rather just pull the Band-Aid off and be done with it. It wasn't my choice to have you come back, but I figured if you're going to be staying on here, you'd find out sooner or later. But then . . . I don't know. I chickened out by the time I was standing in front of you. And I wanted to change my mind," she whispered, looking away. "There. Penn Jenkins admits she's a coward. Happy?"

Happy?

No. I'm not happy, Penn.

I'm confused. I'm furious . . . I'm heartbroken.

Needing to center his thoughts somewhere, Court gazed off to the glow through the farmhouse windows. June sat in her rocker by the front pane, rocking and knitting as she and Patrick listened to Lowell Thomas's nightly news broadcast of the chaos beneath Europe's bomb-riddled skies. Those good people—who loved their land and their family and their God—were the last folks on earth who deserved a moment's worth of trouble. Seemed that was all Court had ever given them. Or Penn. Or anybody. Maybe he wasn't responsible for the situation sitting next to him, but deep down, he knew if he wouldn't have left when he did, Penn wouldn't have rebounded in the way she had.

It was his fault.

"You're not a coward, Penn. And you never could be. Not to me." Court tipped his head to the glow of the sitting room beyond the windows. "Do they know?"

"Of course they know. And they're ashamed of their only daughter. Even if they won't say it, I know. It's there every time they look at me."

"I find it hard to believe Patrick hasn't gone after anybody with his shotgun."

"Believe me, he tried. And why do you think Guthrie came in and yanked you off that barstool when he heard you were back in town? Sister's honor and all that nonsense. I tried to tell him it wasn't you. Even if my parents found the truth hard to swallow, he wouldn't. Says he knew how you felt about his sister long before you packed up and hightailed it out of town the day of your momma's funeral. And he said if you ever did come back . . . well," she said, then stopped short.

"I'd be the one running from a shotgun?"

"Or a fist. You look terrible, by the way," she said through a laugh, and wiped at the moisture of a tear that had tracked down to her jaw. "I never thought my brother could manage to give somebody a shiner like that."

"Neither did I, to be honest. I was a little impressed. But don't tell him."

Penn moved then—gave a little groan as she stretched her back and grimaced in pain. And that inner turmoil was swift to sink through his gut. Court wanted to hold his hand out. To help her in some way. To do . . . he didn't know what. Support her back? Brace her elbow to help her up? She wasn't hiding the swell from him now, and her discomfort was only going to increase as the months went by. He didn't even know how many she had left.

"You know, I've been telling Daddy we need a new truck to replace this uncomfortable old thing." She straightened her back again, covering with a false cheeriness in her voice, as if looking for something to say that would take the conversation anywhere else but where it had been headed. "I saw a new one when we went to the Kentucky State Fair this summer. A Ford, which Daddy likes, and I might've been able to convince him of the investment. 'Cept it was turquoise."

"Patrick Jenkins is not buying a brand-new truck. And certainly not a turquoise one."

"I know. He'll drive this rusty rat trap until it falls apart. But you should have seen it." Penn closed her eyes. And smiled—with that pretty profile that said some sweet thing was going through her mind and the joy showed up on her lips. "Blue like the sea. With running boards and whitewall tires that would get eaten up by the wagon roads out here. But it was beautiful. How could you not smile every time you climbed up in a truck like that? It'd be happy blue rolling down the road."

"Happy blue, huh? How do you know? You've never even seen the ocean."

"A girl can dream, can't she? Someday I'll see it. And in the meantime, when we're hauling peach crates down those dirt roads out there, I'd look out at the horizon and imagine I'm looking at the sea. A truck like that would remind anybody."

"Remind anybody of what?"

"That some things are bigger than us. Or our troubles. Or lack of faith that things are going to be alright. You might just have to look harder to find it is all."

Something crashed between them at her words.

Maybe it was the memory of when Court had left her standing on the front porch steps. And why he'd left—loving her all those years since they were kids and then suddenly realizing he'd never be good enough for Penn Jenkins. Not if he tried for a hundred years. And he'd only hurt her in the end.

It felt like a thousand notions were flying through his mind that he couldn't seem to untangle on his own, let alone say to her now. But one thing Court did know—he couldn't stand to watch her hurting. Even more, hurting with something he couldn't fix.

Unless he could . . .

Hands aching to hold hers, Court reached out. Grasped her hand. She rebounded off the edge of the truck bed faster than he'd have thought possible in her condition, until the quilt fell in a heap and her boots hit dirt with their best effort to keep on going.

He held on. Gently, but pulling her back to him. Pleading like the fool he was. "Penn . . ."

"Whatever you're going to say—don't. This is *my* problem." She stepped back and placed a palm over her middle, like those words were untrue or somehow unclean for the baby to hear. "No. Not a problem. But I made choices and now they're mine to deal with. *On my own.*"

"You don't have to do this alone, Penn."

"I'm not alone. There's a difference."

"You know what I mean," he fired back, yanking the quilt up from the ground.

"Maybe. But what I don't know is what's floating around in that head of yours. You're looking for something I can't give you. This baby and me? We can't be the fixers to your pain. And in the end, you wouldn't want us to try."

"Who's talking about pain? I'm talking about standing up. That baby needs a father. You have no idea what it'll be like for that kid to grow up without one. But I do."

"And you're the man who's going to do it? You think you can really make a decision like that, first day back in town? Just change your whole life without even blinking. Can you honestly stand here and say you'd stay this time?"

She'd only asked because they both knew the answer.

Court couldn't raise a child in the same way he'd been raised—sired by one man yet tossed to another. Carrying a suitcase of shame from home to home, with nothing but an old book and a photograph he kept tucked in the binding. It's why he'd left that book behind after the funeral. And it's why, looking Penn square in the eyes, they both knew the truth now.

He'd left her before. And he'd do it again.

"Tell me what to do, Penn," he whispered, as he shoved back the emotion trying its best to make a tough man's eyes tear up. "Tell me what to do and I'll do it."

For the first time since they'd clapped eyes on each other after months of being apart, she initiated touch between them. Penn walked over and eased the quilt from his clenched fist. Then reached up and cupped a hand to his cheek, brushing a tender thumb across the rise of swelling there. She stared up into his eyes like the only person on earth who could truly see into his soul.

"Do your job, Court. Pay off your debts. And then leave us alone."

16 OCTOBER 1943
PORTICO D'OTTAVIA
ROME, ITALY

Brakes squealed as trucks came to a stop in the piazza.

Court looked far off to the street level just above the Portico d'Ottavia, squinting from their hiding spot in the alley as the rising sun pierced the sky behind the Roman ruins. He blinked through a wave of dizziness the bright light caused, trying to focus on the sudden burst of chaos that erupted at the edge of the Jewish ghetto.

Deafening sounds invaded the streets with the roar from truck motors. A chorus of slamming doors. An army of bootfalls and the barks of deep-chested dogs descended upon the tight-packed rows of connected four-story buildings. Residents emerged along the piazza—timid Jews cracking open their doors and peeking out from upper-floor curtains to see what was the matter, only to be greeted by handlers with guns drawn.

"Court?" AJ yanked Court's attention back from the scene with a firm hand to his shoulder. "Did you hear me?"

"Italian police wouldn't take to the streets like this."

"No. This is something else."

"Gestapo," Court said, though the swarm of uniforms infecting the piazza needed no introduction.

"Yeah. Gestapo." AJ tugged on Court's jacket, pulling him back toward the rest of their plainclothes ops team already making tracks in the opposite direction. "Time for us to go."

They'd stepped out at nightfall—all soldiers armed save for the medics under AJ, who kept emergency supplies under their jackets and an Allied red cross armband stuffed in their pockets. They'd swept through the city under cover of night, gaining intel on the state of the bridges interlacing the city, and avoiding Fascist gangs and the unpredictable SS night patrols.

As dawn grew near, they'd split for the trek back—an army officer, two engineers, and Tenor and Dean went one direction. AJ, Court, two combat soldiers, and their prized Typewriter in the other. They were to meet at a rally point to cross the Tiber. Head south. And get out of Rome undetected. But making it back now, with the unexpected swell of Gestapo sealing the streets, made it seem a fleeting possibility.

"They'll meet us back at the safe house?" Court asked, tracking with AJ's stride as they picked up speed.

"Got two hundred yards to the Tiber first. Then we'll think about what comes after."

Court kept close on AJ's heels as they wove past Roman ruins of an ancient colonnade and disappeared into the maze of tight-packed streets—none of their unit making the fatal mistake of stopping. They were to weave around the obstacles of uneven door stoops and shopfronts and backtrack if necessary to remain hidden. Keep to the shadows along the sides of the buildings. And just run until they could hear the river's current.

"This way." AJ pointed them down a side street. "River's up ahead."

But they weren't alone.

Helpless Jews had caught wind of the Gestapo net sweeping over and dared flee their fate. Men busted through doors at shop backs, nearly careening into their path. Escapees flew from building to building on the rooftops overhead, their footfalls disturbing loose tiles that fell and shattered on the ground like terra-cotta rain. Others hurried out front doors and scurried off with suitcases in their hands, escaping in the same direction they were.

Court turned to look back, midstride, making sure they hadn't been spied by the Nazis swarming down the streets behind them. The action threw him off though, his feet betraying his balance. The misstep blasted him into a row of crates with a loud crash and nearly sent him into view of a pack of Nazi uniforms that had rounded the corner up ahead.

Thinking quickly in the pause, AJ yanked Court to the ground.

In unison they melted their backs against stucco, easing into the shadows behind an open-air market stall and an exterior wall shielding discarded crates and piles of trash. Still breathing hard, they froze. And listened as a fresh line of trucks swooped in, cutting off the exit on the street in front of them.

"You good?" AJ asked between the deep drinks of breaths, staring back at Court like he was either furious, confounded by the blunder of a proven soldier, or both.

"Yeah. I'm good," Court said, only to turn and retch with AJ's glare boring into him as his stomach emptied in the dirt at their boots.

"You sure about that, Private?"

"I said I got it, okay?" Court wiped his mouth on his sleeve like it was nothing, putting on a show of bravado as if he was insulted by the mere suggestion of weakness. "Just tell me when we go."

In truth Court needed the respite to focus. His head was swimming. Had been since they'd ventured out the night before. His legs took to falling asleep at times if he didn't keep them moving. And he couldn't for the life of him explain why he was stumbling around like a scarecrow in a windy field when making a straight-line run that should have been a piece of cake.

Should have been . . . but wasn't.

"Alright," AJ whispered and held up a hand as he peered out to the street. "When I say."

"Copy that." Court exhaled and ran a palm over his eyes, trying to find focus through the blur of the street beyond the alcove.

Movement cut his fuzzy vision, revealing the backs of the Typewriter and the plainclothes officers; the rest of their unit had made it. They slipped through the swarm of Gestapo and disappeared into the darkness of an alley across the street. And looked like they were waiting. That meant if AJ and Court were going to have any cover, they had a rapidly closing window—moments only to get low, get fast, and get through without capture.

On another wave of nausea Court closed his eyes.

Leaning his skull back against the wall, he begged for an anchor, and for the tingling in his legs to stop so he could sprint when he needed to. Then the sound of gunfire popped in the streets—too loud to ignore—and he opened his eyes again. AJ had leaned forward enough to stare through a gap in the weathered wood, between the bottom of the market stall and the cobblestone street.

Boots invaded the foreground then. And along the lip of wood, shoes scuffled behind them.

They were pinned.

Shouts overwhelmed the narrow alcove. Italian rang out in the fitful cries of a woman and what sounded like the desperate pleas of a man. A suitcase dropped into view—a little ivory and red-dotted thing that hit the cobblestones with a clatter. After it, the sound of the woman's cries turned to violent screams.

A shot blasted without warning.

Court and AJ flinched when it rebounded against the wall like cannon fire and carried down the curve of the street in a sickening echo. In a blink the man's pleas became desperate howls as a woman's body fell to the ground. AJ splayed a palm against the air to hold them back, even as her cheek smashed to the cobblestones and distant, lifeless eyes stared back at them from under the stall.

With an order shouted in German, a second pistol shot rang out.

The man's voice was silenced with the same booming echo as before. But this blast ended with a new, gut-wrenching sound: the tiny, kitten-like sobs of a child.

God, no . . .

Blood boiled in Court's veins as a military boot kicked the bodies to make sure the people were, in fact, dead. Court pressed his face against the stall, staring out. And heaven help him, but a pair of little girl's Mary Janes and blood-spattered knee socks were washed in sunlight as they stood frozen between the bodies.

Court turned to AJ. Pointed to the shoes.

There's a kid, he mouthed, wishing more than anything he was a soldier with a gun who could fight back with more than just knowledge of IVs and tourniquets.

The sergeant shook his head.

And Court knew what he meant: the Geneva Convention said they couldn't get involved. They'd be taking their lives into their hands even if they'd raised a weapon, let alone used it. If non-combatant military personnel engaged in any offensive way, all protections were off. While they could argue the man and woman might have been merely injured—and as medics they'd have been beholden to check—engaging the enemy even for the sake of a little girl was out of the question.

Streams of crimson ran in the cracks of the cobblestones beneath Court's combat boots, trickling to their hiding space like a horrific, haunting river. More shots followed somewhere out on the main street. The military boots moved off after them, leaving the child behind with the bodies. Maybe she wasn't a threat, seeing as it looked like her parents were gone. So they'd left her.

Alone.

"They're gone," Court whispered, and checked through the slat again.

The Mary Janes stood frozen, caught in the river of blood that flowed between the bodies and their stall. Court repositioned his legs in the best stance to spring, if only AJ hadn't read him like a Sunday paper and grabbed his forearm.

"Look. The back of the last truck." AJ tipped his chin the other way, out to the street. "There's no guard. We can make it."

"Right. I can get her and meet you there."

"No. You can't."

"Yeah. I can reach her. Look—" Court argued back fiercely and muscled his arm free to point out past the stall's support beam. "She's right there. Just feet away."

"I said *no*. You can't. And you know it."

Court shook his head. "But we can't just leave her!"

"We have a job to do. And I have no sidearm with which to do it. That means no matter what thoughts are racing through that head of yours . . . we stand down, Private. And stick with our unit." Those steel eyes were as firm as Court had ever seen them. "That's an order."

Closing a fist at his side, Court gritted his teeth—anything to absorb the furious energy coursing through his body. War was war. It was bloody. And it was merciless. But war made upon children? That burned inside him anew even years into the grisly, no-win hell party. The inhumanity of what they'd just witnessed stirred the same visceral reaction within him as each new atrocity. But this wasn't a battlefield. And what had been done to that little kid was unforgivable.

Something knotted in Court's gut when he imagined Penn's son, standing alone in an alley with his momma's blood splashed on his shoes . . . It was too much. A voice inside told Court as sure as anything he'd known in his entire life—he was there for a reason.

The reason was *her*.

Court blasted out from behind the stall.

He ran and in a fluid motion curled fingertips through the suitcase handle and swept an arm around the girl to lift her from behind. With a palm covering her mouth, he skidded over uneven stones, his boots slipping on blood as he flew back to their hiding place.

No doubt, Court would have to take his medicine with AJ for defying a direct order. And he would very likely face a court-martial back in the States if they ever got out of there alive. But dizziness struck him dumb—this in a wave he couldn't surface from. Court slammed into the wall, forehead ringing a bell against the market stall's stucco.

The last thing he remembered was lying flat on his back under the blue sky, with AJ's face fading out as the kid's desperate little arms clung to his neck.

Court's eyelids fluttered . . . and oblivion stole him back.

Eleven

Winter snow had turned into a dreary, bone-chilling rain aboveground. And some seven stories below it, their ballet troupe waited to take the makeshift performance stage in the East End underground.

"What's come over you?" Anton asked Julia, then shook his head as a group of Sugar Plum Fairies, bedecked in their mismatched tulle and tights and bright little faces, squeezed onto the stage wing around them. "You look like you're actually enjoying this."

Julia wiped the hint of a smile from her face, should he see it in the dark.

"And if I am? It's you who keeps staring at the crowd like you're waiting for the Grim Reaper to appear. Why not try looking a little bit more jovial, like the star in your publicity stills? Surely you'll be recognized then."

No doubt that would hit the mark she'd intended.

A gathering of young ballet hopefuls who would share their

stage for a holiday performance of *The Nutcracker* clearly did not sit well with the great Anton Vasile. And the more they toured England's small hamlets and bomb-riddled neighborhoods, it was the troupe's star who found the audiences increasingly stolid. To Anton, their hovels were offensive. And the requirement to perform on any stage beneath the level of Covent Garden he deemed an unnecessary waste of time and talent.

It seemed his grand idea for a ballet envoy had far less star power than he'd once imagined. And far less joy about it than Julia always seemed to find. At the very least it had given Anton a reputable position in the British Army—a uniform to wear alongside the rest on the train platforms—as they moved from town to hamlet, performing for the masses. And if Julia could place her bets, she'd wager that fact had been the one small consolation out of it.

Nevertheless, Anton saw Tube performances as ancillary evils that forced him to survey the crowds with an air of distaste. This he did now in spades.

"We've endured eight months of bombings. For what? To dance for rabble who have never seen a ballet in their lives and who can't begin to appreciate it if they ever do see it again?" He looked over the audience within the Tube walls, the space now packed with people. "They can't even arrive on time. The curtain is twenty minutes late."

"And who owns their own time in a war? I heard tell from the stage manager that air-raid sirens have blared through the afternoon, and that threw schedules off. Most of these people have families—children who were to be in the show but just couldn't get here until now."

Their prime minister might have beseeched citizens not to shelter in the Tube tunnels, but from the first Blitz bombs in September 1940, Londoners invoked their right of safety regardless of the directives issued from 10 Downing Street. It seemed they believed they'd be a mite safer tucking away from Hitler seven stories underground instead of attempting to hide in plain sight on top of it. And for the months after, an underground world came to life when the sun went down.

The unfinished Bethnal Green Tube station, dubbed the "Iron Lung," where they were to perform that night, boasted an impressive résumé. When their troupe had been escorted downstairs, they'd seen sleeping quarters with metal bunks rumored to outfit some five thousand Londoners. There were nursery services for working women, stocked medical facilities, and a fully functioning café that served a continuous stream of piping-hot tea and ration goods throughout the night. The Bethnal Green Library had even built a lending library in the underground. That had expanded to other arts now, with opera, orchestra, and ballet performances. It was, in fact, why they were there—to keep hearts light and spirits high through the holidays.

"Just look at them."

"I am looking," Julia shot back, watching in wonder the little ballerinas who would share their stage. "All I see is how excited they are."

"You know what I mean. This is common, Julia. And we are not."

"Do try not to be a snob. You cannot expect the costume mistress of Covent Garden. There's no glue. That means no toe shoes for the older girls who should have them. I'm down to two pairs myself. And with no silk stockings for tights or extra fabric for costumes, we must make do. The director told me local seamstresses accepted donations of wares from East Enders' own wardrobes, and they sat about in sewing circles just to make those little girls' costumes for tonight. They're giving everything they have to fight this war the only way they know. And you ought not snub them for that."

"Off you go, now," the director cut in, patting the shoulders of the ballerinas as they stepped past and whisked out onstage for the Stahlbaum family's Christmas party scene.

Anton leaned his back against the underground wall, brooding as usual.

"And remember to have a jolly good time out there. Yes? 'To dance must always be a joy,'" Julia said, whispering the line her mother had always told her, to as many of the young ones as she could as they moved past.

As the swell of Tchaikovsky's overture began and the lights flicked out, a hush fell over the crowd. More young ones filtered past, taking the stage for the next number, an adaptation of the Sugar Plum Fairy dancing through the Land of Sweets. And in the pureness and beauty of the dance before her—perhaps in the innocence she could still remember from her own youth—Julia took a step forward and gripped the side of the curtain, breathless as she watched.

"Look, Julia. I'm sorry."

"For what?" she whispered over her shoulder. "You're always like this. It's part of your . . . nature, we'll say. One gets used to it."

"I'm not talking about nature. I'm saying I've changed. And I wish to apologize for the man I once was." Anton paused, and that pause seemed to carry a distinct weight that had nothing to do with an attempt at ill humor. When she didn't respond, he added, "Did you hear me?"

"Yes. I heard you."

"And . . . ?"

The loss of backstage lights had blanketed them in darkness, so when Julia did turn, she saw only that Anton had stopped mere inches away and stared down with an expression she had no idea how to read. Especially if they were to take the stage in a fraction of minutes.

"You honestly expect me to do this now? Before we must dance for all these people?"

"You won't talk to me anyplace else, so what am I to do? People usually don't see fit to rub someone's nose in it when they're trying to apologize. Isn't that what you've wanted? Why you've avoided me all these months even while we've been performing? There now. I've said it. Let us move on."

She swallowed hard, trying both to find her voice and to remember to listen for her cue that was fast approaching.

"That's you," he whispered with singsong notes and tipped his head to the stage.

Forced out alongside the rest of the costumed little ones, Julia was swept into their imagined fairy world. It was as if she were far away from the plight of war, or brokenness, or the apology he'd so casually just tossed her way. And she didn't even know which offense he was claiming to be repentant for.

Focus, Julia . . . downstage, right.

Glissade. Piqué, first arabesque.

And breathe . . .

Julia swept across the stage, pulling into the *retiré en face* sequence, her heart light even with the difficult transition from arabesque to *en face*. And her feet lighter as they melded with the happy notes of the Sugar Plum Fairy's world. Though, out of the corner of her eye, something drew her back—a sudden vision of a figure who'd joined Anton in the stage wing.

Turn. Spin . . . and spin . . .

Fouetté to tendu, back facing.

Julia looked again, finding the same figure watching with Anton from their place in the shadows . . . Winston?

Pas de bourrée.

And breathe . . .

Arms high, open to second. And finish in third.

The rest of the performance was a blur of fairies and faces, of music and the melodic cheering of the audience. And Anton, of course, mesmerizing the crowd with a performance as the heroic Nutcracker. But as lights dimmed and children were swept off to sleep the night away in the Tube, Julia knew why Anton had been so keen to watch the crowd before. And it was only a matter of time before Winston Peterbrooke arrived backstage to explain.

He stepped forward at Anton's side, offering a bouquet of blooms. "For you, my dear."

Julia accepted the gift, drinking in the sweet scent of winter-flowering honeysuckle before looking up again. "Thank you. But, Winston, whatever are you doing here?"

"Ah. Mr. Vasile has not shared the good news?"

"I was waiting until after the performance to tell her."

Julia glanced back and forth between them. "Tell me what?"

"To sell out an East End show in these circumstances is quite a feat. Even Markova and Fonteyn have not managed that." Winston clapped. It appeared nothing alleviated his sullen moods better than ticket sales. "The brochure for tonight combined with a standing-room crowd was enough to convince the higher powers to grant Mr. Vasile's request."

"They saw it then?" Anton chimed in, his tone velvet.

"Who saw what?" she asked, only to be drowned out by the eagerness of Anton's guile.

"And they weren't turned off by these underground doldrums?"

"Quite the contrary, my boy. Members of the War Office cabinet attended tonight's performance and were thoroughly impressed. And given the reminder of Julia's family association with the prime minister himself, they have ordered a reassignment of your duties."

Julia looked to Anton, aghast, as her insides clenched like she'd just been served a fist there.

"That's what the apology was for—not for past wrongs. You were smoothing over what you'd just raked. You used my late father's name to secure a commission because he was once a physician to Winston Churchill?"

"Not me, Julia. *Us*. I secured it for us."

"And this tour we've undertaken through the provinces. Am I to assume that was you as well?"

Winston cut in, his propriety in manners of business taking over. "Now, now. To put it plain, my dear, Anton remembered that you'd grown up alongside Mary Churchill at Chartwell. That is all. Amid the horrid bombing raids that could continue at any time, we believe a higher commission is warranted. Where you might have ample security to alleviate any concerns of safety during your performances."

"But I have no concerns. I've said as much. The underground is filled with people all doing their best to get on with it during this war. This is my post with the ATS—to dance among them. And I *love* it."

"Of course you do, brave girl. But when the office of the prime minister was made privy that the late Lord Chatham's daughter was in such a predicament, it seems those in authority agreed that a change is in order. And I have been sent to fetch you to be a part of a cross-country peace envoy beginning in the new year. A larger stage where your talent will not be squandered and your safety could be better assured than what the Tube can provide."

"I hadn't thought anyone's security could be assured in war. And what is this high commission?" Julia exhaled, breath shaky, and delivered a glare to Anton that could have melted stone. "Let me guess. We dance at La Scala? And then perhaps Rome?"

"Yes, my dear. To dance on the most prestigious stages in all the world. Always erring on the side of caution, of course. You shall have a security detail and official appointment from the king himself.

And yes, La Scala." Winston's voice hitched on an unexpected note of emotion. "Just as you always dreamed."

Anton folded his arms across his chest in victory. And this latest move on the chessboard dared masquerade as her dream, when really it would serve both to keep him from the front lines and to bolster his fame in all other spaces—and Julia effectively under his thumb as long as their names were joined in marquee lights.

He'd used her.

Again.

And she hadn't even known.

"And if I should refuse?"

"Julia, surely you remember back to the days at Vic-Wells—we talked then of what war might bring. And our leadership agrees that ballet is how we might best serve our country."

"How *we* might serve," she whispered, thinking only that he'd do nearly anything to keep from taking an enemy bullet and to feed his aspirations at the same time.

"I told you once, our names are tied. Our star rises together." Anton paused just long enough to smile at Winston—the gentleman who had always been her ally now quite unwittingly sold into the ballerino's scheme. "And now it rises higher. But that cannot happen while hiding in the underground. Come up for air, Julia. Do what you were made to do in this life."

Come up for air?

Impossible.

There was no way out but to plunge deeper into Anton's hold on the very air she breathed. Was she never to be free from her gilded cage?

16 OCTOBER 1943
TIBER ISLAND
ROME, ITALY

"Permesso, signora!"

Obeying the doctor's order to step aside, Julia balanced the tea tray in the crook of her elbow and pressed her back to the wall.

A mass of white coats rushed down the hospital hall, wheeling a gurney with a young man laid out upon its top. Dr. Emory—a middle-aged surgeon with spindly, wire-rimmed glasses and a tight crop of thinning ebony hair—flashed Julia a look over the top of his surgical mask, his glance flitting to the doors of the adjoining church.

She nodded as the staff rolled past and disappeared into the depths of the surgery.

A tall, broad-shouldered man in plain clothes attempted to follow but was pushed out, the double doors unceremoniously slammed in his face. He stared back in their wake, his breathing labored, with mismatched woolen trousers, rain-dampened hair, and a drenched utility shirt under a threadbare jacket. It looked as if they could have run all the way to the hospital.

Maybe they had.

One might have thought him a journeyman from the city center or a laborer from one of the vineyards outside of Rome. He was older than the blond man on the gurney though, his profile sporting laugh lines at the outer corners of his eyes and the lightest peppering of gray in the shadow of the beard breaking upon his jaw. Perhaps they'd run into one of the Nazi checkpoints or Fascist sectors that laced the streets at night. Things could have gone badly from any point. The stories Julia told herself made sense, that is, until she looked down and calculated the oddities.

Combat boots? There was no doubt they were military issue.

She paired those with the curious article of a child's suitcase clasped in his bloodstained fingertips and a bundle crooked in his other arm, buried just under the wing of his jacket. A bundle wearing a blue dress with a pair of dangling legs clad in brown socks, far too big for her little size and topped with scuffed Mary Janes.

And . . . a little girl?

Julia pulled her mask down to her chin so the man might see her lips move.

"Sei imparentato con quest'uomo?" she whispered, inquiring if he and the man were related.

"Sto bene. Grazie," he said and turned away.

He gave a canned answer in Italian that said he was "Fine, thank you" and didn't require any assistance, a response that didn't fit with Julia's inquiry. The hints of a language barrier excluded the man from the ranks of the fled Italian Army. And if he was military but wasn't Italian . . . what exactly did that mean?

Julia balanced the tea tray in the crook of her arm, then reached out with a ginger hand to the man's elbow.

"Sir. Is the man ill? With the sickness, I mean."

He snapped his attention to her—steel-gray eyes that searched her face and whispered relief to hear his own language spoken back to him. He edged closer, a footstep of trust carrying him away from the closed surgery doors. "Sickness?"

"No one is allowed entry to the church and quarantine wing unless they are treating a patient or that patient himself has contracted . . ." Julia kept her voice low, as caution bade her glance back at the passage of SS uniforms at the far end of the hall. *"Il Morbo di K."*

There an officer lingered like a wasp protecting its nest,

hovering, watching. With seeming interest piqued by their quiet confidence, his black boots began a slow, measured march in their direction.

"Oh no. The captain mustn't see you like this." Julia pulled her mask up over her mouth and tugged at the man's sleeve, edging them down the hall. "Cough."

"What?"

"Cough. Now. As hard as you can."

The soldier obeyed, hunching over the girl as he let hacking coughs rumble from his chest. Julia placed a hand to his shoulder and patted as she led them away. "We must go."

"Where?" he whispered back, though he still followed.

"This way. Quickly." Julia tilted her head toward the darkened hall connecting the quarantine ward to San Giovanni Calibita Church.

Pew rows lay under soaring arches and high, gilded walls as they rushed through the sanctuary. Rain disrupted the peace of the garden as she led them to the church courtyard. Slowing them up at the colonnade's end before the portal to the rectory, Julia stole a quick look over her shoulder to the stone rail at the second-story veranda.

It lay empty. And she could finally breathe.

Thank You, God.

The SS captain would not stare down from his perch. And those ever-watchful hawk eyes of his would not record the soldier and little girl's entry into the hiding place.

A hall lay behind the door. The soldier followed her inside and waited while she opened the first flat door. "Come. Quickly." Julia ushered them in and bolted the interior lock behind.

With a *clink* of metal to wood, Julia set the tea tray on her writing table and flicked on the desk lamp to cut the dark. She removed her mask and set it aside—only then risking a glance back to her guests.

The soldier didn't stir. The little girl either. They simply collapsed in the leather wingback by the window.

A chill bit Julia, traveling the length of her spine. If she could feel it through her skirt and blouse and the thick-weave cardigan, Lord knew they could in their sad state. She retrieved the jar of matches from the mantel and swiped a stack of old newspapers from the bin, then built a kindling pile in the center of the wood-burning stove. She struck a match head against the tile beneath her oxfords.

Dr. Emory had cautioned Julia that were she to agree to help in the ruse the doctors had undertaken, taking in unknowns—possibly Jews—and providing shelter, this would be her part to play. But now, staring into the melodic growth of flames, knowing the mysterious strangers were sitting right behind for goodness knew what purpose, Julia understood she was in way over her head.

Kilometers over, with no turning back.

Metal hinges cried out as she closed the stove door and turned to find he'd been watching *her*. In the trigger of nerves set aflame under his gaze, Julia reached for the suitcase.

"Shall I find her some dry clothes to—"

"No. Sit. Please." The soldier moved as if to offer his chair, but she waved him off midrise and moved a stack of books from the seat of a spindle chair leaning against the wall. He slumped back down against the corner of the leather chairback, as though exhaustion was quick to befriend him.

"Would she drink tea?" Julia pulled her chair close and reached for a cup and saucer on the tray. "It's licorice, but it might warm her up."

"Thank you."

The soldier attempted to rouse the bundle as Julia poured the steaming liquid, but the girl burrowed her head deeper against his neck.

"What is her name, please?"

He shook his head. "I don't know."

Curious. But Julia brushed it aside as she retrieved one of the tea biscuits from the tray—a honey-sesame sweet dusted with icing sugar—and moved to stoop before the wingback. The little one looked up. Doe eyes peeked from behind a wave of damp chocolate locks that framed an olive-skinned fairy nose.

My, but she was tiny. And couldn't have aged more than four or five years at the most.

"*Tesoro? Qui. Biscotto?*" Julia whispered. She held her breath as the girl blinked back but didn't move. "Hmm?"

"You're British." The soldier's voice was rocky and deep. And those eyes a fraction too direct for Julia's comfort. She noticed a small crescent scar, just visible over one brow.

"And you are a soldier, who I'd wager doesn't speak Italian? Or at least not much." She sighed and nudged the sweet closer to the girl. "When was the last time she's eaten?"

"I don't know that either."

This time his answer ended on a sigh that said something had tipped him over an edge of anger. Maybe frustration. But then, a hospital full of Waffen-SS could cause that in a thrice.

"Well, I don't know where they come about finding sugar in our world right now, except that the SS officers have pull with what comes in on supply trucks. I'm glad the kitchen staff found the sweets, if only this little one might enjoy them."

"Where are we? I know Tiber Island, but . . ."

"Fatebenefratelli Hospital."

The man shifted his glance to the swath of linen Julia had discarded on the tea tray. "There is a sickness?"

"Yes. You're in the church adjacent to the quarantine wing, but

I can assure you that you do not need a mask in here. You're not at risk. Neither of you are."

"And why is that?" He readjusted his bundle, sitting them a little straighter again. "What kind of contagion requires a mask only part of the time?"

"It is *Il Morbo di K*—Syndrome K. You entered through the quarantine unit, so naturally I assumed you'd been made privy to the danger in coming to the hospital right now." When the statement didn't strike the same flash of fear that it did for others, she asked, "You mean you really didn't know?"

Though Julia didn't need an answer; his eyes told her he didn't.

He glanced at the door and then to the other portal in the corner—the one he couldn't know connected the sitting room to adjoining bedchambers.

"It's safe here?"

"Quite safe. *They* scatter like jackrabbits in McGregor's garden whenever our masks appear. But we ought to keep our voices down as a precaution." Julia finally relented with the girl, placing the biscuit back on the tea tray before retreating to her chair.

"And that stone-eyed Waffen-SS. He's in charge?"

"Captain Patz. Yes. He is the chief who's assumed the Reich's leadership over the hospital. Alongside Dr. Borromeo, the administrator." Her heart longed to reach out to the little one. "The sick man you brought in . . . is he the girl's father?"

"No. I am."

Of course he wasn't. Their coloring was as off as winter to summer. And he'd already stated he didn't know her name. The lie was admirable given the circumstances but poorly done. No doubt he had few choices in the matter and went with the best option.

"My brother . . . he collapsed near the Portico d'Ottavia." The soldier paused, as if calculating his next statement. "And I was unable to revive him."

Julia was certain she couldn't have hidden the shock from her face, even in the faint glow of lamplight. They knew of what had occurred at the ghetto just the day before, and she knew what he must be telling her now because of it.

"You carried this child and an injured man all the way from there to here?"

"We had to wait until dark, but I had help. Men on the street said Father Bialek would take us in." Those steely eyes stared back—sure and immovable—saying nothing further yet working to confirm her suspicions one by one. "You trust that doctor? The one who looked to you in the hall?"

He saw that?

"Dr. Emory." Julia cleared her throat. "Yes, I do."

"And would he turn us over to them if we did, in fact, come by way of the Portico d'Ottavia?"

"Well, Dr. Emory is an anti-Fascist." And that ought to have put punctuation to it.

"I'm not venturing into Italian politics. A truthful yes or no will do."

"No then. All I meant was, politics draw clear lines here between the Fascists and partisans. Either you submit to Nazi rule or you're arrested and sent to the Via Tasso Prison. Or executed on the spot. Dr. Emory joins Dr. Sacerdoti as the other in charge over our quarantine wing. And the doctors here share views that can only be in vehement opposition to all the Nazi uniform stands for, no matter what outcome those views might bring them."

The soldier nodded. He ran a palm through damp waves of ebony, until it caught and rested in a weary pause at his neck.

"Then tell the doctor I believe my brother has shell fragments lodged in his spine. He's had surgery to remove them once, but I believe myelopathy has set in as a result. He's been trying to hide it."

"And how do you know this? Are you a doctor?"

Evading that, he continued. "He'll need the remaining fragments removed by a skilled surgeon. That is, if he even wakes up at all after this. He hit his head when he went down. It doesn't look good."

"Alright. I'll seek out Dr. Emory and tell him what you wish. But I'd venture to say he already knows what is needed to help your brother. He is the most trusted surgeon in all of Rome. The Germans even bring their most serious officers' cases to Fatebenefratelli for treatment, just because he is in residence. And that is even with Syndrome K plaguing us."

"I'm sorry," he said, the hard edges of his tone smoothing out. He leaned forward to pick up a biscuit from the tray and held it out, rolling it over outstretched fingertips. "I should have thanked you for taking us in instead of giving you the third degree. But if I told you why, you'd understand."

"You needn't say more. Not in wartime. We're here under asylum the same as you."

It was his turn to register shock, his brow cutting sharply. "Asylum? For what?"

The little girl turned thief then, swiping the biscuit from his fingertips. And lay her head back upon his shoulder as she nibbled the sweet's edge.

The soldier smiled then—wide. And quite genuine it seemed.

Julia couldn't help but return the gesture, as the tiny flicker of normalcy in their broken world had proven infectious. It appeared the soldier understood some constants—that children, sweets, and unbidden smiles between strangers might transcend even the darkness of war.

"What is your name?" His voice was softer now, his guard lowered.

"Julia. And yours?"

The door in the corner creaked then, swinging wide until it smacked the wall—loud enough that the soldier shot to his feet and the girl dropped the biscuit to skitter in a parade of broken crumbs upon the tile.

"Anton." Julia stood as the ballerino anchored a shoulder to the doorframe and leaned heavily upon a knobby wooden cane with the other arm. The gunshot wounds and his subsequent infection had eased, but certainly not to the point where he ought to be trekking around on weak legs. And certainly not with refugees trying to hide in plain sight. "You ought not be up."

"I heard voices . . ." Anton eyed the unknowns quite openly. "Who are they?"

"A family whose brother was lately admitted to the hospital."

"Yet they are in the rectory?" Anton edged back a step, as if the Syndrome K infection could leap across the room and reach him from there. He stared back, addressing the strangers with an icy glare. *"Il tuo nome?"*

"Athenos Rossi," the soldier replied, somehow understanding enough Italian to give a false name. He fused a palm to the girl's tiny back and set her down in the wingback, adding, "Calla."

Anton stepped toward Julia, authoritative even as his cane dragged across the tile. But in a surprise move, the soldier advanced, too, and met them. As if on instinct he closed the space between Anton and her, cutting off the ballerino's attempt to whisper in her ear.

"The rectory is private, Julia." Anton stared daggers at the soldier and tipped his head to the hallway door. "They shouldn't be here. Especially not if someone in their party was admitted to the quarantine ward. There is a surgery waiting room for that."

At such a direct challenge to report them, Julia would have expected the soldier to gather the suitcase and the little girl and be off. But he stood firm, center of the sitting room, staring back as if Anton were the one interfering in a private conversation and not the other way around.

"Yes. I know we've not allowed family here, but Dr. Emory wished them to stay because of the child. I will give them my bedchamber for the night and sleep in the chair by the stove. So you shouldn't be disturbed in your room." Julia offered a serene, confident smile—even as it made her skin crawl to do it—and reached for the teapot. "I'll just go and fetch more hot water. And I will send Dr. Emory in to check on you before his shift ends for the night."

Anton eyed the pair of intruders but turned with an imperious manner and disappeared back through the portal, the door left ajar.

Julia turned to the soldier, cheeks warm in anger, embarrassment, or both. That her dance partner should take the liberty and suggest he had any claim over her as to question guests in her own sitting room. It inflamed her cheeks all the more.

"I'm sorry," she whispered low, thinking it best to keep the secret of English speaking between them. "He can be . . . abrupt at times."

"Your husband?"

"*No.* Good heavens . . . no."

It was the soldier's turn to register surprise with a tiny uptick of the corners of his mouth.

"I meant he is an associate who doesn't much like the injury that has left him confined to bed and at the mercy of Father Bialek's goodwill to allow us to stay."

"I understand." It was a courtesy that he looked away in an attempt to hide amusement at her first answer. He reached down, took another biscuit from the tea tray, and offered it to the girl. She accepted without coaxing this time.

"We thank you for the room, but we'll take the chair for the girl. And I'll sleep here on the floor. When my brother is out of surgery, if you could please let me know? I don't care what time it is. We'd like to stay with him."

"Of course. And I'll see that you're brought a basin of water." She glanced to his hands without thinking first, then turned away. "So you can wash."

"Thank you."

"Good night then, Mr. Rossi," Julia said, barely audible as she stumbled through the awkward air and turned toward the door.

"Julia?"

"Yes?"

He'd taken a soundless step behind her when she turned around. He stood holding out the mask. "You'll need this."

"Oh. Quite. Thank you." Julia affixed the strings of her mask to cover her nose and mouth. Left shaken, she hurried toward the courtyard.

Perhaps it was the way the soldier had been ardent in watching over the girl . . . the look of agony upon his face when the man was wheeled through the surgery doors . . . the way he'd broken and smiled, offering a flash of something genuine in their war-torn world . . . even the way he'd stood up to Anton was illogical for what a man ought to have been in his shoes. The glimpses into the soldier's character were rare. And unexpected. And if anything gave her hope that the monstrous war would one day end, it was that men like that might bring about its cessation.

Julia turned the corner to the hospital, wondering how a single interaction could make such a marked impression. And she didn't even know his name.

Twelve

A Roman sunrise demanded notice—almost as much as the hint that a man might be waiting for you at a breakfast table right after it.

Light poured into the great room from the courtyard, as if the villa's back doors remained open at all hours. Delaney fell under its spell, following it as she turned the corner, only to find Matteo was indeed seated at the table. He was in a casual tee and jeans, bare feet stretched out, and wearing a pair of thick black-rimmed glasses as he clicked through something on his laptop.

"Buongiorno." Matteo looked up, then did exactly what Delaney hadn't expected—gave her his full attention. He nudged the laptop she'd forgotten the night before, inviting her to take the open chair next to his. He turned his phone over on the table, pushing it away like he was ready to discard whatever he'd been working on and instead offer his time to her. "Wasn't sure whether you'd be an early riser or not."

"I am, thanks. If there's coffee."

"You're in luck." Matteo pointed to the stocked sideboard nearest the kitchen door. "Sabine thought of that too."

The regard was a good sign. As was the presence of laptops. Maybe he'd already started translating their letters. And Delaney's choice to wear comfy jeans, a black ballet-neck tunic, and her blonde waves tied back with a jade paisley scarf at her nape was fortuitous since it seemed as if they'd be heads down at a table all day, poring over Italian letters and old photographs. If that was the case now, it was just fine with her.

Delaney glanced around at the empty chairs. "No Finn this morning?"

"Not on your life." Matteo shook his head. Smiled a little as he focused back on the laptop screen. "I'll check in with him this afternoon. He'll be sleeping it off until about the time he has to get up and catch a plane home."

Delaney tried not to smile too, thinking that described Finn to a tee.

"And the rest of the guests?"

"Americans are the only ones up with birds around here. And even if they do wake, they usually head outside to enjoy the sunshine."

Right. And Delaney had been up for an hour, wishing she'd had her laptop to run some intel on the internet-absent family. As it was, she only had her phone with an expensive data plan, and that meant no real way to dig any deeper into the questions Finn had stirred about Matteo and his nona the evening before.

"So . . . I'm going to need some help here." Delaney took a plate from the stack of porcelain at the end of the buffet and lifted golden tongs to the horde of pastries. "Where do I start?"

"Go with the frittata and crostini with pancetta on the end.

Cornetto is the one that looks like a brioche. Try it with the fig jam and pears. And the one that looks like a lobster tail is Sabine's lemon, rum, and raisin *sfogliatelle*. You'll want to take two of those before they're gone." He popped a crumb of pastry in his mouth and turned his focus back to the laptop screen. "Trust me."

Delaney poured steaming coffee from a pitcher into a cup, checking the view of the courtyard outside to see if his nona had slipped out and was anywhere near the garden gate. But no elegant former ballerina was to be found.

"Is Mrs. Santini coming to breakfast?"

He looked up, those ice-blue eyes a little unsettling even from across the table. "I think after that greeting last night, she'd invite you to call her Nona. As would I."

Good heavens. Delaney didn't expect him to say that, or to read the compliment of genuine tenderness in his gaze when he spoke of it.

"Of course. I'd be honored."

Except for that look. Was it purposeful? It was like he felt a little too much ease in her presence. And if Delaney knew anything about flirting after having been seated next to world-champion Finn at dinner the night before, she had the tiniest wonder if something of it existed in the quieter of the two men now. Only his brand of choice appeared to be all in the eyes.

Warmth tinged her cheeks and Delaney looked out the open doors to the garden walls, cutting their sharp line across the backdrop of the great room's leaded-glass windows. "The, um, garden looks beautiful in the daylight. Are those lemon trees?"

"Sì. My grandfather planted them. Years ago."

"Could I have a tour?"

He shook his head to that—no pause needed to consider what

was another flat denial where Nona was concerned. "No guests allowed. Sorry."

"Oh. Of course. I understand."

"No, it's just . . . that part of the villa actually is private. But believe me, there are enough views along the river and in Tivoli's old town to make up for it. And of course when you venture into Rome. That'll take your breath away faster than a family garden ever could."

"Yes. So you said last night you're here working—something about a photography job in the city?"

While she had been dropping a hint about Finn's mysterious mention of some grander story behind who Matteo was in his private life, Delaney took a first bite of the sfogliatelle and had to actively work not to close her eyes in savory appreciation.

She lost.

"Right?" Matteo laughed. "Wars have been fought for less than those."

"Pity. I'll never be able to go to an American donut shop again—at least not without knowing the truth is out there in Italy somewhere." How fast one could get used to breakfasts like this. She leaned back in her chair to sip rich Italian roast with it.

"To answer your question, sì—I do have to sneak in a quick shoot this morning. In the city. But it won't take long." He closed the laptop and tossed a nip of pastry to Ghost, who'd lain under the table a perfect distance away to receive what seemed like the common practice of handouts. And without warning, Matteo looked over to her again. This time with a gaze that didn't seem to care about laptops. "Unless . . . Do you want to come?"

"To Rome? With you?"

"Sì." He took his glasses off and set them on the table—casual, leaning against his chairback, as if he could wait all day for her response. "I could knock off work early. Give you your first Rome experience. Then we come back and put in a full afternoon with those letters if you want."

Of course Delaney wanted to read over the letters.

The one encounter with Calla had opened a vault of new questions Delaney absolutely wanted answers to. And she'd need his help to untangle it all.

But Rome . . . It was tempting. And close. And inviting her to pause on the legal business, if only for a couple of hours.

"I did want to see the city while I'm here, I guess."

"I'm sorry—*see Rome*? Del. No one comes to Italy to just see Rome." Matteo laughed under his breath as he folded his glasses and hooked them against his shirt collar, then began packing up his things. "There's a phrase you need to learn before setting foot in my city: *essere incantato*."

"Your city? Didn't you say last night you live in New York?"

"Touché. Now I do. But does every summer spent in Rome from birth until thirty-two years old and working in this city for more than a decade buy me enough clout to know just a little of what I'm talking about?"

"Okay. You win." Delaney set her coffee on the table and held up her hands in surrender. "I'll give it a chance, Mr. Philosopher. What was that phrase again?"

"Essere incantato."

"*Ess-ere in-can-tato*?" Delaney repeated, wincing when she butchered the romantic notes of the accent so thoroughly.

"It means to be enchanted. And we Italians are nothing if not passionate. So you can appreciate Rome. You can even learn from it. But if you really want it to leave you enchanted in the way only it can, you have to be prepared to listen. That's what awaits the first-time sojourner who thought they were just going to stop by and 'see' Rome."

"You listen to a city?" She'd never thought of it before. Not like that. Not in the way he seemed very serious about at the moment. "Alright. And what would Rome say if it could talk?"

"That's up to you. Rome gets under your skin when you're not looking. And then it goes deeper—into your heart—and never leaves. If I'm honest, the best advice I can give is to say you'd better get ready to fall in love." He swiped up his laptop and stood, edging out from his chair around the corner of the table. "Meet you back here in ten minutes, and I'll show you what I mean."

Curious choice of words.

If she was honest back, Delaney would have said the only voice she heard at the moment was the one in her head warning that when in Rome, falling in love somewhere along the line could be the biggest temptation of all.

PRESENT DAY
PIAZZA DELLA TRINITÀ DEI MONTI
ROME, ITALY

Delaney might have been reluctant to believe Matteo's philosophy on his city while at a breakfast table, but Rome was unashamed to boast once they were actually walking through its streets.

To arrive in the city center was to be transported into Rome's own breed of time, where it marked no distinction between long past and cutting-edge present. Storied streets owned a stunning mix of art and history and modern day, as centuries-old structures intermingled with automobiles and Vespas and tourists who snapped selfies against the backdrop of Roman ruins.

Matteo drove them past the looming shadow of the Colosseum and wove through the streets and roundabouts to show Delaney around. He talked of the iconic Fontana di Trevi not far from where they were, Michelangelo's *Pietà* at St. Peter's Basilica in Vatican City, the Pantheon, and a list of other notable high spots. He offered to make reservations if she had a mind to visit any of them as he parked the car behind a swanky mid-city bistro owned by a longtime friend. It was there they took to foot not far from the Piazza di Spagna's lively shopping district.

Within minutes Matteo led them to his assignment for the day: tourist shots of Rome's famed Spanish Steps and bustling city views against the Renaissance masterpiece Trinità dei Monti, with its twin spires piercing the sky.

The travertine mountain began to climb at the base with the Fontana della Barcaccia—or as Matteo translated, the "Fountain of the Ugly Boat"—a half-submerged fountain behind them. Tourists stopped in at the famed Keats-Shelley House museum dedicated to British romantic poets in Italy, its open doors to the right of the steps, or at the old tearoom on the left. And they could move along the throughfare that cut through or pause for the obligatory photo with the Steps' famous rise climbing behind.

Delaney stood on the cobblestone floor of the grand Baroque staircase and took a deep breath as she stared up.

"So this is it. Delaney Coleman, meet the Spanish Steps."

"And we're going up?"

"That's right. We're going up." Matteo nodded, pocketed his lens cap, and adjusted the camera strap around his neck. Then he pulled his hat a bit lower over his brow. "All 135 steps. Ready?"

They started up, the climb taking them higher over the view of the bustling cityscape below.

"Why isn't anyone sitting on them? Wouldn't it be worth it to stop and admire this view?"

"Ahh. A point of contention. Used to be that's what everyone did. But imagine thousands of tourists trampling the spring azaleas or their spumoni gelato melting on the steps in the summer heat while you're trying to keep your shoes clean on the way up. So came the no-sitting law, which *la polizia* will be all too happy to enforce." He pointed out the uniformed watchmen in bright yellow vests standing at points mingled through the crowd. "To the tune of 450 euros if you're cited. Same price tag if you act on the notion to jump into one of the fountains, by the way. That one always gets the first-timers."

"So no sitting. And no fountain swimming either. All that 'when in Rome' stuff . . . Got it."

Matteo paused at the wide landing halfway up, edged over the balustrade, and must have seen something through the lens because he snapped photos while Delaney peered out at the palette of hues splashed across the piazza below. The arteries of tourist-packed streets were lined with buildings in ivory, salmon, rose, and saffron yellow, with terraces and lush rooftop gardens climbing stories around the steps and vendor-covered street corners. The face of the church was bathed in sunlight, transforming the white marble to gold as they climbed on again.

"What are those windows back there? With the terraces?"

"Private flats."

"Really? People can actually afford to live here on this piazza?"

"Some do. Sì."

"Like who? Movie stars?"

"Maybe. Investors. Business owners. Athletes." He turned his attention back to the climb, clicking a photo every now and then as they went. "The flats come with a hefty price tag. But you might say it's worth every cent for the view. Because you take these steps one at a time, tourist or not, and when you finally do reach the top . . ."

"You realize why." Delaney drew in a deep breath when they tipped over the edge to a stunning view from the top.

"Because there's this."

"Right. All of this. So what you're saying is, this place is special."

"Maybe." He stared out. And really seemed to believe it more than just for a "maybe" answer. "I guess climbing up says something about change. The end of a journey. Start of a new one. That sort of thing. Even if it has a complicated, uneven history, this still might be my favorite spot in all of Rome."

"What was your favorite spot in Brazil?"

"Brazil?"

"Well, Finn mentioned it at dinner and then you never said anything else about it. It seemed important to you, so I wondered."

Something shifted in his profile and Matteo leaned against the balustrade, inspecting the camera cradled in his hands like it was a new toy instead of a trusted old friend. Then it seemed he gave up on the easy banter and turned away from the grand view. He leaned an elbow on the marble rail and instead turned to look down.

At *her*.

"I'm sorry. I shouldn't have said anything."

"No—it's alright. I just ask myself if I should be telling my secrets to a would-be enemy. What about our suitcase? Does that fight play in this conversation at all, or should we still try to be friends while we duke it out?" He smiled, adding a touch of teasing to his eyes in mentioning the tug-of-war between them.

"What if we agree to a truce? We won't be enemies, no matter what happens with the suitcase in the end."

"I might be interested." He tipped his hat back off his brow. "But if we decide not to be at odds, then there's something I've got to ask you first. And I've wanted to ask it since the video call. Even more since dinner and your meeting Nona."

Delaney swallowed hard, surprised to find it wasn't the Spanish Steps working to steal the breath from her. A touch of wind brushed a lock of blonde hair to dance against her chin, and she swept it back behind her ear. Was it the suitcase, Calla's greeting, or something completely different that he wanted to peel back the layers of?

Delaney shifted her stance a little. "Okay."

"I got the feeling you don't know a lot about our family—or about me. Is that true?"

"I don't know much of anything except you take photos and you're good at it. I know Rome's your city. You're obviously comfortable with the cardinal sin of feeding a dog from the breakfast table—which I suspect you keep hidden from Sabine. And that you have a remarkable nona you love very much."

"Sounds like you've got me pegged." He nodded and looked down for a breath. Toyed with the camera a little in distraction. "Even about the cardinal sinning. Anything else?"

"Finn did tell me that Nona's connected to a ballet company here in Rome. And I saw photos of a ballet school hanging in the upstairs hall, next to your photos of the dinners. Was that her? Was she really a dancer?"

"She was. And a gifted one in her day."

"I think I could believe that. And I've been wondering, maybe she'd tell us more about that time—and about my grandfather—if we ask her?"

"I'm sorry. She can't talk about it. Not now."

Something said not to press him, though the protective barriers he always put up around his nona made Delaney want to all the more. What was it he refused to say?

"I understand. It might not be the right time. But if she could tell us why my grandfather would have a connection here, it would really help my family." *And it would help me.* "We were close, he and I. And Grandpa was a good man. He'd made some mistakes early in his life, but he changed. He never spoke of his time in the war, so I don't know if that's why. But when I think back on it now, even as a child I could see when he'd grow quiet. He'd sit on the porch and his gaze would fade off over the orchard hills, like he was somewhere else entirely."

"And you think he was here? In Rome?"

"I do. At least some of the time. But now that he's gone, I can't ask him about it. Do you think we could check in the letters, outside of what we're looking for about the suitcase? I mean, would you mind if we did?"

"No," he said softly. And low. And with far too much tenderness to ever be an enemy now. "I wouldn't mind, Del. Not if it's what you want."

"*Mi scusi?*" A hand with manicured fingertips tapped Matteo's shoulder between them, and he turned.

A small circle of young women stood behind, one out front with her bottom lip caught in her teeth with suppressed elation. She rattled off some animated words in Italian. Delaney heard "Santini," but beyond that, all she could read between the lines was giggling, blushing, and the thrill of just talking to Matteo.

And Delaney was altogether invisible.

"Oh—sì." Matteo nodded and took a receipt and pen from the

woman's hand. Leaning against the marble balustrade, he began a quick scrawl over the paper.

Wait . . . he's signing an autograph.

And then he scrawled another. And another.

"Could you?" Matteo asked, pulling Delaney out of her stupor. "I'm sorry. She wants a selfie." He lifted his camera from around his neck and held it out to Delaney before he eased into the center of the group, looking like he seriously considered losing his breakfast.

"Um . . . of course. Yes. I wouldn't mind at all." Delaney hooked his camera strap over her shoulder and stepped back out of the way.

The girl leveled the scene with the sprawling Piazza di Spagna down below and clicked a couple of photos. The group thanked him and one chanced a bold hug around his neck before they scurried off, but not before other tourists took notice. A few pointed. One man snapped a photo, and Matteo looked like he wished nothing more in that instant than for the marble beneath their shoes to swallow him up.

Matteo took his camera back and swept it crossways over his chest, then pulled his hat brim a little lower. He glanced over his shoulder at the piazza down below. Twice. Like an animal backed into a cage.

"I think I have what I need." Startling Delaney by clasping her hand in his, he gave a gentle tug to move them away. "You want to walk? Let's walk."

"Okay. We'll walk." Delaney kept pace with his long strides and head-down posture as he held on—trying not to read into the fact that his fingers clung to hers for dear life as they marched back down the stairs and away from the crowds clogging the piazza.

"Ready to leave?" He pointed up the street, past the bustle of shoppers flocking to the names *Gucci* and *Bulgari* shining out from upscale façades. "We can go back to the car and then head out if you want."

"Matteo? Please—wait." Delaney took the impulse of the moment to reach for his elbow. Slowing him up on a street corner and pulling him back to the shadows of a small alcove against a building, she let go. And chanced looking up, finding those eyes of his clearly afflicted by something.

"Maybe we don't really know each other, but that was one of the strangest things I've ever seen up close. Should we talk about that, or is it just a normal day at the office for you? Photographically speaking."

"Uh . . . sì. So that was just . . ." He tugged his hat brim a shade lower on his brow, revealing that a touch of nerves had set in. "I've lived in Rome on and off over the years, and so sometimes people . . . I'm usually on my own when I'm shooting so I can move around pretty fast. That back there doesn't usually happen. But I haven't been by the Steps in a while, so it's probably just . . ."

"Matteo Santini. What in the world is going on? I'm not stupid, you know."

"I don't think you are," he said, though still observing tourists like the slightest glance from a human would cause him to bolt. "Far from it."

"Then you might as well be out with it, because if not, I'm just going to stand here and search on my phone until I find out why you're signing autographs."

And then something else pinged in her mind. The driver. The first moment Delaney had stepped out of the car at Villa Adriano. This was something bigger.

"Wait—so was it a tip you signed for the driver at the villa?"

"No."

"Right. And that's why it feels like everyone in this city knows something I don't. So what is it? Are you a famous social media influencer or something?"

"Or something." Matteo braced his hands on his hips and sighed. Looked past her. Then tipped his head down the street the direction of his friend's bistro with outdoor tables shielded by flowering baskets and potted hedgerows. "You want to get a bite?"

From autographs to hugs from strange women, and then straight on to food. Such a guy way to respond. The jumps were enough to give her whiplash. "A bite?"

"A slice of pizza on me? Fabrizio's place is just around the bend here and has a private terrace so we could be alone. And when we sit down, I'll tell you I'm sorry I didn't mention it before. I don't always tell people. But you're here for something completely outside of all this. And that's new for me. I just find it's easier to keep that part of my life, you know . . . quiet. What I'm trying to say is . . ." He shrugged and drew in a deep breath. And slipped reluctant hands in his pockets like an underclassman asking the captain of the cheerleaders to prom. "I'm Giorgio Santini."

"Oh. Okay." Delaney breathed out. And he searched her face as she processed it, seeming relieved for the first time that the truth was finally out. "Giorgio Santini."

"Sì. I've always gone by my middle name with family, so I didn't have to change anything with them. It's Matteo. Or Matt at home. But you know that from dinner, so . . . The other one—Giorgio? It's just a professional name. I don't use it now."

Delaney glanced around. How many of the tourists filtering in and out of the posh shops knew who was standing right in front of them? And then, finally, she chanced looking up in those eyes that searched her face from under the shadow of his hat brim.

"Right. And who's Giorgio Santini?"

Thirteen

26 October 1941
St. John Road
Starlight, Indiana

What are the two things an orchard fears most?"

"Everybody knows that. A late frost and an early freeze," Court said to Penn as he lifted crates of speckled swan Lagenaria gourds and pie pumpkins onto the bed of the tractor wagon.

"You have been listening."

"A country boy knows a little something about frosts and freezes, even if the family business is medicine." He muscled the last of the crates in a row next to the load of hay bales they'd be setting up for the evening bonfires.

The hills had been touched by Midas all around them, with hay rolled in great rounds in the fields. Leaves drifted in the apple orchards and fell from fruit trees in a cascade of ocher and rust and blazing orange. The peaches were long gone—eaten or canned for winter. Or made into a hundred pies placed on red gingham tablecloths for judging at county fairs. Now sweaters and shawls were hanging on hooks by the mudroom door, and mulled cider perfumed the air.

Court secured the gate and chain at the truck bed. Patting the wood for good measure, he walked around to the front of the tractor. He took a bandana from his back pocket, wiped down his face and neck, then shoved it back in.

"We lucked out. October mornings cold as ice and afternoons hot as blazes, but we've still managed to get this harvest in before the frost. All we have to do now is load up this last bit and your daddy'll have sold it all. He should feel proud."

"Everyone should. We worked hard. And it's been a good harvest in a tough set of years. I'm happy for him."

"Me too. Patrick is a good man. He deserves the fortune to match."

Penn drifted a palm over the high arc of the tractor wheel as she looked out at the fields. "You'll be finishing up then, when the season's over? Did Daddy say?"

"No, he hasn't. But I expect I'll know my time is up when Patrick says it is." Court posted his hands to his hips and surveyed the span of fields to see Guthrie hauling the other wagon and waving them on to join up at the barn. "Seems like we're being summoned."

"Right." Penn stretched her shoulders before she fired up the engine. "Let's get going then. These hay bales won't move themselves."

Penn didn't say a word as she adjusted her body in the metal tractor seat, but he could see she was uncomfortable. Court was fighting the urge to disable the tractor engine when she wasn't looking, just to keep her safe on the ground. The thought of her suffering a tumble getting in and out of that high seat had him feeling sick all day long.

"Penn? Would you do something for me?"

"We've managed to get along without fighting for weeks now. I'd like to keep it that way. So don't be asking me anything we'll both regret."

He sighed. And laughed as he stared down at his shoes.

Lord, but she had spirit.

"I'm not proposing, if that's what's worrying you. At least not in a dirt suit in the middle of your daddy's field." He swung up on the side of the tractor, easing higher so he stood next to her seat. "No—I want to ask you not to drive the tractor anymore."

"Courtney Coleman . . . not you too."

"Just listen. On a normal day I'd never say a word, knowing you can work harder than most men—myself included. I'm not supposed to tell you this, but Patrick's about to put his foot down on his only daughter's stubbornness. Even June has backed off as your supporter, and that's saying something."

"If anyone would be on my side, I thought it would be you. Expecting a baby doesn't mean I'm completely helpless."

"Not helpless. Just needing to take extra care." He braced his palm on the wide round of the wheel, just edging his hand alongside hers. She eased hers down seconds after, folding her hands against the round of her lap. "This is what I'm here to do. To work. Let me do my job, even if a very small part of that is looking out for you?"

She gave a reluctant nod.

"Alright."

Thankfully, Penn's tenacious streak didn't extend to his helping her to step down. Court made her a good spot in the back of the hay wagon—safe, hemmed in by pumpkins and sturdy hay bales on both sides—and drove like a snail through water so she wouldn't be jostled on the ride up to the barn.

He joined Guthrie and the others in stacking bales and unloading crates of apples and gourds and pumpkins until the sun drooped lower in the sky and his arms screamed for relief.

"Court? Come on!" Guthrie shouted as he hurried up the porch steps. "We gotta make tracks."

Penn looked up and nodded, a little sparkle in her eyes.

"Saturday night, hmm? And everyone goes to town."

"Yeah. We're supposed to see the new Roy Rogers film." Court shrugged. "Guthrie hasn't shut up about Annabelle Fisher wanting to see a picture show, and I guess he needs an extra man alongside in case it turns out to be an early screening of *How Green Was My Valley*. Sure you want to miss all that small-town drama?"

Penn laughed a little, catching her bottom lip on her teeth. Maybe because she was remembering those times it was them heading to town and she'd been the girl on his arm.

"Somehow I think I'll survive without it. But you've certainly managed to win Guthrie over. No more trading punches?"

"No. That's done. I think we have an understanding."

Guthrie popped his head out of the kitchen door to tap the ghost of a watch against his wrist that said time was a-wastin'.

"Looks like it. You'd better go."

"Yeah. I'd better." He slipped away to wash up at the pump.

Splashing cold water on his face did nothing to ease the nagging pit in Court's gut. Neither did touching up his shave, running a comb through his hair, or putting on Guthrie's good shirt, which June had washed and starched for him. Court couldn't help but think that going to town on a Saturday night with everyone else in their part of the world didn't matter much. Not with rumors of a war coming. And not when he was starting to think the only person he'd ever felt at home with was staying behind.

And the nagging still weighed him down later as he sat with his elbow propped up against the truck cab window and stared out the windshield. Court hated being trussed up. And didn't particularly care to listen to Guthrie's gabbing on about Annabelle. Or to smell his aftershave stinking up the cab like they'd brought a burlap sack with a dead skunk inside.

"Stop!" Court shouted over the engine and pressed Guthrie's arm until his foot hit the brake.

"What's the matter?"

"Look." Court pointed to the orchards.

In the field a vision appeared through the peach grove . . . moving alongside the dusty orchard lane . . . Penn walked an orchard row in a soft gauze dress with her hair spilling free over her shoulders. "What's she doing out there?"

"I don't know. She likes taking walks. Says it helps with back pain or something. Look, I don't really know and I don't think I want to." Guthrie squirmed, seeming a touch squeamish at the mention of birthing. He sighed and tapped the steering wheel like he was putting out a fire.

"Is it safe for her to be out there alone?"

"What do you mean 'Is it safe?' Penn's out here all the time. Likes to be on her own. She never did enjoy town much." Guthrie checked his watch. "Which is where we need to be with tickets in hand in exactly twenty-five minutes, or I'm never gonna hear the end of it."

"But if something happened and she needed help . . ."

"Oh, saints preserve us. I'm going to be shoveling stalls from now until eternity for this." Guthrie exhaled. Reached over. And with a muscled push, flung Court's truck door open from the inside. "Go on."

"What do you mean?"

"Get. Before I change my mind."

Court's heart raced as he sprang out of the cab, and he didn't even know why. He just got out. Closed the door. Stood in the road.

He didn't think to ask if Guthrie would cover for him or what he'd say if he did run into Patrick and June outside the theater. And Court didn't look back to watch how long the truck hung on before driving off.

He just started down the road. "Penn?" Court shouted as he headed into the orchard row.

She turned, and he exhaled deep, his breath stolen at the sight of her walking out in front of him—barefoot, smiling, reaching back—fingertips drifting a dance along the uneven tops of orchard grass.

Court ran up to her, stopping a few feet away. And heaven help him, but nerves from somewhere inside were trying to make him a fool. He didn't care.

"You're going the wrong way, aren't you?" She pointed to the dust kicked up on the lane from Guthrie's exit. "Town's that way."

"What if I'm already where I want to be? Where I want to stay?" He reached out. Took the hand she'd been hovering over the orchard grass. And on a whim that yielded to the longing he'd been trying to deny those weeks they'd been in the same space again, he moved toward her slowly, with careful intention, and laced his fingers with hers. "Is this alright?"

The breeze toyed with her hair, dancing it above her shoulders and across her brow. She swept it back out of her eyes—those green pools trying their best not to tear. He could see it.

"Yes, Court." It meant something that she didn't pull away. "You can hold my hand."

Something told Court to get out of that truck when he had the chance, and not just because Guthrie popped the door open. That same something had said *go*. Get to her. That maybe Court was a wrecked man and had been as long as he could remember, but there was still a chance to make things right.

Did he always have to be the one causing hurt? Or could he do something to help instead of harm in this life? If he could see anything in the beauty before him—in the sunset and peace and simple stillness of her presence—a voice inside whispered that he didn't dare lose the chance.

It was time to dig in his heels for what mattered. That same something told Court not to lose the memory of this place. Because somehow . . . he might need it later.

18 OCTOBER 1943
TIBER ISLAND
ROME, ITALY

Waking in an actual bed was the stuff of every soldier's dreams.

Or that was Court's best guess judging by a soft mattress beneath him. The sterile tang of antiseptic in the air and his head pounding like a jackhammer was trying to escape his skull from the inside out only confirmed he wasn't dead—yet.

Cracking his eyes open, he found a plain and peaceful room. He obviously wasn't on the front, not with a window allowing sunlight to warm ivory stucco walls and a plain wooden crucifix hanging on the wall. A tray sat on a side table by the bed, with a glass pitcher and tumbler, a plate of cookies, an apple, and a vase with a sprig of pink posies staring back at him.

Ah . . . my head. Too much looking around.

Curiosity punished Court and he squinted against the pain of bright light, then turned away. His reward was hot coals that exploded in his neck. He groaned, reaching up with fingertips that fumbled over rows of bandages under his jaw. Seemed he'd woken in the same state as this not too long back.

The squeak of a wooden chair signaled someone was in the room.

"Best try not to move, Court."

That voice. Unmistakable—*AJ*.

Court cracked his eyelids again to find the sergeant seated in a chair by the bed. He'd leaned forward, elbows braced on his knees. Somber and silent—as was his way—it seemed he waited for Court to gather his wits before speaking again.

Lord, AJ. Is that you?

You're a mess.

Unshaven. Eyes brimming red like he hadn't slept for a month of Sundays. And somehow, that forehead was creased enough that his leader could have aged ten years instead of how long? Hours? Days? What happened, and how long had it been?

"Where . . . ?"

More hot coals seared his throat. Court winced through the echoes of pain.

"Probably shouldn't try to talk either." AJ walked over and poured water into the tumbler, popped a straw in, then held it out. "Just wet your tongue. It's gonna feel like daggers for a while."

Daggers was right. AJ helped him swallow and Court fell back on the pillow, spent already by withstanding a plague of knives. "So . . . I'm alive."

"Last time I checked."

"That's something. But why do I feel like I've been run over by a—?"

"Because surgery tends to do that. Even with morphine to dull the edges. Couple that with a knock on the skull, and I'd say if you were a cat, you just used all your lives. Probably a few of mine too."

"What happened?"

"Don't remember? You went rogue. Ran out right in the thick of a Gestapo raid. I thought you'd been shot by how you fell back. And cracked your head against a pile of rubble on the way down."

"That explains the headache . . ." Court reached a hand up to the source of the pounding and felt a bandage taped to his forehead. "Where are we?"

"A hospital. On Tiber Island."

"We made it then." Well, halfway back at least. Surely Tiber Island was better than being pinned in Rome's streets with Gestapo hot on their heels. Court looked over again to the chair and saw the slow burn of fury on AJ's face.

This was bad.

The kind of bad that meant someone had died—or was about to.

"Go ahead. Give it to me straight. I'm dying."

"Not today. But that means we only solve one problem. There's a slew of others in line right behind it."

Forget the pain. Court remembered now and dug an elbow into the mattress to lift himself up against the metal headboard.

"Where's the kid?"

AJ pointed to a Mary Jane and military-issue sock sticking out beyond a mass of pillows on a bench at the foot of the bed. Her suitcase sat on the floor nearby, the cherries peeking out from the corner of a dangling blanket.

"You gave her your socks?"

"Had to. Couldn't keep the other ones or they'd get too much notice. She's been asleep for a while. Waiting for her hero to wake, I think."

Court ignored the backhanded quip and settled back into his pillows again, relief escaping on an exhale. At least she was alive. But the rest of it . . .

Flashes began to streak through the muddle of his mind. Hiding in the market stall outside the Portico d'Ottavia. Shots fired and bodies falling . . . The sight of the girl . . . And he and AJ helpless but to watch as the piazza was bathed in the blood of fallen Jews.

Court tightened his jaw over the rush of emotion. Pain stabbed his raw surgical wounds, and he clenched his fist to fight through it.

"What about the rest of the Jews?"

"I don't know. Shot. Shipped off to some work camp. God knows what the Germans do. The trucks pulled out and the poor souls still alive went with them. They carted bodies off and that's the end of it."

"What about our unit?"

AJ shook his head. "No word. I'd guess they've radioed in we're captured. Or facedown in an alley with bullets in the backs of our skulls. At least that's what they'd think with your heroics back there. They'd have had to move on fast or risk being caught themselves."

"They wouldn't leave us behind. Not without medics for the Typewriter."

"You think the Allies will hold up an invasion from Naples because a pair of American medics go missing? You're dreaming if you think we are in any way that important." AJ stared back, his jaw flexed to a chisel point as he folded his arms over his chest. "So when were you going to tell me?"

Court felt his gut lock up a little—on top of the pain of talking. Somehow, the former felt worse. "Sir?"

"You know what I'm talking about. Loss of balance. I'd wager there was tingling in your legs. Probably dizzy spells. Am I hitting any marks here? Because I know you saw the signs in your own body. You knew what was happening, yet you ignored that and put your entire team at risk because you wanted to come back. And after you said you'd be straight with me when we stood in that field outside Altavilla. But it seems you couldn't do that. Do I paint a clear enough picture?"

Fine. Okay . . . maybe deserved that smack of truth.

"They'd have shipped me Stateside. And I can't go back. Not yet."

"But you don't get to decide that. You're a medic, Court. A non-combatant. It means we don't get involved. And you don't get to just ignore that when it suits you. I'm your superior officer and the unit is my responsibility. Yet you made a decision that affected everyone else—could have taken the lives of any of the men around you. And I don't take that lightly."

"You say we're not involved." Court pointed to the girl. How could they discount everything she stood for? *"She* makes us involved."

"No one knows where we are, Court!" AJ's voice was a ragged whisper, and he pounded his palm to his knee, stirring the girl. She didn't wake, just burrowed into a corner of the bench as her breathing went back to even in sleep. "This place is under some kind of quarantine with a plague on top of halls crawling with SS, all eager to keep their trigger fingers in practice. I don't even know who this girl is to help her, let alone what to do to hide her from all of that. You've just handed me a stack of impossible problems I have to solve before you can even get out of that bed."

Wasn't like AJ to lose his cool.

Still, if Court were honest, he got it. If another member of their unit had been sick or hurt and tried to hide it, AJ would have lit into them too. Par for the course. But even when Court had considered owning up, that moment in the ghetto had changed everything. And things couldn't change back now.

"What was I supposed to do?"

"So help me—if something happened to Tenor or Dean because

you wanted to go out there and play hero . . . I can't forgive that. Or forget it."

"Look at that girl and tell me you'd have done anything different. You'd have left her standing in the street with blood on her shoes? 'Cause if you could . . . then you're not the man I thought you were. *Sir*."

AJ groaned a sigh and leaned back, the chair protesting with a labored creak as he rubbed a tired palm over his face. He stretched his legs under the lip of the metal hospital bed without another word on the matter.

There we go. Hit the mark. You know I'm right.

Court exhaled. Not forgiven, but at least he'd earned a shred of understanding. "You look terrible. When was the last time you slept?"

"Compliments really aren't necessary at the moment."

"Probably right. For both of us. I need a drink."

"Water's by the bed."

"Not exactly what I meant." Court stared up at the thick woodbeamed ceiling and ran a hand over the stubble on his own jaw. "How long's it been?"

"Going on two days."

"Alright. What next? How do we get outta here?"

"It's a little more complicated than just waltzing out the front doors."

"What then?"

"For starters, you're now my brother. We go by Rossi. And other than what hospital staff here have already guessed, we keep our background hidden. We'll have to pick a name you can remember and answer to without hesitation. I'm Athenos. She's Calla—my daughter."

"*Your* daughter? That'll be the day."

"Yes. Mine. Now, they're going to get you up and walking soon. When they do, you don't leave this wing. You wear a mask in those halls. And don't talk to anyone unless it's in Italian."

"And how'd you come up with that? You realize it excludes me from talking at all. Which we'll probably both be glad of, seeing as it hurts like wildfire just to keep arguing with you." He paused, swallowed over daggers, then winced.

AJ rose and crossed the room to a sideboard against the wall. He pulled an old book from the pocket of the jacket on top, the edges worn and spine held together with a rubber band stretched over faded oxblood leather.

"Where'd you get that?"

"The moment I needed a name, this thing you always carry around came to mind. If we were headed to the hospital, I couldn't take a chance someone might find it on you, so I emptied your pockets in the alley. It was still weighing down my coat that night we came here." AJ set the small primer of Homer's *Odyssey* on the bedside table, exchanging it for an apple as he turned toward the door.

The rest was easy enough to figure out. Court took the book, turned it over in his hand.

"Don't tell me. Athenos . . . Athena? Of course you'd make yourself the war leader of this little operation." Court rolled his eyes and dropped his head back on the pillow. "And her. Calla—Calypso?"

"Where do you think the stuff on that table came from? That little girl has nothing, yet she's saved anything she's been given all for the hero who saved her. Sounds exactly like a nymph falling under the spell of Odysseus if you ask me."

Court groaned. And clamped his lids shut against the vise squeezing his head.

The door creaked open and he thought AJ had gone, until something landed on the bed, just grazing his fingertips.

He opened his eyes. Felt the weight of the token on the blanket and then reached for it, his fingertips just able to pull the pocket watch safely into his palm.

"There. You lived, so I owe you that. But don't you dare think I'll take it from you again. 'Cause that was the last time."

"You could have left me behind. Why didn't you?" Court knew there was a better question. "Why'd you stay when I went against your orders?"

"Because I made a promise at the start of this war, Court: Any man under my command is going home. Even if I don't. And I'm a man of my word, even if he tries to fight me on it."

"And why is that exactly?"

AJ looked to the girl. "Just keep an eye on her. Okay? I'll send someone in to give you a shave. And get some rest. You're gonna need it."

The sarge stepped into the hall and clicked the door closed.

Court stared up at the ceiling. Closed his fist around the metal just to feel the lifeline against his skin.

The token had worked. By all accounts he should have died. Twice over now. And even though Court had defied a superior officer's order and had run out into the street to pull the girl back, God had seen fit to watch over his sorry hide.

Again.

The only question left was, why?

Fourteen

T he train slowed its roll into the devil's city.

It's what it felt like for Julia, peering through the window of their passenger car, watching steam rise in a fog against wall cutouts paved over with colorful ceramic murals in Milan's Central Station. A shiver ran over her skin as she stared at the images of goose-stepping soldiers with the Fascist straight-arm salute to their king and the mural's elevated bust of Benito Mussolini watching over the activity that passed by on the tracks.

"You are actually going to speak to me sometime this century, hmm? Now that we're finally here?" Anton checked his wristwatch.

When Julia remained silent, he sighed and stretched long legs out in front of him, taking up the free space left in their row.

"No? Fine. Then I'll talk. We have to wait for the mail and supply trains to go through first. I assume those are the cattle car–looking monstrosities on the tracks down the way. Then they'll let us out.

We'll have the security team escort us to our motorcade, and I presume then it's on to Teatro alla Scala."

La Scala . . .

The train crawled on, and steam rose to envelop another mural. Julia imagined the horror of the bust suddenly becoming real, with the dictator and his mistress at his side, awash in diamonds and sitting in the famed opera house's audience for their evening performance. Perhaps he'd watch alongside King Emmanuel III and the queen, with ladies in opera dresses and men decorated in military uniform, and the presence of blood-red Nazi insignia intermingled in the crowd.

It was never how Julia had imagined dancing when she was young. That had been a beautiful dream. All it took was to close her eyes and she was back—eight years old and listening to her father play his favorite, *Clair de Lune*, on the baby grand and watching as her mother opened the parlor doors to their garden allotment. And suddenly, in a little girl's grandest aspirations, the hardwood floor become La Scala's theater and Julia was awash in lights. The little fairy, dancing . . . dreaming . . . flying free on Italy's grandest stage. And every morning she'd go there in her mind, doing her warm-up routine in the safety of that long-ago world.

How different now, in Milan's darkness.

In London she'd danced in an old pair of toe shoes and a hand-sewn costume of flocked fabric. But for Milan, she'd be outfitted with a faint rose tulle encrusted with white-and-gold crystal beading. Her auburn hair would be twisted in an intricate braided bun and laced with the sparkle of little diamonds winking out from the tiara frosting her crown. Those wares were secured in a special trunk somewhere in the baggage car. And with them, the none-too-gentle pinpricks of shame that increased in her midsection every time she thought on it.

Yes. It must be the devil's city, if she must dance for those who would do his bidding.

"I don't want to dance tonight."

"Ah—she speaks." Anton unfurled his arms and legs, then clapped his palms together as he sat up on the bench cushion. "But only to say you don't wish to dance at La Scala? Whyever not? That is why we're here."

"Look." Julia pointed a gloved fingertip to the window and the murals beyond the glass. "That's why. I don't feel right about this."

"The only view I'm interested in today is the sight of Italy's king and queen sitting in the box of the center mezzanine. Another sovereign to watch the great Vasile and Bradbury perform." He leaned back again and laced his fingers behind his head with that little wink of arrogance that came so easily to him.

"Is that honestly all you see?"

"What am I supposed to see? Hmm? Swirls of paint on dirty tile? If we ace this envoy, we're set for life. After the war is over, we can dance on any stage in the world. And everything we've gone through will have been worth it."

"Maybe it is not worth it to me."

The train stopped and Julia tore her gaze away from him, instead looking down the aisle as passengers moved to and fro, flowing out to the platform. Anton slid into the seat next to her, waiting until the other dancers collected their gas masks and travel cases and began to leave them behind.

"Julia, listen to me. If you're scared—"

"I am not afraid."

"Good. Because you needn't be. There were no bombings in

Milan at all last year. And none this year. By all accounts we could be safer here than in London. And even if there was concern, Britain would focus efforts on industrial areas. Factories. Municipal buildings and ports. Churchill isn't going to bomb a famed opera house in the heart of the city. Even de Gaulle ensured the treasures of Paris were safe before France capitulated to the Germans. And their opera house and Eiffel Tower still stand. So I ask you. What is there to be afraid of by dancing here? Really?"

Julia closed her eyes and pinched the bridge of her nose for a breath.

"I find it impossible to believe we are discussing the virtues of a Nazi invasion. And that you've diluted war into camps of elites who are above or below threat based upon talent. I'd wager Churchill's cabinet hadn't been made privy to all the details of your little plan for an envoy or they might have seriously reconsidered whether to send us on this train. Regardless, I assure you that I am not here for you. Or to build the notoriety of our names. Or anything of the sort to wish to see a king and queen in the audience tonight."

"We are to dance at La Scala. Just think about that. This moment will make us. You know it's true."

"Maybe the only thing I wish to be is a person whose life should matter more than for simply thinking of herself." She stood and shrugged past him to collect her things. Thankfully, he backed off or he might have met with a travel case to the ear. "Let's just go."

"Fine. I give up. But you always do that."

"What?"

He waved a finger at her. "That thing with your nose. When you're stressed and you needn't be."

"It is not stress to wish to be useful in this war. I speak Italian and French and was to train as a telephonist to work with communications.

For goodness' sake, I am a member of the British Army. I stood in an ATS uniform and vowed to serve my country. As did you in yours. And I believe in my heart this is not the way. How easily that has been forgotten when we travel in civilian clothes again and wear finery to dance on an enemy's stage."

"Shh. You can't talk like that here." He lowered his voice, looking around at the remaining passengers as if all were a band of spies. "Maybe we were members of the armed forces—for about five minutes before we got out. And I speak Italian. Russian and German too. What of it? That is the result of fine tutors, not some master plan to have us behave like plebeians. You are serving your country. We all are. And this is how we do it."

"Then perhaps I want to do something with my life that matters more."

"And dancing doesn't? Entertainers are traveling and performing all over—including actors and musicians, and ballet envoys. It is not a crime to have a privileged situation. This is what we were bred for—you, daughter of an heiress and a Harley Street physician. And me—son of a Russian diplomat and his bride, a cousin to the king himself. What else are we to do in this life but live it well? Where is that idealistic young woman I met back in New York? She lived for ballet. Breathed it. And was always the one who'd have done anything to achieve her dreams. Whatever happened to her?"

Julia froze. A shuddering breath escaped her lungs.

"What happened to her? You know exactly what happened," she spat out through gritted teeth. "Don't you ever say that to me again. Not ever. We are required to dance—not talk. In future I'll ask you to remember that. And keep your distance."

She turned, grateful to have left his warped sense of duty behind as she moved up the train car aisle.

Relief proved fleeting, however, as the drumming of Julia's heartbeat was replaced by a rumbling outside the train. It grew closer—a roar overhead that penetrated the car with each step she took, the windows next to her rattling in their frames. The remaining passengers peered out the train car. A woman gasped and covered her mouth with a gloved hand, then pointed up.

Julia looked up, too, through the station's skylights, to formations of tiny plane birds that streaked the sky.

Oh no . . .

The RAF?

She turned in a split second, meeting Anton's gaze across the train car. Terror lay in his eyes—the truest emotion she'd ever seen bared there. He dropped his bags and ran, rushing down the aisle in her direction. But it was already too late to run . . . or think . . . or move out of any bomb's way, should it wish to claim them.

A whistle cried out in the razor-thin second before a blast shook their world.

Julia was thrown to the floor of the train car as windows shattered and glass blew into her hair. She coughed through a cloud of choking dust. With ears ringing, she rose up and glanced around, not recognizing where they were or even who belonged to the bodies tangled on the floor with her own.

Singed mail-car letters fluttered on air, drifting down like snow over a jumble of concrete and twisted metal. Sparks flew from a dangling electric light into a chasm that had ripped the front of the train car wide. And flames sprang to life, illuminating Milan's triumphant war murals that in a blink had crumbled to ruin.

18 October 1943
Tiber Island
Rome, Italy

Julia no longer dreamed of La Scala's stage.

When she closed her eyes, the memory of ladies frosted over with diamonds and designer opera gowns and the fear of seeing men with litzen collars in Milan's grand concert hall faded from her mind. Instead, rose hips became her audience. With birdsong. Remnants of summer oleander that lingered beyond their season. The second blooming of juniper perfuming the air. And the protection of burnished trees that sheltered her escape in the Fatebenefratelli Hospital garden.

Julia drank in a deep breath and rose into the challenging pose, attempting to sweep through the "Rose Adagio"—*The Sleeping Beauty*'s technically demanding *pas de cinq* dance with four suitors vying for Aurora's attention—without the usual counterbalance of a ballerino's hand.

Toe point . . . pirouette.

She bade herself to mentally transport to a performance stage.

Balance, Julia.

Now . . . développé.

The sun warmed her face as she arced back slowly, into the controlled leg extension. Thankfully, the garden had dried out some from the rain, so she hadn't worried her last pair of toe shoes would be soiled. It mattered more that she was fighting to remember the music inside as she swept from pirouette to développé, and imagined accepting the first suitor's rose each time before floating to repeat the complex step sequence with the next one.

Hold, rise. Now, soutenu en tournant . . .

Balance! She chided herself through the double-toed spin, battling for focus when she wobbled.

Now, développé à la seconde.

Suitor one lets go . . . and I receive the second.

The slam of a door jarred her.

Concentration broken, she fell out of the extension and stood. Flat-footed. Hands on her hips. And breathing hard through the shattered focus.

Impossible . . . to think I could do it on my own.

The real world yanked her back as an ambulance skittered off beyond the trees. And the indistinct conversation and hooting laughter of SS soldiers lingered where they'd gathered beyond the iron gate, stealing a few moments tucked back by the garden walls to smoke an outlawed cig.

Julia shifted away, frustrated that the music and its matching steps were still lost somewhere within her. Instead she headed for the towel she'd left on the stone bench nearby.

And there he was—the soldier.

He stood in a casual lean with his back against the hospital wall, turning an apple over his propped knee. And without any wariness that she'd caught him watching her dance.

"You shouldn't be out here." She swept the linen towel around her neck and sat to change out of her toe shoes.

"You're here."

"Yes, but I have permission." Julia untied the satin from her calves, sending a cautionary glance to the SS moving beyond the stone gate. "Father Bialek would not approve otherwise."

"I have yet to talk to the father, but I'll take my chances. Especially as it's been a long time since I've seen anything like that. I almost forgot beauty still exists in this world."

Her heart tripped a little in its unexpected thumping.

Julia looked up. "Beauty?"

"Yeah. The hospital garden, I mean." He gestured to the foliage behind her and the downward slope of the hill just visible beyond the stone walls. "You can see it from the window in my brother's room."

"Oh yes. It is beautiful here." Julia slipped into her flats and glanced around at their garden surroundings too. "I often come in the mornings to . . . be alone."

"I'm sorry. Should I go?"

"No. It's alright. I'm just finished. And how is your brother faring this morning? I was relieved to hear he is in recovery. Apparently improving by the hour."

"He's alive, thanks to Dr. Emory. In fact, it's the doctor who requested I come find you."

Julia stood, not remembering until then how tall he was—even at a slight lean—until she was once again standing before him and was forced to look up.

"I see. And little Calla? Is she well too?"

"She is, yes. And grateful for the treats you found her. That little one has an unselfish heart. Seems she's taken a liking to my brother, so he's received the majority of what you've doled out to her."

"I don't mind. I'll find more for her if I can." She looked around the path. "And where is she?"

"Inside. Waiting with my brother while he gets a much-needed shave."

"Seems like you could use one too," Julia said before she could think better of it, then swallowed over the impertinence that such a personal remark had slipped out. "I'm sorry. I meant nothing by it."

He ran a hand over his chin. "No harm done. Especially when

someone else already suggested it to me this morning." He paused, then in an abrupt shift said, "So you're a ballet dancer. You never said."

"I'm not sure I had time to. But I dance a fair bit."

"That's a bit?" A smile broke free on his lips. Something told her that even under normal circumstances, he didn't allow it all that often. "Seems talent worth mentioning, if you ask me. And if you had, I'd want to know how you do that."

"How I do what?"

"Dance. Without music."

No one had asked Julia that before. And she wasn't prepared to share the intimacy of her answer that somehow she *could* hear music. Or she used to be able to, before she'd left London. Before war had gotten the better of them all. And long before she'd begun to battle the swell of emotions that was ever present since her parents had died.

"What was it?" he asked, like he genuinely wished to know.

"A sequence from *The Sleeping Beauty*. But it seems I can't do it alone. And I'd have much preferred to dance to *Clair de Lune*. It was my father's favorite. I'm starting to forget those notes now, it's been so long since I've heard them," she said, though not exactly sure why. And she immediately regretted sharing the vulnerability.

Even without the actual melody, her memory fought to hear Debussy's piano piece caught up in the wind through the trees. In the cadence of birds flying overhead. Or the drumbeat of the Tiber's current toiling beyond the garden walls. How in the world could a soldier—or a stranger—understand all of that stirring inside her?

"Perhaps I'd ask you something similar—how do you step onto a battlefield, Mr. Rossi?"

He looked down at his boots—caught out—then back at her. "I'd wager we go with as much care as you do when you dance, Miss Julia. Every time." He stood out of the lean and tossed the apple from one hand to the other even as he walked closer. "I'm afraid I came on another matter though. We need to talk."

Julia glanced back to the rectory's rear door. The hall of windows held no shadow. Good—no Anton hovering with his cane like the pettish specter that he was. But she couldn't guarantee that for long. "Not here, please."

He nodded, and they moved off until they were ensconced in the garden, well away from view.

"Thank you. It's just . . . Anton. The man you met the other night? I'd rather he not see us speaking."

"He doesn't know you're working with Dr. Emory then?"

She stopped short and wrapped her arms around her middle, startled at his knowing. "Who says I'm working with Dr. Emory?"

"He does. Is that not true?"

"Oh," she whispered, and let her arms loosen their tense stance a little. No need to put up a false front with him. "Well then. Yes, Anton knows I'm helping Father Bialek at the church. But that is all. He's had a very serious injury that's kept him confined to bed since we arrived here. And now that he's improving, I suspect he'll be searching for a way out of here as soon as he can arrange it."

"Does the British government know you're here?"

"They do. But we must bide our time at the church, until it is safe enough to leave. So for your own safety as well, I'll ask that Anton be kept ignorant of anything we discuss. And he should not know why you're here. I'll do my best to keep him within the confines of the rectory. It's better this way."

"You have my word," he said, though it was easy to detect a glimmer of interest in the way he said it.

"Thank you. And what is it you need to discuss?"

"It'll be some time before my brother will be up and walking much. And could be weeks before he can leave the hospital, even though he's brash enough to think he could drive a tank out of here right now."

"Yes. I imagine he'll need time to recover."

"Time we may not have. Dr. Emory says you can be trusted, so to be frank, I need to get word to our unit as soon as possible. They need to know my brother and I are still alive."

"So you are Americans—Allied soldiers."

"Yes."

It was what she'd known from the first night—from the first moment he stood in the hospital halls. But now, as they stood together on the garden path, it felt different to hear the truth confirmed.

"Forgive me, but does that mean the Allies are close? It's all we've prayed for since we learned you'd taken Sicily over the summer. It would give such hope if the staff—and the patients—knew that the Allied armies are closer to freeing us from the Germans."

The sun behind his shoulders and the overhanging trees cast a shadow on his face as he looked down at her, then gave a firm, "I can't say."

"No. Of course not. I'm sorry." She shook her head. "I shouldn't have asked."

"You misunderstand. I can't say because I don't know. My brother and I are medics. I don't have information beyond what our team does to support casualties already in the field. We were on assignment as medic support for a unit that had gone ahead of the Allied line the night I brought my brother to the hospital. Almost a week ago that line was at Naples, when we crossed the Volturno River. I have no idea where it is now."

"You're a medic? So that's how you knew—the myelopathy."

"Attending medical school helps, too, even if you don't graduate."

"But not a physician?"

"No. I'm not." Bracing a hand on his hip and rolling the apple over in the other like he was thinking with his palm, he sighed. And turned his profile so the light reflected on the small scar on his brow as he stared out at some point of sky over the wall. "Right. You'd already guessed who we are. That means the SS could too. We need to get word to our unit—wherever they are—and wait for new orders to come through. Is that possible?"

"Um . . ." Julia glanced over her shoulder, checking again that no shadows followed them on the path.

"I'm guessing your hesitation is because you've made a vow of secrecy about it. Which I applaud you for. But when Dr. Emory saw my brother's surgical scars, he'd guessed who we are. And he told me the truth about the quarantine ward because of it."

"And what truth is that exactly?"

"Kesselring and Kappler."

Two words, and Julia's heart slammed in her chest.

The soldier had just evoked the names of the Nazi commander in chief in the south and the Nazi chief of policing in Rome respectively—stationed out of Via Tasso prison and the men responsible for unspeakable atrocities, including the clearing of the ghetto just days prior. It was a discreet slap in the face to use the *K* of the officers' names as inspiration for a deadly sickness meant to keep the SS fooled about their real activities.

"We're on the same side, Julia. About Syndrome K and the patients in the ward. But if you'd rather check with Dr. Emory, I take no offense. Given what's going on, I'd be skeptical too."

"No. The circle of those involved is intentionally small. If Dr.

Emory has taken you and me both into that confidence, then he must have good reason. What do you need?"

"He suggested you could provide information on the SS patrol and supply schedules—that you speak Italian. This could help us keep Calla safe as long as she's here."

"I can."

"And there's a transistor hidden in the boiler room?"

She shot a glance over her shoulder, making sure they were still alone before continuing. "Yes. The SS confiscated everything the first day, including radios in the rectory. All except for the transistor Dr. Borromeo had hidden prior to their arrival. Father Bialek has taken to sending transmissions from the basement in the middle of the night. Captain Patz has given the SS full charge of the hospital switchboard, along with what trickle of post comes in, so it is the only connection we have to the outside world. They manage all deliveries of foodstuffs and medical supplies, then confiscate as they see fit. Nothing comes in or goes out without their notice or their approval. Or next to nothing, that is. The doctors have a few secrets of their own."

"It's too risky to try to contact our unit by telephone. So it'll have to be the transistor, as soon as we can chance it."

"Alright. Give me your message then. I can relay that to Father Bialek today."

He looked back at her, waiting. Those eyes firm as stone.

"Was there something else?"

"We're working out how to keep my brother under the SS radar while he heals, but there's another complication that can't wait . . . with Calla. I need you to try to talk to her."

"Talk to her. What about?"

"She doesn't speak English. And I don't speak Italian well enough to get through to her. Dr. Emory has offered to help, but she fears him. Even fears me a little. The only one able to calm her so far has been my brother. Until, that is, she warmed up that first night because of you."

"Alright. I suppose I could try. What should I say?"

"Calla's not her real name. I need to know what is."

"Forgive me for asking, but why on earth would that little girl be with you—two Allied medics at a hospital in Rome? Where is her mother?"

"That's just it. I'm trying to find her family, if there's any left." He stopped. Swallowed hard. "She's a Jew. And I need to know who her parents were before she saw them shot dead at the Portico d'Ottavia."

Fifteen

Present Day
Villa Adriano
Tivoli, Italy

While Matteo Santini preferred to hide away from the world in rural Tivoli, soccer phenom Giorgio Santini had quite the online footprint.

Delaney sat in her room by lamplight, clicking through internet headlines on her laptop, one after another chronicling the prominent career of the now-retired superstar Giorgio Santini. Scores of photos showed him on field as the famed striker for Rome's Società Sportiva Lazio football club. Others showed him at red-carpet appearances with a string of modelesque companions, while still others showed all angles of the three goals that helped his team take a world championship in Brazil several years before, which cemented his icon status worldwide.

But for all the highs, those moments were followed by a trail of downward tumbles.

A mug shot in Italy for what looked like something akin to a DUI arrest in the States . . . A career-ending knee injury in a match that took place the season following the world championship win . . . And a high-profile divorce, his wife and now ten-year-old daughter having packed off for a new life in New York . . . That led to an abrupt disappearance from the public eye and subsequent years of obscurity that still seemed a shock to the international sports community.

All of that, and Delaney still hadn't had a clue who the man was.

The way the headlines told it, Giorgio Santini had been one of the biggest footballers the world over for several years. He'd even played alongside one Finley Hunt—Finn—who was still a forward for Ireland's Shamrock Rovers. And while it spoke volumes that Matteo could have chosen to walk with a monumental chip on his shoulder, he seemed to live an opposite life by choice—a complete reversal for a guy who once had the world dangling from strings on his fingertips.

The last photos Delaney clicked through were a series of paparazzi snaps of Matteo and his daughter, Carly, in Central Park. They started out cheery. Normal even, with Matteo beaming and jogging alongside as she rode her bike down a paved path. But the smile soon faded, and the same look of frustration Delaney had seen on his face at the Spanish Steps featured in these photos too. By the last photo Matteo held up a palm toward the photographer and stepped in front of Carly to shield her from the camera's intrusion.

Delaney closed the laptop and flicked off the lamp, not even checking the time. She lay there in the dark, listening to the trill of cicadas and the gentle sounds of an old villa settling its bones, wishing she could somehow carve the last image of Matteo out of her mind enough to sleep.

The jagged cry of rusty hinges cut the silence, and Delaney popped her eyes open.

The glass of the terrace door couldn't muffle the gate's cry that repeated seconds after. And Delaney was certain she'd heard it that time. She rose, padded across tile, and parted the terrace drapes to peer down on the courtyard below.

The garden gate stood wide.

A ghostly figure hovered in front of it as mist swept in from the River Aniene, wrapping the stone walls in a wreathy fog. Delaney's breath caught to see the petite woman standing there, barefoot and in an ivory cotton nightdress flowing to the ankles, with her white hair spilling, wild and soft, about her shoulders.

Calla . . .

The woman remained frozen upon the cobblestones. As if transfixed. Watching through the silence. Waiting for goodness knew what. And though Delaney looked behind the figure, expecting to find Matteo or Sabine trailing somewhere along the garden path, there was no one.

No one else to see.

With the grace of a former ballet dancer, the old woman balanced one careful step upon the stones. And then she took another. And then slow as a ghost entering a forgotten silence, Calla moved through the gate and disappeared into her private world of lemon trees and parasol pines.

"Matt?" Delaney pounded her fist on the bedroom door. Sabine had said the family's rooms were all ground floor, so she was hoping beyond hope that the one on the end was his and didn't belong to some poor, unsuspecting guest who'd be startled out of sleep at nearly three in the morning.

"*Matt!* Are you awake? Please wake up."

She heard a bump in the room. Footsteps followed. And then Matteo cracked the door. Delaney tried not to notice as he pulled a tee over his athletic build down to his soccer shorts and adjusted sleepy eyes to the light cast from the hall.

"What time is it?" He ran a hand through his unruly hair and yawned. And then he must have realized Delaney would only be standing here if it was really important and asked a little sharper, "What's wrong?"

"It's Nona. She's outside."

"Not again," he muttered, and looked past Delaney down the hall. He shifted back and sat on the end of the bed, giving a rough loosen to laces enough to pull trainers on his feet.

"I saw her from my window. It just didn't seem right for her to be out there alone. I know Sabine doesn't stay in the house overnight, and I don't know which is Finn's room to try to get him to help—"

"No—he's gone. Flew out for a match tomorrow. And he doesn't know about this. No one does, except for Sabine and me. You did right, Del. By coming to find me." Matteo slipped past, ducked his head through the open door of the bedroom next to his to give it a quick check, then fled toward the kitchen. "I don't know how she got past me and I didn't hear it. I told Sabine we needed locks higher up on these doors."

"Why do you need locks on the doors?"

The kitchen door stood open, the cool night air tingling the skin of Delaney's neck. She pulled her cardigan tighter around her camisole and jeans as they slipped outside.

"Come on," he said, and Delaney followed, her flats hitting the uneven stones in the courtyard alongside his long stride.

Delaney pointed out across the courtyard. "She went this way."

"To the garden." Though he said it like he already knew.

"Yes."

The moon hung low and full, casting a silvery glow upon the stone walls before them. Matteo trotted through the gate, the hanging lanterns still and cold as they swept into the private garden world.

Olive trees lined the stone walls, alongside the lemon trees that had been trained to stretch over a pergola. Delaney's leg brushed colored blooms that slept in manicured beds along the cobblestone path, their bright poppy and rose shades muted by darkness. Statues stood guard with their weathered exteriors and mossy patina, and a fountain rose in the center of the path with trickling water that wove a soft melody through the sounds of night.

Matteo turned them as the path curled around a bend, to stone benches where a lone lantern cast a halo over the ground like a Roman version of Narnia. The villa's back wall loomed up before them, blanketed with vines of Italian roses and water that tripped over stones from a wall fountain and a wide stone basin. Delaney looked to the perimeter of the garden wall, its slope drifting lower against a sweeping view of lights pin-pricked across Tivoli's valley below.

There, edged up to the wall with her hand gripping the stone balustrade as if she'd lined up against a dancer's barre, was Calla. She stood in a firm dancer's position—first, if what Delaney remembered from her own childhood ballet classes was correct. And then with effort, and the lifetime of artistry that muscle memory couldn't erase, Calla lifted her foot inches above the stones and gave a toe point on an invisible line out in front of her.

Matteo reached for Delaney's arm, stopping them together on the path.

"What is she doing?" she whispered, watching as Calla swept

her arm in a soft arch over her head, her hand shaking with an aged tremble as it came down and extended at her side.

"Steps." Matteo sighed and braced his hands at his hips. "It's the ballet warm-up she does every morning."

"But why here? And now?"

"She's not here."

"What do you mean?"

Matteo flexed his jaw, vulnerability sweeping over his face.

For the intensity in all the photos of the soccer star, with the passion and competitive drive that had followed Matteo through the top levels of international play, Delaney wasn't prepared to see the opposite from him now. Even in the dim cast of moonlight she could see he was wracked with pain.

"Nona does this. Not every day, but more now that the dementia is taking over." He looked down at the ground and cleared his throat, it seemed, before he could answer. "She's dying, Del. It's a slow fade, but we're losing her."

"What?" Delaney breathed out, the truth saddening her more than she'd have thought it could in so short an acquaintance.

She looked to Calla's tragic form, the arched arms that moved in slow, tottering movements over the stones as if the garden haven were a performance stage.

It was easy to see what Matteo had said was true; Calla was lost in the innocence of a ballerina's dream world.

"Every time I come out here to get her, I don't know if this is it," Matteo whispered, closing his eyes over the pain for a moment. "I don't know if this is the moment she leaves and doesn't come back."

Delaney turned to him, her heart taking in the brutal honesty of his slumped shoulders.

"Matt . . . I'm so sorry." She eased a palm over his hand and squeezed until he opened his eyes and looked back. It was in the manner a friend might show support and offer sympathy when emotion hit. But he turned his hand over, his palm meeting hers, and held on tight. "What can I do? Can I help?"

"Do you have your phone?"

Delaney nodded. And pulled it from the back pocket of her jeans. "Yeah. Right here."

"Good. Keep it close. And stay here, okay?" Matteo sniffed through emotion. And it nearly killed her to see him look away, fighting back tears as he stepped forward, leaving Delaney in the shadows of the path. "Please. Stay back, unless I ask you to come?"

"Of course. I'll be right here waiting."

Delaney pressed back into the shadows of a lemon tree as she watched Matteo step out into the moonlight and begin a slow walk in the dancer's direction. "Nona?"

Calla froze.

"Nona . . ." Matteo said it again, this time with so much emotion packed in the single endearment that Delaney's heart nearly shattered for it. "It's me. *È Matteo.*"

Abandoning the beauty of a dancer's pose, Calla braced both feet on the path and turned in a slow arc. But instead of greeting her grandson, she raised a frail palm, erecting an invisible shield between them. "No!" she cried out.

"Shh. Va bene . . . Va bene." He cooed gentle words with each step he advanced toward her. *"Non ti farò del male."*

Delaney could guess along the lines of what he'd said, just by the easy reassurance of his tone. And he continued coaxing in Italian, emotion choking his voice more than once as he whispered calming words. But to no avail.

Calla's demeanor slid in a quick fall. Her eyes grew wide, flashing with fear that mounted as he approached. And with a furious shaking of her head, she peered over her shoulder as if looking for help from a phantom she saw waiting in the shadows.

"*Non verrò!*" she cried out, edging back as she pointed down to the stones at his feet. "Salvatore! Salvatore!"

Calla turned to the wall and collapsed against the tangle of vines as Matteo rushed forward to catch her. He crumpled to his knees before she fell on her own, though her fingernails clawed down the stones like she was being dragged away instead of gravity simply doing its work.

"Del! I need you," Matteo called out, cradling Calla as she fought him, her fists pounding against his chest and feet wild as they kicked the cobblestones.

Delaney ran out and met them, then knelt at his side.

"Per favore, Dio! Salvatore!" Calla cried out.

Instinct told Delaney to brace her palm behind Nona's head so she'd not hurt her spine or neck in the fit. But Delaney's heart squeezed as she touched the soft white hair of Nona's crown and chanced looking up to meet Matteo's eyes.

He locked his gaze on her too. Staring back. Whispering, "Shh, shh," in Calla's ear as she shook. And cried. And battled against the caring hands that tried only to help her.

"*Dio. Dio! Vedi?*" Calla called out in between sobs, crying over and over, "*Vedi?*" And finally with knotted hands covering her face, she let go of a guttural cry: "*Dove sei?*"

"God sees you, Nona. He knows. And He is here. I promise . . ." Matteo shook his head as Nona weakened, giving in to his strength overpowering the fight. "He knows what happened."

"Matt?" Tears had caught upon Delaney's lashes, and she wiped them away. "What is she saying? What's happened to her?"

Matteo shook his head again, as if unable to answer.

"Del—call Sabine. Please?" he said, after long seconds had ticked by through the silence. He wrapped his arms tighter around Calla, who wept in faint cries now and had fallen limp in his embrace. "We need an ambulance."

Sixteen

Curse the wind. And the bitter December temperatures with it. Wind gusts shredded Court's coat, further punishing him as he and Patrick muscled a cut spruce into the Ford's truck bed.

How he got himself talked into such a mess in subzero temperatures, he didn't know. To be coached by Penn on how to pick out the perfect evergreen from the woods adjacent to the orchards. Not a pine but a *spruce*, because they smelled better? Or some such nonsense. Then to be poked and prodded to bleeding by spiny needles as they sawed it down and wrestled the gangly thing into the truck bed. All for a Christmas tree Court wasn't even allowed to see from inside the Jenkins's parlor.

He pulled a rope down taut over the tailgate and tied it off in a double knot against the wooden slats, Patrick mirroring the same on the opposite side.

"That's it. It's in." Court tucked the bow saw in the bed and headed for the driver's side as snowflakes began falling. He tossed sap-covered work gloves on the dash and blew warm air into his palms before even trying to touch the steering wheel. "I hope to high heaven Penn's happy, 'cause we're never doing this again. I don't care if she does find a bare spot on that thing."

Patrick slid into the cab and reached for the thermos he'd left on the bench seat. "She'll be fine with it. Better get back before this snow flies. And to the radio before June because she'll never let me switch that New York Philharmonic blather off once it's on."

Court fired up the engine and cut through the back field to the road in the direction of the warm farmhouse waiting on the hill. His wrists burned as he turned the steering wheel, the pinpricks from the spruce reminding him they were still there. But the pain set him to thinking of Penn. How a few scratches would be worth it if he could just see the joy cover her face when she got a look at this tree they'd picked out for her.

Then he realized he was grinning like a fool and tried to cover before the man next to him noticed.

"Something got your attention over there?"

Too late.

"No, sir."

Patrick rubbed at his own wrists. "Or is all that smilin' 'cause you're not hurting as much as I am?"

"Nah. Just a couple of scratches is all."

"It's a tough task though, isn't it, dealing with something that stings more than you thought it would?"

"I suppose." Court watched as heavier snowflakes drifted down to earth and bounced off the windshield. "Wait—we are talking about trees, right?"

Patrick unscrewed the thermos cap and took a swig of coffee. Then, as nonchalant as he pleased, asked, "What else would we be talking about?"

"I don't know. It's just the way you said it. Thought maybe it had something to do with me. And my working here these last weeks."

"You've done a fine job for us. To be honest, I'm not sure what we'd have done without your help getting the harvest in. But now that the snow's flying, you're probably wondering when you're through."

"The thought had crossed my mind."

Clearing a debt was something any man would want off his shoulders. It's what Court had wanted since the first moment he'd turned down the road to the Jenkinses' land. Until, that is, he'd walked that dirt road right back into Penn's life. These last weeks of working side by side with the Jenkins family had made him rethink . . . a lot. Too much, maybe. The thought of cutting ties with his hometown roots didn't pull as much as it once had.

"And you'd be moving on again if you're free?"

"Maybe," Court said, then thought better of it as soon as the word was spoken. He sighed roughly. "I don't know."

"What about your father? And Penn? You'd leave them behind?"

Court sighed again, even if he did try to keep it respectful-like. "Look, sir. I don't know what Guthrie told you about that night I came back—"

"Not much. But it's a fair question. Why did you come back?"

"There are . . . reasons." More like a heaping pile of complications. Court shook his head. Last thing he could do was say them aloud now, even if he was trying to own up to things with Penn—even if that had to start in his own mind. "All I can say is, Penn and I are not on the best terms. Come to think of it, I'm not with my father either. So I'd say unless I want to spend the rest of my life living out there in your barn, laboring on your land and causing too much trouble for this town to swallow, I should be moving on. Seems like it'd be best for all concerned."

"Don't lose yourself here. This isn't an interrogation. And I'm not pointing a shotgun at you—*yet*. Just hear me out."

"Alright."

"I've known your father all my life—since we were boys. And I know losing Maddie like to have knocked every bit of breath right out of him. Must've been agony, being a doctor and the one person you couldn't save was your own wife. Surely was agony for you, too, seeing as she was your momma. But out here, on land that's been passed down for generations, there's something to be said for family. About the people who stick by you in this life. And you don't just cast folks off when times get tough."

Patrick paused, fist braced at his chin as he stared out through the windshield. Court chanced it, glancing over, expecting to find anger or judgment there. Or even fury covering the man's face, if he knew half the backstory between Court and his daughter. Unexpected, though, was that he seemed . . . kind. Firm but honest. And forgiving even, which, under the circumstances, was astonishing.

"Out here? We *stay*, Courtney. That's why I paid your bail."

"I didn't ask why."

"Maybe not, but I bet you've been thinking on it. And that tells me there's a good man living under that tough skin of yours. A man who can make peace with his family. With his God. Even with himself, if he'd only see fit to try."

When Court opened his mouth, Patrick held up a hand to silence him.

"Now I don't know what's caused you to choose this path you're on, son, but I'd wager the people in your life aren't ready to give up on you. Not your father, no matter what he says. And not Penn. Now it takes about every ounce of restraint for me to say this to you, because I'm still not convinced I'm not sitting next to the boy who got my daughter in trouble. But I will say, she needs a man to step up, for her and for this child. Do you understand what I'm tellin' you?"

"Yes, sir. I agree."

"Fine. Do you love my daughter?"

"What?" Court swerved, barely keeping the truck tires from sailing off the narrow shoulder into a deep ditch. How was he supposed to explain to anyone else what he couldn't work out for himself? "You gotta ask it—just like that? You're her father."

"That's *why* I'm asking. And it's a question with a one-word answer. Either you do or you don't."

"Yes—alright? I do!" Court raked a hand through his hair, frustration mounting, then slammed his fist on the steering wheel.

"Then if that's true, don't you think she oughta know it?"

"Yes. Or maybe. It's just . . . it's not that simple."

"I think it is. You love Penn, then you'll fight for her. And now that you've paid your debts to me, it's time to make a choice. Are you gonna stay in this—all the way—or are you going to turn around and walk away? Because you can't have it both ways. And if you do walk out that door, this is the last time. It won't be opened to you again."

Wow. Like father like daughter. Why did this family feel it necessary to confront every last uncomfortable space a man had hiding in his bones?

"Look, maybe the issue here is your daughter."

Patrick shot him a glare this time that could have melted stone. Court could feel it burning into his profile and tried like wildfire not to fidget in his seat under it.

"You sure that's how you want to answer my question?"

"All I meant was, I tried to do the right thing. I was going to ask her to marry me. First day back. She knew it and stopped me, flat out."

"And why is that?"

"I don't have the foggiest idea. But she's made a point about me not saying it since, even when I get close. It's clear she doesn't want my help. And she sure doesn't want me."

"And if she changes her mind?"

"Well, that'd change everything, wouldn't it? But I wouldn't count on her doing that. Penn has the most stubborn spirit God ever put on this earth. And believe me, I mean that as a compliment. So I'd say the way things are . . . is the way they're gonna be."

The old man paused. Nodded real soft-like. And screwed the thermos lid back tight as Court eased the truck to a stop in front of the barn and cut the engine. "Alright, son. That's fair. As long as you know helping isn't the same as loving." Patrick slapped him on the shoulder and opened the door. "Let's get this thing unloaded."

They moved in silence, Court slipping work gloves back on as he moved to the truck bed and worked to untie the needly beast.

"Care to come inside?" Patrick offered after they'd muscled the tree down to the ground and held it up in a lean against the tailgate. "June can warm the coffee and we could offer you a slice of pie while you watch us fight over the radio dial."

Court looked to the house. It was easy to see what Patrick was offering—a seat in the parlor where only friends and family had a place. Tempted, he thought about it for a good long minute before he finally shook his head. "I'll just get the tree on the porch for you and then call it a day."

"Dad!" Guthrie charged out the front door, the screen swinging open to the December wind.

Instinct told Court to look for Penn.

In the seconds it took Guthrie to wave them down and come running through the snow, Court scanned the porch . . . the open doors to the barn . . . even looked in the glow of the windows along the front of the house, hoping to find her sweet smile appear through the glass. But all he saw was June darkening the doorway with her apron in her hands, mopping tears away on primrose fabric.

Heart beating like a thunderclap in his chest, Court abandoned the ropes at the tailgate and ran out to meet Guthrie halfway to the porch steps.

"Is Penn alright?" Court glanced over to June again, panic making a fast rise through his insides. "Where is she?"

"I don't know."

"She's not in the house?"

"Out in the barn maybe. No—it's the Philco. Washington news bulletin." Guthrie stood still, a hand braced at the back of his neck as he released a deep breath. "The, uh . . . Japanese have bombed Pearl Harbor."

"What?" Patrick left the tree in its lopsided lean against the truck and took a step forward. "Are you sure?"

"Wish I wasn't. Ships . . . planes . . . airfields—they're gone. Bombed flat. Everything's on fire and it's still going on. Radio says hundreds of American servicemen are dead in Hawaii. Maybe thousands. It has to be war now. There's just no other way."

Court shot a glance to Patrick that said wherever Penn was, he'd go get her. Their place was together in the parlor—all of them, family or not—huddled around the Philco as snow fell on the abandoned spruce outside and the world waited for more news of the agonizing turn of events.

"I'll find her." Fool that he was, Court sailed into the barn.

Seeing no strawberry-blonde locks peeking out over the tops of the stall rows, he ran on and tripped over a milking pail, about landed on his duff in a heap of hay. And then he heard it—a long, shuddering exhale. And then another. And muffled crying from somewhere in the back. That from a girl who never cried if she could do anything to help it.

"Penn?" He stepped around the corner to the shadows of the stairs. There she was, propped against the door to the tack room, fingernails of one hand digging into the wooden doorframe, and pitched over with her other hand bracing the small of her back.

"You okay?"

"I'm fine."

She lied of course. This was nothing close to fine.

"No." He edged closer. "You're not."

"Get out of here, Court. Go in the house. Just leave me be."

He peeled off his coat, wrapped it over her shoulders. "If you think I'd leave you now, then you don't know me at all."

Instead of the fight he expected, Penn gave in. Easy. She collapsed against him and wrapped her arms around his neck.

Court lifted her off the ground, brushed the hair out of her eyes. He started walking and pressed a kiss to her forehead—restrained but intentional so she'd know he meant it. And soft. So soft, when his lips touched the delicate skin of her brow, it felt like an invisible string tugged someplace deep in his chest he didn't even know existed. And if Patrick had dared to ask the questions from inside that truck cab again, he'd have had an easy answer for every single one.

"I've got you," Court whispered against her temple. "Do you hear me? I won't let go."

She nodded, head bobbing up and down against his chin. When tears wet his neck, Court squeezed tighter. Moved faster as he marched them out of the barn. "Come on. Let's get you two inside."

Between the shock of war, the bitter cold of snow hitting his skin as he hurried them across the yard, and, God help him, the scariest thing he'd ever experienced happening right before his eyes . . . For the first time since the day Maddie Coleman had died, Court prayed to a God he desperately wanted to believe in.

Penn was in labor.

The only thing left to do was to telephone his father.

18 OCTOBER 1943
TIBER ISLAND
ROME, ITALY

Court had a false name to go with Rossi. And AJ would hate it because it came from the kid.

It might have hurt to stretch his neck because the nurse had nicked his skin with the straight blade during his shave that morning, but even then Court couldn't feel that bad. They were alive. And Calla was safe. They just had to figure out a plan to keep things moving in that same direction.

Even if they couldn't talk, it seemed the kid liked him.

Court awoke from a fog earlier that morning to find her still in his room. Snacking on an apple. And nose pressed up to the window as she watched something beyond the glass. An Italian primer had appeared on the bedside table. Probably AJ's doing, after their last conversation. Court struggled to sit up in the hospital bed, his back propped against the metal headboard as he thumbed through the pages, trying to find a way to communicate with her.

He tried words like *le mela*—the apple she ate. *Valigia*—that little suitcase she always kept close. And *ciliegie*—the cherries that decorated the outside of it. And he'd started to give his name by saying,

"*Mi chiamo . . .*"—*my name is*—and was going to try to find out hers. But she pointed at him and dubbed him "Salvatore" with a firm interruption.

It sounded like a fine name to him. So Court gave up. Tossed the primer on the bedside table just as the door opened and AJ walked in. A man with round, wire-rimmed glasses and a doctor's coat came in behind. They both wore white surgical masks. But AJ had said something that morning about a sickness in the hospital. And a quarantine. Must have been why.

More interesting, though, was the pretty woman who entered on the doctor's heels. That and the fact AJ was acting off. He waited until she walked in and lowered her mask, revealing a stunning smile to Calla, and then he double-checked, looking out into the hall before he clicked the door closed. AJ stuffed his own mask in his pocket and stood like a stone, as if he were some sort of personal guard assigned protection duty.

Okay . . . Extra protective. That's new.

"You can speak freely," AJ said to Court from his post by the pretty lady. "These are friends."

"I am Dr. Emory. I performed the surgery," said the lab coat—obviously Italian, too, given the accent—and began a quick check of Court's vital signs. "You are making good progress, Mr. Rossi. Sì? And how do you feel?"

"I don't like to say, sir, with a lady present."

Court glanced over to Julia, who seemed to take issue with the insinuation of a fairer sex, even though he was trying to be polite, knowing his tongue could sometimes be on the brash side. But her quick response was sure interesting. In fact, he understood it. Penn might have done the same thing.

"But I'll just say feeling a little rough yet. Grazie. And it's Salvatore."

"What?" AJ pulled two chairs up next to the bed. He eased down onto the closest one.

"My name. It's Salvatore Rossi."

Calla spoke up then, repeating the "Salvatore" with an enthusiastic nod and a little cherub's grin. Court gave a light point in her direction and winked at her. "See? She likes it."

Dr. Emory cleared his throat as he checked Court's bandages. The woman, for her part, seemed a little less concerned about putting on a cheerful face. She glanced from AJ to the girl—an obvious level of familiarity there—and rubbed her lips together in what appeared disapproval of something. And the smile that had been so welcoming was now all but wiped away.

The doctor sat in the open chair next to AJ.

"Miss Bradbury? Would you mind?"

"Of course not, Doctor," she said—curious that this one had a British accent—and then fired something off in lyrical Italian. Calla's face brightened. Immediately. And that ghost of a little girl's grin he'd suspected she owned returned.

Nice—the kid was more comfortable with them now. And that meant they'd have a better chance of helping her.

Calla tapped the windowpane with a tiny index finger.

"La danza."

The woman nodded. "Sì. That was a dance you saw."

Court didn't know what that meant, but the woman's face warmed toward the kid again. And she fired off more Italian to Calla in response.

Whatever she'd said sent Calla to hop down from the bench, crimson ribbons bouncing on lopsided braids and a knee sock sinking to her ankle with the jump. Calla crossed the room with her little suitcase in tow. And the woman knelt to pull the sock back up before she took Calla's hand and led her and the little cherries to the door.

"Excuse us, gentlemen. We will leave you to your conversation. And we shall have one of our own." The woman stopped. Looked to Court. And then whispered something to AJ, who nodded, adding, "I'll see you after," before she stepped out. And seemed to succumb to the battle of not letting his gaze follow the beauty as they walked out the door.

Oh, yep—right on the money.

AJ, you're a goner.

"She didn't have to leave. I'm sure we'd both be more than happy to have her stay. Some of us more than others." Court narrowed his eyes just enough to say he'd noticed AJ's reaction to the elegant British miss in the skirt.

AJ shook his head, telling Court he'd better not open his trap and say a word about it.

"Miss Bradbury is needed elsewhere at the moment," the doc cut in matter-of-factly with English that was quite good even as his bedside manner left much to be desired. "I have come that we may discuss your stay. As soon as you're able, you will be moved with your brother and the girl to the quarantine wards. For your safety."

What flew through Court's mind was one of the first rules he'd learned in this war: Don't trust a stranger. And the second: Break rule one and you don't live to find out if there's a third. Maybe it was the fog of morphine muddling Court's brain, but AJ seemed a little too cozy with this lot of outsiders. And just forty-eight hours after Court had been dead to the world, it seemed all of his superior officer's attention to those rules had been cast off.

"Quarantine ward. Why? Is someone sick?" Court asked.

The doctor didn't flinch. "No."

"Then the kid's not going anywhere near that place."

"This is not up for discussion, Mr. Rossi. There is a ward for the men. Another for women and children. She will be safe with women to look after her."

"No, sir. She stays with us," Court shot back, this time looking to AJ to back him up. "You got anything to say about this? Could use a little help here, sir."

AJ leaned forward in his chair, palm extended. "Close your mouth for once, Private. And just listen. Doctor—go ahead."

"Mr. Rossi. It will be weeks before you can leave this hospital. In that time the safest place for you, your brother, and the girl is in the quarantine ward. There will be no discussion on this point."

"Why not?"

"Because she is a Jew."

AJ's eyes widened, with a *See?* about them, and he folded his arms over his chest. If the doctor wasn't fazed by the truth, seemed rule one really could be tossed.

Court exhaled. "Alright. We're listening."

"I am asking for your assistance, Mr. Rossi. You and your brother. As well as your vow to protect the information I am about to share with your life." When Court nodded, the doctor continued. "I need help to administer protection of the wards—eyes on the inside to ensure the patients are safe when I cannot be with them. In return, we will seek to notify your military unit with information on your whereabouts so when you are able, you might rejoin them. And for the girl, we will try to discover if any of her family escaped the ghetto that night."

"But why a quarantine ward? Isn't it a risk for Calla? I'll go. You let the kid stay here."

The doctor sighed. Took off his glasses and folded them in his hands. "There is no medical risk, Mr. Rossi."

"And why is that?"

"Because Il Morbo di K—Syndrome K—is a farce. An invention of this hospital. And the quarantine, a ruse to support it."

Court laughed in the doctor's face.

That Hitler's elite Waffen-SS force would buy into a ridiculous notion like that? It was fiction beyond even the likes of Homer's tale on his bedside table. And that was saying something. He glanced from the doctor to AJ, expecting to find something different than deadpan next to deadpan.

"You're serious."

"I assure you I am. Some of the Jews who fled the Gestapo that day came here. Father Bialek and the friars agreed to take them in—sixty patients so far, not including the girl and yourselves. As this is not a state-run hospital, it affords the ability to render care under certain . . . protections of the church. Our administration has devised a plan to see these refugees to safety. That plan is Syndrome K. When written on the chart, every doctor, nurse, and member of staff knows what this code means. Except for *them*. We must keep the SS in the dark about our activities to provide a haven for the Jews of Rome, in any way that we can."

"And those Germans buy all that nonsense, about some fake sickness?"

"They have no reason to doubt. And every patient in the quarantine ward is the same as the little girl. There is no sickness here beyond the plague of being born a Jew."

"Now what kind of talk is that?" Court looked to AJ again. Sat up, though doing so made his neck burn like fire. And wished more than anything that he had all his faculties about him so he could issue a fist to that doctor's mug for saying such a thing about an innocent kid.

"It is *their* talk, Mr. Rossi. And their belief. Not ours. And when the time is right, we will see them safely from these walls. Every single one that we can help—including the girl—it will be done."

Dr. Emory rose. And it seemed that was that.

No bedside manner. No frills. Just facts.

"I will leave you now. To talk this over." He looked to AJ, who rose, too, and shook the man's hand. "Please do give me your decision soon, Mr. Rossi, or I will need to find a replacement for the ward."

AJ nodded. But there was no question about his answer. Court knew his leader well enough after surviving the last two years together in the field to know that when he hardened his jaw like that and extended a hand, his decision had already been made.

When they were alone, Court wagered the answer. "So that doctor asked for your help. And you're going to give it?"

"He did. And I am."

"What's your job? Doctoring?"

"Something like that. He doesn't want any more information about us. Doesn't even want to know our real names. Father Bialek will make the transmission, so the friars will be the only ones to have that knowledge. They thought it would be safer that way, the less they know. And I have to agree."

"And what about the skirt? Does she know about us?"

"Uh . . . Julia. She knows some, yes."

Pretty obvious. AJ looked about as uncomfortable as if he'd just swallowed a buffalo. Which made Court a little relieved to know the man was actually part of the human race. Seemed he could manage to feel something outside of duty in a uniform, and that was refreshing.

"And . . ." Court tipped his eyebrows. Waiting.

"And that's all you're going to get." AJ cleared his throat, cutting off the awkwardness. "Dr. Emory has asked for our help with getting three of the refugees—a man and his wife and child—out of the wards. Partisan contacts at Lazio are falsifying documents for their transport. Once they're discharged from the hospital, they're to be released to the partisans in Rome who will see them safely out of the city. Those documents will be hidden in a shipment of supplies due to the hospital soon. It's Dr. Emory's job to get them from the supply truck without the SS noticing. I've said I'll help."

"Sounds risky. And since when do you speak Italian?"

AJ paused. Good—maybe getting some sense through that thick skull of his.

"I speak enough to get by. But in this place, even the friars could be searched. If they were caught with the documents, everything they're trying to accomplish would fall apart, and the people here would have no protection. It's best if they appear neutral. The supply trucks—and those for the quarantine wards in particular—are the only ones where not every crate is checked. If we can get the documents in through the quarantine supplies, then the patients can be discharged with them. And that at least is what I can help with."

"And where will the kid be all this time you're, uh . . . what is it? Playing hero?"

"I really don't have time for this, Court. We'll say it's the pain medication making you loose-lipped to talk to a superior officer like that. But when Julia brings Calla back, she needs to stay in the women's quarantine ward with the other children."

"No, sir. The kid stays with me."

"She can't. Men only."

"Then find a way around it. I'm not leaving her with strangers and that's flat." Court folded his arms across his chest.

"And we're not strangers to her?" AJ walked to the bedside table.

"Not anymore."

AJ opened the drawer on the bedside table. Pulled out a sidearm and checked that the cartridge had a live round—handling the pistol with the confidence of a soldier, not a medic prepared to stay out of things.

"Where'd you get that?"

"One of the engineers. After the ghetto. Left us with it when they had to keep going, and I had to get you and the girl someplace safe." AJ moved to the window. He parted the drapes, saying nothing more as he stared out. Odd, but that's exactly what the girl had done, looking out for the longest time.

"And you plan to use it, sir?" Court sighed when the question was met with no response. He shifted, thinking that silence was worse than if he'd reprimanded him again for getting them into this fix. AJ's silence spoke of disappointment, and that from a leader he respected just about did Court in. "So what is everybody looking at from that window anyway? What's out there? Flying monkeys?"

"There's a garden. Behind the hospital." AJ paused for a moment, eyes centered through the glass. "It's where Julia dances. Ballet."

"Oh, I see. So she's a ballet dancer, huh? Trying to get free tickets for the next performance?" He couldn't help it. A snicker flew from his lips. Leave it to AJ to never show a glimmer of interest in a female until they were up to their eyebrows in trouble with a troop of Waffen-SS.

"Right now, Julia's down there teaching that little girl how to dance. She's making sure there's still room left for beauty and something innocent in this busted-up world. And that's no laughing matter. I wish either one of us could say the same about our place in this war. So I'll ask you to keep your jokes to yourself."

There's still innocence in this world . . .

No jokes needed when Court thought of the most beautiful thing he'd ever seen up close—Penn's baby. That had been more than two years back now. And quite a while since he'd stopped opening her letters. When Court thought of the baby—probably a little one teetering around the Jenkinses' kitchen, causing all kinds of trouble by now—the pain that stirred in his chest kept him from reading or even learning the boy's name. Not if Court wasn't worthy to be a father to him in the end. And he wasn't. Not by a long shot.

Still, he wished he could see that innocence again. Just once.

Leaning back against the pillows, Court chanced pointing out his leader's obvious about-face. "I thought you said we shouldn't get involved."

"And you said she makes us involved," AJ said, still staring out. "So each man makes a choice. If we're caught, let's just say we won't have any more problems to figure out. And if we're not caught, the US Army might have a thing or two to say about that instead."

"Oh. A death wish, is it? Or a court-martial? Well then. You put it that way, you know it's gonna be too tempting for someone who's skirted death twice over now. That's a definite yes."

"Fine. I'll tell the doctor. And I'll see that Julia brings Calla back to you when they're finished. You'll have to keep her out of sight until you can be moved to the quarantine unit. After that, we'll take things as they come."

AJ turned back to Court, only this time the look on his face was one Court had seen before. That same distant gaze Court had seen in the ambulance at Blue Beach. He slid the pistol into the back of his belt, readjusted his jacket to cover it, and turned toward the door.

"That dancer told you, didn't she, before she left? What *Salvatore* means."

AJ stopped. Gave a sharp nod. "She did."

"Couldn't find it in the primer." Court waited for a breath, hating that he felt like a kid asking his dad something he somehow should have already known. "So what's it mean? Am I a hero, or something else?"

"That doesn't matter, Court. The only thing that does is a little girl is looking to you to watch over her. And whether you wanted the name or not, you're about to get the chance to prove to her you're worthy of it."

Seventeen

S he says you may go in." The doctor stepped out but left Julia's dressing room door cracked to the hall.

Anton entered in his lavish performance costume, the white crystal-bedecked tunic taking up the narrow space between the wall of makeup mirrors and a counter spanning one side. Julia sat in one of the chairs along the row, her reflection backdropped by muted pastel satins and tulle stage costumes hanging behind.

Turning her face in three-quarter profile, Julia leaned into the row of makeup lights to inspect the wound the doctor had stitched at her hairline. She dotted more powder to cover evidence of the bruise, even while trying not to wince when the puff touched the tender swell there.

"It won't show onstage," she said, knowing Anton was inspecting her from the doorway, and adjusted the tiara, hoping it instead would receive his notice.

"I wasn't worried. At least not about that." He reached for the door and her insides pinged with alarm when it clicked closed.

"The door was open for a reason."

"I know. And you needn't worry about that either." He forced a slight smile that faded a shade too fast for comfort. "There are things to say and I shouldn't think the whole troupe needs to hear it too."

Anton was certainly not standing before her as the proud peacock ready to make a triumphant La Scala debut. His hands drifted to his sides, and as he waited, as far from her as the room would allow, his glance avoided hers in the mirror's reflection.

"You're alright then? The doctor said you can dance."

"I can. Leastways I've been cleared. And I didn't lose consciousness, so there ought to be no worry about my balance onstage. I am well enough to perform, which is more than the poor souls can say who lost their lives on that train platform today."

"It was close. We were lucky."

"I should think 'lucky' a poor choice of word. But yes—it was close." She let a fingertip toy with the side of the makeup compact on the counter. A memory struck her, of a night when she'd once used makeup to cover bruises in much the same way. "So close that it served as a reminder of what I've been reluctant to say for quite some time."

"Me too." Anton took a step forward. And heavens, he fidgeted his hands—one inside the other—like a timid schoolboy. "Julia, when I saw you on the floor of that train car . . . covered in blood . . . God help me, I couldn't breathe and—"

"Stop."

He did a double take, the swift cut obviously not what he'd imagined while rehearsing his speech in the hallway. "Stop what? You don't want me to be honest?"

"Don't say another word."

"I must, if only to tell you how I care for you and have all these years. I can't keep it in any longer. So I'm here. Honestly and freely saying it."

"Well. That is one thing we can agree on, that honesty would be a virtue just now."

He turned away, shifting his stance and shaking his head in a little tell that suggested he didn't take to the conversation going any way but as he'd favored.

"You're not making this easy."

"It is not my job to make things easier for you."

It would have been weak to face Anton in the mirror's reflection; that was too literal for the moment. A performer never feared what she must do. So Julia stood tall, stepped out from the row of chairs, and held her posture as if she were already standing center stage and just waiting for the swell of orchestra music to begin.

"If we're being honest, Anton, then tell me—would you have noticed a young ballerina from the chorus line if you hadn't first learned she was Lord Chatham's daughter and grew up spending summers at a country home near Chartwell?"

He snapped back to attention, eyes boring into hers. Goading her on in his disbelief.

"And when the young ballerina learned her parents had been killed in an automobile accident on their way to see her perform in New York, how long did it take to uncover the existence of a trust fund that had been set up in her name? And who telephoned Whitehall and supplied the ATS with information as to my background? Who ensured I hadn't a choice in my own endeavors? And whose manipulations worked to bring us both here, to this very moment, where I now demand answers. From you."

Anton blinked back, his glare fixed on her.

And therein was every answer.

"I've tried to apologize, Julia. In London. Two, three times since. And now here. You won't let me speak to you. You won't even allow me to explain."

"I do not require an apology. Though a genuine one would have been the gentlemanly thing to do. On the night I learned of my parents' deaths, I came to you looking only for comfort."

"I tried to comfort you!"

"No. You tried to coax me into warming your bed with brandy and the pain of fresh grief. And in that fragility, I nearly lost my virtue by force, only to find the word *no* was not in your vernacular. My world was shattered long before we entered a war. And what I seek now is not a tossed-out apology."

"I meant no harm that night."

"No harm?" She raised her chin higher. "And when I told you to stop?"

"I did! How many men do you know who would have done the same? You ask too much, Julia."

"Once you'd decided your pride had been wounded enough? Yes—you did stop. And I went onstage with an extra layer of makeup to hide the bruises you left behind."

"Then that's it? One moment of losing control and you can never forgive?"

"I can forgive you. I have. But I could not forgive myself if I were to allow this farce to continue between us, for you to believe you have any such claim to manipulate the course of my life ever again. So I will dance with you tonight. And for the remainder of this tour, you will speak to me only onstage. And after this war ends, we will never speak again. From that day on I will dance on my own stage and I will stand on my own two feet. And the only name that will rise with mine will be a man's of my own choosing. If I so choose *him*."

"And if I said I'd never allow you to be hurt again?"

"I'd be a fool to believe it."

"And if I said . . . I love you?" He edged forward. And the saddest thing was, the raw emotion on his face said he actually believed he meant it. "What of that?"

"I would pity you above all men. You don't know what love is."

"I know that if we break now, we would never see what heights we could have reached together. And you may never again dance on La Scala's stage. Your dream—our dream together—would be lost."

Once Julia had considered it a sadness to live a life devoid of dreams. But with a fresh cut hidden at her hairline and nothing in the world left for her to lose, Julia stepped past him. She opened the door and looked down the long hall with gilded chandeliers illuminating the path that would take her to the lush red curtains of the La Scala stage.

"Nothing of worth is lost. And I will dance, Anton. Just never again with you."

6 November 1943
Tiber Island
Rome, Italy

It was all about confidence now.

Julia mastered an iron façade as she stepped into the bright afternoon sun, even though her insides churned as if she were on a ship tossed at sea. With her head held high and clipboard in hand, she marched down the gangway at the hospital's stone loading dock as if she had dominion over the alley space.

As she'd hoped, smiles faded swiftly and the sea of SS uniforms parted when they caught a glimpse of her nursing uniform and surgical mask in place.

"Aus dem Weg!" Captain Patz barked orders as Julia approached, perhaps to warn the other soldiers off that those exposed to the sickness were coming through. "Aus dem Weg! *Schnéll!*"

Soldiers dropped crates from their arms and abandoned supplies in haste to put as much distance between themselves and the potential disease carrier as they could.

Only a doctor was authorized to retrieve medical supplies from the truck shipments. For the few times they'd managed the task before, Dr. Emory had accompanied Mr. Rossi—referred to as Dr. Rossi now in the weeks since his arrival to the quarantine unit. It had been their arrangement that either he or Dr. Emory would be on hand to ensure they found the crates with forged documents undisturbed. But by the time the supply trucks had pulled up that day and the SS began their unloading, neither man had shown.

They couldn't dare risk the SS uncrating supplies and finding forged documents among them. So Julia was forced to walk the gangway—and face the SS—alone.

"Supplies for the quarantine wards . . . ," the captain shouted in Italian, no doubt for her benefit. He checked a paper on his clipboard, then motioned down to the far end of the alley. "There. In the last truck." He snapped his fingers and barked an order at a uniform.

The young Waffen-SS hesitated, no doubt weighing the balance of contracting a terminal plague from Julia versus incurring the captain's wrath, which could be equally lethal. Choosing to submit to the latter, he loosened the submachine-gun strap so it slid off his shoulder and gripped the weapon in white-knuckled hands. Pointing the barrel to the last truck in the line, he bade her to go first and he'd follow, several steps behind.

Regardless of the wide berth, it would never do to have him in such proximity.

Don't argue. Ask.

Make the captain think any suggestion is his idea . . . Just keep them away.

Julia turned around and raised a hand for effect, palm out, holding the soldier and his weapon at bay.

"Captain?" she inquired in Italian. "We've new patients in the quarantine wards this week. And I fear there is a risk of infection if you or your men were to come too close. I couldn't account for their safety from Il Morbo di K."

The last words stopped the soldier cold. Maybe they didn't speak Italian, but they all knew those words meant death. He stared between her mask and the captain's form, his eyes wild as he asked without words what he was to do.

"There are more patients in the quarantine wards now? How many?" Captain Patz lowered the clipboard to his side. He tilted his head, calculating, with a sharp cut to his brow. "Is it spreading?"

Oh no. They must always choose their words with the utmost caution.

It was a great fear to be caught hiding Jews. But even greater was the fear of wards full of patients being cleansed to control the spread of a deadly microbe—which the staff would not put out of the scope of the Reich's evil to employ.

"No, Captain. But Dr. Borromeo has instructed that our staff alone should assist with the quarantine supplies. As we are under orders to ensure your men are kept safe at all costs. I couldn't account for the risk."

The wind caught the edge of the paper to flap it against the captain's uniform trousers, his glare cutting the deafening silence of the soldiers, whose eyes remained pinned to their discourse.

Julia stared back. Chin up. Immovable, because assurance was all the captain would respond to.

He muttered something in German—perhaps a curse—for his mood darkened still further. "I will speak with Borromeo about this."

"Yes, of course."

Seconds ticked by, until Julia thought her insides would melt from the heat of his glare.

"*Ja.* Fine." Patz waved her off, as if he couldn't be bothered any longer, then turned back to his clipboard to keep them tracking on schedule. "But be quick about it."

Julia was quickly forgotten. The sun warmed her skin and the light autumn breeze rustled the strips of mask linen tied at her neck as she turned away and hurried to the tailgate.

She rounded the corner, hoping . . . praying she'd find him there . . .

Empty.

Looking left and right, Julia saw only garden walls, SS uniforms, and crates being carried in like ants marching from a picnic. But no Mr. Rossi. Something must have kept him away as well.

Julia examined the crates. Some had been marked in Italian. That helped. And German—that didn't. And it appeared some supplies had been procured from the black market—goods pilfered from the Allies and then confiscated by the Germans within the city. Julia shuddered to find English and the jarring symbol of the Union Jack staring back in stamps on some of the rations.

"*Chirurgische maske,*" she whispered, noting the German that might have indicated "surgical mask" on the shipment log, praying she'd find the right one.

Dr. Emory had coached that they'd find the crates of note near the middle of the register. An SS officer would most often skim the top and bottom of the list, and those lines noted for Syndrome K would be given little notice if unassuming and buried in plain sight, somewhere in the middle of the pack.

Julia searched the lot, her heart beating faster to see some crate lids had already been pried open.

There was formalin solution. Iodine swabs. Boric acid. And potassium permanganate—apparently used as a disinfectant. It would fit the ruse of their ward, so Julia grabbed one of those on a whim and marked off her checklist, thinking she could give it to Dr. Emory for real use elsewhere in the hospital. She passed over the various gauzes and cotton, syringes and packed sponges, and synthetic rubber used for surgical dressings. Until finally, in the corner, she spotted a crate holding the linen swaths she sought.

It was stamped with simple Deutsche "chirurgische maske" and the Reich's emblem in Nazi red. And it was still nailed shut, thank heaven. Julia had no clue how their partisan contacts had managed it, but Julia didn't question. And couldn't care. She just reached for the medium-sized crate, slid it over, and began stacking smaller boxes on top of it.

"Nurse? Answer me!" The captain's voice rattled Julia from her thoughts, booming as it was from his perch above.

She turned, her breath locked on the sharp interruption. "Yes, Captain?"

"I said have you Condy's crystals there?" He stared down at his clipboard again, running his gaze the length of the paper and looking up when he reached the end. "Surgery is missing a box. Look. Now."

Julia kept her hand on the crate of masks, desperate fingernails boring into the wood while she tried to think.

Condy's crystals . . .

Oh Lord. What in the world is he asking?

"Of course." She turned her back on him, searching the truck bed for anything that might fit the request.

"What is the matter with you?" he shouted and took a step forward on his perch, a testy glare drilling into her. "There's but a small stack. Are they there or aren't they?"

"What did he say?"

Julia looked up at the voice and the sudden comfort of familiar steel eyes greeting her over the top of a surgical mask.

Mr. Rossi stood by, with his ebony hair combed and in the ruse of a lab coat amongst the sea of SS uniforms, clearly stepping out now to impersonate one of Fatebenefratelli's doctors. And bearing enough confidence that he had every right to stand by her side, though she was certain he didn't understand a word of the language being tossed about and if questioned he surely wouldn't have a believable answer.

"Sorry I'm late," he whispered.

"Condy's crystals?"

"It's this one." He nudged the box she'd picked out earlier. "Potassium permanganate."

"I didn't know it was called anything else." Julia exhaled, relieved for a split second before realizing she ought to turn back to the captain. She did, holding the box up. "It is here."

Of course the captain didn't move to retrieve it—he was too valuable to risk exposure. But he snapped an order at one of the less fortunate uniforms, and that soldier was forced to retrieve the box with a pinch of his fingertips at the comical length of an eagle's wingspan in front of him. He walked that way, like Dr. Frankenstein's odd creation, in a stiff march the length of the gangway, and disappeared into the hospital.

Julia turned back to Mr. Rossi, whispering as she stacked his arms with boxes. "I can't pretend I'm not thrilled to see you. The doctors thought you'd gone out to the trucks—alone. And then I learned they're moving your brother and Calla to the quarantine ward today. When you didn't come back, I was worried. So I came to find you. For heaven's sake, you don't speak Italian."

"I know. But you do." His eyes smiled over the mask and he went to work sorting boxes. "Nice uniform. Where'd you get it?"

"Do not attempt to make light of the situation when we have submachine guns trained at our backs."

"I'd never do any such thing. Not when you're wearing a mask and I can't see you smile back at me."

"Please," she whispered low, so as not to stir notice by the uniforms. "Don't you realize what kind of risk you're taking by coming out here without Dr. Emory? You ought to go. Now."

"I'm not leaving you." He ignored her protestations in favor of getting down to business by examining the boxes she'd been stacking. "Besides, looks like you could use help with the supplies. Between the two of us, we should be able to make sense of what's here, get what we need, and return to the ward in one piece."

"Alright." She checked boxes off the list as quickly as she could account for them.

"There's something else." He flitted a glance to check on the captain in his roost, then looked back to her. "A change of plans. One of the families has to be discharged today. Seven more have come in the last hour, and we need every bed to keep them. It's why Dr. Emory isn't here. He was pulled away to sign off on the Syndrome K diagnoses for the charts before the SS could look over them. It's by pure luck he remembered the shipments and sent me out for them."

"Right. We ought to hurry then," she said as he loaded his arms with the prized crate of linen at the bottom of his stack.

They walked in tandem, his arm just brushing hers as they moved up the gangway. The SS left them the wide berth they'd expected. When they crossed the threshold of the hospital doors and entered the shadow of the halls, Julia realized she'd been holding—and finally released—her breath.

"*Halt!*"

They froze at the captain's order. Desperate, she looked up. Mr. Rossi met her gaze, assurance in his eyes telling her without the necessity of words that it would be alright.

Julia nodded and gave a swift turn. In Italian she offered, "Captain. Thank you for stopping us. It seems we do have another box for you. I didn't realize it before now."

She remained a respectful distance away but pulled a box from the top of the stack in Mr. Rossi's arms. This was the only failsafe the staff knew of, should they ever be stopped by one of the SS. And why Julia had swiped it from the truck, just in case. It seemed that forethought would be their savior now, as the box with the word *Pervitin* stamped in blood red across the side lay outstretched to the officer.

"If it had gone to the quarantine wards, I fear it might have been disposed of. We know how important this one is to the well-being of your men."

Take it.

Take it, her insides coaxed. *You know you need it.*

Though he seemed cross about their having touched anything that he must then put his own hands to, the prize was too valuable to forgo. The captain took the box. He shoved it under his arm and gave them a pointed glower. "Next time, leave it on the truck."

"Of course, sir. My mistake. It won't be repeated."

He dismissed them with a nod, and she turned back with Mr. Rossi. Their pas de deux saw them move in silence all the way to the haven of the quarantine wing. And for how close they might have come to disaster, one realization brought comfort: This man had shown up the exact moment Julia needed someone she could depend on most. He'd been there for her, and she for him. And in a time of war and uncertainty and on the long road Julia had already taken on her own, it could mean nearly everything to find one soul you could completely trust with your own.

For the first time Julia could remember since her parents' deaths, this was one performance in which she didn't dance alone.

Eighteen

R ain cried down Calla's bedroom window.

    Delaney found Matteo lounging in a chair pushed up to the bed, his fist braced at his chin, like he was lost somewhere between trying to sleep and staring at the watercolor world through the glass.

Delaney gave a light tap to the doorframe with her shoe and raised a mug of coffee in each hand. "May I come in?"

"Please." Matteo nodded. And then he did that old-school thing guys sometimes did at a fancy dinner—standing when a lady entered the room. Delaney tried not to like it. And hid the smile that little measure of nobility generated while he dragged an ivory wingback from the corner and set it beside his. He patted the chairback. "Here."

"Grazie," she said, and stepped in.

Tivoli's rainy October weather had cast the bedroom in shadows, even for midmorning. But Delaney found that like the upstairs hall, Calla's room revealed a trove of treasures, hidden until you walked inside. Seemed the entire house was holding stories it could tell.

A painting above the fireplace was reminiscent of a Degas masterpiece, with Impressionist-styled ballet dancers in pastel hues lined up to a barre. A built-in under the windows held a cushioned seat over an eclectic row of Nona's books, the aged spines of which Delaney would have loved to walk her fingertips over and explore. And the most beautiful feature yet was the mosaic of frames that chronicled Calla's life, hung in a visual display on the far side of the room.

To enter into someone's private world required an invitation. And Delaney had been offered one. But how far the liberty extended, she didn't yet know. So she passed by the lure of the memories spanning the wall, offered Matteo a mug, and sat down. "Sabine made breakfast, too, if you're hungry."

"No." He took a sip of the coffee and closed his eyes for a breath, like it was saving him. "This is good though."

"So where were you just now when I came in?"

"Would it be cliché to say a million miles away?"

"Not if it's true." Delaney wondered if his thoughts were in New York, perhaps. With his daughter. Or certainly with the form sleeping so peacefully in the bed opposite them. After what had happened the night before and with Nona slipping further into the locked world of a heartbreaking dementia diagnosis, surely the entire situation would set him thinking on family.

It had done the same for her.

Delaney looked to the air cast on Calla's wrist and the elegant fingers curled around the Velcro securing her palm, feeling the tiniest wish to breach the space and cradle the beautiful aged hand in her own. For whenever someone was in a hospital or sickbed, even if they were gone from the world in sleep, they ought to have their hand held.

"How is she?"

"Nothing's broken—thank goodness. The cast is just a precaution for swelling at her wrist. And the doctor who came by after the EMS service is a family friend, so he said he'd check in later. See how she's doing. At least she's been able to sleep for a while now, which is good."

"And did you . . . sleep?"

"A little. In the chair." He shrugged. The answer looked more like a flat *no*. "I just want to be here if she wakes."

"She doesn't need to go to the hospital?"

"If Nona woke in a hospital, rest assured I'd be the one trying to get out of there alive. She'd never let me hear the end of it. She wants to be home, as long as we can keep her here." Matteo smiled at his nona, a little pride trying to peek out from a grandson's profile. But it faded almost as quickly. "What you saw last night, Del . . . Nona would hate it if she knew. What she said and did—that's not who she is."

"I know. She seemed so confused. So hurt. I just wish we could have explained it so she'd understand."

"It's more what she said. I know you couldn't translate it, but she cried out to God. Almost accusing Him of not hearing her—or not helping when she called to Him? I don't know. It doesn't make sense." He sighed. Weighed down, as if coffee and conversation alone couldn't begin to unload his burdens. "It was like she was crying out for someone to save her, but we were right there."

"Does she know what's happening to her?"

"When we got the diagnosis, she understood then. But she's a proud woman. A religious woman. Always has been. And in the years since, this disease is stealing everything, so now she's just . . . lost. Sometimes even when she's in the same room she can't find us."

"And your family? What do they say?"

Surely he wasn't going through this alone.

Matteo raked a hand through his hair and caught his palm at the base of his neck, as if thinking through some decision. Maybe whether to let Delaney into the private life he kept so close to the vest? It would be a marked departure from ducking off street corners and avoiding autograph sessions for strangers. But just sitting there beside him, talking about Calla's diagnosis after what they'd shared the night before . . . it made Delaney hope he could trust her.

He seemed to agree, because he turned the mug in his hands and just started to talk. "My father and I are not on good terms. Haven't been for as long as I can remember. His Jewish faith faded somewhere. And he left us. Divorced my mom when I was too young to understand anything. We moved back to the States and she passed a few years after. Then I came home here to live with my grandparents. Nona never made excuses for her son's decisions. And she does still love him. As I was growing into a man, she wouldn't let me hate him. Even when I wanted to." He paused, then added, almost as an afterthought, "He has a new family now, in upstate New York."

"So close to where you live. Do you ever see him? Or does Carly get to see her grandfather?"

He shook his head. "That's my fault. It took her a while just to want to see me again, let alone a grandfather she's never met."

Delaney hated that for Carly—and for Matteo.

Loss was so different than she'd once imagined. It didn't only arrive with a funeral. Sometimes it was a longer journey. A deeper pain. And the road to forgiveness an uncharted trek through years of one's experiences. She felt even more grateful that Matteo had Calla in his life. And that she herself had loving grandparents in her life too. Because wherever loss was found, it was much more bearable when the memories of your beloved ones were so kind.

"He came around again, my father. Just once. About the time I signed my first big contract to play professionally."

Delaney watched his profile, looking for the okay to keep going. "And?"

"And he said he wanted to reconnect with his family. And his Jewish heritage. But I told him I was only going to say it once—he doesn't have a son. And as for his faith? That's on his shoulders. It's Nona who's been the rock in my life. My grandfather, too, at least until he passed and we started down this road with her diagnosis."

He reached out. Stroked his fingertip over the air cast on his nona's wrist, doing the same thing Delaney's own impulse had wanted.

"I don't know why I thought things could keep going on the same way forever, just because I wanted them to. Leave it to the arrogant footballer to think he could control the whole universe."

"You mentioned your grandfather. When did he pass?"

"Four years ago now."

"What was his name?"

That was an intentional ask. If Delaney had learned anything from her family's losses over the years, it was getting used to the absence of your loved one's voice. And then no longer hearing their name spoken aloud. And that was only in a matter of months for them. What must it have been like after four years?

Matteo looked up. "Adriano."

"Oh, I see. Villa Adriano. That was nice of her to name their home after him."

"She didn't. *He* did." Matteo laughed and reached for a frame from the table by the bed, handing Delaney the image of a handsome couple bathed in sepia and sun-kissed smiles. "You'd have had to know him, and then it would make every bit of sense that he wanted to rival Tivoli's famous Roman ruins with a strikingly similar name."

"Sounds like he was quite his own man." Delaney ran her thumb over the glass holding the couple's image. "They're beautiful. And look like they were so happy together."

"They were. Sixty years married. She Jewish. And feisty. And he Catholic and feistier. From two different worlds but they made it work. They made their own world here. Together." He took the photo and set it back in place. And then looked over to the crown of white resting on the pillow. "After he was gone, that's when the decline really began. And then these episodes started—not as often as they happen now. But I'm sorry, Del. I should have realized what that would feel like for you, being a guest here. Not knowing any of this."

"You don't need to apologize."

"No—I do. I was rude on that first video call. On purpose. I thought you'd figured out who I was and . . . Well, there goes the athlete ego again, always thinking everything is about him. Sabine told me as much while we were on the call, that I was being a prideful—"

Delaney tipped her brow when he paused and backtracked with a smile.

"Right. You know, I'll spare you the word for it, even if it doesn't sound as bad in Italian."

"Now that I've met her, somehow I thought it might have been Sabine sitting next to you. Giving you what for." Delaney laughed, hiding her smile behind the lip of her mug. It sure sounded like the woman to keep his priorities in check.

He laughed a little, too, soft and light, until the reality of the situation took its hold back and his smile faded.

"The truth is, I wasn't ready to see the suitcase that day. Up until the call, it had just been a big question mark from the past. But I thought if I could find it, maybe it would stir something. Maybe pull Nona out of it, you know? Enough to bring her back, just for a little while."

"I'd already decided last night to give it to you. Before any of this. So it's yours, Matt—or hers—whenever you want it."

"I don't know now. I worry that seeing it again could cause her more harm than good. Because if it exists, then whatever terrible thing is locked somewhere in Nona's mind might actually be real. And I didn't want to consider that. I still don't."

Delaney's heart squeezed. "Do you think this crying out to God is Nona's way of dealing with losing your grandfather? Or something entirely different?"

"I did. But now . . . I don't know. This feels like more than delayed grief. And why would an old suitcase help with that?"

"Grief is an unpredictable foe. My mother says there's no easy way around it and no fast way through. You just have to walk in pace with it, however long that takes." She tipped her shoulders in a little shrug, then pulled her legs up, curling into the corner of the chairback. "You know, it's silly. But for a while, I thought God was mad at me."

"Why would God be mad at you?"

"I told you it was silly. It's all because life didn't meet up with my expectations. Nothing went the way I'd planned. First my grand-mother passed away years back and it broke everyone. My grand-father especially. And now he's just passed too. A few months ago now. My aunts and their families all live away. So our small, tight-knit family feels cut straight down the middle."

"I'm so sorry, Del." He set his mug on the nightstand and turned, really looking at her this time. "What happened?"

"A heart attack. Our family owns an orchard, and that's where my dad found him when he didn't come in one evening. He was out in the orchard row. Just gone . . . I'm my parents' late-in-life only child, so it felt right to come home and help. I went on an extended leave from my job. Left my life in Seattle—" *Leave out the broken relationship part.* "But I never thought it would be like this, you know? A funeral stretching out for months. And now everything's changed."

"So that's what you meant at dinner when you said you were a writer between pens."

"Yes." She laughed. "Although I don't know what I am anymore, except starting over without one of the steadying influences in my life. I didn't even get to say goodbye—Grandpa was just here one day and gone the next. And I've had a hard time with that. Even though my head understands that death is a part of life, I wish someone could explain it to my heart. If that's not too weak to admit."

"Not at all. Look where I am. And who hasn't questioned God when everything falls apart? At least once, if they're honest with themselves. I know I have."

"Me too. But then again, I did wake up in Rome this morning and I hadn't planned on that. And I'm learning a beautiful story of Nona—and maybe some connection to my grandfather, too, that I wouldn't have ever known otherwise. It's like bringing him back to me in a way. And I believe in the healing power of restoration. And rebuilding. So if God is behind something as small as an old suitcase coming to light, I could believe He's looking for ways to heal us in our brokenness. And certainly to be there with us in our grief."

"Well, that settles it, Del Coleman. I just don't know if we can be anything but friends after this."

"Really?"

"Friends do have deep conversations over coffee," he said, mock accusation in his tone as he held up his mug. "Check. And you did call me Matt. And that's reserved for my inner circle, so . . . Check. Check."

"I guess I did. Sorry. Finn's a bit of a talker, and I think the nickname just got in my head. I was only concerned about getting outside to Nona and—"

"No—I liked it. Not being Giorgio for once, to someone outside this house."

"Well, I'm not going to ask you for an autograph, if that's what you're worried about. No big friend expectations here."

When the glance softened and then went on a little long, Matteo cleared his throat and reached for the tablet on the bedside table. He flipped the cover open and tapped in his code. "So, as friends who don't sign autographs, I should tell you I've been reading over your letters and trying to match them in sequence with ours."

"You have?" She sat forward, leaning in to look over his shoulder. "And? What did you find?"

"That's just it. They're what a child would send to a parent. Or a friend. I'm guessing that's how Nona must have viewed your grandfather. She tells him about her aunt and cousins here in Italy— Mirena's mentioned in one. And about her school studies and her excitement to attend a ballet school in Rome not long after the war. While some of the details of her life give a picture of postwar Italy, they're more like diary entries. Your grandfather promises when she's ready, she can have back the gift she'd given him. But there's nothing about a suitcase. And he tells her he'll keep the story safe until she's ready to share it."

"I don't understand. What story?" She leaned in closer to his side. "What else was in my grandfather's letters to her?"

"Those you'll like. Look." Matteo opened the drawer in the

table. He sorted through the stack and pulled one out, pointing to a line in Italian. "See this? He's talking about his wife—Penn. Was that her name?"

"Yes . . ." Delaney breathed out slow. To see her grandmother's name in Grandpa's familiar looping script was a bit of magic she hadn't expected.

"And here." Matteo's fingertip brushed over another line. "He mentions his son. He's writing to Nona about your father."

Delaney's eyes teared without any effort at all now, as he handed her the letter and she pressed the delicate paper between her palms. "I'm sorry. I just didn't expect to be so moved by it—I can't even read what it says. But just to know . . . he's here. In these words? I can't tell you what this will mean to my parents."

She paused for a moment, feeling a deeper sense of familiarity wanting—and trying—to grow under the openness of Matteo's gaze. And she didn't want to push those feelings back. "I can't tell you what it means to me."

"I don't mind helping, Del. I want to. I could translate all of them if you want. And you could take the originals home with you when you leave."

"Thank you." Delaney wiped at a tear trying to drop off her bottom lashes. "I'd like that. Is this all of them then?"

"Sì." Matteo flipped through photos of the letters on the tablet, checking dates as he flew through. "The rest are in the drawer. But looks like the last one goes up to 4 Novembre 1967. It's the latest date I could find. But then they stop."

"Did either of them mention how Nona came to know my grandfather? I mean, if the letters were so mundane, surely something like that would stick out."

"That's where we're flying blind. Nona has never talked about the war years. She wouldn't. Not even to her husband. We know she was an orphan—her parents were killed in the war and she came to live with relatives here in Tivoli after it. But we don't know much else."

Matteo stood and crossed the room to the mosaic of photos on the far wall. Delaney followed. He pointed to one near the center—a sepia photograph in an antique oval frame. "Nona asked for her suitcase in one of her first episodes in the garden. That's when Sabine and I started digging in every corner of this house. We found the letters from your grandfather and then looked at all of her photos closer to see if we could find it. If it was real. And there it is." He pointed out two men and a woman standing next to a little girl in a sailor dress, with bold ribbons holding back twin braids and the suitcase in her hand. "I think the photo is from a church in Rome, and the people who found her relatives after the war. But she's never spoken of them, so we only know one of their names. And at least that the suitcase did exist."

"Matteo, I don't think those are people from the church. At least not one of them." Delaney breathed out. Stepped closer. And dusted a shaking fingertip over the bottom of the frame, staring at the man with the blond hair and all-too-familiar smile. "That's my grandfather."

Matteo eased in close at her side. "You're sure?"

"He's younger, but yes. I can't believe it. It's really him."

"Okay . . . then there might be something there. Because that man"—he pointed to the taller gentleman—"is Andrew, an American. He was a physician, and all I know is, he thought of Nona like a daughter. He lived here in Italy until he died in '79, and was always there for the big moments in her life. He even gave her away at her wedding. But obviously that's all before my time, so I can't fill in any gaps."

"And what about the woman? Who is she? Andrew's wife?"

"Your guess is as good as mine. I don't know if he married or not." Matteo stepped back, surveying the wall and all its stories. Until in the bottom corner, he found another framed photo, in faded color, and pointed it out. "But no doubt that is Andrew. And it means if he and your grandfather were in a photo together, they had to have known each other. The mystery woman too."

The same man in the horn-rimmed glasses and suit from the photo in the upstairs hall looked out from this snapshot. And in it was the same 1960s-style dress. The same smiling, adult Calla. The same aged Andrew, with his arm around her and the stone wall of a ballet school looming behind.

But this one had something the other didn't: a date, penciled at the bottom.

"Matt—the letters. What was the date of the last one again?"

He went back to the tablet by the bed, swiped through images until he came to the last one, and returned. "Uh . . . 4 Novembre 1967."

"Look." She pointed to the photo. "We have a match. So what happened on that day in particular?"

"I'd never have put the dates together, but I do know what that photo is. Everybody does. It's the grand opening for Nona's ballet school in Rome. It was one of the biggest days of her life. She said she kept a promise and it meant the world to her."

Delaney looked from the photo of Calla and Andrew to the aged form sleeping so peacefully in the bed. It made her think on the passage of time from the letters to the photographs and what they'd witnessed in the garden the night before . . . There had to be a connection. And she couldn't leave now without finding out what it was.

"I'm supposed to board a plane tomorrow," Delaney whispered, turning her gaze back to Calla as she clutched her grandfather's letter in her hands. "But I don't think I can. Not now that we've seen this. I wonder . . . could I stay a little longer?"

"You don't have to ask, Del. Stay. As long as you want." Matteo stood there in the quiet at her side as rain tapped the windowsill and Calla's breathing continued evenly in sleep. "Because I think you need to see the ballet school. And I need to see it with you."

Nineteen

The walk down the farmhouse hall was torture.

But not as agonizing as the hours Penn had been in labor the day before. Or the pacing Court had done, near walking the paint off the Jenkinses' front porch while waiting to hear a baby's cry. But by the next day and the first chance Court could find a few minutes alone with Penn—and for what he had to tell her—the hallway felt a mile long from beginning to end.

Even more so when he stood outside her bedroom door, trying to collect his wits before entering, only to have it open and Dr. Henry Coleman walk out.

"Courtney."

"Sir. Is she alright?" Court darted a glance to the door, then back again. And found out just how fast a man's heart could start beating near out of his chest. "The baby? Is he . . . ?"

"Miss Jenkins is just fine." And this wasn't like Henry Coleman—at least not the hardcase Court had always known—but he held up a hand meant to arrest his son's fears. "They both are. There's nothing to worry about."

"Then you're just—?"

"Doing what doctors do. Checking to see that all is as it should be with my patients. And it is."

Court's breath returned. And God help him—was it always going to be like this now? Worrying over Penn and the baby with every single breath he'd take? Court didn't know how he was going to get through what he'd come to tell her, let alone what would come after. He sure hadn't bargained on bumping into his father and having to say the same thing twice over in the span of five minutes.

"Patrick tells me you've done a good job for him these last months."

"If I did, he deserved it."

"And he says you've paid off your debts. So does that mean you'll be heading out soon?"

Court tightened his brow. *What are you sayin'?*

"I spoke with Patrick and June in the kitchen before I came back. Guthrie already told them he's signed up." Dr. Coleman looked to the door—almost as if he could see through it to the girl he'd just visited on the other side. "Does she know about you?"

Court shook his head. "Not yet. It's why I'm here."

It was then his father noticed what Court had brought—the book he held at his side.

Henry stopped. Eyed Court. But not with the usual coolness that came from disappointment. This time the man actually seemed . . . tired. Bone weary, if Court had to judge, in the way he removed his glasses and took an extra long time to rub his eyes. And though he wore the same white linen shirt rolled at the wrists and that usual black-striped waistcoat Maddie had sewn for him ages ago, something about the man just seemed different. Almost like he could be done fighting if they both tried hard enough to step out of the ring.

"I was planning to stop by the house before I go. And the cemetery. I have a few days at least before I have to report to basic."

"That's kind of you. Maddie would be, uh, glad to know you stopped by before you ship out." Dr. Coleman nodded. Firming his lips like he couldn't talk. And heaven help them. Was he choking up? The man who'd always seemed made of stone? "I could make supper. Won't taste good but it'll be filling. I don't think June's in a fair fit to be serving company tonight, even with the joys of the new baby."

"Alright. I'll come on after then."

"Good," he said, and pointed at the bedroom door. "You can go on in. They're waiting on you."

Court nodded and his father moved past him down the hall. He waited until the sound of the old man's steps stopped creaking on the hardwood, then took a deep breath and rapped his knuckles on the bedroom door.

"Come in." Penn looked up when he stepped in.

There was that greeting he'd hoped for. She smiled. So beautiful sitting there with her back against the headboard, the fire in her hair matching the crown of russet on the baby in her arms. He extended his little hand from the blue yarn blanket wrapped around him, gripping tight to the pinkie she offered.

Court walked over to the rocking chair June had pulled up next to the bed. He moved her knitting basket from the seat to the floor and sat down.

Penn glanced at the copy of Homer's *Odyssey* he was turning over in his hands. "Isn't that a little advanced? If you were thinking of reading to him."

"Maybe later," Court said, and then added, "You did good, Penn. Real good."

"He is beautiful, isn't he?" She pressed a kiss to the sleeping babe's forehead. "He's perfect."

It liked to have killed Court, seeing something so innocent and perfect like that and wishing he'd done different. Wishing he'd done right by her. But at the same time, glad he'd messed up because now Penn held a precious dream in her arms. And she wouldn't have the gift of that baby if it had worked out any other way. He wasn't sure he'd ever understand how a man could untangle his pride from his biggest mistakes. Maybe he'd always wrestle with it.

"What's his name?"

"There's time for deciding on that. I'm content just admiring the view." Penn looked down, rocking the bundle in her arms with the rhythm of a tiny jostle back and forth. "Your father just left."

"I know. I saw him. And I'll tell him goodbye."

"Goodbye?" She stared back, the only sounds between them the crackling fire in the hearth and the sleeping baby in her arms. "Somehow I knew I'd hear those words again. Daddy told me you've worked off your debts."

"I have."

"So is that what you came to tell me? That you're moving on again?"

"Yes. But it's not what you think. Guthrie and I went to town today. We, uh . . ." Court swallowed hard. Turned the book over in his hands a time or two. *Just do it. Say what you've come to say.* "We signed up."

"Oh . . . I see. So you're not just leaving. You're leaving to go to war."

He nodded. "Now that FDR's declared it. Guthrie signed on

with the marines. He ships out in a week. He's in the kitchen telling your parents now."

"And you?"

"Uncle Sam doesn't know what to make of me. Story of my life. Even though I have an arrest record a mile long that says I'm a man willing to fight, seems the US Army needs medics. And I do have medical training already from my father. Seems that's more valuable to them at the moment than a pair of fists. Or a trigger finger."

Here's where any other person in the world would have judged him. They'd have looked at the arrests . . . the pattern of drinking and brawling . . . They'd have stacked it all up and said Courtney Coleman wasn't worth the uniform they'd give him.

Judgment would have been easy there.

But not for Penn.

"Is that what you've come to tell me, too, then? To say goodbye?"

"Not only that. I wanted to tell you why I have to go. Why my leaving is different this time." Court opened the front cover of the book. He pulled out the photo of the glamorous raven-haired beauty—the Louise Brooks look-alike in the flapper dress and pearls, standing next to a towheaded gentleman in an ivory-striped summer suit and straw hat, with a stern glower for the camera.

He handed her the snapshot and then ran a hand through his hair. "That's the only photo I have of them."

"Your parents."

He nodded. "The book was my father's. And before you ask, I don't know his name. And I don't remember him. After he left, my mother was hired on as a dance hall instructor at Rose Island. We came here to Indiana when they opened in '23. And tried to make it work, just the two of us."

"I remember Rose Island. It was an amusement park on the

Ohio River, right? Momma and Daddy rented a cottage there one summer. And we all used to go swimming at the public pool as kids. Remember?"

"Yeah. Until the flood took out the entire place in '37. Feels like a lifetime ago now."

"But you never said a word, those times we all went there. It must have been hard, going back."

"It was. In a way."

Penn handed him the photo, and he slipped it back inside the front cover. "I consider my real mother—the woman who raised me—to be Maddie Coleman. I'm grateful she and Dr. Coleman agreed to take me in after my birth mother skipped town. She'd hopped on a train due west, touring as a dancer with a carnival outfit. Or last I heard. And never came back. The Colemans couldn't have children, so they gave me their name. And raised me as their own."

"Some of that I knew. I'm sorry about the parts I didn't." She smiled, supportive-like. It was enough to urge him on. "Why are you telling me all this, Court?"

"Because I have to tell at least one person who I am. And my person has always been you." He cleared his throat over the emotion that surprised him, trying to make him a fool by tripping up his words. "Maddie talked to me the day she died. Gave me that photo. Told me never to hurt another person the way I had been. She told me to use my life to help—not harm others. And if I could just do that, I'd finally be happy."

"So that's why. After the funeral? You thought if you left first, it would save everyone the trouble of one day getting hurt. Because you think you're like them. Your real parents. You think that's what you're marked to do, don't you? To leave."

Court stared at his shoes for a second and gave a flat "Yes."

"I see." Penn reached out for the bedside table, stretching for the knob on the center of the drawer she couldn't quite reach. "Could you? Please."

Court pulled the drawer open. She retrieved a small object—no bigger than a fifty-cent piece—then closed the drawer again and held her hand out to him. "Here."

"What's this?" He took it, finding an antique chronometer, and turned the embossed silver over in his palm.

"It was my father's. He took it with him to France—a wedding gift from my mother before he shipped off to war in '17. He said on more than one occasion it's what brought him home. I asked him for it, to give to you. And he agreed you should have it. To mark your time until you come home."

Court clicked it open, expecting to see a smooth cover or perhaps an inscription engraved on the inside. Instead, there was a tiny snapshot of Penn, her sepia smile cut into a circle affixed to the inside of the silver cover.

"You knew why we were going into town?"

She nodded. And wiped an honest tear from under her eye. "Of course. All the local boys are signing up. And you forget, Courtney Coleman—*I know you*. And I'd like to think I understand you after all these years." Penn sighed, a soft smile on her lips as she extended her arms, offering the now-sleeping babe to him. "So here. If we don't have much time, let's use it well."

"No—I . . ." Court fumbled with his hands, dropping the watch on the quilt as she moved to settle the baby in his arms. "Penn . . ."

"There. Not as scary as it seems, is it?"

But it was. Every last lovin' bit. Court had never felt anything so scary. Had also never seen anything so beautiful. And had never felt something so worth fighting for in his life, until that very moment.

"Now, you tell me how anyone could bear to leave something so fine, so precious and dear, unless they cared so much that they'd do whatever was best for *him*."

He dared to glance up. Eyes searching hers. Heart thumping a drumbeat and hoping a little more than it should. And a sight near to cryin' himself. "Penn, would you do something for me?"

Her eyes glazed a little, like she was trying to hold back tears too. "Of course."

"Look after my father? And this baby. And if I do come home one day, I swear I'll live the rest of my life trying to be worthy of you. If you'll have me."

"*If* you come back? No, Court. I have no doubt you'll come back. I trust God to keep you safe over there because I have faith in something bigger than us. Remember?" She paused, all the compassion in the world shining out from those beautiful greens as she gazed at him, then reached out to cradle the hand he'd braced under the baby's head. "And I have faith in you. You can't keep living for yourself, Court. Once you figure out what that means, you'll finally find home . . ."

6 NOVEMBER 1943
TIBER ISLAND
ROME, ITALY

Syndrome K patients fell like dominoes as Court shuffled by.

They'd been instructed to cough violently if ever approached by an SS uniform. Court couldn't say he looked much like one of them in a hospital gown and with a nurse wheeling an IV tower behind him. But seeing a stranger enter the men's quarantine ward might have seemed a touch too close for their comfort. So men clutched their chests. Bent over hacking. Even turned away to bark into their pillows just to avoid meeting his eye.

The hospital ward itself looked like the nave of an ancient Roman church, minus pews and worshippers, and the Sistine Chapel's finger of God painted overhead. Court kept thinking these Italians really knew how to make things that last. But at least the old space gave him options. Windows might be used for escape, if there was a semi-soft landing space down below. A metal cage that lined the front of the ward could be suited for protection, if they could figure out a way to lock it from the inside. And a steel door dominated the stone wall at the back—looking like it was bolted shut from the inside too—making any entry seem unlikely unless someone could chew through metal.

His bed was down at the far end of the row.

Court surveyed the space, finding a window high on the wall behind his headboard. He tried to steal a glance out before the nurse wheeled a metal divider screen around the bed and moved to help him climb in. Did no good though. They were on the second floor, and to see more than sky out the window meant he'd have to climb up on that metal headboard to get a peek.

The nurse pulled sheets over Court's legs and adjusted the pillow behind his back. She tinkered with the IV drip. Checked his bandages. And pointed to a broom closet hidden behind some wood paneling where she'd put his clothes—all without pause or a word. Probably because Dr. Emory had given fair warning that Court didn't speak a lick of Italian. So she did her job and ignored any pleasantries on top of it.

Court was glad to be past the worst of the pain, even if his energy did still bleed away like water down a drain. He leaned against the headboard, feeling the twinge in his neck as he sank into the pillow and scanned the ward.

"What is that?" He got her attention and pointed at the chained metal door in the wall. "The door. Where's it go?" He made a motion like opening a door and pointed at what could be behind it.

"*No.*" She shook her head. "*Una scala rotta.*"

Whatever that means.

"Grazie," he said, giving up when it seemed like she was ready to move off.

She nodded, checking past the screen panels before she took a round tin, a compact mirror, and a comb from her apron pocket. Then set them on the bed.

Court shook his head. Could be she thought he'd care what he looked like at the moment.

"*Dal dottor Emory.*" She pointed to his hair and slipped away around the screen.

"Oh. That Dr. Emory said something, huh?" He lifted the tin.

Couldn't read a word on the lid, but the image of a shoe in the center did the trick to explain. He tossed the shoe polish to the little bedside table. The comb and compact mirror with it. Court didn't care what Dr. Emory wanted. Putting shoe polish on his head wasn't going to do anything except get him noticed for looking like a fool.

A throbbing started in his neck. He could feel it with his heartbeat. Must have been from tensing up again. Court closed his eyes, clutching the pocket watch as he battled through the pain. It wasn't until he felt the odd sensation that someone was watching, staring him clean through, that Court realized he'd even fallen asleep.

That nurse must have given him something for pain before moving off as she did.

Court jolted awake to find that darkness had fallen. The ward was still, save for the sounds of coughing men. Wall sconces had been lit, giving a faint glow to the high walls. He couldn't see movement through the screen linen shielding his bed, except for shadows passing back and forth. And he had no idea what was happening, until he turned and focused on the figure standing at the foot of his bed.

There was the kid, suitcase clutched to her chest like a shield.

He sat up. "Calla? What's wrong?"

She shook her head, swinging little braids and bows, then pointed to the screen and whispered, "*Il soldato.*"

Il soldato? He sure wished he'd known to look that one up in the phrase book. "I don't understand . . ."

"*Cattivo soldato,*" she whispered. "*Scappa!*"

Minus the translation, Court didn't need to see much beyond the fear in her eyes. Those pupils were fixed on him. Staring back a little too desperately. Seemed like the bows on her head were even trembling.

Court yanked the sheets back and swung his legs over the side, putting feet to cool tile. Squeezing into the space between the bed and the wall, he could just see past the linen screen to the long span of bed rows behind them. Men coughed down the line, looking like they were hacking against death's door. But behind, far off in the shadows behind the metal grating . . . there he was.

An SS officer.

The uniform looked young for a man presumably in charge. Thirty, maybe. Trim. Tall, athletic build. And light hair just like Court's. He stood with his hat firmly on his head, pristine litzen shining in the lamplight and with a bright white surgical mask tied over his nose and mouth. He talked to a lab coat—a nearly bald man of maybe sixty years of age, glasses, and quite a bit shorter than the officer.

It wasn't Dr. Emory, that was for sure.

Court didn't recognize them, but the sight of Nazi gray watching like a hawk-eyed fixture behind that metal grating was enough to lock up the breath in his chest. He could only imagine what kind of terror must be racing through the kid's mind after what she'd been through, just to see another one of those uniforms appear.

"Soldato?" Court pointed toward the screen. "Is that him?"

Calla nodded and readjusted her suitcase in a tighter grip.

Soldato . . . soldier.

Court wheeled the IV over with him, gripping the metal tower in his palm and the wheels making an ever-so-slight squeak as they rolled.

"Kid," he whispered, motioning for her to come to him. "Come here."

Calla obeyed, walking around the bed with fast little steps that brought her huddling into the corner with him. She stepped around the IV tower to turn her back to the wall, too, and leaned into his side.

Court put a hand on her shoulder, just to let her know he was there.

They watched the officer together. And waited. And all Court could do at the moment was flex his jaw, hoping that would be the extent of it. He was shocked to feel the child's soft fingertips reach up in the midst of it and find his hand. Calla gripped tight and held on, long after the uniform and lab coat moved off again.

Something snapped inside.

It left Court fighting mad as he had been that night in the ghetto, that a little girl should have to fear for her life just for the air she breathed. He made a decision then and there. Being laid up in a hospital bed wouldn't work forever. Neither would putting shoe polish on his head do a thing to save them. He needed traveling clothes before it was over. Sturdy boots. Food. Forged identification papers for them and the girl. An understanding of Italian phrases. And most important, in case their hiding place was threatened by the devil stepping into their midst again, they needed a solid plan to escape.

Calla slept curled up in the chair next to his bed, tucked in the shadows behind their screen. But Court stayed awake all night. Looking at his pocket watch from time to time. Seeing Penn's face smiling back. Checking to see that the shadows beyond the metal grating were clear. And reading his book by lamplight.

Turning pages, Court read through the Italian primer he'd ripped out of its binding and hidden inside the worn leather covers of Homer's *Odyssey*. He took in all he could. Searching for words like the ones the nurse had said earlier: "una scala rotta"—which seemed to translate to a broken stairway. And he kept looking for answers until at last he found what Calla had said, and his heart splintered all over again.

She'd been trying to warn him, saying three things:

Bad. Soldier. And . . . *run.*

Twenty

25 JULY 1943
VILLA SAVOIA
ROME, ITALY

The door to her guest chamber flew open and Anton rushed in.

"You ought to knock." Julia set her brush on the dressing table, then turned on the velvet tufted stool.

"You can be icy to me later. I'm only here to relay a change of plans," he answered, though his attention was on parting the gold-hued curtains so he could peer out the second-story window of King Victor Emmanuel III's royal eighteenth-century hunting estate.

"What do you mean a change of plans? The car will be here any minute and I still have to—"

"Come here. You'll want to see this."

"See what?" Julia joined him at the adjacent window. She stared out, too, finding that all lay still. With not a bird in the sky, the sun beat down on the long arc of pristine villa walls lined by manicured hedgerows.

"What exactly am I looking at?"

"That." Anton pointed to the front gate just as an auto turned down the long gravel drive. Then he checked his wristwatch. "It's exactly as I was told."

When he didn't elaborate, she added, "Anton, you're scaring me. Told what? What's happening?" Julia stared out, her fingertips in a nervous flutter over the string of pearls at her neck.

Anytime automobiles—and stately ones at that—appeared without warning, it set one's fingertips to clutch pearls. And it certainly wasn't the usual transport as a row of cars came rolling along the path that cut between parasol pines and holly oaks. And with a sleek Alfa Romeo at the rear looking a shade too luxurious to have been at all common.

"The king is set to make a maneuver here today. And lest Italy should stoke the Allies' anger with an international ballet company caught in the crossfire, the captain of the carabinieri was just sent to give our road manager notice. They said if it would indeed happen, it would be at five o'clock today. And that's what it is now."

"What would be at five o'clock?"

"Mussolini's arrest."

"What?" Julia turned back to the window, palm touching the glass in a panic as she studied the tree line down below. Though with that news she'd have expected to see Italy's national police force lingering in the shadows, nothing stirred. "You cannot be serious. Here? Right now?"

All was still as a figure stepped from the Alfa Romeo at the back of the line. With his fedora-clad head held high, the figure bade a small envoy of guards to wait outside the gate. He walked toward the villa's front doors and disappeared inside.

She breathed out. "But I don't see any police."

"That's him. Believe me, the carabinieri are out there. And they won't wait long for his resignation. Either Il Duce will go quietly . . . or he won't."

"And if he doesn't?"

Anton stared back. And she knew even if he didn't say it. They'd all been lucky in Milan, and lightning didn't strike twice.

"How much time do we have?"

He shook his head. "Ten minutes. Maybe less."

Thinking fast, Julia hurried to the wardrobe and tossed in whatever would fit into a durable travel case. The last pair of silk stockings and the only pair of toe shoes she had left. A blouse. Extra skirt. A cardigan, a pair of woolen socks, and a change of underthings. A pair of serviceable T-strap shoes, the kind—*shudder*—she could most easily run in if need be.

She kept talking and tossing, if only to keep her hands busy and frayed nerves at bay. "Alright. We must have a plan or you wouldn't be here right now."

"Yes. The royal family has made arrangements for us, as a precaution. Their private secretary sent me to fetch you and then we'll be led out. Because we don't know what will happen, we're to go down the service stairs . . . away from the activity in the front wing."

"I assume we'll all go to the train station. And what then?" Julia reached for the paisley mint headscarf and fumbled as she knotted, untied, and knotted it again over her hair. Then she grabbed the Italian primer she'd kept in the vanity drawer, and the little silver-framed photo of her parents to toss on top of the rest.

When he didn't answer, she looked up in the mirror's reflection. "Anton?"

"No trains this time, Julia. It's just us. Our manager will take us out by car. We go south, as far as we can. And now that the Allies have taken Sicily, we hunker down until they meet up with us."

"What?" She stood, the travel case forgotten for the moment. "But the rest of the company. The dancers and the crew . . . We cannot leave them behind—"

"You remember what I told you that night we danced at La Scala?"

Of course she did. Yet Julia refused to remember with anything but revulsion within her.

Anton stared back now, his gaze searching hers from across the room, as if he understood anything of love. And perhaps Julia couldn't conceive of it entirely either, but at the very least she knew what it wasn't. Love did not harm. Nor did it manipulate or threaten.

Real love didn't do the breaking; it restored the broken. And that was something he could not possibly understand.

"I remember what you said. And that you believe you meant it."

"I assure you I meant every word. I won't let you be hurt again." Anton left the window. Took a step and reached toward her until she flinched back, and he stopped short. He dropped his hands at his sides in defeat. "You must see we're not leaving anyone behind. Just dividing. The stars of this envoy have a name that could be used for ransom or worse. And the Italian royal family does not want an international incident on their hands. They have a bunker, not far from here. On the property. We can stay there until dark if need be."

"And if the Fascists demand a reprisal for this action? What then?"

"We leave. Tonight."

Thunderstruck, she looked over to the costumes hanging in the wardrobe—rose tulle and ivory satin and crystal beads glittering in the sunlight. In war, such finery mattered not at all. Julia unclasped the pearls from around her neck and slipped them in the suitcase's satin lining, then lingered for a breath, running her fingertips over the etched silver-framed photo in the travel case. She said goodbye to the warmth of their smiles, then clicked the lid closed.

"An ambulance has arrived at the gate. The carabinieri have come out," Anton said, leaning half hidden by the curtain as he again peered out. "That's it. They've put him in the back. Mussolini is done."

Julia stood, suitcase in hand, not at all ready to brave the road through the pines. "Is this the end? Do we hold our breath and wait? Or let out a sigh of relief? I don't know what to do."

"We go." He eased the travel case from her grip. "Together."

Together.

They fled under the cover of darkness, descending the stairs into bunker tunnels as Julia pushed away the thought that she must place her trust in the one man she could not. And with their road manager acting as driver and one royal guard positioned in front, they were whisked into the only auto available—a luxurious black Isotta Fraschini with royal insignia on its front and sides—and sent out into the night.

They drove through the streets at a breakneck pace, heading south through a pitch-black Rome. The deeper they went, the darker the world became. And the more Julia dared to cling to hope. She sat in the back seat, palm clasped tightly to her suitcase handle, trying to convince herself the drive was all a matter of precaution as they passed buildings and Roman ruins and avoided the known check-points by bands of Fascists still loyal to Il Duce.

It seemed they'd cross the Tiber unscathed until fears turned into reality.

A motorcar lay stalled on the Ponte Cestio, idling at the bridge's far end. Their manager slowed to a stop in the center rise, making the fatal error to pause, even as Anton shouted for him to sail them back in reverse.

Too late.

Headlamps flicked on, washing their car in a blinding light.

Anton shoved Julia down a breath before gunfire swept across the windshield. She heard her own scream as she clamped trembling palms over the paisley scarf on her head. Anton's weight pressed her deeper into the floorboard of the vehicle, covering her body with his own as bullets pinged metal, shattered glass, and pierced human flesh. And it's where they remained when the motor's headlamps were doused and the assailants finally drove off with a screech of tires to cobblestone.

Julia lay in the dreadful silence for long seconds after.

Reeling. Body shaking. Not even knowing whether they were alive or dead—just listening to the sounds of steam from the auto engine, of busted metal settling, and of the River Tiber's angry current sweeping down below.

6 NOVEMBER 1943
TIBER ISLAND
ROME, ITALY

Julia looked through the crack parting the double doors topping the steps of the San Giovanni Calibita Church and peered out to the Ponte Cestio, remembering that awful night all those weeks ago.

The clearest memory she had of it now was seeing the silhouette of Father Bialek peering down through the busted window of the Isotta Fraschini, with Rome's starry sky a backdrop to his shoulders. She hadn't known how long she lay on the floorboards of the auto. Dazed and covered in blood. Shaking from shock. And unable to move or scarcely breathe at all for fear gunmen would return and rain bullets over them again.

"Can you hear me, miss?" he'd asked in Italian, pulling at the body suffocating her own. "Can you hear me?"

She nodded from beneath Anton, his body still a deadweight on top of her.

"Are you hurt?"

"I . . . I don't know." Her limbs took to shaking like she'd been left in the cold all winter. It was a fright to lose control of her limbs like that, but at least she felt no pain. "I don't think so."

Church friars had appeared then. And people in white uniforms—medical personnel? They pried open the auto doors and wasted no time checking the bodies inside.

They lifted Anton's limp form to a stretcher first, then reached for her after.

The father swept a blanket over her shoulders, attempting to shield her from the gruesome sight of their manager and the guard, whose bullet-riddled bodies still lay bloodied in the front seat. She'd thought Anton was dead, too, until medical staff rushed him through the doors of a nearby building while holding pressure to stains on his trouser leg—the only wounds she could rightly see through the dark.

It was only later that Julia discovered they'd been saved by friars of a church with an adjoining hospital on Tiber Island and learned from a surgeon there—a Dr. Emory—that Anton's injuries would render him incapacitated for quite some time. He'd taken several bullets, and even if he did survive, a severe wound to his thigh made it likely he'd never dance again. Or at the very least, not at the level of a proficient.

And they'd have no possible means of escape. Not for some time. And if the war dragged on . . . maybe not ever.

Julia had been rushed through the church doors to safety under cover of night—the same doors the Waffen-SS soldiers had marched through when they took control of the hospital weeks after. And the very same doors where she stood now with Mr. Rossi, waiting for partisans to show in the side street and retrieve the Jewish family they were attempting to help flee the quarantine ward.

"So . . . to clarify. You're not actually a nurse?" Mr. Rossi's words cut into her thoughts, bringing her back.

"What?"

"I said you're not actually a nurse." He stood at Julia's side, looking out, too, a smile just peeking out over the surgical mask to show at the corners of his eyes.

"Of course not, Professor. One role is quite enough for my dance card, thank you very much," Julia whispered behind her mask, then checked back over her shoulder that the alcove was clear. "And do keep your voice down."

With their false names assigned and forged travel documents received by Father Bialek, the Castellano family had been discharged from Fatebenefratelli Hospital. They huddled now in the shadows just through the doors to the church, waiting for the quarantine staff to transfer them over to the hands of Father Bialek's partisan contacts.

"Gutsy thing though, waltzing out in front of the SS like that today."

"I'd rather walk out there than fear the supplies on the trucks would fall into the wrong hands. And I wasn't going completely without my wits. My father was a physician, so I do know something of what goes into a doctor's bag."

"And that's not at all like saying owning a cow makes one a dairy farmer." He laughed under his breath. "We'll have to think up a better story for you in future, Ms. Dancer. And me, too, if I walk out there again before learning to speak Italian."

"I agree. My insides were knotted enough after our close call this afternoon. We should prepare better for next time."

He paused, the moment of lightness broken when he nodded and braced an arm on the door handle as he scanned the street outside. "That's just it. What about next time, Julia? Dr. Emory could be called into surgery or more refugees could show up at the hospital doors. What then? We're walking a very thin line here. And I don't like putting you at risk."

She pulled her mask down, staring at his profile. "We'll do as we must, like we did for you and your brother. And for Calla. And for the family leaving these doors tonight. Isn't that what matters in the end?"

Turning to her, he pulled his mask down too. "You'd really try to help more people like this—without a plan?"

"Syndrome K is the plan. And it's working right now. So yes, I would."

"At risk to your own life?"

Again, a one-word answer. "Yes."

With a nod that looked like hesitation, he seemed to tense his jaw. Like he was working out something in his mind and wasn't sure whether he could say it without a tinge of frustration emerging too.

"Why?"

He stared back, without quips or humor this time. And with the oddest sense of familiarity that said he understood something of the answer yet wanted to hear it from her lips all the same. Of course, Julia must have seemed terribly naive to him. Or obtuse, for what right had a ballet dancer to instruct a soldier on the particulars of war? He could have put her in her place but didn't. He just waited in the silence, patient in a way no other man had been with her before.

"What does a ballerina have to give? Truly?" Julia tipped her shoulders in a delicate shrug. "I'd dreamed all my life of dancing on the grandest stages in the world. I thought to achieve that would bring me happiness. Or purpose. And it did, for a time. But I stand here with you and find what we're doing in this one moment matters more to me than all the years of dancing that have come before it. I'm not even certain how I know that, except that I've found the most beautiful things in this life to be not of my own hand. And I can see a plan in all of that. Can you?"

"I honestly don't know."

She swept a stray lock of auburn hair back behind her ear. "I'm sorry. I suppose that was my roundabout way of saying I believe in what we're doing here, so much that it matters more than any risks we might take."

"Don't be sorry. It's just . . . I've never heard anyone speak that way."

"About ballet?"

"About anything." What was it about the earnestness with which he always seemed to look at her that could make her believe he truly meant what he said? He gave a little tick of the brow as he gazed down on her, like curiosity had captured him. "But if that's true—if Syndrome K is being made up as we go along—then how did you know . . . ?"

"About the Pervitin?" Julia raised an eyebrow.

"Yes."

"There are rumors the Waffen-SS were fed a steady diet of the drug to keep the army moving with Hitler's swift invasion of France. No doubt they've used it here in Italy as well."

"We knew that. Rumor is that's how the Germans made their blitzkrieg through the Ardennes. I never agreed with the use of Benzedrine or similar drugs in the Allied units. But even our higher-ups were seeking to battle the combat fatigue of our men. And something to ward off the shell shock seen in the last war. But there's risk. It's been shown to create a severe apathy, dulling the feeling center of the brain. Over time, it has violent side effects. And the risk of overdose is high."

"I know. Dr. Emory has confirmed that too. Still, the captain and his men use it, even here at the hospital," she whispered, checking the shadows growing in the alley as the sun was trying to set beyond the bridge. "But he says that once stopped, the drug causes a wicked withdrawal. It's come to our attention that Captain Patz has a habit of use that has grown to a monstrous degree. That makes him both controllable on one hand, if we can manage the supply . . ."

"But completely unpredictable on the other."

"Yes."

"How do you know all this? I mean, you're willing to put your safety at risk for these people. But how did you even come here? You never said."

"It's a long story." Julia looked out at the bridge. "I'll tell you sometime, if you ask me again."

A shadow of a car rolled into the alley then—old, and a dull black with dents in the front fender.

"They're here." Mr. Rossi replaced his mask and leaned out, opening the outer door.

The rounded door to the sanctuary creaked open behind them, causing Julia to jump nearly out of her skin. Father Bialek emerged, ushering the family through from the church.

"*Venite qui.*" Julia beckoned to them. "Come. Come now . . ."

The mother stopped before she descended the steps to bow her head to Father Bialek. And then she pressed kisses to Julia's hands, whispering her thanks, unashamed that tears of gratitude wet her cheeks. Mr. Rossi stepped forward and handed the discharge papers to the husband, who tucked them deep inside the front of his jacket and ushered their young son forward into the waiting car.

"God be with you," Julia whispered as they closed the doors and the motorcar disappeared out of sight.

Father Bialek locked the outer doors behind him, pausing only for a few words with Mr. Rossi, and then took his leave through the courtyard. Mr. Rossi joined her in the alcove tucked off the nave, into the space lit by the amber glow of prayer candles flickering down to the wicks and the last of the evening sun streaking through rainbow-stained glass.

"Well? What did Father Bialek say?"

"He'll send a transmission tonight, confirming they got out."

Julia exhaled in relief. "That's jolly good. Anything else?"

Instead of answering right away, he pulled his mask down again and looked at her with a comforting regard that was much more than she'd ever expected.

Steel eyes softened, as did the contours of his face. Like he understood Julia might be coming down from the same peak of adrenaline he was and needed to address it before anything else could be spoken.

"That day, uh . . . in the garden, when you were dancing. You asked me what it's like to step onto a battlefield."

She pulled her mask down too. "I did."

"It's like this—what we did for that family. What I tried to do for other families while in medical school and failed. I made a mistake once. A schoolboy error. And no matter how I wished it, I couldn't ever take it back."

"What happened?"

His jaw flexed and he stopped. Long enough to find the words that obviously pained him. "I didn't listen to the people who knew the patient best. Who were trying to tell me their son was sick. I knew it all back then. I knew *better*. And in the end, turns out I knew nothing except how to miss a congenital heart condition and watched as those parents had to bury their fifteen-year-old son."

"I'm so sorry."

"I'm not telling you for pity. If not for the war, I'd have never picked up a piece of medical equipment again. Not without pressure. And certainly not with any pride in what a medic has to do on a battlefield. You step out there and come upon a soldier who's relying on you, a complete stranger to see him through the worst moment of his life. And that life could end. Right there. In your hands. You learn pretty quick in those moments that we're not the ones in control."

He shifted his glance to the effigy of Christ in the stained glass behind the altar. "After what we did here today, there's something I feel the responsibility to ask you."

Now it was her turn to hold him in a careful regard.

"What would you say to joining forces—you and I? And my brother, when he's able. Not just for the people here, but for Calla. I help with medical supplies. You with the Italian. And we work together to get Calla to her family before my brother and I have to leave. You already said you're doing what you can for the Jews while you're here. So I'm asking you to let us do the same, and to do it with you." He held out his hand, offering Julia an American shake on it. "What do you say? Partners?"

"I'm sorry. I can't." She eased into the faintest hint of a smile. "I can't work with someone until I know his name. His *real* name."

He nodded. And flashed a heart-stopping grin in the shadows.

"Sergeant Andrew James Nelson, US Army, Clark's 5th Division, ma'am." His hand still hovered on air. "But it's AJ to my friends."

Julia eased her palm into his. But instead of shaking, he held fast there, her palm absorbing the blissful connection and the warmth of his. "Well then, AJ. I'd say that's a yes on both counts—to work as partners and live as friends."

Twenty-One

She's here! Honey? Come get on the call." Delaney's momma popped up on the cell phone, her bright smile and front porch rocking chair bobbing up and down in the video call. And then her dad squeezed into the frame, his kind eyes and quiet presence welcome as he gave a wave in return.

"Hey there, Del," he said, so much like Grandpa that she hadn't realized it until that moment. The distance and the memories both seemed to crash together, and Delaney almost felt their Dr. Coleman was back on the other end of the line.

"Dad—how are things? With the harvest and all?"

"Don't you worry about that. We're holding our own. I'm just here to say hello, and since you're staying on in Rome a bit longer, I'm not to give you any reason to cut the trip short. I think that's what I was supposed to say?" He winked and edged out when her momma gave him a playful slug on the shoulder and took over the frame completely.

Delaney gave a quick goodbye and heard him off to the side,

259

adding, "I'm handing this off to your mom now. I just wanted to get a *ciao* in to my girl before you two have your talk. And we'll see you soon."

"Yes, and as her mother, I've been wondering what she isn't saying between the lines of the few texts I've received," Edie shouted after him, then turned back to the phone. "But if you're staying on longer in Rome, I think I can guess."

Delaney shrugged down to the side of her bed and kicked off her ballet flats. She let out a loud sigh—to make a point—and stared back into the camera.

"Hi, Momma. Nice to see you too. And it's not what you think."

"Who's thinking?" She lowered her voice. "But now that your father's gone . . . all I'm saying is it makes sense after I saw that young man on camera. And saves us a trip to pick you up at the airport tomorrow, so we're all winners here. Especially you."

"If you wipe that lovely smirk off your face, I'll tell you what's been happening." Though Delaney couldn't keep her own smile back because of the frolic in her dear mother's grin. "This isn't about Rome—though it is kind of magical here. The villa and these dinners they have every night. And then there's the city itself and this incredible garden they have that covers the whole back courtyard. And the food . . . I wish I could say you don't have a rival with your cooking, but I was not raised to lie."

"Oh, hilarious." Edie took a sip of tea, the little paper label dusting the side of her mug against a breeze that swept across the porch. "So what about the suitcase? Have you learned anything that might connect it back to us?"

"That's just it. You won't believe this, but I saw Grandpa! In a photo on the wall right here in this villa."

"They have a photo of your grandfather? Really?"

"Yes! It's one I've never seen before. Here—I'm going to send it." Delaney ticked through photos on her phone until she found the right one, dropped it into their text thread, then sent it off. "And you should have it."

Edie set her mug down. "Alright . . . Looking." And in a moment, with a little wave of surprise that washed over her face, she said, "You're right. That is him. Would you look at how young he was? Just wait until your father sees this. And your aunts. They'll love it."

"The little girl with Grandpa is Mrs. Santini—with the suitcase in her hand. See? And we aren't sure about the woman, but we know the other man was American too. Do you remember Grandpa ever mentioning someone named Andrew—like he was a friend or maybe someone he fought with in Italy during the war?"

"No. I can't say as I can. But your grandfather wasn't one to talk about those years much. If he said anything, it was that he preferred living in the here and now after all that—at home with his patients and his family. And your father's never mentioned anyone named Andrew either. Your grandfather and he must not have been too close of friends if we've never heard of him."

"I guess not. It just doesn't make sense. The photo obviously means something to Mrs. Santini or she wouldn't have it hanging on her wall. That makes us believe there's something more to it. A lot more. And that suitcase is important somehow."

"And it might also just be coincidence. People take photos all the time, Del. And in a long life like hers, Mrs. Santini would have many of them to display. Maybe this was just some moment captured in film, and your grandfather happened to have been there. Did the letters say anything about it?"

"Well, no. And that's gotten a little complicated. Way more complicated than we thought, actually."

"Mm-hmm. More complicated than *we* thought?"

"Yes. And Matt was wondering whether going to the ballet school might—"

"Oh, Matt, is it?"

"*Matteo* thinks there's something to the photo too. Together with the suitcase. So we're going to his grandmother's ballet school this evening. They have more photos there, and we think maybe they could tell us something about what happened in the war. Or how Grandpa was connected to this family. I mean, it's worth a try."

"Can't Mrs. Santini tell you about it?"

A knock sounded on the door.

"Oh—just a second." Delaney dropped the phone on the bed and walked over, slightly relieved to open it and find Sabine instead of Matteo standing there. At least she'd have a little more time to think through how to respond to the unexpected presence of little butterfly wings in her middle before she had to play it cool again under his smile.

Sabine presented an ivory garment bag and held it out to Delaney. "Here you are, my dear. For you—a gift from Mrs. Santini."

"A gift? For what?"

Sabine looked back, authority in her expression. And Delaney could believe everything Matteo had said about the matriarchs who ran that villa. They were a force to be reckoned with when they wanted to be.

"You are going to the city tonight. Sì?"

"Yes. But just to the ballet school. And we might grab dinner while we're there, but that's all."

"Exactly what Matteo said. But you know men—they can forget to think things through. At least in the same way a woman would. You cannot have dinner in Rome without a proper dress. Every good Italian girl knows that." She held the garment bag up, the tarnished gold hanger top hooked in a graceful arc over her fingertips. "American size six, sì?"

"Uh . . . yes."

"*Va bene.* This is good. It will fit. And Mrs. Santini never misses a trick about that. *Never.*" Sabine handed the bag over, and Delaney's heart leapt a little to see the lettering of *Valentino* shining out in gold foil print. "Buona sera, dear."

Sabine winked and swept off again down the hall, leaving Delaney gaping at the end. The phone still lay on the bed with her momma chirping, "What? What is it?" at the ceiling.

"I'm not sure what just happened," Delaney said, hurrying back to the call. "But I think Mrs. Santini gave me a dress."

She dropped the bag on the bed and opened it up, carefully because the old zipper was in fact very old—vintage, no doubt—and looked like its teeth wished nothing more than to snag whatever masterpiece might be hiding behind the ivory exterior. And as the tines parted, she had to catch her breath or lose it completely.

Inside wasn't just a dress . . . it was *Roman Holiday.*

From the square neckline to the all-over ivory Italian lace, a belted waist, and the elegant A-line drape. This was the dress of every Audrey Hepburn–loving, little girl's fantasy. And the woman had just presented it to her.

"What is it?"

Delaney grasped for the phone again.

"It's a dress. Uh . . . And I think it might be real. Like, a real vintage Valentino. Look." She held it up, her hands actually shaking a little as she panned the camera to the block letters on the front of the bag. "It must have been hers. I can't believe she's given it to me. Should I accept? How can I accept something like this?"

"My dear, how can you not? It's for tonight—I did hear that little secret float over to the phone speaker even if you didn't want to tell your mother." Edie smiled, arching her brow just enough to punctuate the point. "So, dinner. In Rome. With a young man. Isn't that unexpected?"

Delaney didn't mind the teasing. Or the reality of how life didn't care much to make sure it followed any of her plans. Not when she'd just stepped over to the floor-length mirror and held the vision of such a dress up against her. "Have you ever watched soccer?"

"Soccer?"

"Yeah."

"Well, let me see. I don't think so. Your father always has been more of a college basketball man. Or sometimes football. But then, don't they call it football over there?" Her mother's voice lifted from the phone as she talked on about football—the American kind or what it was to the rest of the world. And then let Delaney go so she'd have enough time to get ready for a night out in Rome, only because she gave a solemn promise to send a long and very detailed text after.

Delaney tried to imagine Rome at night and couldn't help but wonder which man would show up to escort her through it: the world's version of Giorgio Santini or the Matt few people really knew.

The thought she'd had on the first video call with Matteo came back to mind as Delaney stood in front of her reflection in the mirror, running her hand down the length of the midi skirt.

It was breathtaking . . .

It was Rome . . .

And if Delaney dared imagine this time, it just might be *perfect*.

PRESENT DAY
PIAZZA DI TREVI
ROME, ITALY

•

Leave it to Rome to convince a girl she'd just stepped into a dream.

Exquisite cuisine, a vintage Valentino dress, night lights illuminating the famed Trevi Fountain piazza, and leaving a restaurant with Matteo looking like he'd just stepped from a Milan fashion ad as he slipped into an easy stride beside her. It almost made Delaney forget what in the world they were supposed to be doing—together—on a night out in Rome, and the counterbalance of Giorgio Santini's acclaim set next to Matteo's wish for anonymity.

Diners idled over wine, Mediterranean fare, and laughter and lively conversation, filling restaurant tables that framed the piazza. Lovers walked hand in hand alongside tourists snapping photos of the Trevi district's famed Baroque masterpiece at night. Buskers played Pachelbel's Canon on violins for couples who slow danced nearby. And as the evening sun tucked into bed behind the buildings, Delaney and Matteo faded into the throngs of tourists moving along the cobblestone streets, the storied setting doing every bit of whispering possible to her heart.

"Sorry about the table being in the back room. I just didn't want . . . you know. To be on display. I don't go out to restaurants much these days."

"It's alright." Delaney smiled. "After the Spanish Steps, I understand. And I don't blame you. It seems like it would be easier having your dinners at home."

"Sometimes."

They walked past the fountain's iconic mix of water and light and tourists snapping their selfies, its stunning turquoise-and-gold painting a vision under a starry night sky. They paused at the fountain's edge, and he pointed them to a street that opened off the piazza. "So the ballet school is this way, in the Jewish ghetto."

Matteo glanced down at her Italian stilettos—another delicious procurement from Sabine—noticing her feet had never looked so incredible in public. But also noticing the cobblestone streets seemed a bit treacherous and she wasn't exactly prepared for a footrace through them.

"If you don't mind the walk?"

"I don't mind." Delaney offered him a little backhanded smile as she took a half step and promptly wobbled her ankle against the edge of a cobblestone. "And . . . if I can stay up on two feet, that would be a good start."

"Don't worry. I'll catch you if you fall."

The course to the Jewish ghetto wasn't that far—but it seemed long enough for a girl in some serious heels and a boy trying to watch her wobbly steps. But the views were sterling. And the conversation even better. Matteo led them along the ghetto district's thoroughfares with shops and homes, the site of Roman ruins, and a centuries-old street market, and then there it was. A stone building with tall windows illuminated by long mirrored walls, the soft glow of light inside, and a black awning with *Accademia di Balletto* in brass lettering at the top.

He slipped a key in the lock and held the front door out for her, adding, *"Benvenuta,"* as she walked by.

"What does that mean?"

"A way of saying come in. And that on behalf of Mrs. Calla Santini you're welcome here."

The halls slept—no little dancers about, of course, after dark. But Delaney could imagine them in such a place, with their laughter rolling off the high arched ceilings, toe-pointing across the polished floors, and filling practice rooms with the birth of artistry.

It felt right to stay hushed, so she peeked down the hall's darkness and whispered, "Can we be in here?"

"They won't mind. Mirena's family runs it now. I mentioned her before. The woman you met at dinner that first night?"

"Yes. I remember."

"She's Nona's cousin. With her daughters, they took it over fifteen or so years ago. And this is it." Matteo stood back. Looked up at the span of wall photos before them, all framed in classic black, and all in deep contrast shades of ivory and black, and the older ones in sepia tones. "Given the walls in her villa, you can guess whose idea this was."

"I can. And it's breathtaking." Delaney pressed her fingertips to what looked like an Italian quote painted on the wall. "What does it say?"

"A rough translation of something Nona has always said: '*To dance must always be a joy.*' Ballet was that to her anyway."

She smiled. "'To dance must always be a joy' . . . I like that."

"So here it is. Nona's life's work on a wall." He pointed down the length of the hall. "The photos go all the way down, around the curve, to the back doors. We can head that way if you want."

In snap after snap, memory after memory from all the time Mrs. Santini had taught in the space, the photos painted a portrait of the school's long history. Delaney and Matteo followed the arc of the glass wall, beyond stilled rehearsal rooms and quiet hallways, studying the images of Calla with her students. They showed prima ballerinas who'd gone on to find success in the performance world. And candid shots showed the everyday grit and grace that was ballet, in delicate poses set against taped ankles and toes, perfect postures alongside the weariness from hard work, and graceful lines of balle-rinas whose poses were broken up only by reams of tulle and lace.

Delaney pointed out a charming snap of a young lady with a pert bun sitting atop her crown and a dimpled smile she'd flashed for the camera. It looked as though it captured the moment she'd received her first pair of toe shoes.

"Just look at her."

Matteo nodded. Maybe in a little too revealing way—she caught something in his profile as they came to the end of the line. A photo from the dedication showed Calla with Andrew again, a black-and-white photo similar to the ones they'd seen before. But with nothing else of consequence, he braced his arm to the windowsill and stared out to the inky night beyond.

"So, not exactly anything that helps, is it? I was hopeful but worried this might happen too. That we'd get here and find ourselves right back where we started."

"No—it does help. It shows us who Nona is, and that's what we really came for, isn't it? The rest we'll figure out. If it's not here, it'll be someplace else."

Delaney looked out with him, through the wall of windows spanning the back of the school. It was dark now, light glowing from nearby flat windows and string bulbs drifting over rooftops like fireflies dotting the sky across an empty space. "What's out there?"

"A garden. Nona just couldn't have a proper ballet school without one." He unbolted the double doors, then pressed them open at the center. "Want to see?"

"Yeah, I do." Delaney followed Matteo out, to a garden space very different from the one at Villa Adriano. This had no grand lemon trees or flowering beds. No trickling fountains or grand valley of Tivoli's old town as a backdrop. This place was reticent and refined, with hedgerows and manicured pines, storied buildings on all sides, and walls lined with stone rails, climbing vines, and benches bracketing the path.

They stepped out, following the semicircle path around its border.

Delaney watched her shoes on the cobblestones, taking careful steps with him. "Would you answer something if I asked?"

"Of course. I'll try."

"Did that wall of photos in there make you think of Carly?"

Matteo paused on the path and she did too. He turned to her and slipped his hands in his pockets. "I'd be lying if I denied it. Or said I wasn't surprised you caught that. It's not what I expected you to say."

"Really? Then what did you expect?"

"I don't know. I'm conditioned to the questions about my past. The money. Fame. And then the failures splashed across the news headlines. You know, when a man's poor decisions mean he makes his bed in life and can't feign shock when he has to lie in it."

"Ah. So Giorgio Santini is used to public scrutiny. You are . . . famous."

"I hate that word."

"I know you do. It's why I haven't said it."

"And it's why I left that life. Finding out what we can for Nona . . . and going home to Carly—they're what I have right now. They're what matters to me. That feels important in a way that so many other things no longer can. And that's private, so I don't usually let people in enough to learn it."

"Then that's something you and I have in common. I hadn't expected to let anyone into my family's pain. Or mine after losing my grandfather. I came home for a funeral only to find that nothing in my life makes sense. And I still don't know what comes after all that."

"But you will."

"How are you so sure?"

Matteo sighed like he was shifting away from a straight answer. And braced his hands at his hips while shifting tracks to something else. "I'm sorry, Del. I had no idea the suitcase would cause this. All the questions you must have now . . . I never meant for you and your family to get pulled into this when you already have so much you're dealing with. I wish there was something more I could do to take it back."

"It's okay. We're here, you and me. And we're trying to set it right, aren't we? We're trying to help Nona. You said it yourself—that's what matters."

Somewhere in the distance, a melody drifted up, breaking the garden's slumber.

It could have been from one of the flat windows or a radio left piping from a rooftop. Or, if Delaney had her bearings at all, it might have been from buskers and their speakers at top volume, still playing out in the street for Rome's nighttime revelers.

Matteo pointed to the sky. "Music."

If Delaney had been even a fraction younger, nervousness might have turned her stiletto at the ankle, in a little tell of a girl waiting for a boy to ask whatever it was catapulting through his mind. As it was, she smiled. And prayed she could withstand the wait.

He held out his hand, palm open. "Dance with me?"

"Now it's my turn. I really didn't expect you to say that."

"Goes against principle, you know, to visit a ballet school and not try dancing at least once."

"When you put it like that, I guess. But first . . ." Delaney took Matteo's hand and balanced to kick off her shoes. "That's better. They're stunning, but I can't withstand another minute of the torture."

"I did say I'd catch you if you fell."

"You did."

"And I stand by it," he whispered, and swept a hand to the small of Delaney's back. Stealing her breath away when his thumb moved, the caress burning through the fabric of her dress. And with his other palm still curled around her fingertips, he pressed their joined hands against the front of his shirt. They swayed to the music—her bare feet brushing the tips of his shoes. And she felt sure he must have been able to feel her heartbeat pressing into his.

"I've made mistakes, Del. And I have to own them. That's what you saw on my face in there, staring at those photos: regret. I don't see it the way the Finns of this world do, that Brazil was some monumental achievement I should be proud of."

"But it was. Your goals in that match? I watched the videos—they were incredible. *You* were incredible. I've never seen anything like it. And you can't downgrade what you've accomplished just because you made poor choices in your life. We're all human, Matt. We all make mistakes and we learn from them. You have to allow for forgiveness in there somewhere. Without grace, none of us would make it a day."

He furrowed his brow a little. "Wait—do you mean to tell me you've been reading up on Giorgio Santini?"

Oh, how Delaney wished a vintage dress had the power to make a woman feel so much more polished than she was. But here she stood in bare feet. Dancing in the dark. And caught for having spent hours staring at photos of his heart-stopping smile.

And he looked like he could read every last bit of it playing over her face.

"Maybe," Delaney snapped back. She prayed he couldn't see her nervous smile in the dim light shining down from the rooftop terraces. "But I'd never admit to it in a million years."

"As much as I hate to admit it either, I'd gained a lot at the start of my career, but I lost what really mattered. I just didn't see it. And then one day after Brazil, I woke up in a hospital bed. Alone. With my career in a freefall and not knowing how to be anything other than the world's version of Giorgio Santini. It sounds like a small thing, but when I was discharged from the hospital, no one was there to pick me up. I took a taxi home that day, to the Spanish Steps."

"You mean that's how you knew about the flats? You actually lived there?"

"I did, even if I was hardly ever home. I had the driver stop out front of the building, and I just got out. And that's how I know there are 135 steps to the top. Because I counted every last one of them as I fought with crutches to climb up. When I finally got there, I realized I wanted a different view in this life. I didn't want to be that man anymore. And even if I couldn't make up for the past and have everything restored, I could choose a different road than my own father did. And be a good dad to my girl."

"So you moved to New York."

"Sì. I retired. Moved to New York. Then I came back here to be with Nona for a while when things started getting bad. For the second time in my life, it felt like everything could change. Like I could lose it all again. And I wondered, after you and I talked this morning, if you might understand all that. If you might understand . . . me."

Delaney swallowed hard. And looked up at him as a tiny breath of wind danced a blonde lock to wave out across her cheek.

Of course he caught it and tucked it back to the soft side of her neck like a trained Casanova. Charming ex-footballer that he was with umpteen tabloid articles to prove it, Matteo had more than enough practice wooing girls who wore Valentino. Though inside, Delaney wanted to forget all that. Maybe shout a "yes"—she understood failed expectations and broken plans and wanted nothing more in the world than to be the girl who'd crash into a kiss with him despite all of it.

Matteo stilled their swaying, and under his gaze, she forgot how to be afraid of tomorrow.

Light blasted the garden like a spotlight from above, with a party that had just moved out to a covered terrace overlooking their solitude. Delaney stumbled back with the flood, nearly tripping over her shoes. He caught her, held her up at the elbow—enough that she could right herself with her palm pressed to a stone bench nearby.

She eased back upright, trying to catch her breath under the glow of terrace lights that shone down. And somehow she saw it when they hadn't before—a patinaed plaque embedded in the stone.

"Are you alright? I didn't think I'd actually have to catch you. I was sorta just saying it."

"No, I'm fine. But, Matt, look—" Delaney reached for his hand, tugging him closer to her side. She stopped short, breathless, and whispered, "4 Novembre 1967. Same as the photograph."

They leaned in together. Delaney ran her fingertips over embossed letters that spelled out the ballet school's dedication in aged bronze.

"The dedication of your grandmother's school? It was for someone named Julia Bradbury. You don't think she's the woman in the photo?"

"I think she could be. But we never knew about a dedication. This must have come later. Or maybe Nona did it on her own." He laced his fingers with hers, holding tight as they stood together and the terrace melody continued its dance through the night. "But now we have to find out why."

Twenty-Two

"**M**r. Rossi? I have a gift for you."

The greeting pulled Court back to the present. He snapped the pocket watch shut and slipped the metal circle into his pants pocket as he sat up on his bed.

Julia stood before him in the nursing uniform she wore more often now and used the false name still visible on his medical chart. She held a stack of clothes and pair of shoes in one arm, and metal tools gripped in the other hand.

He swung his legs over, shoes to the floor.

"Well, almost. And this isn't exactly a gift, but Dr. Emory did ask me to deliver it." Julia did the same thing they always did in the ward—looked past the screen shielding his bed and made certain no one was watching as they conversed in English. She handed the wares over. "So here it is. Everything we discussed."

Court checked them over. Warm traveling clothes and sturdy boots, in case they had to make a run for it during the colder months.

He lifted a chisel from the top of the stack—the cobbler's tool weathered but good quality. A wooden round ball handle and dull, lean blade was set off by a slight hook at the end. The mallet was antique brass, solid and sturdy in his palm.

Looking up to the steel door, he judged the thickness of the hinge knuckle, and the thinner chisel was a good pairing. She'd done well.

"This'll work fine. Thank you." Court knelt to slide the tools under the lip of his mattress, hooking them in the metal tines of the bed frame. "And the key for the metal grating?"

Julia nodded, arms crossed over her middle, as she kept an eye beyond the screen.

"In the pocket of the trousers. Dr. Emory was able to have a copy made for both wards, just in case. And I have one as well."

Court found the key and pocketed it, then tucked the clothes into the shadows between the radiator and the bed. He stood before her.

"Good. I'll keep it on me. And you have everything you need for the women's ward?"

"We do. Yes. The same tools on our side. All that is needed now is what we hope never happens—for Father Bialek to sound the alarm. But we're ready, in any case." She kept her voice low but allowed the ghost of a smile to linger upon her lips. "I've also come bearing ill news, I'm afraid. I regret to inform you, Mr. Rossi, that you've just been diagnosed with Syndrome K. Officially. It's on your chart."

"You don't say?"

"I'm very sorry. You'd been discharged from your surgery recovery, but now, learning this . . . Well, you understand why you have to stay here in the quarantine ward until your symptoms abate. It is standard procedure with a Syndrome K diagnosis."

He nodded. And coughed a little for good measure.

"We also need documentation before we can officially discharge you from the hospital. And Father Bialek is waiting to hear the particulars of how and when your, um, friends plan to meet back up with you. They've assured us orders will be forthcoming, and you and your brother ought to be ready to move when they do."

"Orders are orders."

"And we knew they would be coming, didn't we?" she asked, suddenly not looking as bright as she had before.

"The point is, what do we do about it? I keep thinking about the kid. How we're no closer to finding her family than when we first came here. We don't even know her real name. And no matter how hard I try, she won't budge on it."

"I know. I've been trying too. Every day during her ballet lessons."

"At least she's talking more. I guess that's a good sign. Even been trying to teach me Italian. I tried to argue with Calla that it would be a losing battle, but she didn't understand a word I said." Court smiled, thinking she was a smart little thing with her pointing at objects in the ward and giving him the words, then waiting while his tongue tripped trying to repeat them. "When I mess up, she gives me this look. Only ever seen that kind of thing work on my mother's face, never on a little kid's."

Julia laughed. A kind, genuine laugh that made him think of Penn and the easy way they'd always talked. AJ had obviously turned his eye to this lady; seemed now Court could see something of why.

"Calla is a quick study. I should have known she had a teaching heart to go with all that cleverness. And at such a young age too."

The lightness of the moment didn't last.

Court's smile faded from his lips and hers dulled too. Seemed for the complicated paths that brought two Allied medics and a Brit ballet dancer together for the benefit of the same little girl . . . that time could be over soon. And Court's mind always went back to that alley in the ghetto. Replaying those moments in his mind. Feeling a gut punch every time he thought of leaving the kid alone.

"Calla's special, isn't she?" Julia asked.

"Yeah. So how can we go and just leave her?"

"You may not have a choice, Court," she said, referring to him by the real name they always kept so quiet in the wards. But if she'd said it now instead of "Mr. Rossi," she must have meant it. "I'll make certain we find her family, no matter how long that takes."

"And if she has no family left to find?"

"That's something I'm not willing to consider—not yet. Calla has people here who care for her. And who are willing to watch over her, *Salvatore*." Julia smiled at the nickname she'd once bristled over, adding a little emphasis for good measure. "That's the most important definition of family I can think of. And I promise I won't leave her, not unless it's to put her in the arms of one who will look after her for the rest of her life. You have my word on that."

Court sighed. And peered past the screen to the long stretch of the ward—beds full all the way down the line with people just as displaced as Calla. Maybe just as wounded. And fearful of those SS uniforms too.

Whether he wanted it to or not, Court's glance kept returning to the rows of cherries tucked on the floor between the table and his bed. Calla had only just trusted him with keeping the treasure for small increments of time. And when she came back to the ward, the first thing she'd do would be to reach for the suitcase and keep it within holding distance. She even slept hugging it.

For those weeks they'd been holed up together there, it kept telling Court they needed to know why.

Julia seemed to notice it too. She looked back at him. "What do you suppose is in it?"

"I don't know. I was going to look. I about convinced myself to do it ten times already. But it's locked and every time I got close, I just couldn't break it open. Felt wrong to break that trust she has in us."

"I know. She brings it with her to the garden every morning and keeps it where she can see it at all times. It's only recently she's left it with you." Julia sat in the chair next to the bed, reaching down to run her fingertips over the suitcase handle. "AJ and I have talked about it too. Maybe it holds a doll? Or a bottle of her mother's scent? I'm not sure, but it seems it ought to be something like that for how she protects it. That makes it feel like a sacred little thing sitting over there. And makes me want to keep her safe all the more."

"Maybe I should ask her about it, you know? Maybe she'd warm up if I tried to say it in Italian. With that teacher thing she's got going on. Might work."

"Whatever we do . . . it's time to try something."

A flash of movement at the front of the ward caught Court's attention past the side of the screen. Father Bialek stood behind the metal grating, looking over the space in a quick survey of the bed rows. He said something to a nurse walking by, who pointed in the direction of Court's bed at the far end.

"What's wrong?" Julia whispered, popping up from the chair.

"Father Bialek is headed our way—at a run. And that's never good." Court took a step but stopped short and looked down to the tools hiding against the mattress. "Alright. If this is it, we're ready."

"I'll go to the women's ward. We'll lock the gate and set about getting that steel door open as fast as we can."

"Right. And we'll meet you on the ground floor—AJ, Calla, and I will be waiting outside the garden gate. Just like we talked about."

"Yes. I remember."

They met the father at the end of the bed when he came around the screen. Seemed he was searching for Julia, because his whisper was immediate. And though his words were in Italian, his tone was weighted with urgency.

Court didn't like that look at all.

"Oh no," Julia whispered over choked words, but nodding understanding as she covered her mouth with her hand.

Father Bialek swept off down the rows and disappeared past the metal grating at the entrance. Court knelt to free the chisel and mallet from their recent hiding place. And started unlacing the boots to slip on, should they need to run.

"So this is it? We have to get these people out now?"

"No." She pressed a hand to his shoulder to stop the furious lacing of the boots. Tears built in her eyes. Not at all a good sign. "It's not that."

Tension hit his body. Court shot to his feet and looked to the suitcase in the corner.

Not Calla . . .

"You mean the kid? Is she—?"

"No. Calla's fine. And she'll be back shortly. So do what you think is best with the suitcase." Julia wiped tears from under her eyes and let out a deep breath, composing herself for goodness knew what as she edged closer to the screen. "I must go see to this first."

"Okay. We'll hold the fort here. But what is it?"

The dancer who always seemed to walk with grace and poise, in that instant, seemed like she could have melted to the tile beneath their shoes. Her eyes flashed with something that looked like hurt or pain, and she released a shaky breath.

"There's been an incident, Court. And the SS have taken your brother."

Twenty-Three

W hy must her fingers choose to turn all thumbs at the worst possible moment?

They refused to cooperate, Julia fumbling with the linen ties of her mask while she ran from the quarantine wing, heart thumping in her chest as her feet carried her through the hospital halls.

Father Bialek had little information, save that two men had been brought into the hospital, both suffering from gunshot wounds. One was an SS soldier, complicating matters enough. But the other apparently was a civilian caught in the crossfire who'd been gravely wounded and had coughed up blood in the vicinity of the other.

That cough, of course, was feared to be Syndrome K.

In an abundance of caution, both men had been admitted through the quarantine wing. And as AJ had been the first doctor the SS had encountered, they'd whisked him off to render emergency aid.

All Julia could think was thank heaven AJ was worth his salt as a combat medic and would know what to do to convince them he was a physician. But what would happen if he was pulled into surgery with staff who didn't speak English? Or questioned by Patz or any other officer, and she wasn't there to translate the Italian for him?

Father Bialek had run off to secure the quarantine wing from further intervention, leaving Julia and her nursing uniform as the one ally to step into the fray alongside AJ.

Please, God . . .

Don't let Captain Patz get to him first.

Julia whisked around the corner, and heaven help her, but the sight of AJ alive and unharmed hit like a tidal wave. Even if there was a swarm of SS uniforms not far off, it took every shred of restraint to walk up to him as a nurse would—calm and steady—instead of running and throwing her arms around his neck.

AJ stood over a gurney in the hospital hall, his broad shoulders to her.

He worked on a plain-clothed man who was quite still, with skin ashen and his abdomen bleeding like a faucet of red had been turned on over the gurney's side. The SS soldier was laid out on a gurney, too, set off a good twenty feet behind. He moaned over a wound in his thigh. It, too, spread a stain of blood beneath a tourniquet to run down his uniform trouser leg, but it didn't seem as grave a situation as the other—yet.

Julia eased up next to AJ's side.

He didn't look up, just kept applying pressure to the man's wound. "What are you doing here?"

"I'm here to help, Doctor," she said, loud and in Italian so anyone close by might hear the ruse. Then softer, in English, she asked, "AJ. What . . . what do you need?"

The sight of his blood-red hands and the crimson leaking from a hole just under the man's ribs caused a wave of nausea to wash over her. Julia drew in a steadying breath.

"I want you to go, Julia. *Now.*"

AJ flashed a sharp look to her that said there was truth in what she'd guessed, that by being here she was at as much risk as he, and that he refused to accept.

She could not leave his side. The only thing to do was grasp the injured man's palm. So she held his limp fingers in hers as she shook her head. "I'm not leaving you. So tell me what to do for him, and I'll do it."

"Please, Julia."

"Doctor?" An SS officer cut in behind them, barking in Italian. "That one is dead, ja? He looks dead to me."

"What did he say?" AJ whispered to her.

"He wants to know if this man is dead. I think he would insist you render aid to a German soldier before an Italian civilian, who may or may not be a partisan in their eyes."

"Then he won't like where I'd tell him to shove that opinion."

"Doctor!" The SS officer bellowed this time as he looked from his wounded comrade to advance a step forward. "This soldier is still alive. You will see to him. *Now!*"

"You must stay back, sir." Julia turned to the SS officer, as authoritative as she could be without crossing the line of insubordination that would not be forgiven. She raised a hand, with respect but enough firmness to hold him off. "We suspect Syndrome K. This patient has the symptoms."

Blissful words. The Waffen-SS halted. Even backed up a step, the threat of the plague doing its job to put distance exactly where they needed it.

"There's nothing more I can do for him," AJ whispered to her but kept his hands moving over the wound like he was working in a feverish attempt to save the dying man. "I have to go to the other one."

"What? No—you can't."

"Julia, I have to go with them or they'll know something's not right, and I won't risk them questioning you. Or Calla."

She looked at the growing swarm of uniforms filtering into the hall. "Then I'll go with you."

"You can't. I appreciate the sacrifice you're willing to make more than I can say, but you can't bluff your way through surgery. I don't even know if I can. I'm doing no less than you told me you would, remember? To save those in the wards, I have to go with them."

The resolve in his eyes said he was right, and she knew it.

He was forcing her to see differently, that he was risking his life for Calla. For the people here. Even for her. And those eyes were telling Julia why, just as they were saying the one thing she wasn't ready for . . .

Goodbye.

She reached for his hand, gripping tight to his crimson fingers over the man's wound.

Though she tried to stifle it, the word "no" came out on a tiny sob behind her mask as Captain Patz marched down the long hall, speeding toward them with two nurses in tow. He rarely ever breached the line of the quarantine wing if he could help it, but now an injured SS soldier meant he wasn't likely to back off.

"I . . . can't let you go."

"Just stay with him. Please? He shouldn't be alone. I'll come find you after," AJ whispered, squeezing her hand until she looked at him. *"I promise."*

Julia stared back, wishing she'd have said something—anything—if those were the last seconds between them. But hopeful words died on her tongue, and the void between them became a chasm as AJ squeezed her hand again . . . and let go.

She followed the sight of his strong shoulders down the hall, as he hunched alongside the gurney to see to the soldier's wound. They rushed into the surgery. And then the doors closed behind. And the hall was still again.

Suspected partisan or not, the SS didn't seem to care what became of Julia's dying patient after that. They didn't stop her as she wheeled the gurney back into the depths of the quarantine wing. She walked on until the peace of the empty church sanctuary opened before them. It felt right to wheel down to the end of the pews. Should the man open his eyes, he'd look up and find the painted image of heaven staring down.

An alcove against the nave was cast in the warm glow of flickering prayer candles. Julia couldn't guess where the friars had found them—wax had disappeared in the early days of war. But with shaking hands still bathed in the man's blood, she followed the glow and reached for a taper stick.

She lit a candle and said a prayer. There was naught else she could do for the poor man behind her. Or for AJ. Or for all the people hiding in the quarantine wards, seeking their own reclamation now that death hunted them.

"*La ragazza . . .*"

The man's words jarred Julia from her entreaty. She dropped the singed taper stick and rushed back to his side.

"It is alright," she whispered over him in Italian. Not knowing what else to do, she reached out and held his hand. "I'm here with you."

He cracked open his eyelids, eyes of brown staring up at the vault of painted stucco.

"The girl . . . ," he repeated on a weak breath.

"What did you say?"

"*. . . con la valigia . . .*"

What?

The girl with the suitcase?

"Sir?" Julia patted his cheek. "Look at me. What did you say? You're searching for a little girl? One with a suitcase? Sì?"

His eyelids fluttered and drifted shut again as his breathing slowed.

"No, please!" She patted his cheek again. "Wake up! Tell me about the girl."

The man shook his head. "She is lost . . ."

"No. The little girl with the suitcase. She is not lost," Julia insisted, handing over whatever she could to keep him talking as long as possible. "She is safe. She is here! Do you know her?"

"Sephora . . ."

"Sephora? Is that her name?"

He shook his head. "No. For . . . the girl."

What energy remained in him was summoned for the action of releasing the clenched fist of his right hand. It was then Julia noticed what she and AJ hadn't in giving attention to the wound on his left side—a scrap of paper was concealed, crumpled in his other hand. Julia took the paper and, desperate, read it—just a few words scrawled over the margin of a torn newspaper advertisement.

A woman named Sephora was seeking a little girl . . . her niece? She'd carried a suitcase at the ghetto but was lost. They were looking for her.

"This Sephora—is she in Rome?" Julia pointed to the scrawled words, her fingers fluttering the paper before his eyes as they drifted closed. "Please! Who is looking for the girl? What's the girl's name?"

"The girl . . ." He squeezed tears out of the corners of closed eyes.

"Yes? What about the girl?" Julia gripped the scrap of paper in between their joined hands. "I promise we'll save her. Just please, tell me her name."

His breathing weakened.

"Please . . . ," she sobbed, hands gripping his. "Sir? Don't go."

Painted stucco and flickering candles were the only witnesses to Julia's vow that they'd save the little girl without a name. The man let out a last deep, rattling exhale and stepped into the painted image of heaven beyond.

"Julia."

The rough and beautiful sound of AJ's voice left Julia's thoughts and suddenly became real as it carried across the stillness of the hospital garden. She turned, her breath puffing out a cloud as she exhaled, and the silver glow of moonlight that had shone upon empty cobblestones and leafless trees was instead cast upon him.

AJ was alive. Whole. And waiting on the garden path.

Whether it was a declaration or the wild faith in him Julia hadn't even known existed until that instant, it didn't matter. She picked up her feet and ran, not stopping until she was safe in his arms. He enveloped her waist, holding tight for long seconds as he buried his face against her neck.

She gripped back, lacing the hair at his nape between desperate fingertips.

It wasn't planned, heaven help her, but seeing him released a flood of emotion Julia hadn't the first clue how to untangle in her heart. And she certainly didn't know how to withstand the butterflies dancing frenziedly in her middle when he held her. They just came together—she to him and he to her—in a desperate kiss, as if they'd shared such a thousand times before instead of only in that first breathless instant.

They stood still. Silent and safe. Melded. Fears allayed for the moment. And everything else in the world was forgotten except what existed in the space between them.

"You're alive," she whispered against his lips, eyes closed, trying not to cry. And then she leaned back to look up at him. "How are you standing here right now?"

AJ nodded. Somehow in a flat way that said he wasn't quite certain how to feel about what the SS had forced him to do.

"It's alright. Dr. Emory was coming out of surgery as we headed in. He took over and let me assist. Patz backed out of the surgery due to the risk of exposure so there was no fear of being discovered, even if they did watch us through the surgery window."

"You saved the soldier's life then?"

"We did. He's quarantined in another part of the hospital, so he'll be kept away from the other SS but separate from our wards too. So you're safe."

Julia nodded but shivered. Maybe it was from relief, but he released her and shrugged out of his doctor's coat to slip it over her shoulders.

"Better?" He ran his hands over her arms to warm them up. "Court said you came out here a while ago."

"I couldn't bear it. Pacing in the rectory. Watching the clock. Listening to Anton go on about being a prisoner in the church and that we ought to leave this place now. But go where? The rumors in the streets do not bring confidence. And he can barely walk as it is. We couldn't survive out there. Not now. We must wait for the Allies. And all the while, I knew they had you and there was not a thing in the world I could do about it."

"I'm alright. I'm here. And I'm not letting go now." AJ lifted his forefinger and brushed back a lock of deep amber that had come loose from the waves pinned at her temple. "Besides . . . I made someone a promise. And I wasn't about to break my word to her. I'm just sorry it took me so long."

"That's all that matters," Julia breathed out, looking him over. And taking the liberty to trail a fingertip up to the scar on his brow, like she'd wanted to do so many times before.

"Tell me about these rumors. What have you heard?"

"I don't know all of it. Just what Anton was able to overhear from the church courtyard. He said Patz often brings his officers to the balcony to relay orders, thinking no one will overhear them. Or if they do, they won't understand what they say. But Anton speaks German. And he says the SS have reason to believe the partisan presence is building in Rome, perhaps planning to overthrow the Reich when the Allies break through. And they believe they're coming. That's what happened to the wounded SS soldier tonight—another partisan skirmish. And it seems Patz is fortifying supply trucks here at the hospital. In the event the Allies should close in, they'll be ready to escape. And if they have to, they've made a plan to clear the Syndrome K wards before they go."

"To stop the disease from spreading. God help us." AJ shook his head, his expression growing somber again. "What about the other man? The civilian?"

"He died." Julia bit her bottom lip, the swell of emotion that accompanied the words almost too much to bear. "Hours ago. I stayed with him but . . . I couldn't help him."

Feeling her chin give away her thoughts with a blasted quiver she couldn't control, Julia stared down at her oxfords. Shame gripped her that she could not steel herself against tears that betrayed her, showing weakness. AJ had seen men die on the fields of battle in the most horrific ways. It wasn't likely one ever got used to it, but how could she tell him that the man had been the first time she'd watched a life slip away and felt the guilt that she hadn't been able to do more to stop it?

"Julia?" His thumb found her chin, coaxing her eyes back to him. "I'm so sorry. I wish I could tell you death doesn't rip your heart right out of your chest every time, even with a stranger. But I haven't figured that part out yet. And I hope to God I never do. I don't want that part ever to become easy."

"I know." A rogue tear tracked down her cheek. She swept it away with the side of her palm. "It seems we could break apart here at any moment. It's all so fragile. Tonight made me realize that even more. This is not a game. What we're doing for the people, and for Calla? It is everything to them. And to us."

"Court said the man gave you information—a message of a woman claiming to be Calla's aunt? Is this true?"

"I believe so. Her name is Sephora. It could be coincidence, but I've been thinking . . . What if it was more than a random gunfight in the street? If the man was looking for word on any of the un-accounted Jews from the ghetto, why would he try to come close to the hospital unless whispers are circulating on the streets that we are a haven for Jews? If that's true, it terrifies me all the more because the Germans could know too."

She glanced around the empty garden, praying its walls didn't have ears. And wishing more than anything that the sleeping winter garden would see them through safely to spring.

"We need to share this news with Father Bialek. And Dr. Emory. Court's waiting in the church now so we can talk it over with him first. We agreed to let Calla sleep a little longer before he asks about the suitcase. But it might do well for us to be there, too, so you can translate."

"Alright. And then . . . come sunrise." Julia gazed up at the span of sky. Reams of gold had just begun to invade the horizon over the top of the garden walls. "Court told me. Orders came in over the wire. It's time for you to go."

"We'll have to return to our unit at some point—yes. But we talked it over. It's right to stay and make sure those we care about are safe before we walk out those doors, not knowing what will happen. The Allies are pushing hard against the Germans' Winter Line, but that's all we know. It could be days before they get here. Or weeks. Or longer."

"You'd stay without knowing? Are you sure? The US Army could prosecute you for this. AJ—you'd go to prison for desertion."

"And what makes you so sure they'll ever get the chance to send me?"

No need to elaborate the reminder. He was a soldier. And soldiers died.

AJ looked down on her, steel eyes having gone so tender, as if he, too, was considering the same unspoken fears. "Alright. Given what's happened, we should be ready." He ran his hand through his hair, like he was thinking with his palm. "Okay. We'll ask Father Bialek to send a transmission to the Allies that's truthful—technically speaking—so he doesn't risk them thinking he's playing both sides. It'll buy us some time at the very least."

"And what would it say?"

"Private Coleman has been diagnosed with Syndrome K, hasn't he?" AJ smiled. Wide. And brilliant—that look she'd seen the first night they met. "No one knows it's fake. It just means he can't be discharged. That'll give us enough time to learn about Calla's family before we have to go back. We'll have Father Bialek reach out to the partisans. See if they can verify any existence of Sephora. And in the meantime, it could give the Allies enough time to get to Rome."

"And if it doesn't?"

"We do what's right. For Calla. For the people here. I won't leave while that's still on the table. And I won't leave you in the middle of it."

"We finish what we started then." Julia reached over and grasped his hand, lacing his fingers tight with hers, finding strength in the connection. "Like we said? Partners."

"We did shake on it." He lifted their hands, pressing a quick kiss to the underside of her wrist. "I don't know how they do it where you're from, but we Yanks take a handshake very seriously."

Julia looked around them, seeing the darkness of their garden haven breaking in the light of dawn. "You know, we've been thrown together in this place and in the oddest way, it feels like we've become family. That makes me believe everything we're doing here is worth it. And I'm grateful we get to be a part of that. Maybe we should inquire with Father Bialek if we might take a photograph of us with Calla? I know they've hidden a camera in the church."

"We could ask. It'd be nice to mark a good memory out of all the bad." He brushed the curl of his knuckles against her cheek, then pressed a soft kiss to her lips. "And it's a good idea. This is family. It's home, for now at least. And I promise you—we'll make sure what's happened to the Jews of Rome doesn't stay buried. Calla will leave these doors alive, and the story we're living will go on with her when she does."

Twenty-Four

Night blanketed Tivoli with a starry sky and an autumn breeze stirring the courtyard lights in the trees out the villa's back doors.

Inside the great room Delaney and Matteo had made a spread on the farmhouse table with laptops and notepads, mugs of coffee, and the last of Sabine's pastries from that day. Matteo kept his glasses on as he scrolled through articles on his tablet. And Delaney sat at his side, legs curled under her in the dining room chair, and her hair twisted on her crown with a pencil stuck in a messy bun, working late into the night as they pored over any research they could find on one ballerina named Julia Bradbury.

Delaney popped another bite of sfogliatelle in her mouth and dusted her hands on a napkin, then scrolled back through the article she'd been reading. "Okay—here's another one." She placed a hand on Matteo's forearm, pulling him away from his search to see her laptop. "Look. This photo of her onstage—it's the same woman from our photograph. The article talks about how she was a ballerina in

London before the war and was supposed to debut at Covent Garden in the spring of 1940 . . . But the Vic-Wells Ballet closed down. And instead, she toured with a troupe across England for the next couple of years. It says here she performed with other famous names during the worst of the Blitz. They even danced in the underground—the East End Tube stations—and she did it for free."

"What about Italy? Or the end of the war? Does it say anything about her after that?"

"No. That's just it—I scrolled all the way down and nothing." Delaney jotted notes on her tablet, of names and dates they could cross-reference. "I don't understand. There's no mention of her after 1942. It's as if she just dropped off the face of the earth. And she never danced again. At least not professionally. There are no performances that name her anywhere in the decades that followed."

"It makes sense on one point, though. I looked up the other dancers' names, the ones who were listed as part of the troupe performing in the provinces. Margot Fonteyn was one, and she danced for the Sadler's Wells Ballet at the Royal Opera House after the war. The rest of the list went on to dance . . . in London. Milan. St. Petersburg. New York. All except for one other—a dancer by the name of Anton Vasile."

"Wait a minute. He was her partner in those early years of the war, wasn't he?" Delaney flipped through her notes, scanning through until she found it. "Yes—here. They were famous at Covent Garden, the pair that was supposed to be the lead dancers in *The Sleeping Beauty* in 1940. This doesn't make any sense. Why would two world-renowned ballet dancers never take the stage again after the war . . . ?"

Delaney stopped, not wanting to say it out loud.

"You mean unless something happened to them?"

"Yeah. I hope not, but what else makes sense?"

"I don't know. But I'm starting to wonder. All it says here is that those records were sealed by the British government in the years after the war, at the request of the Vasile family and by agreement of Miss Bradbury's estate, through her London representation—a talent agent by the name of Winston Peterbrooke." Matteo sighed and leaned back in his chair. "Why would they agree to that, unless something did happen during the war? And maybe they wanted to keep it quiet."

Delaney had considered it.

You only seemed to find a bench or plaque or building dedication when something had gone terribly wrong for the honoree. Finding that stone bench in the ballet school's tucked-away garden was a huge step forward to connect the suitcase to Calla's story, but it didn't come without bittersweet tones. For young Calla never to have mentioned Julia in the letters . . . The suspicion formed a pit in Delaney's stomach, and she didn't much care for how that felt.

"What should we do?" Matteo broke into her thoughts.

Those eyes held her in a steady gaze while he braced a hand at his chin. Like he was thinking—maybe a little too much. And something flip-flopped in Delaney's middle at the realization that he was being so open about it.

And was sitting so close.

Out of desperation she reached for her mug—the coffee left in it now ice cold but enough of an excuse to shake off the nervous energy and get her bearings in the next room. "I think I'll just go . . . make a fresh pot."

"When did we hit three o'clock in the morning?" He took off his glasses, tossed them on the table, and rubbed his palms over his eyes as she walked by to the kitchen. "Why don't we take a break?"

"A break is good," Delaney called back, quiet enough not to wake the whole house as she stepped into the kitchen.

The open shelves and long butcher's block island were bathed in the soft glow from the wall sconce, and light from the dining room pierced a stream down the stucco hall. She turned to the sink.

Okay, Delaney. You can do this.

Wash the carafe. Fill with water. Find coffee . . .

Delaney nosed about the open shelves, checking canisters and bowls for coffee grounds.

And try to ignore him when he looks at you like that . . .

Things always seemed harder when she was trying not to admit something had completely tangled her heart with her mind.

It must have been Rome—intoxicating old city that it was. Or that silly dress that had Delaney wondering if she could ever do it justice by wearing it again in any other place in the world. Or maybe it was dancing in a garden with him . . . Who did that? Who tried to fall in love the first week she'd met a man, unless meeting that man was as unexpected or as wonderful as a whirlwind trip to inarguably the most romantic city in the world?

"Del?"

"Yeah?" She whirled around, dropping the carafe with a clatter to the bottom of the sink, splashing water against copper walls. "What?"

Matteo walked over. And seemed to notice the fact that she could lose track of . . . everything when he was around.

The water still gushed from the faucet as she pressed the back of her hands to the sink lip.

He stopped in front of her. Leaned over, arm stretching around her body to shut off the flow, his face coming dangerously close to hers in the process.

And not moving away. "You alright there?"

"Yes," she whispered. Nodding like a nervous fool. And not breathing when he stood only inches away. "I'm fine. You?"

"Did you want to just take a break?"

"A break?"

"Sì. Do you want to keep working, or call it a night?" He leaned in. Braced a hand to the lip of the copper sink, the warmth of his skin brushing the side of her palm in the process.

"A break is good, I think."

He reached over, taking the liberty to pull the pencil from her hair, and smoothed the waves with his palm as they fell to her shoulders.

We should definitely take a break . . .

Or not.

Because one instant they were two business partners standing in a kitchen, and in the next, Delaney had lost the battle to stay untangled from him. Rome or romance or vintage Valentino . . . whatever she could blame it on, Delaney pushed herself an inch forward into the tension zone between them and pressed her lips to his. He met her in a blink—thank goodness, with the same idea—his arms encircling her waist as they leaned together into the sink.

And that was what it felt like to be lost.

"Ahem."

A light flicked on.

What was it with them and lights trying to interrupt every last little wonderful thing they tried to start?

Delaney turned to the sink again, hand clutching her mouth, and Matteo left a void between them, stepping back so fast he must have bumped the center island enough to jostle the olivewood bowl of fruit on top. It crashed to the tile, scattering Italian lemons around

Delaney's bare feet. She stooped, chasing them with her hands before they rolled under the skirted counters.

"I'm sorry to push in at this hour, you two," Sabine said from the doorway. "Please do beg my pardon."

"No—it's alright. We've just been working late . . . I'm sorry if we woke you." Matteo ran a hand through his hair. He knelt by Delaney, helping her retrieve the runaway fruit and put the rescued pieces back into the bowl. "Is, uh, Nona alright? I can spell you if you want to go home."

"No. Mrs. Santini is fine. But we were not asleep. That is why I've come to find you."

He stood, discarding the bowl on the counter. Delaney did, too, the rest of the lemons forgotten as they found resting places on the kitchen tile.

"What's wrong?"

"She is asking for Miss Coleman."

Delaney swallowed hard, and even after the humiliation of being caught in a serious lip-lock in the dark like a couple of lovesick teenagers, she took a step closer to Matteo. Maybe it was instinct, maybe not. But it felt right to stand alongside him for whatever Calla might want.

"Mrs. Santini asks for you both." Sabine folded her hands in front of her. "She wishes to go to her garden."

"Now?" he asked.

"Sì. Right now. You have the suitcase?"

Delaney nodded. "We do. Upstairs. But it's locked."

"Va bene. Go and get it, per favore. She asks that you bring it. And both of you must go with her."

Matteo must have felt Delaney grasp his forearm, because he reached up with his other hand and pulled her palm down until his fingers laced with hers. "I don't understand. Why now?" He squeezed her hand. "Is Nona . . . here? Does she know what's happening?"

Sabine nodded. A soft smile pressed her lips. "Sì. Mrs. Santini may not know all that is happening, but she knows her suitcase is close. And she says she would like to have it now. As long as this lasts, you may wish to bring your phone to record it. It is time to tell a story, and she needs your help in order to do it."

Twenty-Five

Court had been about the same age as the kid when he carried a suitcase too.

Memories flooded his mind from that time. Those flashes of moments, of his birth mother putting on lipstick in the mirror of their Rose Island summer cottage. Of him tooling around the resort grounds—a little kid unwatched and untethered—as she escorted men across the dance hall floor. And a memory of her driving away while Court stood in the road between the Colemans, gripping the handle of a suitcase with little else but ratty clothes and an old book tucked inside.

He couldn't guess what Calla would remember like that, of the war. He hoped it wasn't only what she'd witnessed in the ghetto. Maybe there was something to help inside the suitcase, so she could cling to the good memories of her family in the midst of all the bad that had happened to her.

Court looked to Julia, sitting opposite them in the last church pew, with AJ behind.

"Well? What did Calla say? Will she tell us what's in it?" The kid nudged up next to Court as he asked, leaning into his side with the suitcase gripped tightly in her lap.

Julia sighed, though keeping her features warm and approachable, it seemed, for the little girl's benefit. "She says no."

"Not surprising." Court patted Calla's shoulder, hand resting on her blue sailor dress. "This kid's got spunk. It's what I like about her."

"She says no, that is . . . unless she can show you. And only you."

Court tipped his brow. "Me? Why me?"

"She seems to understand why we need to know what's inside. But Calla says she's made a promise not to share the contents of the suitcase—or even her name—until it is safe. And her family is all back together again. So if she must break this promise, she says she will not do it for anyone but you."

"But aren't you her teacher? It's been little-girl dance recitals in that garden every morning for weeks now. Or you—" He looked to AJ, protesting because wouldn't their leader stepping in give them the best chance of getting out of this mess? "You're the one who got us out of the ghetto that night. You were the one who brought her here. Who saved us. And who made sure the doctors hid her while I was knocked out. Doesn't that mean anything?"

AJ shook his head, that steady combination of strength and forbearance always in his steel eyes staring back. "But you were the one who ran out to save her that day. You picked her up and pulled her out of a nightmare. That's the part she remembers. And that's what meant the most to her."

Court sighed when Calla hugged her suitcase a little tighter—they obviously weren't getting anywhere with the current conversation. But how did they explain what she didn't know? Best Court could say was they were on borrowed time. He was leaving. AJ too. And could be soon. Calla should put her trust in anyone but him. Not when all Court would do is hurt her on top of how she'd already been broken.

He wasn't worthy to accept anyone's steadfast belief in him.

Not like that.

Not when leaving was what he did best.

"Private Coleman." Julia cleared her throat softly. "Calla understands what is happening here, but only as she sees it. As a child would try to understand war. And of the few words she has said, she's told me that she believes you to be her savior that night. She prayed to a God she could not fully understand when her parents were killed in the alley. And you were the answer. God used you to save her. And that's why she gave you the pet name that she did."

"I'm nobody's hero or protector, and certainly not a savior. It sounded funny at the start, but I think the kid's serious." Court shook his head in fierce denial. And feeling close to pleading with them if need be. "And I can't be that. Not to anyone. She doesn't know who I really am."

"Regardless, she's chosen to trust you. And it's her decision to make."

"Come on. Let's leave them to it," AJ whispered behind Julia, brushing his hand over hers to help her up. "We'll be just outside in the garden if you need us. Come out when it's done."

Julia and AJ rose together, leaving them in the pew.

Court listened as the sound of their footsteps faded away, as the door to the courtyard opened and then died with the singing of hinges as it closed again. And in the stillness, with just the kid and him sitting before a gilded altar, Court took a deep breath.

"You sure about this, kid?"

Her answer was to reach under the collar of her dress and pull out a delicate gold chain, weighted at the end by a tiny key. Calla swept it over her neck and slipped the key into the lock, turning it until a *click* echoed out against the sanctuary's high ceiling. And then she turned the suitcase around, presenting the treasure to him.

Court looked into Calla's eyes, so beautiful and innocent as she held her gaze on him. He lifted the lid with a little creak of the suitcase hinges and rested it against the wooden back of the pew. Then Court broke the connection with her gaze and, finally, looked down.

Inside were ghosts: photos filled the case to the brim, surrounded by ruffled walls of white satin.

Calla watched, saying nothing as Court lifted them out. The faces of nameless children . . . couples smiling on their wedding days . . . groups gathered at dinner tables and families standing in front of villa doors . . . He sorted all the images carefully, laying them in stacks on the pew.

Were these families she knew? Were they her family? And were they all gone now?

Laced through the pile was a host of papers. Land titles maybe, with official-looking seals. Or home deeds. Birth registries or wedding certificates. Even a few bankbooks had been tossed in, alongside some sort of travel documents, with photos and stamps from past journeys. Some were in pen and ink. Still others were in pencil— handwritten notes scrawled on the backs of photos. Others were notes on pages ripped from books. One was even from an old, yellowed catalog page, with a message of words scrawled through printed advertisements of shoes and sundries for sale.

Court emptied out the rest, thinking that was all that was there. Until he saw paper wrappings stamped with little pink daisies peeking out from the bottom.

Court connected his gaze back with hers, asking permission without words.

Calla reached in instead and pulled out the package herself, then set the present on the pew in front of her. It was a birthday gift, by the look of it. And while it had been opened already, it appeared new. Someone had taken great care to refold the paper and tie a perfect crimson bow on the outside. She untied it now, folding back paper like it was made of crystal and air, and spread the contents in front of them.

Inside was a perfect new pair of toe shoes. Too big for her, looked like. Must have been something she'd received and hoped to grow into.

Pristine, ballet-pink satin.

"Kid—you had these all along?" he whispered. "You wanted Julia to teach you to dance because it was already on your heart. You want to use these one day. We just didn't know it yet."

Taking the toe shoes in her little hands, handling them with great care, Calla revealed a card and a photo that lay beneath, inside the package. Court lifted the photo. The image of a couple stared back. The mother held a baby in her arms, presumably Calla, and another woman stood nearby, whose features made her seem strikingly close kin to the man.

Calla pointed to the woman. "*Zia* Sephora."

"This is Sephora? Zia? Who—your aunt?"

She nodded, as if understanding.

"I see. You want us to have it so we know how to recognize her if she does come searching for you. Or if we take you to her. Smart girl." Court flipped it to the back to find a name:

Franca Bero

"Franca? Your name is Franca?"

Calla pointed at herself and nodded. "Franca Bero," she whispered, and tapped the photo again.

Data di nascita:
16 Ottobre 1938

And then, with the date and the card, a pang of realization stabbed him.

Court flipped calendar dates in his mind, going all the way back to when he'd first woken at Red Beach, trying to count the passage of time. Then to the days and weeks after their trek to Naples . . . And then Rome . . . And to their operation that morning when they'd fled from the Portico d'Ottavia, and everything that transpired to bring them there, to that very moment.

He was sure of it now—October sixteenth.

And looked up.

"That day in the ghetto . . ." Court swallowed hard, courage crumbling. "It was your birthday?"

She said nothing in reply. Couldn't understand him anyway. Just began the careful job of placing the contents back inside the case.

And it hit him. This wasn't just the sharing of a little girl's treasures anymore. Court had witnessed the worst of war and the most gruesome of deaths, for years now. And he'd thought it had hardened him. Yet Calla had seen the same face of war. And even Court didn't own the strength to do what this little girl had done—offering to trust another, and in it, to bare the very depths of her soul.

Calla closed the suitcase and turned the key in the lock from the necklace around her neck. Then sat back, waiting for his next move.

He didn't have one.

"Look—kid. You don't want me. I can't help you. You think I can, but I can't. I'm too far gone." He wished he didn't sound so much like he was pleading with a little kid—especially one who couldn't understand a lick of what he was saying. "I'm no hero. Not when I'm the one who's lost. I never told anybody this, but I need saving, too, okay? Just like you do. Just like everybody. I've just never been able to say it out loud."

"Salvatore." She looked up at him. "Amico mio. Grazie."

"I don't . . . I don't know what you're sayin'. I wish I did."

Calla pressed her family's photo in his hand and something squeezed in Court's chest. Just like the last time, in the hiding place in the ghetto, he couldn't ignore that whisper inside.

They two were more alike than he'd known.

Maybe Court didn't have a suitcase now, but he carried keepsakes too. A photo of his own. An old book by the bed. A stack of letters Penn had been writing to him since he'd signed up, but he still wasn't brave enough or near worthy enough to read, let alone answer. He had a watch weighing down his pocket and a truckload of memories of people who mattered most . . . all of these things, the story of the years he'd walked this earth. And in all that time, Court thought he'd been battling all by himself.

He didn't want to run anymore. Neither did he want to put up his dukes and fight.

This time, Court wanted peace.

The kid slept at his side through the early morning hours, the suitcase hugged in her little arms. And Court waited with her. Staring up at the images of heaven painted high up on the church ceiling. And holding tight to the photo she'd given him.

For the first time since all the running and fighting—and his own warring—had begun, Court started to believe the busted-up boy sitting in the pew might actually have a chance at becoming a better man. He wasn't sure what faith even was. What it looked like. Or if he even deserved it. But if he could stare up at the cross hanging on that wall and believe redemption was possible for every living being, no matter what they'd done, Court knew he needed it. And maybe the same God who had looked after Calla in her darkest moments could see far enough to reach down in the pit and pull him back to safety too.

The only thing in the world Court wanted to fight for as much as Calla in that moment was to get home and prove he could change. For those he loved, he was willing to give up everything just for one more chance to try.

Twenty-Six

Remember—chin high. Shoulders back. And eyes fixed. Sì?"
Julia adjusted Calla's form as the girl moved through her five basic foot positions, warming up for their morning dance lesson in the hospital garden.

"Now, choose a spot out in front of you and keep your eyes locked there." Julia pointed the direction of the garden wall, with the light drift of morning fog rolling in from the Tiber. "That spot will help you hold your balance as you move. And smile, if only on the inside. You may be called to dance through injury. Through fatigue. Or through an unsettled mind. But to dance must always be a joy, no matter the circumstances. Remember that and it will serve you well."

Winter had been unforgiving, and the skies over Rome cried their tears through spring.

With unamiable weather and an uptick of caution in the quarantine wards since the turn of the new year, the number of days Julia could take Calla outside to dance had thinned. But on this morning, the sun had awoken in a generous mood. It dried out the garden with golden warmth cast upon the shoots of new blooms and clusters of buds on the trees.

The return of spring couldn't help but give Julia hope.

The transmissions Father Bialek took in over the wireless had increased tenfold. It was more than rumor now—the Allies were indeed pushing toward Rome. And Julia dared to smile inside too—just like she'd instructed her student—for everything pointed to the fact that the days left to be sequestered in the hospital might be a blessed few.

Soon they might be able to see Calla home. And Julia's great hope was that the ballet lessons would give her something of this time to take with her, beyond war and loss. Maybe this would give her hope as it had once given Julia. They had a unique pain, they two, both having lost their parents. It was something she ardently wished to help Calla heal from if she could.

"Every ballerina knows to set her feet on a firm foundation. You must commit to do this every morning, even when I'm no longer at your side. Learn it so well that your arms and legs shall remember these positions without you being required to think them through. Do you promise?"

"I promise," Calla said, her words soft. And sweet. And always fewer when she was focused on perfection of her form.

They spent a pleasant hour there, dancing in the grove along the garden path, and took great care not to be seen by the SS as they cut back through the church courtyard. Calla trusted Court to look after the suitcase now so she might cradle her ballet slippers in her arms like a badge of honor, she having been enchanted enough by her garden lessons to insist upon bringing her own toe shoes, even if she was years out from being able to wear them.

That, Calla said, was as a *real* Italian ballerina should.

Pulling masks up over their smiles, Julia led them around the corner from the courtyard to the quarantine wing. But in the time they'd been hidden away in their own garden world, a new darkness had infected the hospital halls. And the terrifying sight of uniforms now blocked the doors to their return.

Calla saw the soldiers and froze, dropping her ballet slippers to the tile at her shoes.

Nazi police stood guard, heavily armed. Masked. And by all appearances, meticulous in their efforts to inspect the identification of all entering the quarantine wing. Just as they'd done for the Jewish refugees who'd already passed through the hospital, Julia must present documentation in order to get back in—when she had none.

Julia stooped, using the action to reach for the ballet slippers and then fixing the buckle on Calla's Mary Janes as an excuse to kneel before her. She caught the little girl's attention and drew her back from the terror of the uniforms, instead trying to smile through brightened eyes over top of her mask.

"Not to worry, darling," she whispered. Giving the air of calm on the outside but frantic as she searched the space for any sign of AJ or Dr. Emory. "I will not let them hurt you. Just hold tight to my hand. Sì?"

"Sì," Calla squeaked out, though pitifully brave.

"I need you to pretend for me. Please? You must cough. Hard. Like you feel quite sick, in your tummy and in your chest. And do not look the soldiers in the eye. Look away, as though you'd much rather be snug in your bed. Can you do that for me?"

"Sì, Miss Julia."

"Alright. Va bene." Julia squeezed her hand. "Let us go."

A soldier barked an order—their turn. They stepped forward.

"Papers?"

This one spoke Italian, indicating they'd gone to the trouble to bring in a soldier who'd be able to converse with the patients and staff. For what purpose though?

Julia obeyed, stepping forward.

And waited, watching as the soldier eyed them both. Praying that she could employ her stage skills to put on a performance that she looked just scared enough to be rightly intimidated before a uniform of the Reich, but not enough to be truly guilty of anything that should require a more thorough inspection. It was a delicate tightrope trek between two worlds and they, caught on its wire.

"I am staff, sir."

"Staff. You still must have papers."

"We have been through a Gestapo check already. And I wasn't instructed there would be a checkpoint at which I would need them in future. Not when I am working. The oversight shan't happen again, sir."

"And the girl?" He glanced back and forth between Calla and Julia, his eyes stone, revealing nothing behind his mask.

"She is a patient." Julia took a deep breath and gave a light squeeze to Calla's shoulder. She responded by coughing and sinking into Julia's side, burying her face in her uniform skirt. "It is Il Morbo di K."

The soldier backed up.

Searching identification papers of those moving through the doors was one thing. But having a confirmed case of the plague a mere foot away caused alarm to flash in his eyes.

"They are with me," a voice cut in from steps away down the hall.

Julia looked up and let out a tiny exhale behind her mask, relieved when she heard his voice.

AJ had answered in perfect Italian—bless him, for she hadn't a clue how—and marched straight through the quarantine doors in a smart suit and tie and doctor's coat, with a confident stride like he owned the entire hospital. And he didn't stop until he'd eased a step in front of Julia and stared the uniform down for the grave mistake of daring to inconvenience *them*.

"This is a nurse in our unit. And my patient." AJ eyed the soldier as he presented falsified admission papers with the Syndrome K diagnosis stamped at the top. "They are allowed through."

"And they have been through a Gestapo security check, Doctor?"

"Sì." AJ reached out to Calla. She raised her arms in the air and he swept her up in his own without missing a beat, like a doctor caring for his young patient might have done with the youngest ones a hundred times before. "You may speak with Dr. Borromeo."

"And your name?"

"Dr. Athenos Rossi." AJ snapped his fingers at another solider holding a clipboard before a small crowd of men, standing before the quarantine unit doors, coughing like death was amongst them. "You there! This is a nurse, and these are Syndrome K patients. They are allowed through as well."

With *Il Morbo di K* on admission papers, the soldier wanted nothing of an encounter with a confirmed diagnosis. And certainly not whatever might come of the ferocious coughs of men or a little girl plagued by impending death. AJ's authority was unwavering. He kept one arm tight to Calla. With the other he held his palm out, demanding that the clipboard fill it.

The Gestapo soldier didn't question. He handed the admission papers and clipboard over, and in a breathless instant their party was through and rushing down the quarantine wing halls.

"How did you do that . . . ?" Julia couldn't make sense of what had just happened, even as they hurried in the direction of the Syndrome K wards. "You've been studying Italian? When do you sleep?"

"Not exactly. It was Dr. Emory's idea. He had us memorize a few phrases a while back, just in case Court or I were questioned. At least we'd have some answer that way." He smiled, took her hand, and led the new patients through at a swift walk. "Looks like it worked."

AJ set Calla down just inside the men's ward, her little Mary Janes hitting the tile floor. Court called out, "Kid!" as soon as they were through, from his place at the far end of the bed row, gripping her treasured suitcase in his hand.

Ballet slippers turned to streamers on pink satin ribbons as Calla ran all the way down the aisle, past curious refugees who sat up, now alert in their beds.

Court swept her up in his arms, muscling her in a tight hold, and waved to them before moving with her back toward the steel door.

Julia turned to AJ. "What's happened?"

"Dr. Emory sent me out to the garden to find you, to try to keep you away from the wards. I was too late." He turned to the first at the front of the group of men—a young man with a tradesman's hat and jacket, leather messenger bag slung over his shoulder, and eyes that had an unmistakable confidence set in their deep amber. "You are Aleksander?"

"*Tak*, Dabrowski." He nodded. And in heavily accented English asked, "And you are Sergeant Nelson, US Army?"

"Yes. Glad you made it through."

"And just in time too." Aleksander turned to look at the men standing behind. He tipped his head to the back of the ward. "Is that Private Coleman?"

"It is."

"Good. I will speak with him. The friars gave us instructions so we know what to do to get our people out."

Our people . . .

You are Jewish too.

Aleksander rattled off something the men behind him didn't hesitate to put into action. They rushed off across the hall, presumably to flood into the women's quarantine ward as he swept back to the long span of men's bed rows behind them.

"Julia," AJ whispered, pulling her into his arms. He shook his head. And pressed his forehead to hers with clamped eyes and a tensed jaw, like a man did when he was in pain and didn't want to own up to it. "Dear God. I thought you were . . ."

"We're alright. Nothing happened, thanks to you."

No matter the stark ratcheting up of energy around them, he placed a palm to her cheek and held it there for a soft breath—as though breathless himself.

She placed her hand on top of his. "AJ, you're shaking."

"Yes." He nodded. Even laughed a little, for how a soldier—with his tough-as-nails reputation, Court had once said—looked just as rattled as she'd been. Yet very rightly so.

"And here I thought soldiers never got scared."

"We're no different than anyone else, Julia. We just know what we have to do and do it. And we always know what we're fighting for when we step on a battlefield. Maybe I didn't really understand that until I met you."

"I'm here. We're with you. So there's nothing to fear now."

Julia gazed around the ward then, as a subdued sense of panic sparked.

Court was moving about quickly, with Aleksander at his heels as they readied the men in the ward for some impending threat. Showing them what they could use as weapons. And as noiselessly as possible, moving furniture about and turning beds on their sides.

"Those soldiers at the entrance have caused all this . . . Who are they?"

"Gestapo—Nazi police from Via Tasso prison. Father Bialek received an urgent transmission that as of today, the Polish Corps of the British 8th Army has taken Monte Cassino from the Germans. That's only about eighty miles from Rome. They've broken through the Winter Line, and the Americans are pushing inland from the coast."

"That's good news though, right? If we can just wait until the Allies get here! Surely that will be soon, and they'll free everyone from these walls."

"We can't wait, Julia. The Allies know we're here and would never intentionally set this hospital in a plane's bombing sites. But the Germans are scared. And Patz is ready to tuck tail and run at a moment's notice, if need be. That means men like him"—he pointed to Aleksander—"are taking up arms to fight. He's a Jewish leader of a partisan band that's built up around Via Tasso, and he was sent to warn the hospital that the Allies are closing in."

"We're out of time."

News of the Allies drawing close should have provided relief. But AJ nodded like it pained him instead. "The Gestapo have come to clear the Syndrome K wards."

"You mean to deport all the people? They don't know they're Jews, do they?"

"Not deportation, Julia." He shook his head. "To kill the disease."

"God, no . . . But surely not the children?"

"Everyone. They've already confiscated the charts. Dr. Emory was trying to hide as many as he could, but anyone who might have been exposed will be arrested. And dealt with. Either here or at Via Tasso."

"Then we haven't a choice." Julia looked around, her mind flying through the paces of what needed to come next. "Aleksander sent his men to help on my side of the ward?"

"Yes. The friars supplied false information to the SS about the steel doors in the wards, when Court first got wind of them. Captain Patz believes they're welded shut from the outside and that the stairwells are bricked off, making no way out but the quarantine wing entrance they've sealed. That's why they probably let you through without a full security check. If they believe you've been exposed—"

"Then we'd be dealt with anyway. And it's easier to have us locked in the quarantine wing."

"Except they don't know of the exterior door that leads to the garden gate. So Aleksander will help you and Court on the inside to get the people through the steel doors and down the stairs. Dr. Emory and I will hold them off at the entrance, at least until you're all out. And the rest of the partisans are waiting to give us cover over the Ponte Cestio. Once we cross the bridge, we burrow in at a safe house with Calla until the Allied line meets us. And then we get her home."

"Alright." Julia nodded. The fear pitting her stomach was not all that different from the pangs of anxiety before a grand performance. If you experience them enough times, you learn to outsmart them. And then overcome, and soon you're dancing through the fear. She prayed she could summon the will to do it again. "We'll get them all out. Then I'll see you in the courtyard."

"Yes. The garden gate. We'll meet you there." He pressed a kiss to her lips. "You can do it. You're the bravest woman I've ever known."

"So can you. Partners, remember?"

Court ran up the bed rows, dodging patients and tipped beds. "AJ! Wait—you need to see this." He tossed a glance over his shoulder to Calla's tiny form, keeping tabs on her from across the ward as the partisan leader worked to free the steel door bolts. "Aleksander gave me this, for the friars. But when he saw Calla with me just now, he asked about her. I told him we're her family here. He thought it should go to us instead."

Court held out a photo before them—a small sepia square showing a family standing in front of a modest villa and stone gate, shadowed by a small olive tree. A man looped his arm around a woman, holding a baby girl in her arms. A second woman with features heavily favoring the man stood to the side with a child's ivory suitcase on the ground at their shoes. All smiling for the camera, the little one they recognized as owner of the cherub face they knew so well.

"They"—Court pointed to the pair—"are Calla's parents."

"It's her," AJ said. "I remember her face from the ghetto."

Julia's heart squeezed, thinking of the horrific moments when AJ and Court had witnessed Calla's parents' deaths too.

"Right. I knew you'd remember. But I also know because they're the same people in a photo Calla showed me from inside her suitcase. This one here is her aunt, Sephora. I believe it's true that this woman really is her family."

Taking the photo in hand, Julia stared back at the beautiful smiles of the family. She turned it over. Scrawled in pencil: Bero, 1940.

"It was no coincidence then. The injured man here at the hospital. He was trying to find her?"

Court nodded. "Seems so. Aleksander's team was pushing through the German line to the city some weeks back, and they stopped at a partisan safe house on the outskirts of Rome. There they came across a family—a man and his wife and son by the name of Castellano— who have been in hiding to evade the Gestapo these last months. The husband told of a hospital in Rome that has become a haven for Jews—a 'House of Life' it's being called. He said that the friars and the staff here at Fatebenefratelli were saving refugees from the ghetto. And that those in the hospital had saved them."·

The family we first helped from the church . . .

Julia handed the photo back.

Court looked AJ square in the eyes as he held the photo between them. "If you tell me we don't get involved now, it's too late. I'm ready to be court-martialed for this back in the States if that's what it comes to. As long as we get Calla home."

"That's not what I was going to say. But how does a photo tell us where her home even is?"

"The man remembered seeing a little girl in the men's ward here—a Jew who carried a suitcase with cherries on the outside. That detail struck Aleksander, because he'd once met a woman desperate to find any news of what had become of her brother's family and the articles in a suitcase that chronicled the story of the Jews of Rome. She has been in hiding, too, since the roundup at the ghetto, with some others. At a vineyard in Tivoli. And she gave Aleksander this photo as proof, begging him to bring back information if anyone in Rome had found the girl and her parents still alive."

"So we have a direction at least. When the Allies come through, there's a chance we could find this Sephora in Tivoli." AJ nodded, decision made. "Alright, Court. Lock the metal grating here after we leave. Calla's your responsibility. Get her out. Meet us at the garden gate. And we go when the Allies clear the way."

"Yes, sir." He pocketed the photo as he offered a genuine smile.

AJ reached in his waistband and produced his sidearm. "Here. Take this." When Court hesitated, he added, "Only for Calla."

"No, sir. I don't need it. We'll be safe." Court looked to Julia then, and she had the oddest sensation of wanting to hug him in that instant—as if he were AJ's brother and hers, too, and they'd once again be a family when it was all over. "Miss Bradbury? It's been a pleasure. See you on the other side, ma'am."

"Court. You too." She nodded and offered her warmest smile in return.

He fled then, meeting Aleksander at the steel door with Calla and her little suitcase at his side. AJ replaced the sidearm at the back of his waistband, and they edged toward the door.

"Wait." Julia pulled him back. She took the clipboard he'd set on the nearby medical cart and tore a sheet of paper from the admission records. She flipped it over, grabbed a pencil from among the wares of unused medical supplies, and scrawled a message on the back, writing as fast as she could.

"Here." She presented it to him. "Sign this."

"What is it?" AJ scanned the missive, then looked up, his brow furrowed in question. "You know I can't sign this. I can't believe you'd even ask."

She gazed at the windows as noise erupted beyond the glass. Heaven help them, but gunfire had begun popping in the streets. It would only be a matter of time before that horror echoed within the hospital too.

"Please, AJ. I need you to sign it, with your name and your official rank. Court too. It's for Calla, and it's the only way the directive will be taken with any credibility. Put it in her suitcase, where it will be safe. Just in case we get separated. We'll need it after—when we get to Tivoli."

"*We'll* need it after?"

"Yes. We will. You don't think I'm going to let you do this alone, do you? We're partners, remember? That's what we said. I'm not about to let you out of that contract now."

"You realize if I sign this . . ." He leaned down over the cart, scrawling his name fast. "I'll have to marry you when this is all over. I can't just let you go now. Not after this."

"Good, Sergeant Nelson. Because I favor formal partnerships." She caught her bottom lip in her teeth. "Though I've never signed a marriage contract."

"Me neither." He stared back as he pocketed the paper. And showed her the flash of a grin that had him looking like a schoolboy staring down his summer holidays. "I, uh . . . Even if that's not how I imagined saying I love you, five seconds before I have to go—"

Julia cut him off, pressing her lips to his.

How could he possibly know that the most romantic of notions to her was not dancing on a grand stage or achieving the world's successes of this life, but only what she could gain by giving part of herself away? And if he could understand that, a proposal before they both fled to save the people in the wards was all she'd wished to hear from him. In that, he'd fulfilled every dream Julia had ever had. And in spite of the whole world crumbling around them, that truth felt like an anchor to her heart.

"I'll see you after," Julia whispered against his lips. And pressed another quick peck for good measure. "At the garden gate. You'll meet me there? Promise?"

"I promise. We'll go together," he whispered back, those steel-gray eyes searching hers, then let go.

Julia watched as AJ fled down the hall back to the quarantine wing doors. He turned. Once. Gave her a hopeful smile, then disappeared through. She waited until he was gone, then turned too— the opposite direction though. Toward the adjoining church.

There was still time. The story that had brought her to Rome could no longer own her—a stark reminder as they readied the wards for a fight.

Whether the Allies came or not, her own war was not yet over . . .

Julia knew what she must do.

Twenty-Seven

Delaney thought back to that first video call with Matteo, when she'd looked at the picture-perfect view of Rome and wondered what all lay beyond the garden gate.

It was Calla who led them through it now, into her world of parasol pines and lemon trees, walking them past manicured beds that slept under the lantern light's glow. She gripped the old suitcase in a hug at her chest as they moved through the private garden, Matteo having anchored a gentle palm under the brace on her wrist. They took careful steps together while Delaney walked at their side carrying the framed photo of a young Calla, Andrew, and her grandfather standing alongside who they now knew was famed ballerina Julia Bradbury.

It was at the fountain that Calla slowed them, where the vines climbed the back garden wall. The same place where memories had sent her into a panic the last time.

She hesitated there now. Without a word. Just stopping short and standing with her suitcase in her arms. Matteo held her steady and whispered something in Italian.

"No." Nona shook her head as she eased away. She set the suitcase on the ground at her feet and gazed up at the vines.

Easing back, Matteo watched and slipped in beside Delaney. She accepted his hand and they waited together, breathless in that moment. Watching as Calla stood in the moonlight, in a nightgown and crochet shawl draped over her shoulders, frozen on the path.

Would she dance?

Would she turn to them, confused and terror stricken, and cry out again?

Calla stepped forward and with careful hands parted the vines' long locks that fell in a cascade over the back wall. Undoing the weaving. Pulling and parting and untwining vines, until finally, she revealed an aged bronze door that reflected in the moonlight.

She opened it—a great *creak* from tired hinges sang out—and reached inside the stone wall's hidden door.

"Did you know . . . ?" Delaney asked, half wondering if she was imagining what she was seeing.

Matteo seemed to read her thoughts and shook his head. "No idea."

Was it there that the story had lived? In photos hanging on a villa wall. In letters long forgotten. And in a little suitcase that for decades had lived on only in Calla's mind. Now the story she wished to tell was lifted out: a large wooden box she gripped tight.

Calla turned back to them. Matteo trotted forward on the path, taking the box from her. And she let him, then picked up her suitcase as she led them to a nearby bench. She whispered something in Italian and Matteo nodded.

"She'd like us to sit with her for a while."

"Alright." Delaney eased onto the end of the stone bench and placed the frame in her lap, then held up her phone. "Should I record?"

"Per favore," he said, the words hanging on air as he looked at Delaney over his nona's bent form.

Calla opened the box, aged hands ever so careful as she reached in and pulled out a key on a chain. She whispered something to Matteo and he obeyed, setting the suitcase on her lap.

Turning the key in the lock, she opened the lid.

Delaney's heart stopped, for though the suitcase was empty, the wooden box was not. And it seemed that whatever she'd held in secret for so long, Calla wanted only to be able to put it back home, where it belonged.

Wrapped in plastic for goodness knew how long or why, Calla lifted a stack of memories from the wooden box. And in the softness of the lantern light and moonlight shining on the garden path, she took each item out. And relayed a story with it—whatever it seemed she could remember.

Matteo echoed her words, translating with each photo she held out.

Some she spoke of from the ghetto—tiny remembrances of neighbors or friends. Of Jewish shopkeepers. Of a couple who'd just celebrated their wedding day. Of a butcher and his wife who owned a small shop not far from the old street market and who would give Calla's family the best cuts they'd had even when food became woefully scarce.

Calla told of a teacher who used to listen to Chopin on a gramophone set by an open window, and that was where she'd first twirled on the ghetto's cobblestone streets at the Portico d'Ottavia and dreamed of one day performing a pirouette on a stage. She remembered the little girl and boy who'd lived next door with their parents, who were supposed to come celebrate Calla's birthday but whom, like her own parents, she didn't see again after that horrible day. And when the war ended, they never came home.

"And who is this?" Matteo said in English first, so Delaney could understand. Then he pointed to the framed photo from the wall in Calla's room and asked the same in Italian. "Can you tell us about them?"

Calla pressed her palm to the photo behind the glass and closed her eyes. *"La mia seconda famiglia."* She closed her eyes as her mouth warmed into a soft smile.

"She says your grandfather, Andrew, and Julia . . . they were her second family."

She carried on with a story Matteo repeated.

A prima ballerina, Julia was beautiful, she said. Kind. Strong. And gentle, like no one she'd ever known before or since. Calla held out a paper torn at the side, and Delaney took it and turned it over. The name typeset on the back of a typed medical chart read: *Fatebenefratelli, Isola Tiberina, Roma.*

Overwhelmed, Delaney fought back tears as she held the paper and brushed her fingertips over the signature of *Private Courtney Coleman, US Army,* written in her grandfather's familiar script at the bottom—alongside the sharp signature of *Sergeant Andrew James Nelson, US Army,* and the elegant, looping cursive of *Julia Bradbury.* Both men had inked their names as witnesses to the penned note, written in English and by Julia's hand:

Dearest Winston,

I, Julia Bradbury, do hereby leave the whole of my estate trust to one Franca Bero—Calla Rossi, by documentation of her medical chart at Fatebenefratelli Hospital, Tiber Island—of Rome, Italy.

Minus a sum of ten thousand pounds to be transferred directly to agency representation, Winston Peterbrooke, of 80A Kensington High Street, London. This estate will be transferred to the name of the recipient and watched over by the soldiers signed herein.

Thank you, dear friend.

All my love,

Julia

"Whatever happened to Julia?" Delaney looked up.

Matteo and Calla talked back and forth for a few moments, until he nodded. "Nona says her second family saved her after her first family was killed. That Julia, Andrew, and your grandfather worked alongside the doctors at Fatebenefratelli Hospital—they found a plague . . ."

Calla interrupted—corrected him, maybe?

"No—not found. She says they created it. Syndrome K. All to fool the Germans and hide the Jews. And it worked. It was so simple, yet they never learned the truth," Matteo said, still listening, and exhaled low, like he couldn't believe what he was hearing either. "She says her second family risked their lives to save the Jews of Rome. They got her out at the end of the war, and they kept a promise to look after her for the rest of her life."

He paused then, eyes growing wide.

Delaney held her breath. "What? What did she say?"

Matteo looked back. Brow weighted. And moved from the bench beside Calla to kneel in front of Delaney. He took her hand, easing the camera from it so the warmth of his skin met hers. He brushed his thumb against her palm. "She calls Courtney Coleman 'Salvatore' because she says God used him to rescue her in the ghetto. She says if not for him, she wouldn't be here. None of us would." He shook his head, in as much disbelief as Delaney felt in her shaking hands. "Your grandfather saved her life."

"He did? He never said . . . I mean, we knew Grandpa had served in the war. As a medic. But in the end he talked very little of those years. We knew nothing, especially nothing like this." She glanced back and forth between them, the sweet woman lost in the photos she was stacking in her lap. "Um . . . How did he save her, did she say?"

"There was a Gestapo raid on the ghetto." Matteo reached over, helping his nona layer items into the suitcase so the stack didn't slide off her lap as he continued talking.

"She says the attack came when the Germans took over Rome. I remember reading about it—the Jewish ghetto was cleared in 1943, I think?" He paused to sniff, emotion building in his voice. "She says she remembers that morning. How her mother had managed to find flour and baked her a birthday cake. And her parents had been so excited to give her the gift they'd found that they woke her early that day. She was eating cake when the Gestapo came for them."

"Oh, Matt. Is that what that was?" Delaney cried. "The episode in the garden the other night? She must have thought she was back there."

He nodded. "Some of the people from the photos had given their documents to her father—marriage licenses, birth records, land deeds—whatever they could, and because he was a university professor before the war, they trusted him to keep the information safe. She remembers dogs barking out the window as her father filled the suitcase. And before they closed it, her mother put her birthday gift inside—a pair of toe shoes they'd found in an old shop and saved for two years to buy. This, she believed, was because they wanted to give their daughter something to hope for. Something for her future. Then the soldiers came. Some of the people from the photos ran away. And she says the Germans were going to take her parents, and her aunt Sephora, too, and all her neighbors away to work in a factory. But then they tried to separate the children. And her parents begged them not to take her away too." Matteo stopped and hung his head for a breath. "They shot her parents in the street. She was there. And she . . ."

"She called out, didn't she? Like we saw here in the garden."

Matteo nodded. "For someone to save her, sì. And she says God sent her Salvatore—her friend. He ran out. Picked her up from the middle of the nightmare. And he helped her. He made sure she had food to eat and a bed to sleep in. And he got her home after the war. And she says some of these items now belong to you because of it."

Delaney looked over to Calla's sweet face and the bright violet eyes that had come alive. Though she didn't speak English and Delaney no Italian, it was as if time stopped between them, in a place where spoken words were not required.

The old woman handed Delaney two rusty bolts—what Matteo translated were the ones her grandfather had forced out of a locked steel door so the Jews could escape down a stairwell to freedom. And Calla shared an old book—a copy of Homer's *Odyssey* by the cover on the outside, but instead the torn pages of an Italian phrase book tucked inside. And said she'd given Delaney's grandfather his first lessons in Italian, though he wasn't very good at the start.

She allowed Delaney to hold the bolts in her palm. To see the penciled name of *Courtney Coleman* written in the book's front cover. And to hold Calla's first pair of toe shoes—in old, faded, but never worn satin—which she lovingly held and then set on top of the stack.

Treasures. Calla shared them all until one item remained in the box.

She handed over a photo to Matteo, asking something in Italian. He nodded, leaning in to share it with Delaney.

"This is Vittorio Bero, her father—my great-grandfather. He was a professor of music at the university. And her mother." He pointed to the woman holding the baby in her arms. "My great-grandmother. Elisabetta. Nona says she used to bake for all the brides and expectant mothers in the neighborhood. And the one on the end is her aunt—Sephora, the woman who raised her as her own, with her daughters. Mirena is the youngest of them."

Delaney stared at the Bero family smiles.

It haunted her, knowing Calla's parents had been taken in such a horrific way and that Calla had witnessed it right before her eyes. And now, flooded by her own childhood memories, Delaney wished more than anything that her grandfather was still there.

Now that a few had been answered, she had so many more questions.

Delaney wanted to ask him about the time he'd spent in Italy. To thank him for being so brave as to save a little girl. To say how proud she was of what he'd done, and to acknowledge the absolute humility he showed in never once seeking accolades for such heroism. In all the years Delaney had known him, he was Dr. Court Coleman—the small-town doctor who'd loved his community, his church, and his family most of all. And in those moments she remembered when he seemed far away and his gaze would drift off past the Jenkinses' farmhouse porch . . . now she knew why.

Calla closed the suitcase. Turned the key in the lock again and slipped the chain over her neck. She pressed an aged hand to its top, with a butterfly's touch of her palm to the leather and faded cherries, patting it as one would a beloved old friend.

She whispered something to Matteo, and he stood quickly to help as she did. "She says she's tired now. But Nona does ask if we could help her with something."

Delaney stood with them. Calla lifted the case, presenting it to her. And she said something in the most beautiful Italian and the sweetest voice, whispering "Grazie" as she pressed a hand to Delaney's cheek.

"What did she say?"

"You heard the thank-you. But Nona says it's time to tell the story of her families—both of them. She wants to know if she can return the suitcase, take it home. To the ghetto. There's a Holocaust museum there, and I know they'd want to talk to her when she's able."

"Tell her yes. Of course. Sì. And there's so much to ask her. About Julia. And my grandfather and Andrew after the war. And what happened to the rest of the Jews of Rome . . ." Delaney looked to the precious soul of Nona, who smiled and began to walk them back toward the path. "I suppose the journalist in me has far too many questions. But I think it's beautiful that she carries their story and now wants to honor them by telling it."

"Va bene. And I think Nona would be glad to answer our questions. But it should be soon." Matteo hugged an arm around Calla's shoulders. "We want to let her talk while the story's fresh. So I'll call the museum tomorrow and see where we go from here."

"Wait—can you ask her one more thing? Why *Calla*? Why has she been called that name all of her life when her real name is Franca Bero-Santini?"

It must have seemed an obvious question to him too. Matteo asked, and in an instant his laughter filled the garden.

"Well? What did she say?"

"She said Calla because she likes it." He shrugged, offering Nona his arm. "And all her life, she's kept a promise to her first ballet teacher, that like dancing, she'd only ever do the things that brought her joy."

Twenty-Eight

A Nazi officer knelt in the sitting room, buttoning his uniform coat down the front.

Julia had opened the rectory door and slipped inside, intent upon warning Anton of the threat to the hospital. But instead of a quiet suite of chambers, she found a glass syringe discarded on a side table, a uniform hat tossed upon the floor, and a tall, blond body that lay sprawled on the sitting room tile.

Before she could process the shock and back out of the room, the officer turned and spotted her aghast in the doorway. But to look upon his face . . .

"Anton?" She gasped.

"Close the door!" he barked on a ragged whisper and stood on his slightly unsteady gait, his hand bracing the wingback's top or he'd fall over it.

She closed the door but pressed her back against it.

"What have you done?"

War, and the dark things intertwined with it, shouldn't have shocked her by now.

She'd lived through Blitz bombings, a Milan train station that had been ripped wide, and a deadly ambush on the Ponte Cestio bridge, so a body on the floor wasn't the first time she'd seen death. But in all of that, death had come for them. It sought them with bombs and bullets and the collateral damage of one enemy vicious to hunt down another.

Not this time.

Anton had been the harbinger of death, as evidenced by a man's partially clothed body spread on the tile behind the furniture. There was no blood but just enough of a distant gaze in his eyes to leave no doubt.

Captain Patz was dead. And by all presumption, he'd been felled by the famed ballerino's hand.

"You . . . killed a Nazi officer?"

"He would have killed himself in the end, with his injections of Pervitin. I just helped him along with an ample supply of the drug—enough to knock him out and drag him down the hall, out of sight."

"You realize they will have noticed their chief Waffen-SS is missing by now and will scour every inch of this hospital in order to find him! And when they do, Father Bialek, the friars, even Dr. Borromeo and the staff . . . they could all be implicated in something you yourself have done. Do you have any idea what their reprisal would be?"

"I needed the uniform, Julia."

"Whatever for?"

"It's our only chance to get out of here. Remember the supply trucks? Patz has one ready to go. And I have the keys right here in my pocket. It's our chance for escape."

"You cannot be serious."

"I've been planning this for weeks. Months, while you've been running around the hospital playing nursemaid. Watching for the perfect time to get us out of here. And I don't plan on us waiting around to find out what happens when they do discover the body. Not when they're helping us by clearing the quarantine wards on their own."

Julia looked back in Anton's eyes, to the vile coldness in their depths. She darted her glance back and forth between the officer's clothes and military boots Anton now wore and the sight of Captain Patz's ashen form lying still in the dark.

"What do you mean they're clearing the wards?"

"Don't you see? A distraction in the quarantine wards will save *us*. It will give us time. The Gestapo will be looking only for plain-clothes patients attempting to flee. They wouldn't think twice to let a German-speaking SS officer pass through security. And it would be easy to believe one of the patients killed an officer while attempting to escape capture. Any of them could be partisans."

"But they're not. Those are innocent men, women, and children in those wards!"

"I said *could* be partisans. It will take the Germans a while to search the whole of the hospital and sort this out. And by then, we shall be gone."

Julia pushed his hand off when he tried to reach for her shoulder.

"Wait. How did you know about the Gestapo? This was you . . . wasn't it? You alerted them! You planted the seed in their minds that the partisans are preparing for a fight. All the while sending inno-cents to their deaths!"

When he didn't deny it, Julia shuddered.

And wished more than anything that she hadn't taken pity on

him, caring enough about the despicable man to have come to warn him about the threat in the quarantine wards. And it was he who'd alerted the Nazi authorities in the first place.

"Julia, this is the only way. The Pervitin may have kept the captain awake at all hours. But it also made him paranoid. I'd heard of it in the Allied ranks as well. All he needed was to believe there was a real threat, and we had one."

Anton advanced on her, his stride far more agile than it should have been for the injuries he'd suffered. And until now he'd needed the cane to get around.

"How did you . . . ?"

"Yes, you're surprised? I'm not my old self yet." He looked to the cane, discarded against the arm of the wingback. "I might be a little more sure-footed than I let on. I thought it may serve me well. And I've been proven right."

"For whose benefit would you lie about that?"

"Why, yours, of course. And theirs. The Germans thought I was a charity case of the church—an Italian citizen. Displaced, like so many others. Like the injured man who arrived at this hospital months ago, with a man and his little girl whom I found in this very sitting room— with you—curiously, not long after the ghetto was cleared. If they'd been infected with Syndrome K, they'd have been either discharged by now or dead. And they are neither, are they, Julia?"

When she refused to answer, he leaned in closer. Every nerve ending in her body tensed, preparing to run even as he whispered in her ear.

"They are not who they seemed, are they? And they could very well be the partisans the SS have been searching for. I wonder what the SS would think, if they knew they've been working right inside this hospital . . . with you."

"Why have you done this? Why? Those people . . . they are innocent."

"I told you. The officers talk. On the balcony, right over the church courtyard, where I could hear their plans." He glanced to the body on the floor. "While the captain knew the hospital would provide sanctuary for those with Syndrome K, he did not know that two were here under asylum from a ballet envoy, and that we've been holed up in this church for months as secret political prisoners. It surprised Patz when he learned of it."

"You tried to bargain with a Nazi officer?"

"It didn't exactly work out the way either of us envisioned."

"I would never take a negotiation with one of them. *Never*."

"Of course not. Nice little nurse that you've become. Without any medical training, mind. I was bargaining for our protection and it went badly for him. But I find it curious that while I've been locked up here, you've been living quite the life in those hospital halls—dancing and meeting lovers in your garden."

The hair at her nape prickled to standing. "What do you mean?"

"Why would you assume if I could become a ghost and listen in on those officers who so often stepped out to the courtyard, or see the activity in the garden from the rectory windows, that I wouldn't see you there with *him* too?"

"Him . . . ?" She swallowed hard, the air in the room becoming thick as the tension increased. "You mean Dr. Rossi?"

"Oh. Is he a doctor now? That explains the blood on his hands that first night, doesn't it?"

He looked to the window as the popping of gunfire escalated again out in the streets. It echoed across the church courtyard, so loud it could have shaken the windowpanes.

"What of your Dr. Rossi's daughter, hmm? Why have they been

in the quarantine ward all this time, unless in some wartime infatu-
ation, you sought to protect them too?"

Fool that he was, Anton didn't know the sickness was an invention. And it set his treachery into motion in a completely asinine
manner.

"Anton, listen to me. You don't know what you're talking about.
I came here only to warn you. To help you get to the quarantine
wards, to get out. Even after everything, I would have tried to save
your life."

"You owe me your life, Julia! After what happened on that bridge,
I will never step onto a stage again. I have had months staring at the
walls of these rooms to think on all that I have sacrificed for you. For
our name. For your future! All I have done up until this moment has
been for *you*. Even pumping that officer over there full of his blessed
Pervitin came with risks. Care to know why I did all of that?"

"No. I don't want to hear anything else. I wish to go."

He pressed his arm to the wall behind her, creating a barrier
sturdy enough that she'd never get the door open in time. The only
chance she had was to make him believe she feared him. That she'd
crumble again and fall to his will.

"I told you once that I loved you. Come with me now and I'll get
you out. I promise—no harm will come to you. And I will forgive
what happened here."

"This is not love." Julia slipped her hand into her skirt pocket.
"You don't know what that is . . . you will never know."

She found the metal key to the women's ward security grating
and gripped it tight as he pressed harder against the door, attempting
to hem her in.

"And if you do not wish to find the good doctor and his little
girl shot by the Gestapo in that courtyard, then you will reconsider,

Julia. You will come with me. This uniform will see us out. And perhaps when we are back in London, away from this place, we will come to an understanding about our future."

Holding her breath, Julia held fast until he was within striking distance. She wedged the key between her index and second fingers—waiting as he stood before her, her fist clenched like a bomb poised to explode at her side.

"I will never go with you, Anton. Ever again."

It took only the split second for Anton to encircle her wrist and pull hard for Julia to let the other fist fly, the metal key catching on his cheekbone in a furious blast that threw him back. He fell off balance with his hand over his eye and cried out, his unsteady footing throwing him against the sideboard in a tumble of books and a furious *crack* as a lamp shattered to the tile in the dark.

Julia flung open the door and ran from the rectory. The only thoughts in her mind as she crossed the courtyard were to hold tight to the key in her palm and to make it back before the Nazi police discovered Patz's body or raised their guns to the souls fleeing the quarantine wards.

The key would save them.

Lock Anton Vasile and the Gestapo out of the quarantine wards, and they'd be safe.

Lock them out . . . and they were all free.

Twenty-Nine

Court had one of those flashes in his memory, of the time he and Penn had gone to the picture show to see the Western *Stagecoach*. In it, a gun had fired. And after the loud *bang*, everybody was checking themselves to see who'd taken the bullet. He did the same thing. Stood. Checked himself over quick. Felt no pain so he reached for Calla. Swept her into his arms. And prayed while he looked her over too.

"You hurt, kid?"

Must have been a warning shot. They were okay. And seemed there was no harm. Except that she was crying, of course—probably scared out of her wits—and stretched her arms out over his shoulders, reaching toward the front of the ward.

He looked back, thinking he'd check before they sailed down the stairs to meet up with Julia and AJ in the garden. Only Calla's cries led to the sight of the Nazi officer, dazed and lowering his gun . . . and staring across the space to a woman's body laid out on the floor before him.

Oh no . . .

Setting Calla down against the stairwell wall, Court turned and ran.

He slowed up as he drew close to the officer and raised his hands with his last cautious steps forward. And then Court's heart sank. He saw the amber hair . . . the willowy ballet dancer's build . . . and, God help him, but her nursing uniform was darkening to crimson— fast—with blood spreading on her side.

Julia—you're supposed to be in the women's ward . . .

The officer wasn't Captain Patz. But thankfully, the uniform looked to be the only one who'd made it inside the ward. None followed from the hall.

"I didn't mean to. She . . . she stepped in front of me!" the officer muttered, pleading in choppy and, curiously, very British-sounding words. Even as tears mixed with a trail of blood from a fresh cut under his eye. "I wouldn't have hurt her. I swear—I'd never have hurt her!"

"I don't care. Just don't shoot, alright?"

The officer did a double take at hearing Court's words—spoken in English instead of Italian. He allowed the pistol to hang down at his side then and let go. It skittered across the tile until it came to a stop against the underside of a radiator against the wall. And left Court enough space to unlock the grating so he could slip through.

"God . . . what have I done?" The officer scraped tense fingernails along his scalp, then crumpled to his knees and buried his face in his hands.

"I just want to help her, alright?" Court took cautious steps forward. Even if the officer was despairing in the corner, best not to make any sudden movements and have him rethink reaching for the weapon. "I'm coming through."

Court slipped the key in the lock and, once he'd passed through the grating, rushed up to Julia's side.

She lay still.

Too still as he eased down beside her and patted her cheek. Court needed to get her attention. Get her eyes focused so he could see how bad this was.

"Julia? Can you hear me? It's Court."

"Calla?" She tried to stretch her neck, turning so she could see the length of the ward.

"She's fine. Don't you worry. You saved her." He turned his mind only to the job he'd been trained for. Tearing off his jacket, Court wadded it loose and propped it under her feet. "And you're going to be alright. I'm going to make sure of that."

He moved to rip the side of her uniform shirt and she cried out, pain causing the back of her head to lift and then smack the tile.

"I'm sorry." He exhaled, hating it. Knowing what he'd have to do to help was likely causing her unbearable agony in the process. "I'm not trying to hurt you. I just have to do this."

She nodded, gritting her teeth as Court tore soaked cotton at her waist. And then he found it—the hole of a 9mm bullet that hadn't grazed but pierced deep in the right side. Under her ribs. And into the worst spot, draining the dark blood of the liver out.

God, help me . . .

Please.

Court jumped up. Ran to the nearest medical cart and wheeled it over.

He fell to his knees and yanked drawers out one after another, cursing the Italian labels he couldn't read. Knocking stuff out of the way as he opened another. What looked like packets of sutures spilled all over the floor.

A tray of instruments crashed in a clatter like it was raining metal a second after. And thank goodness, he flung open a drawer at the bottom and gauze fell out like snow, rolling away in all directions.

Court grabbed whatever he could reach and started packing the wound. Knowing he couldn't cry out for one of the doctors at the quarantine unit entrance—the Gestapo would hear him. And that would only serve to send more guns their way. But he also knew a medic couldn't save her on his own. Not with this wound.

Footsteps thundered down the hall.

Before Court could form a plan, AJ appeared in the doorway, his sidearm raised.

He fired into the darkness of the ward as Court ducked on instinct, falling over Julia's body like he'd been trained to do—like the medics had once covered him in the madness at Blue Beach. When he looked up, a second shot flew behind them, piercing the chest of the Nazi officer who'd pulled the weapon from under the radiator and raised it again.

This time the uniform fell in a hard *thud* to the floor, the pistol going still in the shadows when his grip went slack.

"Julia!" AJ ran and slid across the tile on his knees, dropping his sidearm when he saw her laid out under Court. He pulled Court back, demanding, "What happened? How did an SS officer get in here? We were holding them off at the entrance."

"I don't know. I don't think he's one of them." Court's hands packed gauze in as he peered over his shoulder at the lifeless body behind them. "This one spoke English. He's a Brit."

AJ looked at the dead man's face and seemed to go panic-stricken for a second—like some understanding dawned—then snapped out of it and shoved Court back. "Come on—get me more gauze!"

"AJ . . . ," Julia whispered, her eyelids fluttering open. Her face brightened back to life with a little smile when she saw him.

"Hey there, love. You're alright. Court and I are going to help you."

"I'm sorry . . ." She peered over at the uniform on the floor. A tear squeezed out of the corner of her eye. Court's gut twisted as he watched it fall. "I was trying to help him . . . I just couldn't leave him in the rectory, no matter what he'd done. I'm so sorry . . ."

"Shh. You don't have anything to be sorry for. Do you hear me?" AJ pressed a quick kiss to her forehead. "We're going to get you out of here. Just stay with me."

They'd been trained to do exactly what Court was watching now.

AJ made a *V* with two fingers and pointed at his eyes, like he'd once done with Court at Blue Beach, getting him to focus under the brim of a combat helmet. Minus the red cross and now with desperate tears in his eyes, AJ told her to keep talking to him. If she could. To stay awake. To stay right here with him. They always did that when a soldier's wound had taken him to within a whisker of the grave, and it was all they had left if they didn't want to let him go to it.

The thing you learned in battle, after two years of watching life drain from men's eyes, was when a soldier's number was up.

Either he went instantly and it was a blessed, easy passing, or he fell hard and was gripped in an agonizing tug-of-war between life and death. And if he'd gone too far, nothing a medic did on this earth could pull him back. Even in a hospital. Even if they could carry her, running down the hall to the expert hands of Dr. Emory . . .

Court knew in his gut; it was already too late.

"AJ . . . ," Julia whispered, eyes closed. "Remember what I asked you . . . to sign?"

"I remember. And seem to remember I asked you a question of

my own. You recall that?" He pressed his mouth to hers, kissing as he fumbled over his words. Then packed gauze upon gauze and clamped his eyes shut in frustration as it filled to red nearly the instant he added it.

"Promise me. We'll look after Calla together . . . when we get to Tivoli?"

"Of course. We'll all go. I promise, Julia—I'll never leave you."

Court rocked back on his heels. Hands bloodied. Bottom lip wavering as he took in the sight of AJ working so hard to save the woman he loved. Court felt the watch weighing down his own pocket, forcing him to think how in the world he'd survive it if that were Penn. And he looked up, his heart crushed in his chest to find a little Italian ballerina watching it all unfold from her place at the stairwell door.

He stood, walking slowly to the contents of the medical cart scattered on the floor.

Blessed Dr. Emory. To keep the ruse of the Syndrome K wards intact, he'd always kept them stocked—even if they'd never needed it. Court knelt, examining each vial on the floor. Grabbing the things he thought they could use. Sniffing through tears, he searched until he found what he was looking for. Then went back to his leader, still pressuring gauze to Julia's side. Even as she'd stopped talking. And her breathing was slowing. And AJ had to shake her shoulders to keep her awake.

"Sir?" Court reached out, placed a tender hand on AJ's shoulder.

"Get back, Court!" he snapped. "Go—get Dr. Emory. Bring him here!"

For the second time under AJ's command, Court defied his leader.

Willingly, he did what he knew was right. He knelt at AJ's side, just being with his friend as they stared down at the beauty on the floor, trying so hard to stay with them. She whispered something else through the stillness—maybe AJ's name?

Court couldn't tell.

They sat there for a breath, until AJ stilled his hands. He gripped them into agonized fists. Hung his head. And let out a guttural cry.

"AJ?" Court reached out for AJ's hand. He unclenched the fingers and pressed a syrette of morphine into his palm. "Here. For her. Just in case she needs it. So she's not in pain when we carry her down the stairs."

Eternity ticked by on an invisible clock as Court waited, and gunfire cracked far off in the distance.

"Sir—it's time to go." Court stood and walked to the metal grating, the key still in its lock, and held the door wide. "All of us. Let's go to the garden. Let's take Julia down together."

AJ finally nodded. Sniffed. And slipped out of his medical coat to cover her with it like a blanket. "Come on, love," he whispered as he slipped his arms under Julia's shoulders and legs and lifted her into his arms, cradling her close. "Let's go."

Court closed the metal grating, locking it tight behind them.

AJ carried Julia down the long row of upturned beds and disappeared into the dark stairwell. Court followed, silent and somber, as he swept the kid and her little suitcase into his arms. And as the world of Fatebenefratelli Hospital had proven a haven for the Jews of Rome, it performed a service for one last family—providing a line of safety as they fled down the stairs to the garden gate, leaving the body of London's famed ballerino behind.

Thirty

S abine said I might find you here. Well, in the city, that is."
Delaney slipped in beside Matteo, leaning her elbows on the balustrade of the Spanish Steps to join him and take in the sights from the top. The view was more subdued this time, with fewer tourists and less noise in the early morning and the muted colors of the buildings encircling the piazza under gray skies that threatened rain.

"I seem to remember telling you a few of my secrets." He tipped his hat back off his forehead a little so he wasn't completely hiding under the brim. "And where to find Giorgio Santini in Rome today is exactly where he was the last time."

"Even if I wasn't looking for *him*." Delaney paused until he looked over. "I was looking for you."

Matteo tipped his shoulders in a shrug. "Couldn't sleep. Not after last night."

"Me neither. So when I came downstairs to breakfast and Sabine told me you'd gone, I thought I'd call a rideshare. You know, take in this last tourist stop before I have to fly home tomorrow."

When Matteo didn't respond to that, she looked to the flats and their terrace gardens facing the stairs. Something had captured his attention there, and it must have had quite the pull to lure him back to Rome first thing in the morning. And without a camera in his hands.

"So—which one was yours?"

"That one." Matteo pointed to a flat at the top—a penthouse terrace covered with a wide trellis and flowering plants that offered the owner some privacy with the view.

"Hmm. It's beautiful."

"It was. And ought to be at that price." He flashed a smile, taking a little bit of her breath away when he did that—even in profile. "But that just made it easier to sell when the time came."

"Do you regret it now?"

"No. I was never home to enjoy it. And I don't think I ever stepped out on that terrace, if I'm honest. Not once. My wife and I lived there in the early years. Carly took her first steps inside that flat. But I wasn't there to see any of it. Not while I was off trying to make a name for myself on the field. Or the times I was waking up in a holding cell after an arrest. Or a hospital bed after Brazil . . . And now, after all these years, it's funny what sticks out in my mind. I had the best view of all inside that flat, and I can only remember what it looks like from right here."

"Maybe you can't go back, Matt. But you yourself said that it was climbing these stairs after Brazil and looking out at this view that made you want to change. And that's a good thing. Very few of us can say we've done the same in our own lives."

He turned to her at that.

Lucky there wasn't a steady stream of tourists around, because they'd have spotted the international football star with no trouble this time. Matteo yanked off his hat and turned it in his hands like he'd been working through something for a while. Something he didn't have the first clue how to say.

"Del . . . I've been thinking. About Nona and the suitcase. And all we've been trying to figure out about it since you got here."

"I've already told you—the suitcase is yours. I couldn't keep it now. It wouldn't be right. It belongs to Nona. I'm just glad she has it and I was here to learn why."

"That's not what I meant."

"Oh . . . Okay."

He took a step, closing all space between them. "What if you didn't go?"

"Matt—I have to."

And there was that nervous pit that formed in her middle whenever he stood that close. Or anytime those eyes of his looked down on her. And when the boldness of his words met with the nagging thoughts trying to remind Delaney to be practical.

That they were from worlds far apart.

Delaney was boarding a plane tomorrow. And neither one of them seemed to know what came next. Because if they were being honest, she'd have to admit she'd never had a kiss like that in her life—where a girl could actually forget she was in Rome and only remember what it felt like to be in his arms. But those internet articles said he'd been there before. A thousand times with as many kisses. And red-carpet photos didn't lie.

"I may not know what my future holds at the moment, but I have to move forward too. Like you did." She tipped her shoulders in a little shrug. "I've even been thinking of writing again. But this time, something that stirs my heart like it has been stirred here. I can't shake the fact that Julia's story should be told. My grandfather's . . . Andrew's . . . And Calla's, too, if it's what she wants. For the Bero family, and all the lost Jews of Rome."

"That's just it. I think Nona's been holding on for that suitcase. But now that she has it, I'm afraid she'll just . . . let go. She won't have a reason to stay."

"You're afraid she'll die."

"Sì." He nodded, obviously pained, because heartache etched his brow. "And thinking she'll finally let go makes me wish I'd never tried to find the suitcase in the first place. And then I hate myself for even thinking that. Because I can't be selfish. This is the story of her life—of the lives lost—and it needs to be told. Their story has to be remembered. And that suitcase has carried it all this time just so it would be."

"And it will, Matt. You'll make sure of it. Anytime Nona does come back, you'll be here. You'll give her the opportunity to tell as much of the story as she wants—in her time. And in her way. That's what matters."

"No, Del. I'm trying to say I don't want to learn this story alone. You should be here too. For your grandfather. Isn't it what he'd want?"

"Probably. You know, my grandmother used to tell a story when I was young. About the dashing soldier who came home from war. Grandpa showed up with a brand-new truck for her as a wedding gift. Because he knew he was going to propose right then and there. But he was the one who ended up with the surprise. He already had a family waiting on him. And he found out he really did have a son—my dad. So maybe that's what he thought too. By keeping the suitcase all those years, the story would live on until Calla was ready to bring it home."

Matteo dropped his hat to the ground, freeing up his hands to reach for her instead. "That's why I'm asking you to stay. Because if it hadn't been for the suitcase coming all this way, then I'd never have met you."

"I'm glad we met too. You have no idea how much."

"Then . . ." He pressed in closer. Forehead grazing hers for a breath. And lips looking like they wanted to meet her soft smile. Whispering, "Don't get on that plane. Please. We'll both be sorry if you do."

Rome began to cry then, sprinkling tiny raindrops between them. Even as Delaney looked up. And couldn't keep from getting lost in those eyes that searched her face for an answer. And leaned closer, letting his arms hold tighter, making her forget all about the romance that was Rome, even when it cried.

"But you live in Rome and New York. And I'm just considering packing up my life in Seattle and moving back home to a country orchard. That's nowhere close to being in between where you are. Our lives are in different poles."

He brushed a raindrop off her cheek with his thumb.

"Delaney Coleman . . . Giorgio Santini may want to hide out from the rest of the world, but I can tell you that all Matteo Santini wants is to be a part of yours. Wherever that is. Whatever it looks like. All I know is I want *that* view."

Kissing Matteo in the rain on the Spanish Steps was the answer . . . *This* was breathtaking.

This was Rome.

And to her, it was perfect.

"I guess I should ask again if I can stay a little longer? Just so we can figure out that last part."

Thirty-One

They could see clearly now, the fighting that had exploded along the River Aniene.

Trees were singed, limbs black and smoking alongside a military tank left overturned on the riverbank rocks. Buildings—what looked like an old church—lay in great piles of rubble along the slope. At least the bridge was still intact over the water. Its span was broken up by burning debris piles, but the stones still appeared sound for crossing.

"You ready, kid?"

When Calla peered up at him, somehow Court knew she understood. It was her quiet way, holding on to that little suitcase and nodding as if she could comprehend each word instead of relying only on tone and trust.

He hugged her tight as they stood alongside AJ under the cover of the tree line, watching the landscape of the bridge, the river, and the hills along Tivoli's western slope.

By the time the Germans had pulled out of Rome and the Allies swept in, there was little opportunity to find a girl's family members who might or might not still be alive in rural Tivoli. And though they knew they'd be in a world of trouble with the US Army when they did get back, AJ had whispered the last words in Julia's ear that no matter what, they'd see it through.

He promised her just like Court had promised Calla—they'd look after her.

They'd keep their word. They'd get her home.

Aleksander and the other Jewish Poles had never made it out of Fatebenefratelli Hospital that day. They'd cut across the courtyard and were the lone Syndrome K ward patients apprehended by the Gestapo, once the body of one Captain Patz had been discovered in the rectory and they swept through the hospital halls hunting for the culprits.

The gut-wrenching arrests on the balcony overlooking the courtyard gave Father Bialek enough of a distraction to help AJ, Court, and Calla make it out to the Ponte Cestio in the opposite direction. AJ left with the father's promise that he'd bury Julia in her garden. And Court left with a map in his pocket and instructions on how to find the partisans—and, they hoped, Sephora—hiding at a vineyard in Tivoli's war-ravaged hills.

"Alright. Here we go."

There'd be bodies lying in the carnage. And Calla sure didn't need to be seeing that. So Court covered the kid's eyes, holding her against his shoulder with a palm cupped to the back of her head. He watched the fringes of the landscape beyond the bridge, just in case, turning his head down to shield his eyes from the sun as AJ led them out of the small grove of trees. They crossed over, boots hitting stone as they ran around debris, always watching the riverbanks as they headed in the direction of smoking vineyard rows on the rise.

When they were through, men appeared.

They popped up from behind stone walls and debris piles. One even came out from behind a cow that lay bloated in the road—all armed and pointing submachine-gun barrels in their direction.

"*Non sparare!* Sephora Bero *è con voi?*" AJ held his pistol firm, even as he shouted for the men not to fire upon them. "I have no idea if I'm saying this right," he muttered, then shouted again, "Sephora Bero?"

One of the men in front lowered his submachine gun. He looked to another, then eyed them and called over the rise, "Sephora!" and followed that by Italian they couldn't make out.

Court hugged Calla tight as they waited. Watching the men. And watching the trigger fingers on those machine guns even more keenly.

A woman stepped out from an open door along the street front—no question the same from the photo. She must have been weary. Probably sleep deprived like them all. But she appeared young and strong, too, as stalwart as the men. She stood in a long skirt and tradesman's shirt, in high-laced combat boots, with a submachine gun in her hands and bandoliers crisscrossed over her chest and shoulders. Her hair was knotted back under a paisley scarf tied over her crown, revealing the same warm face and big, bold eyes of the family Bero.

"That's her," Court whispered to AJ. "That's Sephora."

She pulled her gun back, lifting the strap over her shoulder as she peered down to the riverbank, then shouted something in Italian. AJ and Court didn't know what she'd said, of course, but any soldier worth his salt could guess. And the welcome by a horde of submachine guns probably meant they hadn't been the first visitors through that way. These people would take every precaution with strangers crossing their bridge.

AJ moved slowly, palms raised, and set the sidearm down on the ground at his feet. He took steps backward toward Court, then looked at him and nodded, with his hands still in the air.

"*Abbiamo trovato* Franca Bero!" Court called out and released the hold on Calla's head. "Kid? Calla?" he whispered in her ear. "*Guarda*—look up."

Sephora took a step forward as Calla raised her little head. And when the suitcase swung around Court's side and the cherries came into view, she dropped the submachine gun in the dirt and ran all the way down the road that cut a path from the town to the water's edge.

It took everything in him to let go, but Court set Calla down in the dust at his feet.

When the woman came close enough for Calla to see her face, she took off, too, her little legs moving with the suitcase swinging to one side. The woman fell on her knees in the dirt and scooped Calla up. Holding on. Weeping. Palming the back of the girl's head, fingertips holding the ribbons that still tied lopsided braids and then checking her face over again.

"Grazie . . . grazie . . ." Sephora reached out over Calla's shoulder, asking for Court's hand when he and AJ reached their side.

He stepped forward. AJ too. And they accepted her hand—gratitude squeezing their palms as she held her niece, as the men and women protecting the vineyard pulled machine-gun straps over their shoulders and began descending the hill behind.

War was a leveler.

Regardless of age or nation or language spoken, it could not and never would be powerful enough to overtake love. Court hadn't realized it before. And he felt so unworthy, standing there by the river, accepting gratitude from strangers who had only wanted a little girl to make it through alive and come home to live her life.

Court stood off to the side, watching Sephora with Calla. The woman pressing hands to the girl's cheeks and holding her close. AJ turned, looked at him with as much feeling as Court had ever seen in another person's eyes. And the tough-as-nails leader was unashamed to let his tears surface.

"For what it's worth, Court, you were right that day in the ghetto. To save her. She was worth it. For Julia's life. For ours. All of it. And we're here because you went against an order from your superior officer." AJ held out his hand. "And I for one would like to say, no matter what happens to us now—I'd really like to shake your hand. And say well done, Private."

"Sir." Court saluted first. "If you'll allow me. I never thanked you the way I should have . . . for saving my life. Twice. I'd like to do that now." He took AJ's hand, giving a firm shake back.

"Calla was worth it. And so were you."

"What will the kid do now? She may not want to share the story for a while. Maybe never, after what she's been through. But we'll stay in her life, right? Like we promised Julia. Maybe we'll watch over her, even from afar. I don't think I could just let go that easily."

A little shrug tipped AJ's shoulders. "And I don't think I'll be able to stay away. I feel like Julia's still here, in this place." His voice hitched and he recovered. And went on. "She'll always be here. And I don't want to forget that. I can't forget *her*."

"Salvatore?" Calla cried out from the midst of the crowd growing around them.

Court stepped out, weaving through the people, searching to find her again. She ran up to him and he knelt, opening his arms wide. She jumped into the embrace, holding on for a long moment. He kissed her head. Holding too. Until he finally set her down and stared back, eye to eye.

"I want you to have this, okay?" He pulled the weathered book out of his pocket. "*Per te*—for you. *Sì?*"

Homer might not have cared too much to have had his copy of

the *Odyssey* ripped out of its binding and replaced with Italian primer pages. But for the time they'd spent in the hospital ward, and for how the book had carried *Courtney Coleman* written in the front cover from childhood to the man who knelt before her now . . . he wanted the gift to go to her—the person who'd changed all of their lives.

Calla took the book, hugging it in her arm.

"No Salvatore, sì? I'm not anyone's savior. I hope I'm sayin' this right. I don't think so, but *tu sei mio amico*—you are my friend. And I'm yours. For life, okay?" Court looked at the kid, her eyes welling with tears as she stood before him. And she shifted to give him that disapproving teacher look again. Forcing him to laugh. "So I said it wrong. I got it." He smiled. "I'll learn. Okay? I'll learn Italian for you."

AJ pulled the note Julia had signed from his chest pocket and held it out to Sephora. "Read this to her? Uh . . . *leggi?*" he asked, trying his best to get through as he pointed at the names Julia had written. "Sì? And find this man. Winston Peterbrooke. London, England. You reach this man and show him this letter. Have him find us. *Trovaci*. Sì?"

"Sì. Sì." Sephora nodded, taking the letter. She kissed the paper in her hands, then pressed it between her palms, nodding again.

Court moved to stand then, but Calla drew him back. "Yeah, kid?"

She pulled the chain from her neck and turned it in the suitcase lock. Working fast, she emptied everything out, handing the stack of photos and papers to Sephora. Then closed it up again.

"For you," she said in English. "Salvatore. Thank you . . ."

Must have learned something in reverse from all that Italian she'd tried to teach him. Or Julia's lessons in the garden had been for more than dance.

"What?" He tried to push the suitcase back. "I can't take that."

"*Portare a casa.*" Calla pressed the handle into his hand. And smiled—the most beautiful thing Court thought he might ever have seen. "For to go. Bring it home."

Looking down on the kid, seeing those doe eyes staring back, he couldn't say no.

Court nodded and kissed the top of her head. Then watched as Sephora held her hand and led her up the hill to Tivoli.

Funny thing—the kid had kept the key that unlocked it. Maybe she was a far wiser little sprite than he'd given her credit for. Maybe she realized, like his pocket watch, the suitcase had helped her get home. And maybe it would do the same for him.

Court slipped his hand in his pocket. And enclosed his own metal treasure tight in his palm.

I'm coming back, Penn.

I know where home is . . . It's always been with you.

6 AUGUST 1945
ST. JOHN ROAD
STARLIGHT, INDIANA

Penn had been right. Wagon roads were murder on whitewall tires.

Court slowed the shiny new Ford truck to a stop along the lane to Jenkins' Orchard. Guess they'd just have to deal with it now. Because the last thing in the world Court was going to do was take the turquoise thing back. He hadn't saved a soldier's pay for the last few years to show up without a wedding present for his girl—that is, if she said yes.

And this time, he wasn't gonna wait to ask her.

The late-summer sun shone down on the orchard rows, the peach trees heavy with fruit and just catching the last of the evening light. He saw Penn right off. With that gorgeous hair spilling over her shoulders. And that smile that could melt a man at a hundred paces. She was doing what she always did—walking the land that her family had lived and loved and worked for generations.

Only this time, she wasn't alone.

Dr. Henry Coleman held Penn's arm. And Lord help him, but the man smiled at something she'd said. He actually laughed and seemed happy as she helped him keep from walking into a peach-tree limb that was hanging low. He'd lost most all his eyesight since Court had been away, and no surprise but the Jenkins family had taken him in. Especially after they'd lost Guthrie at a place called Corregidor late in the war. It's what Penn had written in those letters he'd finally caught up with reading. And Court hadn't known how he might make it out of a court-marshal for he and his sergeant going AWOL from the US Army while in Rome. Praise be he'd made it and was looking out at them now.

Court opened the door and stepped out of the cab. He unfolded his garrison cap and positioned it just right on his crown, then gave his tie one last check in the gleaming window glass.

He stood there, having been pardoned by some higher-up from the British government. Thanking his lucky stars that AJ had spoken up for them both and had been prepared to take any heat, if it was to be dished out, for what they'd done at the Fatebenefratelli. It didn't matter how, just that he was there. Looking out at those orchard rows. Where family was what mattered. Patrick Jenkins had told him that once upon a time. And Court sure believed it now.

"Courtney Coleman! You come back here right this minute!" Penn called out, and he whipped around, thinking she was calling him.

Instead, a little boy with hair that had lightened to strawberry blond had turned a corner and ran free, arm stretched and flying a little B-17 between the rows. She called him back again, and the boy eased up when he heard his name.

Court stopped—stunned and overwhelmed and almost unable to breathe as he stared at the boy who'd just noticed the soldier waiting up on the hill.

Penn covered her brow with her palm, following the boy's line of sight all the way up the row to where Court stood. Knowing the questions must have bled all over his face. And her eyes didn't deny it.

Court had a son.

The boy was the spitting image of himself at that age. And the hair? A perfect blend of his mom and dad's. And how Court could have dared to think Penn would have fallen for anyone else . . . He really was a fool, wasn't he? To have doubted her for one second. But no more. And never again.

Penn offered a soft smile, then seemed like she caught her bottom lip with her teeth when Court saluted and held an arm out to present the truck. She leaned in, whispered something in his father's ear, and then took the boy's hand. They all started walking the long length of the row to meet Court halfway.

Court took a deep breath, and leaving his Army-issue bag behind in the dust on the road, he instead carried a little suitcase with red cherries on its sides—a gift from a dear friend who knew what it meant to be heartsick and waiting for that one moment you finally found yourself back home.

Epilogue

It was a good day for Calla. She'd awoken. Remembered the past, and said it was time.

The sun warmed the morning dew, making the smoothed cobblestones at the Portico d'Ottavia shine like mirrors beneath their shoes. They knew now, the last time Franca "Calla" Bero-Santini—Holocaust survivor and ballet teacher from Rome's Accademia di Balletto—had stood amongst those ancient stones, it was the last time the Bero family was all together in this life.

Matteo led Calla through the high stone arch at the Fondazione Museo della Shoah, she anchored to his arm with one hand and the weathered cherry-red suitcase handle clutched in her other.

The scene was one from Delaney's dreams.

How Grandpa would have smiled had he been there to witness it. And felt proud that something they'd fought for had such a great impact on so many lives, so many decades later. As the curator met them at the front door, cameras captured the moment the survivor

358

walked through to honor the past she'd once shared with London ballerina Julia Bradbury, US Army Sergeant Andrew James Nelson, Private Courtney Coleman, Fatebenefratelli Hospital's doctors and staff, and hospital administrator Giovanni Borromeo—who for his sacrifice had been named to Yad Vashem's Righteous Among the Nations.

Ancient Roman arches shielded the sun as Calla stood in the doorway, elegant in a vintage Valentino suit and a string of pearls. Calla listened as the curator talked. Nodding from time to time. Smiling once at something the gentleman said, and Delaney could almost imagine her as that little Italian ballerina once again. It was as if time hadn't touched her at all, save for the laugh lines around her eyes and her well-earned snow-white crown.

Calla accepted the curator's outstretched arm to go inside.

Matteo hung back, waiting to hold Delaney's hand as they went through. They stayed joined—her engagement ring pressing between their laced fingers. And they stood off in the shadows as cameras rolled, Matteo whispering every word of the translation in Delaney's ear as Calla talked of a British ballerina who'd given her life, and the two Allied medics who'd saved her in the war, all who made certain a little Jewish girl came home.

As they walked down the hall to the exhibit rooms, Calla remained silent but her heart shone through in every expression that rested upon her face.

She took in the photographs of the lost . . . the letters . . . the memories of the Jewish families she'd carried in the suitcase. She ran loving fingertips over the glass that shielded a pair of toe shoes, and the frame that covered the photograph of a little Jewish girl with her suitcase, and the second family who'd become her protectors in Rome.

Delaney and Matteo stood at Calla's side as she said goodbye, her chin trembling ever so slightly as the curator moved behind the glass of the adjoining room.

Lined floor to ceiling were the suitcases of the lost. Calla nodded approval and watched as the man opened the ladder. Took one step up. Then another. And went the rest of the way until he slipped the little child's suitcase into the space cleared at the very top. In a sea of charcoal and faded black and time-worn brown leather, ivory and little red cherries stood out like a beacon for the lost, that their stories, too, might one day be found.

—La Fine—

Author's Note

German officials in Rome issued the order: "Clear the Jewish ghetto."

On the morning of 16 October 1943, trucks pulled up to the cobblestone courtyard at the Roman ruins of the Portico d'Ottavia (Portico of Octavia). Gestapo soldiers disembarked and began a ruthless raid to seal the streets and round up the city's remaining Jews. The roundup resulted in some 1,600 to 2,000 men, women, and children being loaded onto trucks, deported via a sealed train from Rome's Tiburtina station to the Auschwitz-Birkenau death camp in Oświęcim, Poland, where they are presumed killed en masse upon arrival.

Some sixteen would return to the ghetto after the war.

Two hundred yards away at Tiber Island, administrators of the Fatebenefratelli Hospital and friars of the adjoining San Giovanni Calibita Church (Church of St. John Calybita) became aware of the mass deportation when Jews who managed to escape—by fleeing through the back of shops, jumping over rooftops, and scaling down drainpipes—arrived at the church seeking sanctuary. While Dr. Emory is fictional to this story, real-life hospital administrator Dr. Giovanni Borromeo, fellow anti-Fascist doctors Adriano Ossicini and Vittorio Emanuele Sacerdoti (who was Jewish himself), and Polish Father Maurizio Bialek devised a plan to hide the Jewish refugees.

This plan was Syndrome K.

Prior to the Waffen-SS arrival at the hospital in October 1943, administrators hid a transistor radio in the basement boiler room, setting up a clandestine station for middle-of-the-night transmissions to underground partisan contacts hiding in Lazio and at the Vatican. When the Nazi SS arrived at the doorstep of the hospital demanding to search for partisans, anti-Fascists, and Jews believed to be hiding within its walls, they were met at the doors by the German-speaking Dr. Borromeo. Borromeo handed out masks, advised the Nazi authorities of a deadly and highly contagious plague that was fast spreading through the hospital, and offered an invitation for the quarantine wards to be searched in full.

SS leadership declined the invitation.

Aptly named "Syndrome K," the invented disease was an affront to either Albert Kesselring—the Nazi commander charged with the occupation of Rome—or Herbert Kappler, the SS chief responsible for the devastating raid on the Jewish ghetto. Between October 1943 and the Allied Liberation of Rome in June 1944, the collective efforts of the doctors, hospital staff, and church friars ensured Jewish refugees had falsified documentation as they were filtered through the hospital, with estimates that dozens, if not hundreds—including Dr. Sacerdoti's own cousin, Luciana Sacerdoti—were saved.

While it is believed the Nazi occupiers of the Fatebenefratelli never learned of the ruse of the invented plague, there was a raid upon the hospital in May 1944, in which SS soldiers finally searched the quarantine wards. Hospital administrators provided an escape for the remaining Jews just in time, and the search netted only five Jewish Poles who were caught attempting to escape on a balcony.

In recognition of his efforts to save members of the Jewish Almagià family—and, it's believed, many others—Yad Vashem (the World Holocaust Remembrance Center in Jerusalem, Israel) bestowed its highest honor of a non-Jewish citizen upon Dr. Giovanni Borromeo in 2004, declaring him one of the Righteous Among the Nations. The Fatebenefratelli Hospital was also recognized as a House of Life by the International Raoul Wallenberg Foundation for Holocaust awareness.

While those on Tiber Island fought to save the Jews of Rome, Allied armies continued the arduous push north from Sicily in a grueling Italian campaign that would last from 10 July 1943 until 2 May 1945. With Clark's 5th Army landings at the beachhead of Paestum—a planned US assault of roughly 3,800 yards at beaches dubbed Red, Green, Yellow, and Blue Beach—and the UK 8th Army farther north at Salerno, the 9 September 1943 assault on the German-held beaches became some of the bloodiest fighting of the war. Between 3 September and 20 October, the Allies would suffer some eighteen thousand casualties in Italy—five thousand from these two units alone.

By the time of the Italian Campaign, Americans were used to seeing notable names in uniform, the famed Douglas Fairbanks Jr. and Pulitzer Prize–winning author John Steinbeck among them. Steinbeck's battlefront dispatches were read in syndication and gave American families at home a poignant—and sometimes brutally real—look into the soldier's front-line experiences. As the Germans sought to delay the Allies in a muddy slog of Italy's rugged terrain (by routinely bombing roads, bridges, and culverts), Allied engineers were brought in to rebuild with lightning speed. Though a specific bridge-mapping commando unit including Steinbeck was a construct for this story, the fictional characters of Private Courtney Coleman and Sergeant AJ Nelson give a glimpse into the true experiences of soldiers like them—especially the noncombatants and conscientious objectors who were often placed in some of the most dangerous front-line medic roles.

Keen literary fans might recognize Homer's epic journey, the *Odyssey*, running as an undercurrent throughout this story (even down to many of the characters' names). At the heart of this novel is the life of one Jewish girl—who grows up to become our Italian ballerina—and the individual part each person played in her survival. From AJ Nelson's pursuit to save others, Court Coleman's finding faith and restoration within his own heart, Julia Bradbury's longing for deeper meaning to her calling, and Delaney and Matteo's journey to uncover truth for the grown Calla so many years later . . . All show the impact just one life can have on the lives—and faith journeys—of so many others.

In this way history is powerful. To remember. To learn. To see and understand the human experience through another's lens. And, we hope, to give empathy a foothold to grow in our own hearts. Let us be changed. Let us open our eyes. And let us learn what Jesus meant when He said, "I desire mercy, not sacrifice." For He has come to call sinners—all of us—to wholeness in Him.

Acknowledgments

I watched my very first Steve McQueen movie in the midst of the 2020 global pandemic.

Having loved classic films since I was a girl, I don't know how I lived as long as I have without righting that wrong in my film repertoire. Upon ticking through the list of his films during quarantine months and learning more of McQueen's faith journey in his latter years, I knew the Allied medic who would open this novel must be inspired in part by the Hollywood star.

Private Courtney Coleman's journey to find faith—from home, to storming the beaches of Salerno, to his time in the quarantine wards of Rome's Fatebenefratelli Hospital—emerged from this time in my own life. It's the very personal faith journey we all walk that needed to both begin and end this story.

We wouldn't have this novel without ideas brainstormed with dear friends Sarah Ladd and Katherine Reay: You ladies took the exquisite imagery of a ballet dancer's world and helped me find a story as the smoke of war settled around it. Thank you both for the years of friendship and for journeying together with me on this story road.

The picturesque small towns of Borden and Starlight, Indiana, have been backyard homes for the last two decades of my life.

Many thanks to Irene "Renie" Coffman for research help and inspiration through the Borden Museum (including the name for AJ's character, taken from longtime Borden, Indiana, resident Mr. AJ McKinley). And to Grandpa Bob Mullins: Thank you for spending time with me on the best walk I've ever had! It was the generous sharing of stories from your youth during the war that helped shape this novel. Thanks also to Huber's Orchard and Winery in Starlight, Indiana—which loosely inspired Jenkins' Orchard—for being the beautiful country haven our family has visited for the last twenty-five years and counting. The haunting remains of the Rose Island Resort and Amusement Park—with its former walkways, swimming pool, and zoo structures left in the overgrown woods along the Ohio River—have become a more recent ground of exploration for our family and inspired fascinating research. Though it features only in Court's backstory, I'm wondering whether a future Rose Island story needs to be told of this little-known historical gem . . .

Heartfelt appreciation goes to friends who walked with me through the creation of this novel. I'm so thankful for the encouragement, steadfast support, and fierce friendships: Beth Vogt, Sarah Ladd, Katherine Reay, Sara Ella, Rachel Hauck, Allen Arnold, Marti Jackson, Maggie Walker, my incredible agent and dear friend, Rachelle Gardner, and all in our publishing family at Thomas Nelson. And in particular to my editors: Becky Monds, your grace and your careful handling of the human heart are gifts without compare. I'll never forget your authentic friendship on this journey of writing novels together. And Julee Schwarzburg, thank you for the ever-patient editing and the seriously fun commentary as we polished this story. I'm thrilled to have partnered on another novel with you.

A heartfelt "Grazie!" goes to Brad and Kathleen Charon of Author Fan Travel, for allowing our family to dream of a trip to Paris (for

The Paris Dressmaker) and to the incredible sites of Rome included in this novel. We're ever grateful for your friendship out of this opportunity! "Grazie!" also to Margaret E. Gray, PhD; Mr. Antonio Marvasi; and the department of French and Italian at Indiana University for assistance with the translations in this novel. It is the ongoing support of this academic community that makes me ever so proud to be counted among your alumni.

To the incredible women to whom this novel is dedicated—my mom, Linda, and my high school librarians Marilyn Hock and Harriet Smith: I send my ardent appreciation for the hand you had in cultivating the love of storytelling in my heart. You are brave, beautiful women, and I am indebted to you for life. A special note of gratitude also goes to Margaret Wedge, whose own battle with Alzheimer's so tenderly found its way into Calla's grown-up story: I'm so very proud to be your granddaughter. You're remembered every day.

To the always supportive fab four of my heart: My husband, Jeremy, and our boys, Brady, Carson, and Colt . . . My life is so much richer because I've been given the incomparable gift of *you*. I love you all.

And to the Savior, whom I, too, needed to find anew out of this season . . . You are faithful. You are home. And my heart is ever still—and always will be—Yours.

For Further Reading

Atkinson, Rick. *The Day of Battle: The War in Sicily and Italy, 1943–1944.* Volume 2 of the Liberation Trilogy. New York: Picador, 2007.

Atkinson, Rick. *The Guns at Last Light: The War in Western Europe, 1944–1945.* Volume 3 of the Liberation Trilogy. New York: Henry Holt and Company, 2013.

Bell, Amy Helen. *London Was Ours: Diaries and Memoirs of the London Blitz.* London: I.B. Tauris, 2011 (first edition 2008).

Bettina, Elizabeth. *It Happened in Italy: Untold Stories of How the People of Italy Defied the Horrors of the Holocaust.* Nashville: Thomas Nelson, 2009.

Bosworth, R. J. B. *Mussolini's Italy: Life Under the Fascist Dictatorship, 1915–1945* (reprint edition). New York: Penguin Books, 2007.

DK. *World War II: The Definitive Visual History from Blitzkrieg to the Atom Bomb* (revised edition). New York: DK, 2015.

Homans, Jennifer. *Apollo's Angels: A History of Ballet.* New York: Random House, 2010.

Larson, Erik. *The Splendid and the Vile: A Saga of Churchill, Family, and Defiance During the Blitz.* New York: Crown, 2020.

Mayes, Frances, and Ondine Cohane. *Always Italy* (illustrated edition). Washington, DC: National Geographic, 2020.

Mayes, Frances. *See You at the Piazza: New Places to Discover in Italy.* New York: Crown, 2019.

Overy, Richard, ed. *The New York Times Complete World War II 1939–1945.* New York: Black Dog & Leventhal Publishers, 2013.

US Medical Department. *The Battlefield Medical Manual: 1944.* Gloucestershire: Amberley Publishing, 2014 (first edition 1944).

Discussion Questions

1. Court's story from broken drifter to heroic soldier and faithful grandfather takes him on a journey to find faith in his own life. How did meeting and saving Calla during the war affect his walk with God? What were the pivotal moments that helped him overcome his turbulent past and lean on God instead of himself? How might we discover a renewed faith, especially when ours is tested?

2. Julia was a rare talent—a master artist willing to share her gift with others in a way that profited them instead of herself. How did Julia use her talent of ballet to impact others? What were the choices she had to make along the way that could have derailed her ability to live out her calling and pursue her purpose?

3. Delaney and Matteo meet with the same motivation of uncovering the story behind Calla's suitcase, but it's they who carry their own baggage from past mistakes, regrets, and broken dreams for the future. What do they understand in each other's stories that ultimately brings them together? How does Calla's story intertwine their

own and open the door to a potential future beyond the pain of their past?

4. On their trips to explore the city, Matteo introduces Delaney to some of Rome's most famed treasures, including the Colosseum, the Jewish ghetto and Portico d'Ottavia, the Fontana di Trevi, and especially the Spanish Steps. How does the presence of the modern day mixed with the ancient past impact Delaney's first experience of Rome? How do the more personal sites—the ballet school, the family villa in Tivoli, or Calla's private gardens—affect her differently than tourist spots?

5. Much of this novel takes place within the halls of the Fatebenefratelli Hospital in October 1943, where the staff and church friars conspire to use Syndrome K as a ruse to shelter Jewish refugees from their Nazi overseers. Why was Syndrome K so effective in fooling the German authorities in Rome? What were the risks that Court, AJ, and Julia—and all the staff—were willing to undertake in order to help save lives?

6. Famed writer John Steinbeck—and others like him—captured the real-life experiences of soldiers battling on the front lines during World War II in a way that brought the realities of war back to the home front. From the Jenkins family in the American Midwest, to Julia's entertainment world in the Blitz-bombed streets of London, and to the darkness of occupied Milan and Rome, how did the wartime experiences of everyday civilians differ? Or differ from the heartbreaking experiences of Italian Jews?

7. In stories of tragedy and war—such as Homer's *Odyssey*—there are often clear-cut character roles. Who were the

heroes in this novel and why? Who were the villains? Were there any characters who had a measure of both light and dark in them?

8. A grown Calla is battling the devastating effects of a dementia diagnosis, causing her to lose the ability to differentiate between present day and her early life during the war. How are items from her past—the suitcase, steel door bolts, photographs and letters, and even a vintage Valentino dress—significant to help bring the lost parts of her story back and help her find joy in the memories she still has?

9. Sacrifice is the hallmark of a soldier's duty, from Court and AJ storming the beaches of Salerno to the brave men and women who fought and died on the front lines during World War II. But the same courage is needed for any duty that requires a person to be willing to give of themselves to save the life of another. What were the acts of sacrifice and courage offered by others in order to bring Calla safely home? How did Calla honor those who'd given so much for her?

10. At the heart of this novel is the theme of "coming home" or finding faith through the peace of reconciliation with God and others. How does each couple—Court and Penn, Andrew and Julia, Delaney and Matteo—find hope and restoration in God and in each other, even if they'd struggled with sin, regret, loss, or grief in their pasts? How do we overcome past hurts in order to find peace in our present and hope in our future?

About the Author

Author photo ©
Whitney Neal Studios

KRISTY CAMBRON is an award-winning author of historical fiction, including her bestselling debut, *The Butterfly and the Violin*, and an author of nonfiction, including the Verse Mapping Series Bibles and Bible studies. Kristy's work has been named to *Publishers Weekly* Religion & Spirituality Top 10, *Library Journal's* Best Books, and *RT Reviewers'* Choice Awards; received 2015 and 2017 INSPY Award nominations; and has been featured by CBN, Lifeway Women, Jesus Calling, *Country Woman* magazine, *MICI Magazine*, Faithwire, Declare, (in)Courage, and Bible Gateway. She holds a degree in art history / research writing and lives in Indiana with her husband and three sons, where she can probably be bribed with a peppermint mocha latte and a good read.

Connect with Kristy at kristycambron.com and versemapping.com.
Instagram: @kristycambron
Twitter: @KCambronAuthor
Facebook: @KCambronAuthor
Pinterest: @kcambronauthor